More Praise for

GHOST IMAGE

"A breezy read with just the right amount of thrills."
—*Library Journal*

"A solid, scenic mystery."
—*Booklist*

"From a secluded monastery garden to the halls of power in Washington, D.C., Ellen Crosby leads us on a deadly chase to catch a killer, showcasing powerful and corrupt personalities against a landscape where nothing is as it seems and no one can be trusted. A page-turner to the last, *Ghost Image* is a compelling read that kept me guessing late into the night."
—G. M. Malliet, award-winning author of
A Demon Summer

"*Ghost Image* is the exciting new title in Ellen Crosby's marvelous Sophie Medina series, and positively another winner! An intriguing plot, perfectly drawn characters, and Crosby's thorough knowledge of the world she writes about make *Ghost Image* a must-read for mystery fans everywhere! Sophie Medina is a bright new star readers are going to love."
—Charles Todd, *New York Times* bestselling author of the Inspector Ian Rutledge and the Bess Crawford Mystery series

"Elegant writing and a plot that twists and veers like creeping ivy, *Ghost Image* is a smart, engaging read."
—David Riley Bertsch, author of *Death Canyon*

ALSO BY ELLEN CROSBY

The Sophie Medina Mysteries
Multiple Exposure

The Wine Country Mysteries
The Sauvignon Secret
The Viognier Vendetta
The Riesling Retribution
The Bordeaux Betrayal
The Chardonnay Charade
The Merlot Murders
The Champagne Conspiracy

Moscow Nights

GHOST IMAGE

A SOPHIE MEDINA MYSTERY

ELLEN CROSBY

SCRIBNER | NEW YORK LONDON TORONTO SYDNEY NEW DELHI

Scribner
An Imprint of Simon & Schuster, Inc.
1230 Avenue of the Americas
New York, NY 10020

First Scribner trade paperback edition October 2016

SCRIBNER and design are registered trademarks of The Gale Group, Inc., used under license by Simon & Schuster, Inc., the publisher of this work.

For information about special discounts for bulk purchases, please contact Simon & Schuster Special Sales at 1-866-506-1949 or business@simonandschuster.com.

The Simon & Schuster Speakers Bureau can bring authors to your live event. For more information or to book an event, contact the Simon & Schuster Speakers Bureau at 1-866-248-3049 or visit our website at www.simonspeakers.com.

Interior design by Jill Putorti

Manufactured in the United States of America

10 9 8 7 6 5 4 3 2 1

The Library of Congress has cataloged the hardcover edition as follows:

Crosby, Ellen.
  Ghost image : a Sophie Medina mystery / Ellen Crosby. — First Scribner hardcover edition.
    pages ; cm. —(Sophie Medina ; [2])
  1. Murder—Investigation—Fiction. 2. Washington (D.C.)—Fiction. I. Title.
PS3603.R668G48 2015
  813'.6—dc23   2014040750

ISBN 978-1-4516-5937-5
ISBN 978-1-5011-5104-0 (pbk)
ISBN 978-1-4516-5944-3 (ebook)

For Kristin and Claudia,
my beautiful daughters-in-law

Make no little plans. They have no magic to stir men's blood.

—DANIEL BURNHAM, ARCHITECT AND URBAN DESIGNER, 1846–1912

We may know with certainty that nothing belongs to us except our vices and sins.

—ST. FRANCIS OF ASSISI

GHOST IMAGE

GHOST
IMAGE

1

"When the old prince dies they're going to cut out his heart and bury it in a monastery in Hungary. They'll bury his body in the family vault in Austria." The elderly woman who'd spoken helped herself to a glass of Grüner Veltliner from a silver tray held by a white-jacketed waiter.

She sipped her wine, the enormous diamond ring on her finger like a sparkling star in the light of a crystal chandelier that dominated the drawing room of the Austrian ambassador's residence. "It's a royal tradition, something to do with the Holy Roman Empire," she said to the stooped man standing next to her.

He took a stein of pale gold beer from the same tray. "The Holy Roman Empire?"

She frowned. "That can't be right. I think the wine's going to my head. I meant the Austro-Hungarian Empire. That way he can be buried in the two countries his family used to rule. Ursula told me about it."

"Ursula would know something like that. She said both of Victor's parents are still in Europe because his father isn't well."

He leaned in closer to the woman, but his voice carried anyway. "What do you bet she's sticking pins in a doll, hoping the old man pops off before the wedding? Then her future son-in-law gets a bunch of new titles, plus an art collection and a library worth a fortune."

The woman laughed. The string quartet that had been playing in the foyer all evening ended Mozart's *Eine kleine Nachtmusik* and, with perfect timing, slid into *The Merry Widow Waltz* by Franz Lehár. The elderly couple turned as if they were going to leave the room and froze when they saw me standing there holding a professional-looking camera with a large lens attached to it. She turned red, and he said, "You're not the photographer from the *Washington Post*, are you?"

If I hadn't been working, I would have told them I was the gossip columnist and asked them to spell their names. Instead I kept a poker face and said, "No, sir. I'm the wedding photographer." I held up my camera. "May I?"

They posed stiff-necked with embarrassment and forced smiles, knowing I'd overheard their unkind remarks. Afterward, the man leaned in and squeezed my arm. "We're neighbors of the mother of the bride, honey. We've known Senator Gilberti and her daughter for years. And let me tell you, we love Ursula and Yasmin like they were our own family."

I let "honey" go by and nodded. Sure they did. Across the room a dark-haired man caught my eye and gave me a long, slow wink. He was too far away to have overheard anything, especially over the buzz of voices and the music that floated above the din, but he was still smiling as though he'd figured out exactly what had just happened.

Tonight many of the men, including Archduke Victor Hauptvon Véssey, the future groom, and his host, the Austrian ambassador, were wearing loden jackets, the boiled wool collarless coats that were the traditional dress of their country. Among the sober-suited men who kissed women's hands with Old World charm, this guy stood out, too flashy in a black suit, black shirt, black tie, and fashionably long wavy hair that brushed his collar. He was still staring.

The crowd between us shifted as if a curtain were closing, and he disappeared.

A waiter touched my arm. "Ms. Medina, Senator Gilberti would like to see you in the dining room."

Ursula Gilberti had given me a list of the one hundred and twenty guests expected at tonight's engagement party, along with detailed instructions of the pictures she required me to take. In a previous job with an international news agency, I photographed world leaders, two popes, and peace talks where neither country trusted the other that hadn't required this much stage managing. I pulled Ursula's list out of the pocket of my black silk evening pants. Before I saw it, I hadn't realized how many exiled members of royal families—including kings and queens—lived in Washington. A few were here this evening, and everyone else was either friends of the engaged couple, coworkers from the Smithsonian where Yasmin worked, or from Global Shield, the international refugee relief nonprofit whose Washington office Victor ran, and Capitol Hill staff and colleagues of Ursula's.

I followed the waiter into the dining room. What did Ursula want now?

She stood in the middle of a small knot of people that included the ambassador and his wife, gesturing expansively with her glass of wine as she recounted a story. She had probably chosen her floor-length gown, which was the color of amethysts, not only because it looked so perfect against her fair skin and auburn hair but also because it was the color of royalty. Ursula was attractive, but with no softness or girly femininity, and in the Senate she was known as a tough, competent deal maker, which was why her party had chosen her as their whip. Tonight she seemed to be running this engagement celebration with the same capable efficiency she used to deliver votes.

Across the room, her animated, chattering daughter was also the center of attention, provoking eruptions of laughter like little explosions from the mostly male group surrounding her. Yasmin Gilberti looked stunning in a vivid green satin halter dress that matched her emerald-and-diamond engagement ring. She was tall and athletically built, and with her flaming red hair done up in a mass of curls that framed her face, alabaster skin, and enormous green eyes, she had already become the subject of European media interest, the fairy tale wedding of the beautiful American who had captivated the plain, solid-looking archduke.

This evening she and Victor hadn't spent much time together, apparently deciding to circulate separately among their guests. I had seen Victor in the drawing room just now, looking happy and animated as he clapped an arm around the shoulders of the men and, in his courtly way, kissed the women's hands with a small click of his heels. A few times he'd caught my eye as I moved around taking pictures and flashed his warm, charming smile. Royal titles had been banned in Austria when the monarchy was abolished, but other countries didn't respect that edict and there were enough old royalists and members of the aristocracy here tonight that I'd overheard him referred to as Archduke Victor or, if someone spoke to him directly, Your Royal Highness.

Ursula finished delivering the punch line of her story and excused herself to join me. "Yasmin and Victor are going to cut the cake after the champagne toast. I suspect people will start leaving after that. Did you get everyone's photo?" Her eyes roved over the crowded room as if she were looking for someone.

"Except those who aren't here, of course," I said.

"Who's not here?"

"Among the people you wanted to be photographed, only Edward Jaine and the king and queen of Ethiopia. Also, Brother Kevin Boyle hasn't arrived yet."

She turned her gaze on me. "Their Majesties were always iffy, but Brother Kevin ought to be here by now. And I know about Edward. He said he might just drop by, but he promised to come."

She could have told me about the iffy king and queen, but that was Ursula. And I was curious about her relationship with Edward Jaine, though I figured she was probably courting him as a political donor. I'd never met him, but he was in the press so often I knew plenty about him—that he'd dropped out of Harvard after developing what became the gold standard in Internet firewalls, a system so secure it was now used on all U.S. government computers and had made him a multibillionaire. Lately he was better known for his flamboyant and sometimes outrageous lifestyle. Less publicized was his habit of stopping by a soup kitchen or a shelter for battered women or another small charity and writing a large check. But in the past few weeks, unflattering stories had surfaced about a series of disastrous investments he'd made in companies that manufactured computer components. Jaine's Jinx, it was called.

"Pardon me, Senator." Father Jack O'Hara, the man indirectly responsible for my presence at this party, stood behind Ursula and me. "I overheard you mentioning Brother Kevin Boyle. He told me this afternoon that there was a chance he might be late to the party."

Ursula's smile was pinched. "Well, he is."

"I'm sure he'll be here any minute."

"Victor wants him to say a blessing before the toast, and the waiters are about to start passing out the champagne." She gave Jack a pointed look. "Perhaps you could call him?"

I avoided eye contact with Jack because I knew what he was going to say. "Unfortunately Kevin doesn't carry a mobile, or I would have already done that."

It was said about Ursula that she was chosen as her party's whip because she made the trains run on time. Kevin's train wasn't on time. "Then I think you should say the blessing yourself, Father O'Hara. We don't want to keep our guests waiting."

Her smile broadened but it didn't do much to soften what had been an order, not a request.

Jack and I had known each other since we were teenagers, and he was as close to me as a brother. We'd even dated briefly in high school in the days before he realized he had a vocation and left for Rome to study with the Jesuits. Now he taught ethics at Georgetown Law School and had introduced me to Victor, one of his former students, after Victor saw photographs I'd taken a few years ago at a refugee camp in Somalia. Six weeks ago, on Valentine's Day, he asked Yasmin to marry him. Shortly afterward he wrote me a charming letter asking if I would take the pictures at their June wedding at the Franciscan Monastery in Washington. Though I'd never professionally photographed a wedding, let alone a royal wedding, I said yes. Later I discovered I would be dealing almost exclusively with Ursula, who was paying my fee.

I nudged Jack. Through the wide arched doorway we could see a butler greeting Kevin in the foyer. "I don't think that will be necessary, Senator," Jack said. "Brother Kevin just arrived."

Heads swiveled as Kevin entered the dining room dressed in the plain brown tunic of a Franciscan, a knotted rope cincture tied around his waist, and sandals with thick socks on his feet. His salt-and-pepper hair was windblown, and his glasses, as usual, were halfway down his nose.

"Why isn't he wearing a Roman collar and a suit?" Ursula said under her breath. "This is a dressy affair."

"Franciscans always wear their habits," Jack said. "Even to dressy affairs."

Kevin came directly to the three of us and held out his hand to Ursula. "I apologize for being late, Senator. I was unavoidably detained or I would have been here sooner."

She took his hand but didn't shake it. "May I ask why? We've been waiting for you so we could begin the toast. The party's almost over."

Kevin cleared his throat, and I knew this wasn't going to go well. Ursula already didn't get along with him and she'd been hoping for a European wedding at the magnificent Cathedral of St. Stephen in Vienna, with all the pomp and pageantry that would have accompanied it. But over the years Victor's family, who had been exiled from their homeland when the Austro-Hungarian Empire was dissolved in 1918, had developed a close relationship with the Franciscans, as the guardians of the Holy Land, the protectors of Catholic sacred sites. Eventually, after Victor's grandfather renounced any claim to the Austro-Hungarian throne, the family had returned to Austria, where Victor grew up. But the bond between the Franciscans and the Haupt-von Véssey family was still important to Victor, and it was the reason the wedding was going to take place at the monastery in Washington.

"The majority leader called this afternoon and asked if I could drop by his office to go over talking points for your party's all-night floor session tonight on climate change," Kevin said. "By the time I left the Hill, it was later than I expected."

Ursula looked as if she'd just been slapped. "Obviously I'm aware of what's going on in the Senate," she said in a chilly voice. "Yasmin and Victor's party was planned long before that session came up, and I can't be in two places at the same time. My constituents know I'm a single parent and this is the marriage of my only child. Family always comes first with me." Her glare took in all three of us. "If you'll excuse me, I need to find the head waiter and ask him to give us a moment before they serve the champagne."

After she strode off, Kevin said, "That went well, don't you think?"

Jack grinned. "She was too defensive. You really got under her skin."

"I think she's still ticked off about Alaska," I said.

Two years ago, Kevin, an internationally known environmentalist with a PhD in botany, wrote *Reaping What We Have Sown: The Catastrophic Consequences of Plundering Sister Earth*, a controversial manifesto that was still on the *New York Times* bestseller list. When the book came out, he had been invited to testify before a Senate environmental subcommittee, where Ursula Gilberti made an unfortunate comment about the states that bordered Alaska.

"I think you mean Canada, Senator," Kevin had said. "No states border Alaska."

The geographic faux pas had been fodder for late-night talk shows, and Ursula had never lived it down. Now Kevin looked pained. "Don't remind me about Alaska. Look, she had no intention of attending that session tonight, party or no party. She's from a coal-mining state and her primary is right before the wedding. She might not win this time, so there's no way she's going to be part of a conversation about how humans are responsible for global warming and the need for clean energy. It's political suicide for her."

Across the room, a white-haired woman in a teal suit was threading her way through the crowd toward the three of us. She was looking right at Kevin. "There's an attractive woman making a beeline for you," I said to him. "Probably one of your many admirers."

"Or someone else I ticked off with my politics."

"Nope. She's smiling. Definitely a female admirer," Jack said. "You know the old saying, Soph? 'Never trust your wife with a Franciscan or a Dominican.'"

Kevin gave him a friendly dig in the ribs. "The very old saying from the sixteenth century. Along with 'Don't trust your wallet with a Jesuit.' That one's still true."

Jack and I laughed. "Peace be unto both of you," I said. "Here she comes."

She sailed over to us, slipping her arm through Kevin's. "In a sea of Austrian loden, a Franciscan friar is not hard to pick out of the crowd. I thought I would see you here, Kevin." She nodded at Jack and me. "Do introduce me to your friends. Good evening, Father."

"Thea Stavros, meet Father Jack O'Hara, an old friend who's now at Georgetown Law School and a friend of the groom's, and Sophie Medina, the very talented wedding photographer," Kevin said. To Jack and me he added, "Thea is the director of the science division of the Science, Technology and Business Library at the Library of Congress. If I need a reference book anywhere in the world, she knows how to get it. And every so often she invites me over to dig in the dirt of her magnificent garden."

I'd heard Kevin talk of Thea Stavros. With her snow-white hair, I would have guessed her age to be late fifties or early sixties, except that her fine-boned face, as delicate as porcelain, was unlined and youthful looking. The teal suit was old-fashioned, but it had the look of couture, with a low-cut neckline that showed off a glittering crystal-and-gold webbed necklace.

Thea smiled at the mention of her garden and dropped Kevin's arm to shake hands with Jack and me. "My garden is a never-ending work in progress," she said. "I'm always begging friends to help and Kevin is kind enough to oblige."

"Your necklace is lovely," I said. "Is it antique?"

She fingered it. "I wish. It's a knockoff, though it is Swarovski crystal. Austrian, in honor of tonight." She added in a conspiratorial whisper, "Don't tell. I'm hoping everyone thinks it's diamonds."

We laughed, and Kevin said, "We'll keep your secret, Thea."

She gave him a sly look. "Speaking of secrets, you've got one, haven't you?"

"I'm in the business of keeping secrets," he said with a bland smile. "I've got loads of them."

Thea wagged a finger. "You know what I'm talking about. *Your secret*. The new project you're working on. By the way, the latest bundle of documents you ordered is waiting for you on the hall bookshelf outside your study room."

"Thanks. I'll come by the library for it tomorrow."

"Are you writing another book?" she asked. "One hears rumors, you know."

"Never listen to rumors," Kevin said with flat finality. "Half the time they're wrong."

Thea ignored the rebuff. "Based on the information you've been requesting, it's obviously something to do with gardening in colonial America. A history book would be a real departure for you, my dear."

"I'm sorry, but I can't talk about it."

"Oh, come on, you're among friends. No one here is going to say anything, are we?"

In the awkward silence that followed, Jack's face was politely blank and I pasted on a smile.

Finally Kevin said, "Please keep this under your hats. I honestly don't want word to get out . . . my agent is still working out a few things with the publisher. But you're right, Thea. It is a history book, a botanical history on gardening and agriculture in colonial America." He looked at her over the top of his glasses. "And that's all I can say."

"Well, if you're planning to use illustrations, you will come to me for help, won't you?"

"Of course," he said, adding to Jack and me, "I forgot to mention that Thea is the leading historical scholar in the country on American botanical prints. She also has a fabulous private collection in her home that could give a few museums a run for their money."

Thea waved a hand and said with a rueful smile, "Not all of them were considered rare or antique when I acquired them. By the way, Kevin, you must peek into the ambassador's private study. He has two original hand-colored botanicals from the *Hortus Eystettensis*. They must be worth a fortune since the colored plates are so rare. I'd give anything to own something like that."

"What is the *Hortus Eystettensis?*" I asked.

Thea's hand fluttered to her necklace. "An extremely famous book of botanical illustrations from 1613. The name is Latin for 'Garden of Eichstätt,' and it's a massive compilation of flowers from all over the world that were in a very beautiful garden in Germany belonging to the bishop of Eichstätt. The complete book is worth well over a quarter of a million dollars, but many copies were cannibalized and the prints sold separately. Even the prints are still worth thousands of dollars . . . do have a look at them, Kevin."

"I will." He shifted his gaze and scanned the room. "It looks like the waiters are starting to serve the champagne. I believe I'm saying a blessing, and I haven't even said hello to Victor and Yasmin. Will you all excuse me?"

"And me, as well," Jack said. "I'm going to be taking off soon, papers to grade. I need to have a quick word with someone before I go. Sophie, I'll call you, okay? Nice to meet you, Thea."

Jack left and Thea gave me a sideways glance. "So tell me, how do you know Brother Kevin? And the dashing Father O'Hara?"

"Jack and I went to high school together and I met Kevin through Jack. At Jack's ordination, in fact." I left out the part about the dashing Father O'Hara being an ex-boyfriend and changed the subject. "Do you know many people here tonight?"

"The ones from the Smithsonian, Yasmin's friends and colleagues."

"What about that man over there?"

The dark-haired man who'd been watching me earlier had entered the dining room and positioned himself so he had a clear view of Yasmin Gilberti. She seemed aware that he was staring at her because she abruptly swung around to face the opposite direction and nearly spilled her glass of wine on her beautiful dress. Kevin caught the glass just in time and cut a look at the man, who turned away. He said something in Yasmin's ear and she blushed, shaking her head.

"The one in black who's ogling Yasmin?" Thea had been watching the little drama as well. She gave me a coy smile. "That's David Arista. Gorgeous, isn't he?"

"I . . . well. I just wondered who he was, that's all."

"Get in line, darling."

"I'm happily married. Why is he ogling Yasmin, if you don't mind saying?"

"David flirts with all the women he works with. Even me." Her laugh was rich. "It's part of his charm."

"What's he doing here tonight? Besides flirting, that is?"

"He owns C-Cubed. A marketing and media strategy company. I believe it stands for 'create, catalyze, and connect.' He's been working with Yasmin on the Smithsonian Creativity Council."

"The Smithsonian Creativity Council?"

"A group of young creative types—to me, they're practically children—who founded companies in their dorm rooms or their parents' garages and then made a billion dollars. They're supposed to come up with innovative solutions for making the museum's collections accessible to the public, particularly the hundreds of thousands of items in storage." She gave me a droll look and said, "David calls it 'interacting with the physical and the digital worlds simultaneously.'"

So David Arista's relationship with Yasmin was professional, not personal.

"Sounds like you need to be a contortionist."

Thea laughed again. "Yes, maybe. There's a rumor going around that Ursula Gilberti's reelection campaign manager just hired David as well."

Thea Stavros seemed well versed in all the rumors floating around tonight. She took a glass of champagne from a waiter holding a tray and said, "It wouldn't surprise me if it were true. David knows where all the bodies are buried . . . a useful skill in this town."

"No champagne for you, miss?" the waiter said to me.

"Thank you, but I'm working." I pointed to my camera. To Thea I said, "I need to have a word with Yasmin and Victor before the toast. Will you excuse me?"

"Of course." Thea lifted her glass. "Perhaps we'll meet again before the wedding."

The string quartet had stopped playing, and someone tapped the bowl of a wineglass to signal the guests assembled around the large dining room table to quiet down. In the silence that followed, Ursula Gilberti's voice, mingled with a man's light baritone, carried from the foyer into the dining room. Edward Jaine had arrived.

Ursula walked in with him on her arm as though she'd just won Jaine as a prize at the county fair. I raised my camera and fired off half a dozen pictures. He was shorter than I expected, dark skinned with jet-black hair, dark eyes, and a cocky, bantam swagger. He was underdressed compared to the other guests in a cashmere camel blazer, open-neck shirt with a cream and camel paisley scarf wound around his neck, worn jeans, and bright turquoise cowboy boots.

"Victor, Yasmin," Ursula said. "Look who's here."

Victor gave Edward Jaine a polite nod and shook his hand. But Yasmin's face lit up as he took her hands in his and kissed her on both cheeks. He leaned in and whispered something that made her laugh, caressing one of her curls with his finger and giving her a conspiratorial grin.

I heard Ursula murmur Kevin's name as she continued making introductions around the small circle. Jaine held out his hand and said to Ursula, "We know each other. Brother Kevin, nice to see you here."

Kevin pretended not to see his outstretched hand. "Good evening, Edward."

A muscle twitched in Edward Jaine's jaw and Ursula took his arm, as though the little slight hadn't occurred. "Edward, you must meet our hosts," she said, turning to the ambassador and his wife.

Someone touched my arm. Victor stood there holding a glass of champagne. "I saw you turn down the champagne a moment ago, Sophie. Yasmin and I insist that you drink the engagement toast."

I looked away from Kevin, who was now talking earnestly to Yasmin, and said, "I'd be honored."

"Victor, Brother Kevin's going to say the blessing," Yasmin said. "I need you."

He smiled. "I'm being summoned."

He returned to Yasmin's side, slipping an arm around her waist. She smiled, but I still thought she looked tense. I took more pictures, though Edward Jaine had moved away and was no longer standing next to Ursula. Before I could look around for him, the ambassador introduced Kevin, and everyone grew quiet again.

"Heavenly Father," Kevin said, "you have gathered us this evening in joy to celebrate the love of Yasmin and Victor. Strengthen their hearts to keep faith with each other on their journey toward marriage and give them wisdom, guidance, and wise counsel to learn truths that will help them in their life together. May all of us here tonight be witnesses to their love for each other. And may they look forward with joy and anticipation to the day when, in the words of St. Matthew, the two shall be one. Amen."

I wondered if Kevin had inserted the line about keeping faith with each other after watching Yasmin's reaction to David Arista or her flirty exchange with Edward Jaine. But the ambassador had begun talking, a lighthearted and gently humorous toast in English and German that ended with everyone clinking glasses and saying "*Prost*."

Then Yasmin and Victor cut an enormous Sacher torte, which had been flown in that afternoon from Vienna. By the time I finished taking pictures, Kevin was gone as well.

I made a tour of all the rooms looking for him until I heard voices, his and Edward Jaine's, coming from a darkened corridor that led back to the kitchen. I couldn't catch what they were saying because they were speaking so quietly, but it seemed like an argument.

Someone called my name and I spun around. Yasmin Gilberti stood there with a nearly empty glass of wine. I'd lost count of how many she'd drunk. She gave me a lopsided smile. "Have you got a minute? Mom wants a word."

"Sure."

I followed her and she wobbled a little tipsily as she walked. A few days ago she'd turned twenty-four. Victor was forty-one. He was crazy about her, as anyone could tell, but each time I saw them together I couldn't help wondering whether she was really in love with Victor or with the idea of becoming an archduchess with a glamorous European life where she would be known as Her Serene and Royal Highness. Tonight had been no exception.

Ursula said goodbye to another guest in the foyer and joined us in the now-empty drawing room.

"How soon before we have these pictures, do you think, Sophie?" she asked.

"In the next few days. I'll edit them and send you a link like I did with the photos for the engagement picture."

She nodded. "All right, and now I think it's time to start talking about the wedding. Yasmin and I are meeting the florist next week, and we still have to choose the color of the bridesmaids' dresses. It would be helpful to have some venue photos to work with. I'd like the three of us to meet tomorrow at the monastery and do a walk-through of the church and gardens."

Venue photos. Either one of them could take pictures with a camera phone and they'd have what they needed, but if Ursula wanted to hire me for an extra session at the monastery, then fine.

I glanced over at Yasmin. It was her wedding. "What do you think?" I asked, though by now I knew she didn't fight city hall.

"Pictures would help."

"Okay," I said. "What time?"

"Five," Ursula said.

"The monastery and the gardens are closed then."

"I know. We'll have the place to ourselves. Don't worry, my office will call and straighten it out. They'll let us in."

"I think Kevin's still here," I said. "Why don't I find him and we can ask him now?"

And then maybe afterward I could corner him and ask what was going on between him and Edward Jaine.

"No need. Speak of the devil," Ursula said as Kevin walked into the room. "We were just talking about you, Brother Kevin. I presume it won't be a problem if Sophie, Yasmin, and I drop by the monastery tomorrow at five after it closes to go over a few things?"

"You'll need to talk to our guardian. I'm sure Father Navarro can accommodate you." Kevin's smile was strained. "Yasmin, Senator Gilberti, thank you for a lovely evening. Sophie, I'll see you tomorrow morning at ten thirty at the Tidal Basin, right?" I nodded, and he added, "Good night, everyone."

After he left, Ursula raised an eyebrow at me, and I said, "Kevin's helping me with a photography project."

"If we're done here, I'm going to get another glass of wine," Yasmin said in a hard, flat voice. "Excuse me."

She nearly walked into the doorframe, and Ursula, who had watched her daughter leave, pressed her hands together and said, "I'd better have a word with her. We'll see you tomorrow, Sophie."

I gathered up my equipment and left. When I got home, I downloaded the photos from the party and began editing them, but after an hour I quit and looked up the Scripture passage from St. Matthew that Kevin had used to end his blessing this evening—*the two shall be one*—because something had bothered me about it all evening.

He'd used only half of it. The rest was language from the marriage ceremony: *Therefore what God has joined, let no man separate.*

I wondered why Kevin had chosen it tonight and if no man was David Arista or possibly Edward Jaine. And then there was this: Why would a peaceful man of God who often quoted St. Francis of Assisi, that no one is to be called an enemy and no one does you harm, be arguing with one of the richest men in America?

Tomorrow at the Tidal Basin we'd have a lot to talk about.

2

"Someone followed me after I left Victor and Yasmin's party
last night." A gust of wind caught the folds of Kevin's habit,
blowing his scapular and hood so they billowed like a dark sail.
"Halfway down Wyoming Avenue, I ran into a man walking one
of those enormous dogs, a Great Pyrenees, and that scared him
off. The guy was nice enough to walk me to my car."

"Good Lord, Kevin. In that part of town?" I said. In the
Kalorama neighborhood of upper northwest Washington, there
were at least half a dozen embassies within a few blocks of the
Austrian ambassador's residence, and the area was, or should
have been, regularly patrolled. "Did you get a look at him?"

He shook his head. "I had just started walking down the
street when I heard footsteps behind me. He was moving quickly
and it kind of bothered me, so I sped up. So did he. Then I ran,
and he did, too."

We had been walking through the winding Franklin Delano
Roosevelt Memorial next to the Tidal Basin. Now the two of us
stood in front of an enormous statue of FDR draped in a bronze

cape weathered to verdigris and sitting next to his beloved Scottish terrier. Roosevelt, who had shepherded America through the Great Depression and World War II by this point in his presidency, looked worn down and weary.

"Could it have been Edward Jaine who was following you?" I asked.

Kevin shot me a startled look. "No," he said in a firm voice. "It couldn't."

I shrugged and knelt to take photos of Fala, Roosevelt's little dog. "Okay."

"It's the third time it's happened in the past few days, Sophie. I think someone's stalking me."

I stood and stared at him. "Are you serious?"

He nodded. "For all I know, whoever it is could be here right now."

I shuddered and looked around. Washington in late March can be temperamental and unpredictable. Some days the weather is glorious and the warm, silky breeze makes you believe it's finally spring. Or it can be like today, when the wind slices like a knife and the damp chill settles into your bones. There was no one at this memorial except the two of us.

No one.

"Kevin," I said, "we're alone."

"What made you bring up Edward?" he asked.

"Last night when he walked into the room with Ursula Gilberti, you didn't shake hands with him. I didn't know you knew him. And you obviously don't like him."

"I didn't realize you saw that."

I tapped my camera. "I'm a trained observer, remember? I get paid to notice people's expressions and body language."

He gave me a rueful look. "It's a long story, but Edward doesn't need to chase me down a street late at night if he wants to talk to me."

I thought about the darkened corridor where I'd overheard

them arguing. "Maybe he wanted to finish the conversation you two were having right before you left."

"We did finish it. And I can't talk about it, Soph."

Maybe not, but it still bothered him. "The sanctity of the confessional?"

"If I were a priest, yes, something like that. Come on, let's get out of here and go over to the Tidal Basin. It will be easier to spot anyone who looks like he's hanging around watching us with all that water and open space."

"You really are spooked, aren't you? When did this start? Have you reported the other times to the police?"

I followed him down a small flight of steps to the Tidal Basin promenade, where the long branches of the sweeping ring of bare cherry trees arced over our pathway, sheltering us from the punishing wind. I panned the view with my camera, taking shot after shot until I captured all of it in a panoramic image. The top of the Washington Monument was just visible above the distant tree line, and across the choppy, lead-colored water, the dome of the Jefferson Memorial faded into the gray-white sky.

"It started on Sunday. Three days ago," Kevin said. "And no, I haven't reported anything."

"Why not?"

"Because no one else saw or heard anyone."

Kevin was a man of faith, but he was also a scientist. In the real world he dealt in facts, not speculation or conjecture. If he said someone was following him, I believed him.

"What happened those other times?" I asked.

"I was at the monastery. Both times. On Sunday afternoon I stopped into the church at the end of the day after visiting hours were over. There was something I needed to do in the crypt. You know no one's allowed down there even when the place is open unless one of the knights goes with them, don't you? Except the friars, of course."

I nodded and knotted my scarf tighter around my neck, turn-

ing up the collar of my jacket as the wind blasted us a̶
course."

The Franciscan Monastery was a sprawling forty-four-acre compound with a church and magnificent gardens set on a wooded hillside in Brookland, a residential neighborhood in northeast Washington. Unofficially it was known as "the Holy Land in America," a reference to the Franciscans' mission to serve as guardians of places the Catholic Church held sacred. Tourism sites called the monastery Washington's best-kept secret because of the magnificent gardens. The Franciscans' own website described it as "an oasis of peace."

The knights Kevin was referring to—the Knights of Mount St. Sepulchre—were a lay order of Catholic men who gave tours of the monastery and its grounds. They dressed entirely in white except for scarlet sashes around their waists and, on special occasions, white capes with blood-colored Jerusalem crosses emblazoned on them, symbolism dating back to the Crusades. They were also fiercely protective of and devoted to the friars.

"I went downstairs to get something in the catacombs," Kevin was saying. "All of a sudden I heard footsteps, so of course I figured it was one of the other friars. Except as soon as I called out, the footsteps stopped. I went back to the entrance, but no one was there. After that I got what I came for, but as I was leaving I heard them again."

I had been in those catacombs, underground replicas of the original ones in Rome, the mazelike complex where the early Christians used to hide, open graves in the soft volcanic rock under the ancient city where the dead were buried in secret, and Mass was celebrated in hushed voices. It was one of many shrines scattered throughout the monastery gardens and the crypt—all of them exact reproductions down to every detail of places like the Grotto of Lourdes, the house in Old Cairo that sheltered Jesus, Mary, and Joseph during their exile in Egypt, and the Tomb of Christ—built in the late 1800s for

Americans who could not afford to travel overseas to see the real shrines.

Some people thought that duplicating these sacred sites at a monastery in Washington, D.C., was a bit creepy, and I'd even heard it referred to as "Catholic Disneyland." Others found genuine peace and a connection to their faith.

"You never ran into anyone down there?" I asked, and almost added *alive*. The bones and relics of saints and martyrs were displayed in tiny chapels and glass cases throughout the crypt, so in a manner of speaking, you were never really alone.

Kevin shook his head. "I felt foolish, but afterward I asked one of the knights to go back downstairs with me. He searched the place and, of course, no one was there. He . . . well, he suggested maybe I'd been working too hard lately and that I might need some rest."

"So he thought you were imagining it?"

"Not exactly. He hinted that maybe it was someone not of flesh and blood. A spirit." He twirled a finger next to his ear. "I think he was just trying to humor me."

"What about the other time?" I asked.

In front of us, a group of teenage girls in bright blue sweatshirts suddenly spilled onto the promenade in front of the Martin Luther King, Jr. Memorial, giddy and squealing with high-pitched laughter, snapping pictures of themselves and one another on their phones. A school field trip.

Kevin scanned the faces of the laughing, chattering kids. "Same thing," he said. "I heard someone, but I never got a look at his face, just the back of a person in dark clothing."

Except for this school group and two elderly women up ahead of us who were examining the old stone lantern that was lit every year at the opening of the cherry blossom festival, I still hadn't seen anyone who looked remotely interested in Kevin and me.

"Where were you?"

"Walking through the cloisters on my way back to the residence. It was about nine o'clock at night," he said. "Same thing, I heard someone following me. This time one of the seminarians showed up, so I said, 'Come on, let's go after this guy.' Except he said, 'What guy?' And the next thing I knew, whoever was there took off running toward the lower garden." He sounded disgusted. "By the time I reached the top of the stairs, he'd vanished into the woods. I'm sure he left the grounds through the path by the outdoor Stations of the Cross. From there it's easy to disappear into the neighborhood on Quincy Street."

"Kevin, you ought to tell someone about this. I mean, besides me."

"Come on, Soph. What am I going to say? I have no witnesses."

"What about the seminarian who was there? He must have heard something."

"Nope. Paul said he didn't see or hear a thing. Same as the knight who checked out the crypt." He sighed. "Forget about it. Let's talk about your project."

"Kevin—"

"The reason we're here freezing our butts off is that you wanted to talk to me about that book of cherry blossom photos you want to put together, right?"

"Yes, but—"

"So tell me."

He was done talking about his stalker. "It's a fund-raiser for the Adams Morgan Children's Center," I said. "I could use your help."

"Cherry blossom photo books have been done already. A lot."

"This wouldn't be lots of pictures of pink clouds of blossoms wreathing the monuments. I'm talking about photos of the trees like they are today when it's gray and miserable, or in the fall, or covered with snow. And not just the Tidal Basin, but the out-of-the-way places people don't usually think about, like Meridian Hill Park, Scott Circle, Stanton Park." He shook his head. "Come on, Kevin, I think it's a good idea. But I need your help identifying all the different varieties of cherry trees and which ones are planted where."

He pulled down a branch filled with clusters of tightly furled buds from over our heads. "These are Yoshinos, the most common cherry tree in D.C., *prunus x yedoensis*. It's a hybrid. They're the trees with the light pink flowers, very fragrant. When they're in bloom they look like your pink clouds." He released the branch. "Choose another subject, Soph."

A pair of ducks landed in the Tidal Basin and swam under the protection of a low-hanging branch in front of us.

"Such as?"

"Photograph Washington's unknown—or little-known— gardens. I can show you where they are and introduce you to the people who care for them. Everyone thinks they know D.C., but there are loads of beautiful gardens in this town that have either been forgotten or people look at them every day but don't see them anymore. Photograph the places that are hiding in plain sight, so to speak."

I was surprised by the passion in his voice, but maybe he was right: Find the gardens that had become invisible for one reason or another in this city of gardens and show people what was right under their noses.

He reached inside his habit and pulled out a white business envelope as another gust of wind tugged at his long robe. "I brought this for you. It's an article I wrote a few years ago on some of the gardens I think you might want to look at."

"Thank you." I opened the envelope and scanned his list. "It's a good idea, Kevin. Maybe I could talk you into collaborating, since you already know so much about these gardens?"

"I'll be glad to help, but if you want to sell books for charity, leave my name out of it. I have a reputation for riling people up."

I slipped the article into my camera bag. "I'll take my chances."

"Come on," he said. "Those ladies have finished examining

the stone lantern. Let's walk over there. I'd like to look at the old markings. You know it once belonged to a shogun, don't you? It's one of a pair."

"No, I didn't know." I linked my arm through his as we started up the hill. "Do you think whoever is following you might be someone you've riled up? A person who doesn't like your views on climate change or the environment?"

He hesitated a moment too long before he said, "No. I don't think so."

I knew then that he hadn't told me everything about his stalker. "You have an idea who it is, don't you?"

"That's not true. I don't know who it is."

He wasn't going to make this easy. "All right, you don't know who, but you do know why someone's following you." When he didn't reply, I said, "What's going on, Kevin?"

We reached the old lantern. "I don't want to get you in the middle of anything."

"Nice try. We've known each other too long."

A muscle flexed in his jaw as he traced the worn outline of a crescent moon on the old stone with his finger. I waited. Logic dictated that he would tell one of his brother friars, men he should trust implicitly to keep secrets. Instead I had a feeling he was going to unburden himself to me.

Finally he said, "Back in February when I was in London to speak at a conference at Kew Gardens, I came across something quite by accident. When I got home I did some more investigating. If I found what I think it is, this whole thing could be pretty big."

"What thing? And define pretty big."

"Potentially millions of dollars, maybe a lot more. It's complicated. I can't tell you anything else until I'm sure I'm right. There's one more piece of the puzzle I still need to put together."

The Franciscans were a mendicant order and took vows of chastity, poverty, and obedience symbolized by the three knots on Kevin's cincture. They lived a simple life with few possessions. Kevin had given all of his royalties and any money he earned from the publication of his book to the Franciscans, supporting their mission in the Holy Land and helping charities that worked for the poor and the disabled.

Whatever Kevin had discovered, the money would go to those same causes, not his own personal wealth.

"Good God, what is it?"

"I've said enough. Like I told you, it's a huge long shot. I'm not sure I'm right."

"Of course you are. Otherwise why would someone be stalking you?"

He gave me a long, steady look. "No one knows better than you, Sophie, because you're married to a guy who used to be a covert CIA officer, that a person can't talk about what he doesn't know. So can we just leave it at that?"

Nick Canning, my husband, had been with the CIA for years until his cover was blown last fall. The story had been in the press everywhere, and that ended his clandestine career. Kevin was right. You don't have to lie when you don't know the truth.

"At the party last night, Thea Stavros said she heard rumors about a project you were working on," I said. "Do you think she knows?"

He traced more markings on the lantern before he answered, and he seemed uneasy. "I've had to ask a few people for some information, including Thea, but I'm sure she doesn't know or hasn't figured anything out. The project she was talking about last night was the history book on colonial gardening."

"Does your missing puzzle piece have something to do with that book?"

He pressed his lips together and shook his head. "I've said enough."

"That sounds like a yes. Come on, Kevin, you trusted me enough to tell me someone's been following you."

A long look passed between us, and I knew he needed to tell someone.

"All right," he said at last, "but you can't say a word to anyone. I'm serious."

I crossed my heart with a finger. "Hope to die."

He took a deep breath. "If I'm right, I found something of historical importance that nobody seems to have realized is out there, even though it's probably been hiding in plain sight. Like I said, it could be worth a lot of money to the right people. I want to be the person who makes that discovery, solves the puzzle. And be the first to write about it."

At least now I understood the thinking behind his idea for my garden book, since it mirrored his own project: photograph the city's jilted beauties, gardens that were overlooked and ignored. In other words, hiding in plain sight.

"So the reason for all the secrecy is that you don't want someone stealing your story?"

He nodded. "I don't own the information I uncovered. It's in the public domain, and anyone who figured out what I was doing could obtain the same documents. So far no one else has. Right now, it's my treasure hunt."

"Was that why you were arguing with Edward Jaine?"

He gave me a severe look. "In a word; no. That was about something else."

"What did you retrieve from the catacombs?"

He made a zipping motion across his lips.

"Kevin, someone knows something or he wouldn't be following you."

"I know. That's what's bothering me. I don't know who it could be."

"What are you going to do?"

He shrugged, but he still looked worried. "What can I do? Keep searching and watch my back."

"You'd better be careful."

"Whatever happens is in God's hands." He glanced at his watch. "Sorry, Soph, but I ought to go. I promised Thea I'd stop by the library and take a look at those books she was telling me about last night." He grimaced. "Then I'm meeting someone for coffee."

"You don't look too happy about it."

"I have to say something I wish I didn't have to say."

"Then why are you doing it?"

"If I don't, more people are going to get hurt later. And I'll know I could have done something to prevent it. It's better to get this over with." He sighed and pulled his car keys out of a pocket inside his robe. "Are you leaving now, too?"

"I think I'll stick around and take some more pictures. I have a meeting at the Smithsonian, but it's not for an hour."

"Another job?"

I nodded. "An editor from Museum Press hired me to take the photographs for a history book on the National Mall. So I'll see her, and then at the end of the day I'm meeting Ursula and Yasmin at the monastery. She wants to walk through the church and the garden. Again."

"I remember." He made a face. "The kids from Brookland Elementary are coming over at two to clean up the beds in their vegetable garden. We'll be long gone when you do your walk-through with Ursula."

"That school garden is such a great community project."

"Especially when they get to eat what they've grown and realize food doesn't only come from a can or a package." He leaned over and kissed me on the cheek. "If you ever want to take photographs, you're welcome to come by. We could put them on the garden website, get some publicity. You know we're always looking for donations."

"I'd be happy to, but you'd need written permission from every parent," I said. "A friend who works for the *Post* accidentally took a picture for a school story without knowing one of the kids was in the witness protection program. It was a mess."

His eyes widened. "I'll keep that in mind."

"I can take garden pictures without the kids," I said. "You can put those on your website. I'll come by early and check it out."

"That would be great, though there's not much to check out right now. Too early in the season." He gave me a swift hug and left, robes flying as he strode down the promenade. As he disappeared up the steps by the FDR Memorial, my foot kicked something on the ground. A key.

The head was dark gray molded plastic, the same color as the lantern. I picked it up. On one side, the number 58 was etched into the plastic. It was too small and oddly sized to be a house key or a key to a room at the monastery; it looked more like it belonged to a storage locker or a trunk.

Kevin must have dropped it when he pulled out his car keys, or maybe when he passed me the envelope, unless one of the two women who'd just been here had lost it. I shoved it in my jeans pocket. When I went over to the monastery later today, I'd ask him if it was his.

I took pictures for another half hour and thought about my conversation with Kevin. Had he moved whatever he'd hidden in the catacombs to a new, safe place? I hit the Unlock button for my car door and wondered what the little gray key might open.

More than that, I wondered what object could be so precious to a Franciscan friar that he went to such lengths to keep it hidden, especially when he lived in a house whose only other residents were religious men of God.

3

A parking space opened up across the street from the old-fashioned carousel on the Mall as I drove up. In two weeks, the flowering cherries, dogwoods, magnolias, and redbud would begin to bloom, and Washington would be at its loveliest, bringing tens of thousands of tourists in buses and cars that choked the Mall and overran the monuments and museums. But today the city still belonged to the locals. I liked it without the crowds, days when you could get a parking place practically in front of the Smithsonian Castle, and the museums and art galleries were so empty you might have an entire room filled with centuries of culture or the world's greatest paintings practically to yourself.

Nearly eight months ago, my husband and I moved here after living in London for twelve years. Nick's career as a covert operative with the CIA had ended after a nerve-racking, harrowing time when he had been on the run for three months and I had returned to Washington to be near family and friends. It hadn't been an easy decision to leave a city we both loved, but we knew if we stayed in England any longer, we'd be expats forever and maybe strangers to each other because we were together so seldom.

Living with a spy is not easy. I had never been able to tell anyone this, not even my family, who had known Nick only as a geophysicist working for a British oil and gas exploration company that had been drilling for oil in Russia. I knew what Nick really did before the wedding, and I liked to think I wasn't naïve about what his clandestine life would mean for us. I'd grown up around Washington where everyone knew more spooks than they realized. What I didn't understand was how hard it would be to live with someone you could never truly know, who erected impenetrable walls and spun webs of fictitious truths without batting an eye, who could compartmentalize his life with what seemed like ruthless efficiency.

Then Nick's cover was blown and he was PNG'd—declared persona non grata—by the Russian government. But after being in the field for so long, he didn't want to return to a desk job in Langley. Three and a half months ago, after a couple of bottles of champagne on New Year's Eve and a discussion that lasted until dawn, Nick handed in his resignation to the CIA and I left the small photography studio where I'd worked for the past six months. I picked up freelance assignments right away—almost more work than I could handle—but it wasn't so easy for Nick, who got in touch with friends and started calling in favors for job leads at meetings or lunches or over drinks.

Anyone who has been recruited as an informant by a foreign country's intelligence agency can bend over and kiss his ass good-bye if he's ever outed, because professionally no one will trust you again. You're a snitch and you can be bought. It's different if you were hired by the CIA, as Nick was, and had gone through Agency training, because intelligence gathering is your job. You have a regular paycheck, a pension, health insurance, and an annual vacation, and you have sworn an oath of loyalty to your country. But it's still a complicated and fickle world when you leave the life to start over again on the outside. Whatever Nick did next would have to be something unusual, almost certainly not advertised on any website or with a written, well-defined job description.

In the beginning of February, he came home one day and told me Quillen Russell was forming a consulting firm and had asked Nick if he wanted the position as his energy expert. Washington needs more consulting firms like the beach needs more sand, but Quill had been secretary of state in a previous administration and he was godfather to the oldest daughter of the current president. I doubted they would be advertising for clients, and the new office was going to be within walking distance of the White House.

"What will you do?" I asked Nick.

He gave me a dangerous half smile and said, "Whatever they ask me to do."

"It'll be like the Agency again, won't it?"

"Not really. Quill sees it more as being fixers or facilitators for problems or situations that are . . . unconventional."

"Your fee won't be a line item in someone's budget?"

He laughed and pulled me into his arms. "Do you mind if I go away for a while?"

"Yes, I do," I said as he kissed my hair. "I was just getting used to having you home after all the time you spent in Russia."

"Well, don't get unused to it."

"When do you leave and where are you going?"

The Middle East and the former oil-producing Soviet republics for long enough to learn his way around, meet the players, and become familiar with the politics. At least I knew he wasn't going to Russia this time, or he'd end up in Lubyanka, the notorious KGB prison.

Ten days later he was gone. I knew a rough itinerary, and unlike his work with the CIA, we were in touch on e-mail almost daily. Occasionally we even managed a video call on Skype. At the moment he was in Saudi Arabia, and he'd told me the last time we spoke that he figured he'd be home in another month.

Before I got out of the car, I checked my phone to see if he had written me today as he usually did, and for any other messages. Somehow I had missed a call in the last hour, a D.C. area code and a number with a 224 prefix. The U.S. Senate.

The message was from Ursula Gilberti's personal secretary asking me to call as soon as possible. Maybe Ursula had reconsidered today's meeting at the monastery because of the weather.

I hit Redial and the secretary answered right away. "The senator would like you to drop by her office in the Russell Building this afternoon," she said. "She has something she wishes to discuss with you."

"We're supposed to meet at the Franciscan Monastery at five o'clock. Perhaps we could talk about it then?"

"The senator was very specific that she wanted to see you in her office without her daughter present before your meeting at the monastery. I'm sorry, that's all I know. She did say it wouldn't take long."

She was just the messenger, and knowing Ursula, her secretary obeyed without question. My meeting with Olivia Upshaw wasn't supposed to take long, either; I was just picking up a manuscript. But finding parking on the Hill and going through security would chew up at least half an hour.

"I have a meeting in a few minutes at the Smithsonian. I'll try to be there in an hour or so, maybe around one thirty or one forty-five, but don't hold me to it."

"Senator Gilberti is working in her office in Russell all afternoon. I'll let her know." Before she hung up she said, "Thank you."

Now what did Ursula want?

I grabbed my camera bag and got out of the car. The sky threatened rain so I was about to head straight to the Castle when I caught sight of a scrolled wrought-iron bench wrapped around a fountain in a sweet little courtyard. Behind the courtyard was one of the hidden gardens Kevin had written about in his article, a narrow serpentine walkway between the Mall and Independence Avenue known as the Mary Livingston Ripley Garden. But more important to me was the memory of the day I sat on that bench between Harry Wyatt and my mother, when Harry asked me if it was okay if he married Mom and me. A passerby had taken our photograph, the three of us beaming, a happy, soon-to-be new family. I still kept a dog-eared copy in my wallet. Afterward we'd walked through the pretty, sheltered pathway between the Hirsh-horn Museum and the Arts and Industries Building, Harry's protective arm around my shoulders, as he talked about our future after Mom and I moved from our apartment in Queens, New York, to his sprawling horse farm in Middleburg, Virginia.

I walked into the courtyard to take a picture of that bench, remembering Harry explaining how the garden had been slated to become a parking lot until the wife of the secretary of the Smithsonian saved it. She'd turned it into a replica of a sensory garden she'd seen in San Francisco for the blind and disabled, an eclectic collection of plants, shrubs, and trees that filled beds, overflowed urns, and trailed from hanging baskets. Probably no surprise to Kevin, I had it to myself just now, my own secret garden.

Halfway down the path I had company. A man in a black leather jacket, jeans, and a black turtleneck with a leather messenger bag slung over one shoulder had entered the garden from the Mall, just as I had. It took a few seconds before I recognized David Arista from last night's party. I hadn't seen him when I parked my car, and that had been only a couple of minutes ago.

He came toward me, smiling as though we were old friends, and held out his hand. "We met last night. Or almost did. You're Sophie Medina. My name's David Arista."

I'm not good at being coy. We shook hands. "I know who you are. I asked someone about you when we kept almost meeting."

He laughed, and his eyes crinkled into tiny crow's-feet. This close I saw flecks of gray in his long dark hair. It was swept off his face to reveal a sharp widow's peak that made me think of actors who played the devil in old movies. Last night I guessed he was in his early thirties. Today I realized he was probably closer to my age, maybe late thirties or early forties.

"You could have asked anyone about me," he was saying. "I know Yasmin's friends and everyone from her mother's office. Plus a few folks who work with Victor at Global Shield."

"I understand you own a public relations company."

"You really did ask about me, didn't you?" He seemed pleased, and for a moment it flustered me that he had misconstrued my curiosity for another type of interest.

He pulled a leather business card case out of an inside jacket pocket and handed me a card. "C-Cubed. Media, creative strategy, marketing, branding. PR is so twentieth century." His smile was self-deprecating. "And you're the wedding photographer. I know a few people who would love to meet you. Do you have a card? Give me a couple. I'll pass them out."

I had been expecting a fast-talking snake oil salesman, someone who kept looking over your shoulder as he spoke to you in case someone more important moved into view. David Arista was smart, disarming, and nobody's fool. The amused look I noticed last night seemed to be his default expression.

"I'm not a professional wedding photographer." I slipped his card into my camera bag. "I'm just doing this as a favor."

"For Yasmin or Victor?"

"Both, of course. But Victor's the one who asked me."

He pointed to my Nikon and the long lens I had on it. "That camera body and that zoom lens are worth at least five or six grand. You're no amateur."

"No, I'm not. I'm sorry, but I'm going to be late for a meeting. I should be going."

He gave me a shrewd look. "Is your meeting in the Castle?"

"As a matter of fact, it is."

"I'll walk you there. I'm heading over to the Smithsonian metro, so it's on my way."

"Thanks, but I thought I'd take the long way around so I could see the garden in front of the Castle on Independence Avenue," I said.

"No problem." He fell into step beside me. "I'll take the long way, too. You must like gardens?"

"I . . . yes."

"That was a great photo you took of Yasmin and Victor in the garden at the Franciscan Monastery," he said. "I saw the announcement in the *Post* a few weeks ago."

"Thank you." I didn't know too many men who checked out the wedding and engagement announcements, but then, he was a friend of Yasmin's. And, presumably, Victor's. "You recognized the garden?"

He grinned and made the sign of the cross. "Are you kidding me? I grew up in a house with a Jack-and-Jesus wall in the living room. I'll bet I visited the Eternal Flame more than some relatives of the Kennedy family when I was a kid. My Irish mother worshipped Jack Kennedy and she loved Jesus. And the Franciscans. Some people have garden gnomes. We had Francis of Assisi in every corner of our yard like he was multiplying overnight."

I laughed. "She sounds very devout."

His smile turned rueful. "She was."

"I'm sorry. I didn't realize you lost her."

"Three years ago. Lung cancer. She was a smoker; all the radiation and drugs in the world couldn't stop it. And, God knows, my family had the resources to try everything." He shook his head, remembering. "Let's talk about something else."

"Okay . . . why don't you tell me about the Creativity Council? What does it do?"

He smiled. "So you heard about that, too? A creativity council shakes things up. At the meetings, we play games, do some role-playing, come up with a lot of what-if stuff. You start by dismantling everything and then you rebuild it from scratch and see what you end up with."

"Dismantling the Smithsonian?" We turned onto Independence Avenue by the Arts and Industries Building and walked the final block to the Castle.

"Why not?" He pointed to the elaborate designs in the brickwork of the beautiful old building. "That's the second-oldest Smithsonian museum after the Castle. Built in 1879, a terrific example of Victorian architecture. It's been closed for over a decade and it's going to stay closed. There's not enough money to maintain it and there's no plan for what to do with it." He sounded disgusted. "So there it sits, right here on the National Mall in the nation's capital, covered in scaffolding and all boarded up. Tell me, what good is it doing anybody?"

The building looked forlorn and abandoned, the barricades in front of it crisscrossed with bright yellow DO NOT ENTER tape.

"I'm waiting for permission to get inside and take photographs for a book on the history of the Mall," I said. "Apparently there are safety issues."

"Call me. I can arrange it. Wear a hard hat and you'll be fine," he said.

"Thanks. If I don't get anywhere with the calls I've made, I might do that."

"You must be working with Olivia Upshaw," he said, and I nodded. "I know her. We've worked together as well. She's good."

We reached the enormous wrought-iron Renwick Gates at the entrance to the Castle, and David Arista gestured for me to walk through them, ladies first. Inside, the Victorian Enid Haupt Garden was planted in geometric floral patterns that changed with the seasons. Today yellow and violet pansies formed interlocking diamonds across a pale green lawn and more pansies and spiky ferns spilled out of urns on each corner.

Something in David Arista's voice when he mentioned Olivia

made me think of Yasmin Gilberti nearly spilling her drink when she realized he was watching her. Olivia was young, blond, and lovely, a beauty just like Yasmin. And if you believed all the rumors, Washington was more notorious than Hollywood for infidelity and people who worked together sleeping around. Somehow it wouldn't surprise me if David mixed business with pleasure.

"So what brought you down here today?" I asked. "A meeting with Yasmin?"

He shot me a quick surprised look. "Nothing like that. I met a client at the Chihuly exhibit at the Hirshhorn. We both wanted to see it before it left town."

"Really?" I would not have pegged him as an arty guy, certainly not someone who liked Dale Chihuly's fabulous glass sculptures.

That easy, self-deprecating laugh again. "Yeah, I know. You took me for some chump who wouldn't know a Chihuly from a Chihuahua."

I blushed. "I did not."

"I guess I'm what you'd call a museum nerd. Plus I know a lot of the folks who work at the Smithsonian museums since many of them have been clients."

We walked toward the Gothic turrets and towers of the Smithsonian Castle. In the somber light, the lozenge-shaped panes in the leaded-glass windows glittered like black diamonds.

At the entrance, I stuck out my hand. "It was nice to meet you."

He shook it, smiling, and I knew what was coming next. "You never gave me your card. And we ought to get together sometime. Coffee or a drink, maybe."

"That would be great, but I'm awfully busy right now." I laid my left hand over his.

He looked down at the antique diamond and white gold braided wedding ring that had been my grandmother's, and grinned. I knew he'd gotten the message. "Ah, the old brush-off." He let go of my hand.

"No . . . I really am busy."

"Look, I have a feeling we're going to be running into each other if you're working with Olivia. And Yasmin. You and I might be able to do business together, especially if you're involved with the Smithsonian." He was still smiling. "Give me a call sometime and maybe we can get a cup of coffee."

I pulled my wallet out of my camera bag and gave him my business card.

"Thanks," he said. "I'll call you. Coffee. Just coffee."

He left, walking in the direction of the Mall and whistling something cheery and tuneless. Even after he disappeared around the other side of the Castle, I still felt uneasy at the thought of David Arista calling me.

There was more to him than met the eye.

4

I took the cramped elevator near the guard's desk to the second floor of the Castle and walked down a corridor with a sloping worn tile floor to Olivia Upshaw's office. Her door was partially open and she had her back to me, doing something at her computer.

For all the splendor of the public rooms downstairs with their soaring columns, vaulted ceilings, gold-leaf moldings, and other beautiful embellishments, her office was a nondescript, windowless room with greenish-beige walls, metal furniture, and the kind of overhead fluorescent lighting that sucks the life out of every government building in D.C. Books, manuscripts, and folders were stacked on her desk and piled on a long, low bookcase. A mural of pale yellow Post-its festooned with her familiar loopy handwriting decorated the wall above her computer. Three posters of past Smithsonian exhibitions were the only decorations in the room. One of them had been askew the last time I'd been here, and it still was.

Olivia had sought me out for this job through the usual way

things get done in Washington: She knew somebody who knew me. In this case, it was my landlady, India Ferrer, who had met Olivia's parents when they had been overseas together in the Foreign Service. India had filled me in about Olivia, a smart twenty-five-year-old Yale grad who majored in art history and grew up mostly in Southeast Asia and Africa, finishing high school in Switzerland. She was a blue-eyed blonde, attractive in a tanned, lean, outdoorsy way with a habit of reaching around with one hand and pulling her long hair so it fell against her shoulder as if she couldn't stand the weight of it on her neck.

I knocked on her door, and she said, "It's open, come on in," without turning around.

A manuscript bristling with neon flags and Post-its sat on the corner of her desk. I read the title upside down, "No Little Plans." It was part of a quote by Daniel Burnham, a Chicago architect and urban designer who had lived in the late nineteenth and early twentieth centuries. More of the quote, I knew, was on the dedication page: *Make no little plans; they have no magic to stir men's blood.*

Olivia chose it as the title for a book on the history of the Mall because Burnham, who played an important role in designing the master plans for several major American cities, had served on a Senate commission that took a hard look at Washington at the beginning of the twentieth century and was appalled by what it saw. A mediocre town with nondescript architecture and poorly planned public spaces, nothing that could hold a candle to London, Paris, or Rome. The commission resurrected the original grand plan of Pierre L'Enfant, the French architect hired by George Washington in 1791 to design the city, after it had been scrapped for more than a century. They razed the hodge-podge collection of buildings, a Victorian park, and even a train station that had overrun the Mall, and started over. Since this was Washington and Congress had been involved, it had taken decades.

Olivia spun around in her chair and smiled when she saw me. "Sophie, sorry I kept you waiting. There's always so much work here. Please sit down. I've got the manuscript ready for you, as you can see. The Post-its and flags mark the places where I want photos. I've also made notes in the margins."

I realized when we started working together that she was going to be a hands-on editor. What I didn't know was whether she would feel the need to change "puppies" to "young dogs" just to have her imprimatur stamped all over this project. She stood and handed me the manuscript. Then she picked up a book that had been sitting on top of her bookcase.

"I think you should read this. It's a biography of Pierre L'Enfant."

"Thank you, but I know who Pierre L'Enfant is."

A look of annoyance crossed her face, and I knew that she was a "young dogs" editor.

"Everyone studied Pierre L'Enfant in high school," she said in a cool, firm voice, "for about fifteen minutes. This is probably the best book I've read on his life, why he wanted Washington to become a grand capital like Paris and London, and the problems that caused him with Thomas Jefferson, who hated that idea." She held it out. "And why George Washington finally fired him."

"Olivia, I'm taking photos of what's here now, not what should have been or didn't get built. You're getting those pictures, the historical photos, from the Library of Congress and the Smithsonian."

She held the book out to me. "I think it's important for you to understand L'Enfant's vision for Washington. It's important for this book."

I didn't take it. Long ago I learned to pick the battles worth fighting and let the other ones go. She was trying to do my job, or at least get me to do it the way she wanted. At some point she needed to trust me, or this wasn't going to work.

"And why do you believe I don't?"

"Would you please at least look at it? As a favor to me?"

"I'll make you a deal," I said. "Let me go through your manuscript first. You've got a lot of notes here. Then we can talk about the book."

She set it on her desk and gave a little one-shoulder shrug. "Fine. I know you're busy. You're the photographer for the royal wedding." She sat down and avoided my eyes. "Everyone's talking about it around here. I heard about the party last night at the Austrian ambassador's residence."

She hadn't been at the party. "Do you know Yasmin?"

Her smile was brittle. "Oh, sure. Everyone here knows her. And her mother. Senator Gilberti's on the Smithsonian board."

It sounded like a dig at Yasmin, implying Ursula pulled strings to get her daughter a job at the museum.

"I didn't know that."

She nodded. "How did you end up with the job, if you don't mind my asking? I didn't know you photographed weddings."

"I don't. A mutual friend introduced me to Victor. He liked my photographs, so he asked me if I'd do it as a personal favor."

"I should have guessed it was Victor. I heard Yasmin was looking for a celebrity photographer, no disrespect to you."

"Olivia," I said, "they're my clients."

She leaned toward me, elbows on her desk, fingers interlaced. "I wish you the best of luck. Yasmin went after Victor because she wanted his title and all the glamour and wealth that come with who his family is. That's all there is to it. She wants to appear on the cover of magazines because she's such a fashion icon or she went skiing in Gstaad or vacationed on Richard Branson's private island or partied with some rock star after his concert." She sat back in her chair and folded her arms. There were two bright pink spots in her cheeks. "I wonder how long it will be before she finds a lover."

Teddy Roosevelt's daughter Alice Roosevelt Longworth, a flamboyant woman who had been known as "the other Washington monument" because of her sharp-tongued political zingers, owned a needlepointed pillow that read, "If you can't say something good about someone, sit right here by me."

"I think we ought to change the subject," I said. "I'm meeting Yasmin and her mother at the Franciscan Monastery at five o'clock. This is more information than I want to know."

She looked embarrassed. "I apologize. I shouldn't have said anything, though all of it is an open secret around here. I met Victor last year at a Smithsonian lecture. He's a doll." She stood up. "Be in touch if you have questions about my notes. And let's get together again when you're done. Maybe the end of next week? I need your spring photos and all the interior shots by the last week of May, by the way."

I nodded. "I'm still waiting to hear from someone about taking photographs inside the Arts and Industries Building. Though I met a friend of yours who said he could cut the red tape. David Arista."

Her eyes flashed when I mentioned his name, but she said in a cool voice, "David? Really? How did you meet him?"

"At the party last night and then I ran into him walking through the Ripley Garden."

She straightened a pile of already tidy papers. "Last year right after Museum Press hired me, we worked together on publicity for a book on the history of the National Portrait Gallery." She fiddled with the pages until the edges were aligned. "Now he works with Yasmin. They're very close."

The pink color had returned to her cheeks. "Tell me," she said, "did he invite you for coffee or a drink?"

I smiled. "He did."

She didn't smile. "Want some advice about David Arista?"

"Sure."

She pointed to the corridor outside her door. "Walk down that hall. There are a couple of women who could give it to you."

I thought about what Thea Stavros had said to me last night: *Get in line, darling.*

"I'm not interested in anything except speeding up my request to get into the Arts and Industries Building."

She reached around and flipped her hair off her neck again. "I wouldn't ask him. Then you'd owe him a favor. And David always collects." Her phone rang and she glanced down at it. "Sorry, I need to take this. Good luck."

I left and wondered if she had been talking about the book or David Arista. And if Olivia Upshaw was also one of the women who could give me firsthand advice about the danger of getting involved with him.

I left the Smithsonian by the Mall entrance and stood under the portico. Across from me, the enormous green dome of the Natural History Museum rose behind a line of bare trees. The rain had come and gone during my meeting with Olivia, and the frigate-sized clouds piled overhead now streamed west toward the river, leaving a swath of bright sky behind. But the streets were still wet and slick, and the slant of the rain had made dark-ringed stains on the curves of the sand-colored American Indian Museum at the far end of the Mall.

As predicted, it took half an hour to find a legal parking place on Capitol Hill and then pass through security in the Russell Senate Office Building. Ursula Gilberti had an office in the Capitol as a member of the Senate leadership, but her secretary had told me I was expected in her private office on the fourth floor of Russell.

It was the oldest of the three Senate office buildings, and to me the two other buildings—Dirksen and Hart—lacked its character, history, and elegance. They also didn't have the magnificent two-story columned Rotunda or the grand Kennedy Caucus Room, where the sinking of the *Titanic* had been investigated and the Watergate hearings had unfolded.

I made a point of detouring through the Rotunda, which was

silent and empty except for a security guard. Daylight flooding through the oculus in the dome softened the severity of the gray-and-white-hued marble, and I stopped to take photographs of the arches and columns and the carvings in the coffered ceiling while the guard watched me. Then I took an elevator to the fourth floor.

Ursula's state flag, the flag of West Virginia, hung from a stand in an alcove in the corridor outside her suite of offices; bright colors against more gray-and-white marble. One of the young female receptionists in the visitors' room took me back outside and walked me to a door that led to the secretary's office, where she handed me over to a white-haired no-nonsense woman. She, in turn, led me into Ursula's office.

The large room was furnished with a quirky mix of modern and antique furniture, the walls painted a buttery yellow and covered with art, mostly avant-garde modern, which surprised me, along with numerous awards and rows of photographs of Ursula with the good and the great, which did not. On the mantel of her carved marble fireplace next to a modern sculpture of what looked like a bronze elephant was my framed engagement photograph of Yasmin and Victor.

She got up from a paper-strewn desk and shook my hand.

"Can I get you and Ms. Medina a cup of coffee, Senator? Tea?" the secretary asked.

Ursula gave me a quizzical look and I shook my head. "Not just now, thanks. Can you buzz me when my two o'clock arrives?"

I glanced at my watch. One fifty. Whatever Ursula had to say wasn't going to take long.

"Sophie, please have a seat." She gestured to a pair of leather mission-style armchairs across from her desk and I slid into one of them. "Thank you for coming by."

Last night, the golden light of the candelabras that graced the dining room table and the glittering chandeliers in the formal rooms of the Austrian ambassador's residence had somewhat softened Ursula Gilberti's hard-shell demeanor. She had been a proud mother at a family celebration, not the tough get-the-deal-done woman she was known as on the Hill. Today she wore a severe black suit with a white blouse and a pearl choker, and any softness I'd seen at that party was gone.

"I have a proposal for you." She smiled, but it lacked warmth, and already I knew I didn't like where this was going.

She put on a pair of thick-framed reading glasses and picked up a piece of paper from her desk. Though I couldn't see through it, I thought it looked a lot like my contract. "It concerns the fee you're charging."

It was the fee we'd agreed on after a round of horse trading. I gave her a tight-lipped smile and waited for her to go on. She wanted more sessions for the same price or something like that.

"I'd like you to do this job pro bono."

"Pardon me?"

"Pro bono. It means you wouldn't charge me for it."

"I know what pro bono means, Senator."

"In return, I will recommend you to everyone I know, and believe me, I know a lot of people."

She had somehow managed to make it sound like she was doing me a favor.

"Thank you for the offer, but I'd prefer to stick to the agreement we have."

Ursula took off her glasses and rubbed the bridge of her nose with her thumb and forefinger. "I'm not sure you understand. Do you realize how much publicity you're going to get just from being chosen as the photographer for this wedding? A royal wedding in Washington? You couldn't pay for that kind of exposure. Already the guest list includes royalty from just about every European country, senators, cabinet secretaries, a Supreme Court justice . . . not to mention that we're juggling publicists from a couple of rather big names in Hollywood whom I've met over the years and would like to be here." She folded her hands. "The president and the first lady are on the guest list."

"It sounds like it's going to be quite an event. But with all respect, I didn't volunteer for this or compete with anyone else. Victor asked me because he likes my work and I said yes."

Ursula blew out a short-fused breath and looked up at the ceiling. "Oh, for God's sake," she said, focusing on me again. "Do you have any idea how much this wedding has cost me so far? I'm also in the middle of a primary where I'm being out-spent by an opponent who's got deep pockets all the way to China, and then there's the election in the fall. When all is said and done, I'm a working single mother, not a millionaire. The expenses for all of this are absolutely crushing. Can you possibly understand what I'm saying?"

Sure I could. I had bills, too. That's why I worked for a living and expected to get paid for it.

"I'm sorry to hear that—"

She cut me off. "I need you to do this, Sophie. I'm not really asking you. I'm telling you. I can't afford to pay you anything beyond what I've already given you. You were well compensated for last night's party, and I trust you'll be sending a link to those photos soon because I'm fending off press queries with a stick until I get them. I'm not asking for charity, you understand, because I assure you what I'm offering will be very much in your financial and professional interest. And I always keep my word."

Except for the contracts she signed. And it certainly felt like she was asking for charity. Before I could open my mouth, her phone buzzed and she reached for it.

"We're almost through here. Ask him to wait." She put down the phone and said to me, "If you don't want to do it, I'll find someone else. Any other photographer would kill to be in your position. And I don't want Yasmin to know, either. Or Victor. This conversation needs to stay between us."

Gloves off. Now I knew why she was so good at her job as her party's whip.

"I'll have to think about it," I said.

"Fine. You have until five o'clock, when we're supposed to meet at the monastery. If you change your mind between now and then, let me know. I'll need to start looking for another photographer right away." She paused and gave me a halfhearted smile. "I certainly hope it won't come to that."

I stood up. "I'll let you know. And I can see myself out. Good afternoon, Senator."

Before she could reply or buzz her secretary to escort me out and admit her waiting two o'clock, I walked over to her private door, which led directly to the outside corridor.

"You need to use the other door—" she said.

I had no intention of waiting to be escorted out by the secretary and I didn't hear the forbidden door click shut behind me until I passed Ursula's state flag at the entrance to her suite of offices. This time I took the spiral staircase with its winding bronze balustrade. When I reached the first floor, I was as breathless with anger as I'd been a few minutes ago in her office.

By the time I walked outside, it was ten past two. I had fewer than three hours to simmer down and decide what I was going to do.

I reached in my jacket pocket for my phone, ready to call Ursula and tell her she could find another photographer. But it was the wrong pocket and my fingers closed around the little key I'd found this morning by the Japanese lantern. I thought of Victor and the sweet letter he had written me, asking if I would do him and Yasmin the honor of photographing their wedding. Could I really face him and tell him I had changed my mind?

Whatever I decided to do about Ursula's ultimatum, I had to stop by the monastery anyway. I had promised Kevin I would take pictures of the community garden and I needed to ask him if he'd lost this key. It was too early to drive over there now. Kevin was probably still busy with the children from Brookland Elementary. Between the meetings with Olivia and Ursula I had forgotten about lunch, and right now I was famished.

I dropped the key in my pocket and walked down 1st Street past the Supreme Court and the Library of Congress on my left and the Capitol on my right until I got to Pennsylvania Avenue. A few blocks later, I slid into a booth at the Tune Inn, the scruffy, beloved bar that was one of the Avenue's oldest Hill hangouts, ordered a beer and a burger, and tried to forget about Ursula Gilberti. There was a sports program on the television over the bar, alternating between highlights of March Madness and ice hockey, while Willie Nelson, Brad Paisley, and the rest of them sang the old rip-your-heart-out country songs from the jukebox. I ate and drank and listened to them croon about lost love and women who were trouble and the tantalizing freedom of getting in your truck and leaving it all behind.

I thought about ordering another beer and just spending the rest of the afternoon at the Tune until whenever I felt like leaving, but I'm not that kind of girl. I paid the waitress and told her to keep the change, which was almost as much as the bill. Then I walked back to my car and drove to Brookland and the Franciscan Monastery.

It was time to face my own music.

The parking lot across the street from the monastery was deserted when I pulled in shortly before four, even though the gardens and the church were still open to the public. The Byzantine-style Church of Mount St. Sepulchre, built to resemble the Hagia Sophia in Istanbul, always looked to me as if it had been plucked from the midst of the real Holy Land, where it had stood in the shadow of a sacred Catholic shrine, and set down in this working-class neighborhood of Craftsman bungalows and wood-framed houses the way Dorothy's house had landed in Oz. The inlaid gold-and-red Jerusalem Cross, the symbol of the Franciscans since the Crusades, and the gold cupola on top of the dome gleamed in the dull late-afternoon light. I walked through the arched entrance to the Rosary Portico, the cloistered walkway that surrounded the monastery on three sides.

In a few weeks the formal garden beds on these grounds would be filled with hundreds of blooming roses and flowering annuals. Now they were mostly bare patches of earth except for bright yellow and orange pansies around the statues of St. Francis, St. Christopher, and the monastery's Franciscan founder, Godfrey Schilling.

Kevin was either in his room in the friary or somewhere on the grounds. The quickest way to find out was to ask the guard who sat in the small anteroom connecting the residence and the church. But when I checked with him, he seemed surprised.

"I haven't seen Brother Kevin all afternoon," he said. "I don't believe he's here."

"He was supposed to meet the children from Brookland Elementary at the community garden at two o'clock," I said.

The man shook his head. "That was canceled because it was raining."

"I saw his car parked on the street just now. He has to be here."

"Then try the Valley Shrines in the lower garden," he said. "I just came from the church and he wasn't there. He also might be praying at the outdoor Stations of the Cross since it's Lent."

I thanked him and walked through the portico with its multicolored columns and small chapels with mosaics commemorating the mysteries of the rosary. A sign marked the entrance to the lower gardens halfway down the walkway, and a series of blacktop ramps zigzagged down to several flights of stairs that ended in what looked like a large park. From down here the monastery was nearly invisible, hidden by towering evergreens and ancient magnolias, a tangle of brush and vines and high stone walls.

The formal part of the garden was dominated by a replica of the grotto at Lourdes, a place where the faithful believed the

Virgin Mary appeared to a young peasant girl named Bernadette Soubirous, and that the waters of a spring located on that
spot possessed special healing powers. I called Kevin's name, my
voice echoing weirdly off the ivy-covered wall where a statue of
Mary looked down from an alcove on the white marble figure of
St. Bernadette kneeling with her arms outstretched in the middle
of a garden of bare, green-tinged rosebushes.

I made a complete tour, checking all the tucked-away chapels
and memorials. Maybe Kevin was still working in the community garden, which was in a clearing on the upper level near the
end of the Stations of the Cross. I followed the winding path
through the woods until I was at the top of the hill across from
the monastery.

The small garden was enclosed by chicken wire nailed to
posts, presumably to keep out rabbits, with a gate at one end.
Not much was sprouting this early in the year, as Kevin had said,
so it was mostly tilled earth. Someone had left a pitchfork with a
weathered handle in a pile of mulch near the gate, and a garden
hose was coiled on a large hook attached to one of the posts.

Kevin wasn't here, so I finished the path of the Stations until
I reached the final one, the laying of Jesus in his tomb. If Kevin's
car was at the monastery and he wasn't in his room or the church,
where else would he be? Had he returned to the catacombs for
something else he'd hidden?

Then I remembered the Grotto of Gethsemane, a replica of
the garden where Jesus prayed the night before his crucifixion.
The entrance was on the hill opposite where I was standing,
halfway between the upper and lower gardens and so well hidden you couldn't see it from either the monastery or the lower
garden. I ran back through the woods and sprinted up the stairs,
slipping on a slick patch of moss and mud. I grabbed a vine as
thick as a small tree trunk that ran along the wall, but I still
landed hard on one knee. The momentum knocked my camera
bag off my shoulder and it bumped on the ground.

I found Kevin in the grotto, lying on his side at the bottom of a small staircase. The wrought-iron grillwork door to the underground chapel was padlocked and looked like it had been that way for a while. In the viscous gloomy light, the small room hewn out of rock like a cave seemed more like a prison than a place to pray. I knelt beside my dear, beloved friend and touched my finger to the pulse point on his neck.

But I already knew I was too late. Brother Kevin Boyle was dead.

5

A gust of wind blew through the trees above my head, a low, keening sound almost like a child crying. Had Kevin fallen, or had he been pushed? I whipped around in case I'd missed seeing someone come up behind me, trapping me in this dead-end place. But no one was there, only Kevin and me.

I wiped my eyes with the back of my hand and got out my phone to call 911, turning away because I couldn't bear to look at him while I did this. A female dispatcher answered after three rings and thought I was calling to report the death of my brother.

"He's a Franciscan friar," I said. "He belongs to a Catholic religious order. *Brother* Kevin Boyle."

"Okay, I'm with you now. Sorry about that, hon. Spell the name, please."

I did.

"Address?"

I gave it to her and explained that Kevin was in the Gethsemane Grotto of the monastery garden, spelling Gethsemane before she asked. She took down my name and number, confirmed the monastery's address, and told me someone would be here shortly.

"Do you know how long?"

"As soon as possible. Please stay on the scene and meet the officer." She disconnected.

As soon as possible. Fifteen minutes? Twenty? Longer? Kevin was dead, gone, so no police cruisers and ambulances with their flashing lights and wailing sirens were going to come racing up 14th Street.

I turned back to him. He was lying on his right side in a contorted angle in the cramped space. His left hand was thrown up over his face as though shielding himself from something or someone, and his outstretched right hand was clenched in a fist. His eyes were wide open, as though he'd been surprised, and judging by his position, he had fallen forward. Somehow he must have hit his head, maybe on the steps or the sharp corner of the stone wall or the padlocked wrought-iron gate, which had stopped his momentum, because a pool of blood underneath his right shoulder had oozed onto the stone floor and seeped into his habit. Both his feet rested on the last step, and dried mud embedded with bits of mulch was stuck to the bottom of his sandals.

Kevin was a good man, a holy man of grace and erudition and scholarship, fierce in his beliefs, loyal to his friends, devoted in his faith. I didn't want to remember him stripped of his dignity like this, blood spattered, his kind, intelligent blue eyes now staring blindly, his habit rucked up to reveal worn, threadbare trousers and pale flesh, a sense of death already permeating this place like a bad stink.

Fading daylight poured in through a fretted skylight inside the locked chapel. The wind rustled the trees, the shifting shadows rippling like the lashings of a whip on the walls and floor. The spine-tingling feeling that something was crawling on my skin made me wonder if I was being watched. A replica of the tomb where Jesus had been laid after he was crucified was only a few steps from the grotto. I couldn't remember if that gate was locked as well. The air fizzed with a low-pitched vibrating whine. I scrambled up the stairs, needing to get away from this closed-in space with its prisonlike entrance, to the open space of the upper garden and the sanctuary of the church.

Halfway back to the main garden path I skidded on the muddy spot where I'd slipped before, and a branch from one of the vines brushed against me like fingers raking my skin. I whisked it away and ran, the crazy idea flitting through my mind that the spirits of the dead haunted this alcove and the vines and branches that ran along the walls had begun magically weaving together to form a barrier that would imprison me in the Gethsemane Grotto.

I raced up the ramp to the Rosary Portico, colliding with a friar who was striding toward me. He was tall and sturdy, with ruddy cheeks and a mop of dark brown hair, and wore a heavy dark plaid flannel shirt over his habit.

He grabbed my arms. "Hey, what's wrong? Hold on there. Why are you running?"

"Where's your guardian?" I said. "Where's Father Xavier? I just found Brother Kevin Boyle in the Gethsemane Grotto. I'm so sorry . . . he's dead."

The words tumbled out and the friar flinched. He was young, in his early twenties. "What are you talking about? Dead? Are you sure?"

"He's lying at the bottom of the stairs and there's blood. He's . . . believe me, he's dead. I called 911 and the police are on their way."

A scowl crossed his face. "The police? Why did you call them?"

"Because that's what you do when someone dies, that's why." He was staring at me like I was speaking in tongues. "You need to get Father Xavier."

"Who are you?"

"Sophie Medina. A friend of Kevin's. Who are you?"

"Paul Zarin." He let go of my arms and pulled his phone out of his shirt pocket. "Don't go anywhere. Stay right here."

He sprinted away and slipped into the church through a side door. Kevin had mentioned a Franciscan named Paul the other night. He had been walking through the monastery when Kevin thought someone was following him in the cloisters. According to Kevin, Paul had heard nothing.

He was back in less than a minute, accompanied by two knights of St. Sepulchre in white ice-cream suits. They split up, the knights heading toward the entrance to the lower garden and Paul Zarin returning to where I waited.

"I want to thank you for finding our brother," he said. "You're free to go. We'll take care of him. Our guardian will talk to the police if it's necessary."

"Take care of Kevin?"

"He belongs to God now," he said as the two knights disappeared down the ramp.

"What are you talking about? What are they going to do?"

"Bring Kevin to the church to lay him to rest there. It's what he would want. It's where he should be."

I caught my breath. "You can't move him. No one should touch anything in that grotto. Kevin could have fallen down the stairs, but he also could have been pushed. It could be a crime scene."

Paul Zarin's head snapped back as if I had just uttered something that defiled this holy place. "That's not possible. No one here would do such a thing."

"You have visitors, people who come and go as they please. And Kevin was a controversial public figure, you know that. People heckled him at talks all the time. Maybe someone showed up today and went too far."

Paul Zarin gave me another dark look. "Or maybe nothing

like that happened and it was merely God's plan to call Kevin home. Thank you again for finding our brother, but now I must ask you to leave. Please. Go in peace."

I folded my arms across my chest. "I'm not leaving. I can't leave. I'm the one who found him. The police will want to question me."

I thought when he had taken out his phone he'd called his superior, a quick, discreet conversation with Father Xavier Navarro to let him know something was seriously wrong, that this was an emergency. Instead it seemed like he'd alerted the entire monastery. I heard male voices as about a dozen men in Franciscan habits and a few in street clothes ran toward us, some emerging from the church, but most coming from the friary.

He pointed to the entrance to the lower garden and shouted to the others. "Down there. He's in the Gethsemane Grotto with two of the knights. We must pray for him and then bring him to the church."

"Are you crazy?" I said. "You can't send them down there. They'll trample everything. They could destroy evidence before the police get a chance to search the area. Don't do this. You need to get Father Xavier here right now."

"Father Xavier is on his way back to the monastery. He should be here any minute." His clear gray eyes were cool and he pointed to my khaki trousers. "Did you fall or trip on something? That mud stain on your knee is fresh. You never told me what you are doing here or how you knew where to find Kevin."

It took a moment before I realized he was implying I had something to do with Kevin's death. I said, stunned, "I didn't know where to find him. And I came here to return something to him, plus Kevin asked me to take photos of the community garden. Ask the security guard at the residence. I checked with him when I got here."

But Paul Zarin had stopped listening. "Did you bring a friend?" he asked.

"Pardon?"

He pointed over my shoulder. "Her."

Yasmin Gilberti, stylishly dressed in jeans, leather boots, and a Burberry rain jacket with a pashmina scarf knotted around her neck, walked toward us down the middle of the driveway. Her vivid red hair was even more startling against the grayness of the afternoon. Paul Zarin didn't take his eyes off her.

I had forgotten all about our meeting. Ursula would be here at any moment as well.

"Sophie," Yasmin said when she reached Paul and me. "What are you doing here?"

It was an odd question. Maybe Ursula had decided to fire me after all and I just hadn't found out yet. Maybe Yasmin was expecting someone else.

"Kevin's dead, Yasmin," I said. "I found his body . . . found him . . . in the garden a few minutes ago. I'm sorry."

I shouldn't have blurted it out like that, but I was still dealing with my own grief. Yasmin turned pale, a horrified expression on her face. When she finally spoke, she sounded as though she were gasping for breath.

"Oh, my God. That's not possible. He can't be."

Paul Zarin spoke up. "Here comes Father Xavier."

A small black car sped through the main gate and stopped in the driveway across from the three of us. A slight, white-haired man in a Franciscan habit got out.

Father Xavier and Paul Zarin exchanged glances, and a look passed between them that I didn't understand. "Where is Kevin?" Xavier asked him.

"The Gethsemane Grotto. Our brothers are praying for him, and then two of the knights are bringing him to the church. It's where he would want to be. In God's house."

The old priest turned to Yasmin and me. "I understand a woman found him," he said in his gentle voice. "I am Father Navarro and I am in charge of this monastery. Was it one of you?"

"I found him, Father," I said. "I'm a friend of Kevin's. My

name is Sophie Medina and this is Yasmin Gilberti. She and her fiancé are going to be married here in June."

Xavier nodded, apparently recognizing Yasmin's name and possibly mine, but before he could speak, I said, "With all respect, you can't move Kevin. I mean, you shouldn't. All those people who are down there now are leaving footprints everywhere . . . if it's a crime scene they could destroy evidence."

Father Xavier shot me a startled look as the full meaning of what I was saying seemed to dawn on him. "You are right," he said. He turned to Paul. "Go and tell whoever is in the grotto not to disturb anything and that they must leave at once. I will call the police and we will cooperate with them."

Yasmin's face was still as white as bleached bone. I took her arm and said, "You don't look well. There's a bench over there in the courtyard. Maybe you should sit down."

She shook her head. "I'm okay."

She didn't look okay. She looked scared. To Xavier, I said, "I called the police as soon as I found Kevin."

Two blue-and-white Metropolitan Police Department cruisers pulled into the monastery driveway. "So you did," he said. "It looks as though they're here."

The 911 dispatcher was right that the police wanted to talk to me since I was the one who had found Kevin. I caught a glimpse of Ursula's black Mercedes with its blue, yellow, and white West Virginia "USS" license plate pull into the parking lot as a petite African American officer whose name tag said her last name was Carroll walked me into the visitors' lobby of the church.

She pointed to one of the benches in front of a screen where a video usually played before the tour started.

"Please have a seat," she said. "I'll be right back."

I glanced up at the clock behind the reception desk where the knights usually sat. It showed exactly five o'clock.

Officer Carroll didn't return for half an hour. She sat next to me and apologized for keeping me waiting before she asked all the usual questions, how I'd found Kevin, what my business was at the monastery, and eventually, my relationship with the deceased.

I flinched at that word and she looked up. Her short, glossy jet-black hair framed her face in a cap of loose pin curls that reminded me of a cherub.

"I'm sorry," she said. "I know this is difficult."

I told her about my friendship with Kevin as she made notes in a spiral notebook.

"You came here for a meeting with Senator Gilberti and her daughter," she said. "Why were you also looking for Brother Kevin?"

I fished the little gray key out of my pocket. "To ask if this belonged to him. I found it on the ground at the Tidal Basin this morning and I wondered if he had dropped it."

Officer Carroll took the key and turned it over. "You think it's his?"

"I don't know. Like I said, I found it on the ground. Maybe he dropped it or maybe someone else did."

"Do you know what it opens?"

"No idea."

"You can keep it for now." She handed it back to me. "Did Brother Kevin have any enemies that you know of?"

"A lot of people didn't like him because of his views on the environment and climate change, especially after he wrote *Reaping What We Have Sown*," I said. "He told me once someone called him 'a tree-hugging kook in a robe.'"

"Did he mention any names?"

I shook my head. "But this morning at the Tidal Basin he told me he thought someone had begun following him. Last night after the party at the Austrian ambassador's residence and two other times, here at the monastery."

She gave me a sharp look. "Did he know who it was, or why someone would be following him?"

"No to your first question. But he thought it might have to do with a new book he's working on, something he came across in his research."

Officer Carroll tapped her pen on her notebook. The cap looked chewed on, as if she used it when she was thinking things through. "What research would that be?"

"Although Kevin's mostly known as an environmental conservationist, he has a PhD in botany. He was working on a botanical history of gardening and agriculture in colonial America."

She frowned. "Go on."

"He said he believed he'd made some kind of historical discovery and if he was right it could be worth a lot of money. Quite a lot of money."

"Botany." She shrugged. "That's plants. Any chance he could have been referring to something to do with drugs? Those kind of plants?"

Drugs. The word dropped into the silence of this holy place and spread like a dark stain. My God, was she right? Not medicinal drugs but narcotics, derived from plants. Heroin, cocaine, hash, marijuana—what else was on that list? Had Kevin somehow gotten mixed up in something drug related?

I shivered as though a blast of cold air had just passed through the room, a specter moving from this life to the next. "I don't know . . . I mean, no. No way. Kevin . . . he was a good man, Officer Carroll. He would never knowingly get involved in anything illegal."

She gave me a searching look. "You got any idea how many times I hear that? 'I didn't mean it.' 'It wasn't my fault, it just happened.' Usually right before they ask to cut a deal."

"Not Kevin." I was adamant, my hands clasped tightly together so she would not realize how badly they were shaking. "I would bet my life on it."

"I hear that, too." Her smile was grim. "Anybody else come to mind who didn't get along with him? Maybe someone who had a grudge against him?"

I knew this wasn't going to sound good, but I told her anyway. "Last night at a party I overheard him arguing with Edward Jaine, or rather they were arguing with each other."

She looked up. "The Edward Jaine? The rich guy?"

"That's right."

"What was it about?"

"I don't know. They were in a corridor by themselves and they kept their voices down."

"But you're sure it was an argument and you're sure it was Edward Jaine and Brother Kevin Boyle?" When I nodded, she said, "All right, we'll check it out. As well as whether anyone else at the monastery knew about Brother Kevin being followed."

If Paul Zarin, whom I'd just met, was the Paul who'd been there the other night when Kevin heard footsteps in the cloisters, he'd shoot that theory down right away. So would the knight who'd been in the catacombs with him. I didn't want Officer Carroll thinking Kevin was some loony tune who heard voices, or that he was paranoid.

So I nodded and didn't say anything as she flipped back through her notes. "You're sure you didn't see anyone else in the garden when you got there?"

"Positive."

She shook her head in disgust. "Well, now that the grounds around that little cave have been contaminated thanks to everyone and his cousin trampling the place, it's going to royally screw up any chance of figuring out what the hell happened. Whose bright idea was that?"

I gave her a rueful look. "The Franciscan who was with Father Xavier and me when you first arrived. Paul Zarin. I told him that it might be a crime scene and that Kevin shouldn't be moved." I shrugged. "For all the good it did."

"It's not going to make the medical examiner's day, either."

"There'll be an autopsy?"

"For an unattended death with no obvious underlying conditions there's always an autopsy," she said. "Speaking of which, I didn't ask you whether Brother Kevin seemed unwell when you saw him this morning."

"He seemed fine," I said. "Are you saying he might have died of natural causes?"

"Until we have the results of the autopsy, we don't rule out anything. But if the ME finds injuries consistent with a fall and there are no witnesses, plus no obvious motive for his death—" She shrugged. "Then it may just well be an accident. It does happen, you know."

"You mean you won't try to find out if he might have been murdered?"

She gave me a withering look. "Right before I came here I was with a mother whose twelve-year-old got shot walking home from school. He's at Children's Hospital about fifteen minutes from here, in critical condition. Probably not gonna make it. I promised that woman I'd catch the asshole who shot her son whose straight-A report card is now covered in his blood. I make a lot of promises to a lot of people, and I do my best to keep them." She pointed to a small crucifix that hung on the wall. "But I'm not God."

"I'm so sorry about that little boy."

She said with feeling, "Me, too. We do the best we can, Ms. Medina." She stood up. "Now, if you'll excuse me, I gotta talk to a few priests about the death of one of their own. You're free to go."

By the time I left the church, it was just after six o'clock. The temperature had dropped and the overcast moonless sky made it seem later. The lights in the arched Gothic church windows and along the colonnade of the Rosary Portico glowed like lanterns, gilding the gardens so the place looked like an enchanted fairyland. Except for the two MPD cruisers parked at oblique angles in front of the statue of St. Christopher carrying the Christ Child, the Franciscan Monastery seemed serene and peaceful. Ursula Gilberti's Mercedes was gone, and presumably Yasmin had left, too.

After everything that had happened today, I hoped Ursula still didn't expect an answer to whether I would photograph Yasmin and Victor's wedding for free.

Someone called my name. Standing in one of the arches of the portico was a Franciscan, hood pulled low over his face, a dark silhouette backlit by the soft yellow light. I caught a flash of snow-white hair as he pushed back his hood.

Father Xavier. I walked across the lawn to where he stood.

"Officer Carroll said she just finished interviewing you," he said. "I wanted to make sure you were all right after what you've been through. Kevin spoke warmly of you, my dear. He was very fond of you."

"Thank you, Father. I was fond of him. I still can't believe he's dead."

"Nor can I."

"Did you know Kevin thought someone was following him? He told me about it when I saw him this morning. It really bothered him."

The old priest looked troubled, his face lined with fatigue and sadness. "Officer Carroll just asked me about that. I knew nothing about it. I wish Kevin had said something to me. To be honest, I was more worried about his health after what happened the other day."

"What are you talking about?"

"He went to the ER at Providence Hospital complaining of chest pains three days ago," he said. "Thought it might be his heart. They kept him overnight and released him."

That explained Officer Carroll asking me if I thought Kevin hadn't looked well this morning.

I pulled the key out of my pocket. "Do you recognize this, Father? Does it unlock something at the friary? A door or a locker?"

He shook his head. "No. We have few locked doors or cabinets. The church and the chapels are another matter; it is a regrettable fact of life that we can no longer leave the place open as we once did. For insurance purposes and for general safety we installed a security system. But that key does not unlock anything here that I know of. Why do you ask?"

"I think Kevin might have dropped it today. I was going to return it, if it was his."

He took the key and turned it over, rubbing his thumb over the etched number 58 on the head of the key. "Perhaps it opens a locker, as you suggest. Why don't you ask Edward?"

"Edward Jaine?"

"Yes, Kevin's benefactor." He smiled at the expression on my face. "Ah, I see you are surprised. You didn't know about their relationship? He was very generous in supporting Kevin's research, paying for his trips and anything he needed for his work."

"Last night at the Austrian ambassador's home I overheard Kevin arguing with him. And when Edward Jaine arrived at the party and walked into the room with Senator Gilberti, Kevin was really upset."

Xavier's forehead furrowed. "Are you sure? When I saw Kevin this morning at breakfast, he said he had enjoyed himself last night." His smile was tinged with regret. "Not that he would say any differently. Kevin kept himself to himself."

I nodded. Kevin was also a peaceful person. So why had he been arguing with the man who paid for his research?

"Is there something else, Sophie? I didn't mean to upset you further."

"I apologize for asking so soon, but I was wondering if you had any idea yet about . . . arrangements."

"You mean Kevin's funeral?" I nodded, and he said, "Yes, of course. Kevin planned it himself."

"He did?"

"It's one of our requirements," he said with a small smile. "Each of us must specify the readings, the music . . . everything must be on file. Don't look so shocked . . . we all leave this earth to join God someday. So far, I haven't heard of a single soul who's found a way around that immutable truth."

I smiled. "So you already know?"

"His funeral Mass will be here at Mount St. Sepulchre, of course, and he'll be buried with his brothers in our cemetery. But it probably won't take place for a few weeks to give Kevin's colleagues and friends from all over the country—all over the world, actually—time to make arrangements to attend."

"Can I do anything to help?"

"Keep us in your prayers, my dear. I am expecting an onslaught from the press once word gets out. Kevin was an international celebrity, and the media attention we'll likely receive will be difficult for many in this quiet community to handle. In his professional life as a scientist Kevin was revered and admired for his work around the world, but, as you know, there were others who found him a threat for speaking his mind."

I walked back to my car mulling over what Father Xavier had just said, along with Kevin's worry—fear, actually—that he was being stalked. His death was no accident. He hadn't slipped and fallen on those wet stairs or suffered a heart attack.

Someone had killed him.

Possibly someone who didn't like his politics, what he stood for, and decided to deliver his message in person this afternoon. Or had it been someone who knew about Kevin's current research, the discovery he'd mentioned to me this morning that he needed to keep secret?

Edward Jaine, maybe? Kevin said what he found might be worth "millions of dollars." Jaine was a multibillionaire, even though he'd invested in a few flops. He didn't need money, so perhaps that knocked him out as a suspect.

Then who was it? Who had cornered Brother Kevin Boyle, one of the kindest men I knew, in the Grotto of Gethsemane, a sacred place of agony and death, and killed him?

6

I got in my car and turned on my phone. A text message flashed on the screen.

> *Just leaving work. Going straight to Trio's. If I get there first,*
> *I'll order us a bottle of red.*

I leaned back against the headrest and closed my eyes. The message was from Grace Lowe, the first person I met the day I started school in Virginia after Harry and my mother got married. Last week she and I made dinner plans for tonight so I could fill her in on the book project I'd discussed with Kevin this morning.

As kids, Grace and I had been as close as sisters; even our teachers mixed us up, which we thought was hilarious since we looked nothing alike—my dark hair, dark eyes, and olive skin inherited from my Spanish father, and Grace, a cool, fair, blue-eyed blonde. What had cemented our friendship for more than twenty-five years was a bolshie, restless curiosity that occasionally got us into trouble but eventually led us both to careers in journalism, me as a photographer and Grace as a writer. Now she was a senior reporter on the Metro desk at the "other" Washington newspaper, the *Tribune*.

A month ago she covered what was supposed to be a feel-good story about the reopening of an elementary school not far from her home in Adams Morgan after a fire. When the interview was over, one of the teachers took her aside and told her about the kids in her class who missed school regularly because their parents could afford only a single pair of shoes, which all the children had to take turns wearing. Then there were families who lived in their cars, barely a rung on the ladder above being on the streets. Pride, the teacher said, kept most of the parents from asking for help. Grace had been so devastated by that kind of poverty in her own backyard that she came to me and asked if I'd help her raise money for new shoes for every child in the school. We wrote checks and passed the hat among our friends and family. Two weeks later, we had enough cash, so we went looking for a shoe store to sign on to the project. On Saturday, Sole Brothers Shoes in Adams Morgan was closing to the public for the afternoon so the kids and families could buy their shoes.

The idea behind the photo book was that the profits would go toward continuing the shoe project and also to raise money for the run-down Adams Morgan Children's Center, where most of those children went after school. The very last thing Kevin had said to me before he kissed me goodbye was that I could count on his help. The thought of taking this on without him was heart-wrenching.

I pressed the Call button on my phone. When Grace finally answered, I heard the familiar doorbell chime of the D.C. subway and a muffled voice announcing the doors were closing.

"I just got on the Metro," she said. "What's up?"

"Gracie." I raised my voice so she could hear me over the din. "I've got some bad news. Kevin Boyle is dead."

She gasped as though someone had elbowed her hard in the ribs. "Oh, my God, Sophie, that's awful. What happened?"

I told her, and then she said, "I need to call the desk. Actually, I probably need to get off this train and go back to work. Someone's going to have to get out to the monastery and cover this."

I massaged my forehead with the back of my free hand. Father Xavier said he expected to be inundated by the media because of Kevin's notoriety. I had just opened the floodgates. But if I were in Grace's place, I would have done the same thing.

"Are you going to do it?" I asked.

"I don't know," she said. "We're also going to need an obit. I'm sure we don't have one on file. Kevin wasn't that old, only in his fifties, and nobody expected . . . oh, my God, I can't believe he's gone."

"I know," I said, and for the first time my voice wavered.

"Oh, honey. Soph . . . are you okay?"

"I'm fine. Look, Grace, can you keep my name out of the story?"

"I'll do what I can. Have you told anyone else?"

"No. Certainly not anyone from the press. I'll call Nick when I get home. And Jack. This is going to kill him."

"Oh, Jesus. Yes, Jack. He's teaching tonight. I spoke to him earlier."

"I'll leave a message, tell him to call right away. I don't want him finding out on the Internet or hearing it on the radio or television before I get a chance to talk to him."

"I'd better go," she said. "I think it's going to be a long night."

I left vague messages for both Nick and Jack, though it would be awhile before Nick and I spoke because of the eight-hour time difference between Washington and Riyadh. As for Jack, his classes finished at nine o'clock, but he often stayed late for students who needed to talk to him.

By the time I heard from him it was a few minutes before eleven. I knew from his voice that he didn't know about Kevin, but Jack can read me like a book. "What's wrong?" he said. "I hope it's not Nick."

I was upstairs in bed with a glass of wine, channel surfing in the dark. I flipped to Channel 4 to wait for the eleven o'clock local news and hit Mute.

"It's not Nick," I said. "I'm sorry, Jack. Kevin Boyle is dead. I found him today at the monastery at the bottom of a flight of stairs in the lower garden. When I got there it was too late. He was already gone."

His silence went on for an eternity. Then I heard his heavy sigh and what sounded like a bottle being uncorked and liquid splashed into a glass. "My God, Sophie. We were all together just last night. I'd been expecting to hear from him today, so that explains why I didn't."

"I'm so sorry," I said again. "I'm pretty sure it's going to be on the late news. I didn't want you to find out that way. And Grace knows . . . we were supposed to have dinner this evening. She might be writing the story for the *Trib*. Or the obituary."

I stumbled over the last word, and Jack said, "What happened?"

I heard the tinkle of ice cubes. Probably a Scotch on the rocks.

"I don't know for sure. The police came . . . they had to. The officer who talked to me said there would be an autopsy to determine the cause of death."

"The cause of death?" He sounded as if he was still trying to process that Kevin was gone. "How could Kevin fall down a flight of stairs? That doesn't sound right."

"I don't think he fell. I think he might have been pushed."

"Are you serious?"

So I told him about Kevin's fear that someone had been following him. "Unfortunately, Kevin didn't tell anyone else about it. And no one at the monastery wants to believe what happened could be anything other than an accidental fall."

"Why would someone push him?"

"I can think of two reasons. A lot of people hated Kevin's

views on climate change and the environment. Not to mention the businesses he alienated that had to hire lawyers to fight him in court and drug dealers who had to move when he tried to clean up a couple of parks."

"If not liking someone's politics or what he stood for was enough of a motive to commit murder, Washington would be a ghost town, Soph. It's a big step off the edge into the abyss to go from hating someone to actually doing something about it. What's your other reason?"

I heard voices in the background on his end of the phone and glanced up at the television. "Here it is," I said, unmuting the sound on mine. "I'm watching Channel 4."

"Me, too."

We were silent as an attractive blond reporter did a live stand-up in front of the monastery gates. The harsh spotlights lit her and the scenery behind her as if it were daytime while the camera panned to show bouquets of flowers, lighted votive candles, and handwritten notes placed in tribute in front of the entrance to the Rosary Portico.

"The tight-knit Catholic religious community in Brookland, often called 'Little Rome' because of the many Catholic institutions located here, is reeling tonight from the death of one of their own," the reporter said. "Brother Kevin Boyle, a Franciscan friar and internationally known environmentalist, was found— tragically—on the grounds of the Franciscan Monastery's magnificent gardens in northeast Washington, a place he knew and loved so well."

She continued talking as the picture switched to B-roll of the monastery, showing the gardens in full bloom, dazzling sweeps of color against vivid greens, on a sun-dappled day. Eventually, the camera zeroed in on the Gethsemane Grotto, and the reporter didn't miss the opportunity to play up the irony.

I heard Jack's sharp intake of breath. "That's where you found him?"

"Yes . . . shhh, listen. She interviewed Father Xavier."

The brief taped interview was poignant, and the old priest looked more weary than when I'd seen him this evening. The picture cut back to the reporter, who wove together Kevin's pioneering work as an environmentalist into the story of Francis of Assisi, the patron saint of plants and animals, before doing her sign-off.

Then the screen flickered to the story of the twelve-year-old boy who'd been shot, his mother's anguished face. I couldn't bear to watch her raw grief and turned it off.

After a moment, Jack said, "You were about to tell me the other reason why someone would push Kevin down those stairs. And why he thought someone was following him."

"I think it might have something to do with his research." I told him about the key. "I was going to ask Kevin if it was his, but obviously I can't anymore. Father Xavier didn't recognize it. He suggested I ask Edward Jaine. Did you know he was underwriting Kevin's research?"

"No." Jack sounded as surprised as I'd been. "I didn't."

"They were arguing about something last night at the party. I overheard them."

"Sophie," he said, "maybe you should just do what Xavier said and ask Jaine about the key."

I didn't reply, and he said, "Let me guess. You want to keep it so you can try to find whatever it unlocks."

"Not keep it, just hang on to it for a while. If Kevin and Edward Jaine were arguing, Kevin probably wouldn't want him to have it anyway."

"You don't know that."

"I just want to see if I can find out what it opens."

"And if you do?"

"Then maybe I'll know why they were arguing and what to do next."

"And if you don't?" When I didn't answer, he said, "It's a slippery slope, kiddo."

"Come on, Jack. If the key is Kevin's, then why did he have to find someplace that he considered safer than the monastery to store something . . . or hide it? If the autopsy shows he died because of a fall and there are no witnesses who saw anyone with him, the investigation ends there. The crime scene's contaminated to hell. Every friar who was at the monastery went down there to pray over him. It's a mess. The police may never find out what really happened."

"I don't think—"

"We owe it to Kevin. You know that. I know he's with God, but he should still be alive. There were so many things he wanted to do, so much good he could have done."

I heard Jack take another long drink, and when he spoke, his voice was tinged with sadness. "He was an incredible person. And don't think I didn't notice that you've roped me into this."

"Just give me twenty-four hours," I said. "If I don't find anything by tomorrow evening, I'll try to contact Edward Jaine and see if he knows anything about the key."

"If you do find anything, call me. And if I don't hear from you, I'll call you."

"Don't worry. There's really only one place I can think of to look. After that, I'm out of ideas."

Nick phoned the next morning when I was in the kitchen finishing my coffee and reading Grace's front-page story about Kevin. Her byline ran under the obit as well. Nick had already read the story on the Internet.

Long ago when I realized how much Nick would be on the road for his job with the Agency, we made a pact that we wouldn't share news that didn't travel well and would save the rough stuff for when we were together again and could talk it over face-to-face. I didn't tell Nick that I had found Kevin, or any of the rest of the story about him being stalked or my belief that his death was no accident. He knew, of course, that something was wrong. You can't fool a spook, especially if you are sleeping with him.

"Are you okay, baby? I wish I were there."

"I wish you were here, too. Jack took it hard and Grace covered the story for the *Trib*. Everyone's devastated."

"I'm sure." He exhaled the way he did when he wanted to get something off his chest. "Look, love, I know my industry fought hard against what Kevin stood for, that we don't accept his arguments and theories that we are somehow responsible for, or the cause of, climate change."

We had had this discussion before, how industry lawyers and their scientists had come up with an avalanche of data and statistics refuting much of what Kevin had said in *Reaping What We Have Sown*. Nick was veering into the forbidden territory of news that didn't travel well. He and I had had our differences on this subject. Some of them involved shouting.

"I don't think we should—"

"Wait," he said. "Hear me out. Kevin held our feet to the fire, standing there like the reincarnation of St. Francis of Assisi in his quiet, humble way. He never backed down and he wasn't afraid of anything or anyone. Everyone in my business listened to him, Soph. I know a lot of people who rooted for him privately though they couldn't say so publicly, me included. Now that he's gone, there's no one who can take his place. He was a formidable adversary. Everyone's going to miss him, and thanks to you, I was honored to know him as a friend."

I reached for the dish towel and swiped at my eyes. Eventually I said, "I'm glad you knew him, too."

"I'm sorry. I didn't mean to upset you."

"I'm not upset."

"I love you. And I'm afraid I have to go. I'm leaving for the desert tonight and I'm not sure what kind of Internet service I'll have. But I promise I'll call or write as soon as I can."

"I love you, too."

Nick wasn't at all religious—the family joke was that he was waiting for the Rapture—so I didn't expect him to say what he said next. "I guess God decided He needed Kevin more than we did, so He called him home."

If he meant it as a comfort to me, it wasn't. I didn't think God had called Kevin home.

I still thought there was a killer out there who had made that decision.

My solitary idea about what the little gray key unlocked wasn't that imaginative. At the party two nights ago, Kevin and Thea Stavros had talked about a study room he used in the Science, Technology and Business Library at the Library of Congress. I had already checked and found it was located in the John Adams Building across the street behind the main Jefferson library. What were the odds I'd find lockers there where scholars like Kevin could leave books, papers, and other reference materials at the end of the day?

I grabbed my camera bag and the key to my Vespa from a hook on an antique hall rack and went downstairs. Nick and I rented the top two floors of a Queen Anne gingerbread row house on S Street, just north of Dupont Circle. India Ferrer, our landlady, lived next door, and the lower two floors were occupied by Maximillian Katzer, an interior designer who owned an upscale antiques gallery in Georgetown. Our apartment had come furnished, and we'd sold almost everything we owned in England rather than pay to ship it home, so over the winter Max had taken me around town to his friends' galleries and used his professional discount and bargaining skills to help me purchase a number of pieces of vintage furniture that would have otherwise been out of my price range. Nick and I moved India's things to the carriage house in the alley behind the two row houses, and gradually the duplex started to feel like home. In return for

Max's design help and services, I photographed several of his clients' homes for his portfolio and took pictures for his website. So far we both thought it had been a good deal.

An envelope with M. Katzer Fine Antiques engraved in plum-colored ink lay on the floor below the mail slot when I got downstairs to the foyer. The handwritten note looked like he'd written in haste.

Left very early this morning and didn't think you'd be up. My deepest condolences on the death of your friend—saw the story on the news. I'll call you for a drink. I'm sure you could use one. Love.

I took a deep breath, sent him a thank-you text message, and put the note in my camera bag. Overnight the weather had changed from yesterday's late-winter raw chilliness to the soft sunshine and sharp blue skies of early spring. Washington is like that now, seasons that ping-pong back and forth, so it might be seventy for a few days in December, or there will be a brief, fierce blizzard in late March, instead of the orderly trajectory of the seasons that I remember growing up. Kevin had told me climate change evolved over centuries, not decades, but I still thought the weather was crazier and more extreme now.

I unlocked the large sliding doors to the carriage house where I kept my mint-green Vespa in bad weather. It had been one of my first purchases when I moved home after owning one in London and discovering what a godsend it was in a city with no place to park. But D.C. didn't have London's temperate climate, so when the weather turned bad, I took cabs or the Metro, or borrowed Niles, India's late husband's British racing-green Jaguar. Parking the Jaguar was like docking the *Queen Mary*, and within a few months Nick had moved back to D.C. as well, so at Christmas we bought a used red-and-white-striped Mini Cooper convertible from a family friend.

But today was perfect for the Vespa, and after a half-hour trip from Dupont Circle to Capitol Hill, it took only a few minutes to find a lamppost on 2nd Street, a block from the Adams Building, where I chained the scooter.

A guard at the front desk in the empty lobby looked inside my camera bag and asked me to walk through a metal detector before directing me to a bank of elevators down the hall. I was the lone occupant of the car, which went straight to the fifth floor. Unlike the palatial Thomas Jefferson Building across the street, the staid-looking Adams Building, built in the 1930s for the sole purpose of housing overflow books, wasn't a tourist destination. The only people I was likely to encounter in the corridors were employees of the Library of Congress and people who had come to do research as Kevin had done. So far, other than the guard downstairs, I hadn't seen a soul.

The double doors to the Science and Business Reading Room had been thrown open on an enormous high-ceilinged Art Deco space of lighted bookcases and walls of gray concrete block decorated with subtly colored murals and quotations. Candlestick lamps with green-striped copper shades lined rows of mahogany tables and made pools of golden light in an otherwise coolly lit elegant room where half a dozen people read, wrote, or typed on laptops. Kevin must have loved this beautiful place with its air of Old World scholarship and reverential silence.

A cute blonde who looked like she'd just graduated college asked for my reader's card at the entrance desk. The laminated ID around her neck said her name was Logan Day. A few months ago when I was still working at the photo agency in Georgetown, I'd gotten a reader's card when I needed to use another of the library's specialized reading rooms before a photo shoot at the Turkish embassy. I pulled it out of my wallet and handed it to Logan Day. She examined it and asked me to sign in.

"Is Thea Stavros here?" I asked.

"She's in her office. Do you have an appointment?"

"No. Actually, I was just wondering if this reading room has public lockers."

"Around the corner," she said, and I felt a little zing of excitement. "The long teal doors, two rows of them, above the bookshelves. You'll need a library ladder to reach the top row. Unfortunately, ever since the earthquake a few are jammed shut, but you won't have any problem finding one that's free."

"The earthquake damaged this building?" I said.

"It did that." She pointed to a long jagged crack like a lightning bolt in the far wall. "And some of the lockers. But I'm sure you'll find an empty one."

I thanked her and walked around the corner.

A moment later I was back, holding the key. "Those look like storage cabinets. I'm looking for the locker that this key fits, number fifty-eight."

Logan examined it. "It's not ours."

"Don't the people who use your research facilities need lockers to keep their things secure when they leave at the end of the day?"

She passed the key back to me and shook her head. "They're called study rooms, but they're more like individual private offices with doors that can be locked. Everyone leaves their stuff in their own room." She frowned. "Why are you so sure that key belongs to us?"

I'd tripped too many red flags and now I'd made her suspicious. But I was also out of ideas about what the key might unlock. "I'm not. A friend who uses one of your rooms might have dropped it when he and I were down at the Tidal Basin yesterday."

Her eyes narrowed. "So you're trying to get into your friend's locker, rather than returning the key to him?"

"I don't know if it's his, so I thought I would check here first. Unfortunately I can't ask him anymore if it belonged to him."

"Why not?"

"He's dead."

We were no longer speaking in library whispers, and I could feel the eyes of everyone sitting nearby focused on the two of us as though an electrical current had passed through the place.

She turned pale. "I think I should get Thea." She glanced down at my name on her sign-in sheet. "Please wait here, Ms. Medina."

I set my camera bag down and pretended to study the murals that formed an enormous frieze around the room, ignoring the stares I was getting. In a lighted alcove above the reference desk, a fan-shaped painting of Thomas Jefferson with Monticello in the background had an inscription in a corner: THIS ROOM IS DEDICATED TO THOMAS JEFFERSON. By the time I realized that all the murals and all the quotes were in some way related to Jefferson, Thea Stavros had burst through a set of double doors and was striding across the room.

She wore a tailored navy silk shirtwaist dress and held a lace-trimmed handkerchief in one hand. As she got closer, I wondered if she had been crying because her mascara looked smudged.

She didn't bother with a greeting, nor did she seem surprised to see me. "I heard the awful news about Kevin this morning," she said. "I still can't believe it."

"I know. Me, either."

"Logan said you've brought a key that belonged to a friend who died and you thought it was ours. It's Kevin's, isn't it?"

"I don't know."

Logan placed a hand over her heart as though she'd just felt a sudden pain. "Your friend was Brother Kevin Boyle?" she asked me, and I nodded. "He was such a sweetheart, everyone here loved him."

"May I see the key?" Thea asked.

We still had the undivided attention of everyone in the room. I handed it to Thea and she studied it.

"Why don't you leave it with me? I'll ask around at the other libraries and see if I can find out what it opens."

Giving up the key wasn't what I had in mind. "What about Kevin's study room?" I said. "Would it be possible to see if the key unlocks something he left in there?"

"You've got the master key, Thea," Logan said. "Maybe the three of us ought to check it out."

Thea gave Logan an admonishing look. "There are privacy issues, my dear."

"Kevin's dead," I said. "I can give the key to Father Navarro, the guardian at the Franciscan Monastery. He can fill out the appropriate paperwork to get Kevin's things returned. I guess I can wait and ask him."

I held my breath, hoping Thea was as curious as I was about the key. She turned it over in her hand and wrestled with protocol. Finally she sighed and said, "The study rooms are just through those double doors. I suppose we can take a quick look."

A small staircase on the other side of the doors led to a dimly lit corridor of sea-green walls. Glass-fronted doors lined one side of the hallway. A floor-to-ceiling metal bookshelf divided into compartments ran the length of the opposite wall, and a few of the compartments held books, magazines, and reference items bound together in neat bundles.

"After I saw Kevin yesterday morning, he was planning to come by here and pick up the documents you told him about at the engagement party," I said. "Is this where you left them?"

Thea rifled through the bundles that were waiting to be retrieved. "Yes, but Kevin's papers are still here. He never got them. Did he sign in yesterday, Logan?"

Logan picked up a clipboard with a sheet of paper on it from a small table near the stairs. "The last time he was here was Monday. Four days ago."

Thea removed her ID lanyard from around her neck and

picked out a key from a ring that was attached to it. She walked over to the door directly in front of us. "This is Kevin's room . . . was Kevin's room."

She unlocked the door and pushed it open. Logan and I gasped and Thea muttered something under her breath that sounded like a curse. The place had been ransacked—books pulled off shelves and dumped on the floor, desk drawers opened and emptied, the contents of file folders scattered everywhere.

There was no way Kevin had trashed this room.

His stalker had been here.

7

For a moment the three of us stood without speaking, surveying the ruined state of Kevin's study room. Beautiful books splayed open or spine down lay on the floor around us. "What in the world . . . what happened?" Thea sounded distraught. She walked in and began picking up books where they'd been flung haphazardly.

Logan and I followed her. The room was small but efficient, just enough space for an old-fashioned desk and chair, a metal file cabinet, a colorful framed poster from the National Book Festival, a bookcase now mostly emptied of books, and a wooden table strewn with files and papers, presumably reference material for Kevin's new book. No laptop, but he wouldn't leave something that valuable behind.

"The blinds are closed," I said. "I wonder if whoever did this came at the end of the day when it was dark."

Thea nodded, still visibly shaken. "We're open until nine thirty at night so people can come by and do their research after work. But we don't really monitor these rooms. The occupants are serious scholars. They're hardly the sort of individuals who need supervising. I can't imagine anyone among them who would do . . . this."

Logan bent down to retrieve a sheaf of papers from under the desk where they'd slid out of several file folders like a fan, her lips pressed together in anger. I helped Thea reshelve the books. Many were old and fragile, the yellowed pages as delicate as parchment. The person who'd been here hadn't cared about damaging them.

I read the eclectic collection of titles as I picked them up. Aristotle's *Politics*. John James Audubon's *Delineations of American Scenery and Character*. *Thomas Jefferson's Garden Book*. Numerous books on the unpublished and published papers and letters of George Washington and Thomas Jefferson. The history of the founding of Washington, D.C., multiple biographies of Pierre L'Enfant, including a copy of the book Olivia wanted me to read. A plant and seed catalog published in London in the 1800s. Several copies of a pamphlet called *Twinleaf*, published at Monticello, the common thread being that each edition contained an article on the Lewis and Clark expedition.

"I wonder if anything is missing," I said.

Thea looked up from caressing the spine of a book on the history of the Chelsea Physic Garden in London. "I was just wondering the same thing. Though this"—she gestured at the mess around us—"seems like pure malicious vandalism, it's just so awful."

"Maybe someone was searching for something." I didn't say it, but I thought it: for what Kevin had left in locker number 58.

Thea set the book on the bookshelf and swung around to stare at me, one hand on her hip. "Do you know what it could be?"

"No. I don't."

"We've got records of everything Brother Kevin borrowed," Logan said. She leaned against the desk as if she suddenly needed something solid to support her. "I'll go through them, Thea. If anything has been taken, we'll know."

Thea shifted her gaze from me to Logan. "Yes, of course, start there. Though the only person who would truly know what's missing is Kevin. Not everything here might be ours."

I picked up *The Journals of Lewis and Clark by Meriwether Lewis* from under the table. "Your security guards search everyone," I said. "Not just on the way in, but also on the way out, to make sure no one takes something that belongs here."

"If you're wondering whether someone could get something out of the Library of Congress that belongs to us, I think anything's possible if you're determined enough," Thea said. "We're a lot less strict with our security than most of the other government buildings in Washington. You can't just walk into the Main Reading Room in the Jefferson Building anymore, but this still is a library, the library of the American people, not Fort Knox."

"What about security cameras?"

Thea set the last book, a history of English gardening in the eighteenth century, on the bookcase. "I'm afraid there aren't any. There's also a corridor that bypasses the reading room and takes you to the back elevators on Third Street. Someone could have come and gone quite easily without being noticed."

She sat down in Kevin's scarred-up chair. "The lock appeared to be intact when I opened the door, and these are dead bolts so you can't jimmy them. It costs a pretty penny if you lose your key," she said. "I wonder if someone got hold of Kevin's key? Except he wasn't careless about things like that, he never left anything lying around."

Unless it had been taken yesterday in the monastery garden.

"Speaking of keys," Logan said, "I've been thinking. A few of the Smithsonian museums have public lockers, including the Natural History Museum. I know Brother Kevin spent a lot of time there doing research." She shrugged. "It's worth a try."

Thea gave Logan a sharp look. "Kevin knew the entire staff at that museum. If he needed to store something, anyone who worked on the third floor would have let him leave it in their office."

I tried to quash my newly revived excitement and keep my voice calm. "It's also possible the key isn't even his. I found it on the ground by the stone lantern at the Tidal Basin. A couple of women were there just before Kevin and I arrived. One of them could just as easily have dropped it."

Thea fluttered her eyelashes and gave me an ironic *nice try* look. "I presume you're going directly to the Natural History Museum after you leave here?"

I blushed. "Yes, but first I need the key. You still have it."

She looked startled. "Oh, goodness, so I do. I put it in my pocket when we started to clean up and forgot about it."

She gave it to me, along with her business card, which she took out of her plastic ID holder. "I'd really like to know what you find, Sophie. Would you call me, please? The card has my direct number at the library and my cell number."

I nodded, and she added, "Perhaps you could give me your contact information as well?"

She waited while I got my own card from my camera bag and passed it to her. She ran a finger around the edge. "I'm sure we'll be talking soon. And, Logan, dear, I think you should start working on that list of documents and books right away."

Logan stood up and when she spoke her voice wavered. "It's going to be sad going through all this and knowing he's gone." To me she said, "He brought Thea and me flowering Lenten roses after he came back from his fellowship at Monticello at the end of January. I thought it was so sweet. He hardly knew me."

"*Helleborus orientalis*," Thea said. "They're lovely, though Kevin and I joked about it being a plant that's supposed to cure insanity because he mentioned that he was insanely busy with work." Her voice cracked with emotion when she said that, but then she was all brisk business again. "I'll walk you out, Sophie. We can use the back corridor."

An elevator was waiting. Just before the door closed, she said in a soft voice, "Good luck."

On the ground floor I walked down the corridor to the main lobby and stopped at the guard's desk. Something in my demeanor must have put him on alert because he gave my camera bag an extra-thorough going-over. Finally, he said, "Okay, thanks. Have a nice day."

"Do you also inspect the bags of employees when they come and go?"

"We check everyone," he said. "No exceptions."

I walked down 2nd Street to where I'd left the Vespa, but once or twice I couldn't resist looking over my shoulder, even though there was no one around. Kevin's stalker knew about his study room, I was sure of that. And as for Thea, was it my imagination or had she been reluctant to hand the key over to me, as well as a bit annoyed when Logan suggested the lockers at the Natural History Museum? Though I knew Kevin trusted Thea, it seemed to me that someone in her position at the Library of Congress would have been as familiar with that museum as Kevin had been, and that she, too, would have known about those lockers.

Maybe I wasn't being followed just now because someone already knew where I'd turn up next.

And what I was going to do.

I checked the Vespa's side mirrors and kept glancing over my shoulder, but no car cut in and out of traffic tailing me as I drove down Constitution Avenue until I finally chained the scooter to a bike rack across from the Natural History Museum.

A museum guard checked my bag—again—and I walked through another metal detector. Today school groups seemed to be visiting the museum in force, kids swarming the Rotunda or leaning over the wrought-iron balcony railings on the upper floors to stare at Henry, the enormous African elephant that dominated the room, its trunk raised as if calling to the herd. I found the information desk and asked where the lockers were located.

A man with a pale face looked over the top of his horn-rimmed glasses and pointed across the room. "Behind the security desk. Over there."

I thanked him and my gaze fell on a rack stuffed with pamphlets and museum maps. Between a glossy photo of the Dom Pedro aquamarine and a brochure on life in ancient Egypt was another brochure, this one with a familiar title: "Losing Paradise: Our Endangered Biosphere and the Challenges of Safeguarding It for Our Children." It was an upcoming symposium that would take place at the Botanic Garden in a few weeks, part of an ongoing forum on endangered species and conservation science. This year's topic was the alarming number of plant species disappearing from their natural habitats.

I already knew that the keynote speaker was Brother Kevin Boyle, OFM.

I skimmed the names of the other presenters and panelists. No doubt Kevin had known everyone, but I didn't recognize any of the names, though I did notice that someone from Monticello was one of the speakers. Dr. Ryan Velis, director of horticulture at the Center for Historic Plants.

"Help yourself," the man behind the desk said to me. "The symposium's open to the public. You have to register and there's a small fee. But it's quite good. You might enjoy it."

"Thank you." I didn't want to tell him the news about Kevin, so I smiled and said, "It sounds fascinating. I'll keep it in mind."

I put the brochure in my camera bag and walked across the Rotunda past the security desk. The storage lockers were in a room located behind a partial wall, which acted as a screen, creating a narrow semiprivate corridor and softening the din from the Rotunda. When I finally found it, the corridor was deserted.

A locker slammed shut as I pushed open the door. A moment later a man in a Redskins sweatshirt came around the corner of a row of lockers holding a small rucksack.

"Sorry," he said with an easy smile, "didn't mean to scare you."

"It's okay," I said. "I didn't realize anyone was there."

He left and I checked out the room. Most of the lockers weren't being used; only a few had missing keys, including number 58. I put the key in the lock and turned the knob. Something dropped to the ground next to my feet. A quarter. Kevin's quarter. You got your rental money refunded when you returned the key. I picked up the coin and put it in my pocket. The next time I visited the monastery I would put it in the poor box.

The locker door swung open. A canvas bag encasing what looked like a large box sat in the middle of the shelf. At a rough guess, the box was approximately nine by twelve inches and about four inches high. It was heavier than I expected, maybe six or seven pounds. I still had the room to myself, and before I walked out of this building, I needed to know what was in that box.

I set it on a long, low bench, knelt down, and slipped off the bag. The dark gray cloth-covered box was old, centuries old. I lifted the cover, which was hinged to the bottom so it would lie flat when it was open. Inside was a coverless book that fit the space perfectly. *Adam in Eden: or, Natures Paradise. The History of Plants, Fruits, Herbs and Flowers.* It was Kevin's, all right, and probably valuable, to have its own purpose-built protective box. The author was someone named William Coles, Herbalist. At the bottom of the title page was a quotation from Genesis: *Then the Lord took the Man, and put him into the Garden of Eden.* Below that, in red and black, was this: *London, Printed at the Angel near the Royal Exchange, 1657.*

There was more written on the page, including a bit of shameless author self-promotion—*a Work of such a Refined and Useful Method that the Arts of Physick and Chirurgerie are so clearly laid open,* et cetera. So it was a dictionary or an encyclopedia of plants and their proper use for medicinal purposes.

The box slid easily back inside its protective covering. I removed my camera from my bag, did some rearranging, and set the box inside. Here at the Natural History Museum no one checked your purse or backpack on the way out as they did at the Library of Congress, so getting the book out of here wasn't going to be a problem. Nobody gave me a second glance as I left the building.

Kevin had taken a vow of poverty, so he wouldn't have had the means or money to buy such a rare book. I suspected Edward Jaine had purchased it, but whether it belonged to Jaine or the Franciscans now was a matter for them to sort out. What I wanted to know was why Kevin had gone to the trouble of hiding it in a museum locker.

So before I did anything else, I was going to call Max Katzer, my neighbor, and ask if I could pay a visit to his antiques gallery in Georgetown. If he couldn't tell me something about the book's provenance and its value, he would know someone who could.

And, more to the point, was this 350-year-old book that seemed to grow heavier as I carried it down the museum steps important enough to be the reason for someone to murder Brother Kevin Boyle?

8

No one followed me out of the museum to the bike rack where I'd parked the Vespa. Years ago when I began working for International Press Service in London, Perry DiNardo, my boss, sent me and two colleagues to a hunting lodge on the grounds of a semiruined castle in the Scottish Highlands for a week-long intensive training program called Surviving Hostile Environments. The British ex–Special Forces team that taught the course made us work our tails off with endless drills, sending us on excursions to hauntingly beautiful lochs and steep-sided glens where we were ambushed by terrorists, caught up in gunfights, or told that our driver or security guard or a buddy was bleeding to death and help wasn't coming.

What they wanted us to take away from that week was not a set of learned skills but how to keep our wits about us and think fast. "In the military you don't learn, you train," one of them said to me. "Training is what you fall back on in combat."

The habits I developed because of that indelible week were still with me and, on one memorable occasion in Islamabad, saved my life. I put my camera bag with Kevin's seventeenth-century catalog of plants in the hard-shell case on the back of my scooter and checked one more time to see if anyone was paying attention. Then I called Max.

"Sophie, darlin', how are you? Everything all right?" Max had a voice like honey poured over gravel and the faintest hint of an aristocratic Southern drawl. He called every woman he met by some endearment—darling or sweetheart or sugar—and you knew it was just part of his charm.

"I'm fine, Max," I said. "I have a favor to ask."

"Ask away."

A couple of yellow school buses lumbered past me on Madison Drive and I had to raise my voice. "I was wondering if you'd be willing to take a look at a very old book I've come across? From 1657."

"Of course I would, though you know rare books aren't my specialty. I can certainly help you get it to someone who could give you an appraisal, if that's what you want. Where are you, by the way? It sounded like a couple of tanks just rolled by."

"Close. School buses. I'm on the Mall by the Natural History Museum."

"I see. And where is this book?"

"In my camera bag carefully stowed away in the Vespa."

"Good Lord. I hope it's not under your seat. The heat of your engine could do some serious damage."

"Come on, you know I know better. It's in the top case." There were only certain things I could leave under the seat—my helmet, gloves, a rain jacket, items like that. No groceries, unless I wanted the meat and produce to be precooked and the cheese melted when I got home. "Do you think I could stop by now?"

"Sure you can. I'm just catching up on paperwork. What's going on, sugar? Is this something urgent?"

"Yes."

"I see. Would I be correct in assuming the book's not yours?"

"You would, but the owner, or the person I think is the owner, can't ask you about it himself. It's a long story."

"I see. Well, in that case, come on over. I'll make tea."

M. Katzer Fine Antiques was located on upper Wisconsin Avenue in Georgetown, in a historic district known as Book Hill. A neighborhood of wide brick sidewalks lined with art galleries, antiques shops, and home-furnishing boutiques, the long block between Q and R Streets had been the home of the late, lamented French Market until twenty years ago. But the Gallic charm lingered, along with the pleasant, unrushed feeling that you'd somehow left frenetic Washington behind and wandered into the Latin Quarter of Paris. The name Book Hill came from the nearby Georgetown Neighborhood Library, as well as a pretty hilly patch of green on Reservoir Road called, not surprisingly, Book Hill Park.

Max's upscale gallery at 1605½ Wisconsin specialized in eighteenth- and nineteenth-century English and continental antiques and decorative arts, Oriental carpets, and an eclectic collection of art. I liked the fact that he wasn't a snob or a purist, and every now and then he'd display something offbeat like a retro 1950s sofa upholstered in loud avocado and tangerine stripes or, once, a chandelier made of red, yellow, and green Murano glass gummy bears.

The gallery was a secondary business, opened to appease his many admirers who clamored for it. But he'd made his reputation and his fortune as one of D.C.'s top interior designers, thanks to a client list that included diplomats, politicians, wealthy socialites, and even the First Family.

The Tibetan wind chimes hanging on the front door of his gallery tinkled as I walked in half an hour later cradling my camera bag with Kevin's book inside. Max's business partner—and, if you believed the rumors, a former lover—glanced up from a catalog she was reading behind an antique walnut-and-glass display cabinet.

She smiled. "Sophie, how nice to see you. Go on through, he's in his office."

Max was sitting at a mahogany desk that dated from one of the Louises—fourteenth or sixteenth, I could never remember—frowning at something on his computer screen. When he saw me in the doorway, the frown vanished and he switched off the display and came around, smiling, to give me a kiss.

He was dressed as though he'd just come from a meeting at the White House: impeccable charcoal suit, pale blue dress shirt, blue-and-yellow silk tie, and black wingtips polished to a military shine. He was tall and slim, with an air of erudition and seriousness and the bearing of someone who grew up surrounded by privilege and luxury on a grand estate or a historic plantation, a first-class private education, summer holidays abroad. The truth—and he was proud of it—was that he was the only child of a single mother who worked in a school cafeteria in rural Kentucky. The military paid for his college education.

"Sweetheart, do come in. Let me take that from you." He set my camera bag on an English sideboard. "I made Earl Grey. And we've got macaroons from Patisserie Poupon."

I'd completely forgotten about eating lunch. "Sounds wonderful," I said. "And thank you again for the note you left this morning about Kevin Boyle."

He shook his head in dismay. "I read his book. A real shame about his passing. He wasn't that old." He indicated a chair. "Have a seat, darlin'. Your tea's ready."

I sat in a moss-green velvet slipper chair in front of his desk and took the bone china cup and saucer he handed me. Max sat in the matching twin chair across from me and passed me a plate piled with macaroons. When he crossed one leg over the other, I noticed he was wearing socks with a pirate skull and crossbones on them.

"Hazelnut or raspberry?" he said. "Never mind, take one of each."

I took one of each and said, "I love your socks."

"I like 'em, too. Always do one thing that keeps people guessing about you. It's boring being predictable. Suit from Savile Row, socks from Target." He grinned, and stuck out a leg, admiring his sock. "So tell me about this book. We have some time before Bram calls. He won't be free until three o'clock."

"Bram?"

He dipped a hazelnut macaroon in his tea. "Bramwell Asquith. You must know Asquith's, the British auction house? Their Washington gallery is on Cady's Alley."

It was one of the oldest auction houses in Britain, founded in the late 1700s.

"Of course." The studio I briefly worked for was also located on Cady's Alley, a little cul-de-sac in lower Georgetown next to the C&O Canal. "When I lived in London I used to stop by their gallery on Bond Street."

Max nodded. "I know it well. Bram is their senior vice president—and heir apparent to take over—but he's also Asquith's expert on rare and antiquarian books. He works here in Washington, though. I'm not sure how much he'll be able to tell us over the phone, but at least you might be able to get a rough idea of the value." He gave me a questioning smile. "I'm presuming that's what you're after, isn't it?"

"Yes and no. I believe someone is searching for this particular book, and I want to know why."

"Can you be any more specific?"

"I'm fairly certain it belonged to Kevin Boyle. He hid it in a locker at the Natural History Museum, or at least I think he hid it, though I don't know from whom."

Max brushed imaginary crumbs from his perfectly creased

trousers and looked as though we were discussing something as innocuous as what fabric to choose for my living room drapes. "I see," he said in his languid drawl. "Do you believe there's a connection between Brother Kevin's death and the book?"

"I don't know. That's why I'm so curious about it."

Max set his cup and saucer on his desk as though I still hadn't said anything that surprised him. But in his line of work, he probably saw his share of surprises—some of them no doubt jaw-dropping—peeking into the bedrooms, offices, and private lives of his powerful and wealthy clients. I figured he had a lot of practice perfecting that poker face.

"Why don't I pour us some more tea?" he said. "And maybe you can start at the beginning."

I told him everything, including finding Kevin's study room trashed, Thea Stavros's asking to keep the key, and Logan's suggesting it possibly opened a locker at the Natural History Museum.

Max's eyebrows went up when I mentioned Thea. "So you met La Stavros? How interesting. I haven't spoken to her in ages. In fact, I didn't realize she was still at the library."

"You know her?" I asked, as he gave me a practiced innocent grin that fooled no one. "Why am I asking? You know everyone."

"You flatter me. But Thea . . . a fascinating woman, to say the least. We met years ago when a client asked me to create a one-of-a-kind hand-painted wallpaper of eighteenth- and nineteenth-century American botanical prints." He picked up his teacup again and drank, his eyes crinkling as he started to laugh. "Let me tell you, Thea saved my bacon. Refused to let me use two of the prints I absolutely loved because she said they would look like we'd put big green phalluses all over the walls once they were enlarged. Lord, it was a distinguished room in a rather famous home."

I laughed, too. "I don't suppose you'd care to tell me which rather famous home?"

He gave me a look like a cat that just drank all the cream. "Have another macaroon, Sophie, darlin'."

I took one, and he stood up. "Let me wash my hands and we'll have a look at your book."

I cleaned up our dishes while he disappeared into the small bathroom that adjoined his office. Then I took the book in its canvas cover out of my camera bag. Max returned holding a pair of white cotton gloves. He removed the cloth-covered box from the bag and set it on the sideboard.

"Well, the fact that it's in a Solander box already indicates that it's of some value." He took reading glasses out of the inside pocket of his jacket and put them on.

"Why is it called a Solander box?" I asked.

"Because it was invented by Mr. Solander." He opened the box. "I don't recall his first name, but he was a botanist, interestingly enough, who needed a sturdy container to protect a collection of prints . . . let's see what we have here. *Adam in Eden: or, Natures Paradise. The History of Plants, Fruits, Herbs and Flowers by William Coles, Herbalist.*"

He lifted the yellowed book out of the box and set it on a piece of cloth he'd laid out on the sideboard. I took a look inside the box.

"There's an envelope in here," I said. "It must have been underneath the book. No postage stamp and it seems to be quite old. Addressed to Dr. Francis Pembroke of Leesburg, Virginia."

"We'll have a look at that in a minute." Max slowly began turning the pages of *Adam in Eden.* "Well, first off, there's no leather binding, no cover of any sort, just bound pages. Whoever owned this particular volume—it looks like a medical reference encyclopedia of plants and herbs—annotated it extensively. Look at the marginalia. But these beautiful plates of flowers and plants are originals . . . they're hand drawn and hand colored . . . quite unusual."

William Coles had done his homework. The book was nearly

650 pages long, and every chapter referenced a particular plant, herb, or tree in exhaustive detail—its description, history, Greek and Latin names, and a long explanation of its medical uses, which Coles referred to as "the virtues." Chapter one was titled "Of the Wall-nut Tree."

"Does the writing in the margins decrease the value?" I asked.

"Depends on whose handwriting it is. We'll have to ask Bram . . . What a pity. Someone pressed a plant between the pages. Stained the paper so badly you can't read the text underneath." He shook his head and made a *tsk-tsk* sound with his tongue. "It's called foxing when there's spotting or staining like this."

"It's in the chapter about hyssop. Do you think someone pressed a hyssop plant and put it there?"

"Possibly, or just picked this page because there would be enough weight to press the plant flat."

"The stain is at least twice the size of those leaves. It looks like part of the plant is missing." I leaned over his shoulder and started reading: "*A decoction of rue and honey, being drunk doth help those that are troubled with coughs, shortness of breath, wheezings, and rheumatic distillations upon the lungs.*"

"Hyssop does seem like a cure-all for everything." Max turned the page. "*Taken with oxymel*—I believe that's honey mixed with vinegar—*it purges gross humors of the stool, worms in the belly, expels wind, it helpeth those that are stung by serpents, the oil killeth lice.*" He turned more pages. "It appears to be the only thing preserved in these pages, so that's good. Let's have a look at that letter. It might give us a clue about the owner. It would make sense for a doctor to own a dictionary of herbal plants."

Max picked up the envelope and turned it over and we both saw the return address on the back. John Fairbairn, Chelsea Physic Garden, London, England.

"One of the books in Kevin's research carrel was a history of the Chelsea Physic Garden," I said. "And he was in London a few months ago to give a talk at Kew Gardens."

Max unfolded the letter, which resembled a small booklet, and held it open with gloved fingers. The ink had faded to the color of old blood, and the spidery penmanship was hard to decipher.

"Well, the date explains why there was no stamp," he said. "London, 4 April 1807. Stamps weren't invented until the mid-1800s."

"Can you read the handwriting?"

"I believe so." He reached for his glasses again.

London, 4 April 1807
My esteemed Doctor Pembroke,

This is in reply to yours of 12 December to inform you that I am in receipt of the most recent shipment of Seeds intrusted to you by your cousin Capt. Lewis. Regrettably the Plant you refer to as Hesop arrived in poor condition and the one tender Specimen that germinated is not of the genus hyssopus. We therefore entreat you to send additional Seeds, as we are most interested in your assertion & that of Capt. Lewis that it produces wondrous, indeed miraculous, Results in restoring forgotten Memories to your Patients.

At your request, I am sending herewith the final volume of Flora Londinensis to complete your Collection. As you know, it was the Life project of my predecessor, the Praefectus Horti William Curtis, to document all wild Flora within the environs of the City of London. I commend your decision to undertake a similar Project to record the Native American flora chosen by Presidents Washington and Jefferson for the proposed American Botanic Garden in Washington and would be most interested to know a more complete list of the plants and herbs that have been selected.

As ever, we stand ready to offer any Assistance as regards the

*planning of this new American Garden. Additionally, since
your Hesop is to be included among the Medicinal Plants, I
will provide details concerning its proper nomenclature and
properties once I am in receipt of additional Specimens.*

*I await your next Shipment with great Anticipation and I
pray you accept Assurances of my Best regards.*

Most sincerely Yours,
John Fairbairn, Curator,
Chelsea Physic Garden, Swan Walk, London

Max looked up. "Well, I guess that answers a few questions.
The book probably belonged to Dr. Francis Pembroke, and I
would imagine he put the plant he believed was hyssop in the
book to preserve it. Maybe it was his medical reference book."

"Kevin was also reading about Lewis and Clark," I said. "He
had their diaries and some books and articles on their expedition
in his study room. That letter says Francis Pembroke was a cousin
of Meriwether Lewis and the plant came from seeds Lewis and
Clark brought back or sent back from their trip to West."

I gave Max a hopeful look, but he pursed his lips and shook his
head. "Sorry. Obviously knowing about the owner contributes
to the book's history and provenance. But if Francis Pembroke,
a nineteenth-century American doctor, is the one who wrote in
the margins, it doesn't do anything to increase the value."

"Then why did Kevin go to all the trouble of hiding it?"

"Good question." The phone on Max's desk rang. He walked
over and glanced at the number. "Here's Bram. Maybe we're
missing something. He might be able to tell us."

Max hit the speakerphone button. "Bram, thanks so much
for calling back. I've got Sophie Medina here with me now, and
we've had a chance to look at the book she's brought. *Adam in
Eden: or, Natures Paradise. The History of Plants, Fruits, Herbs
and Flowers.* The author is William Coles, Herbalist. Published
in London in 1657."

Bram Asquith's pleasant baritone with its cultured British accent filled the room. "Not a problem, Max. Good to speak with you again. Ms. Medina, how do you do?"

"Sophie, please. Fine, thank you, Mr. Asquith. And thank you for taking the time to do this."

"A pleasure. Anything for a friend of Max Katzer's. And it's Bram. Give me just a quick second and I can look up the most recent sale information for you."

A chair creaked, followed by the sound of computer keys clicking. Max and I exchanged glances. It didn't take Bram long to find what he was looking for.

"Here you are," he said. "The last time a copy of *Adam in Eden* was sold it went for $495. Before that, $267, another one went for $1,100 . . . I'm just scrolling through the records here and . . . well, nothing over $2,000. Only £1,200 five years ago for one in excellent condition, so about $1,800 give or take. Even though it's a rather old book, it's not a rare one. Of course, I'd need to actually see your copy to give you an idea of what it might fetch if you decided to sell it."

So that was it. Max had been right and Bram Asquith had just confirmed it. The book was valuable, but not precious, probably worth a few hundred bucks, a thousand, at most.

"Thank you," I said. "You've been very helpful."

"Pleasure. Please do be in touch if you want to sell it."

"Thanks, but it's not my book. It belonged to a friend who passed away. But I'll let the new owner—whoever that is—know about your offer."

"I'm truly sorry," he said. "I realize this isn't what you were hoping to hear, but unfortunately we're the bearers of disappointing news more often than not and it's never enjoyable. Someone brings us a piece of furniture or jewelry or a work of art they've discovered in a grandmother's attic that they're sure is an original by Chippendale or Cartier or an undiscovered Rembrandt. It's a terrible letdown when we have to tell them their treasure is just some bog-standard item that has more sentimental value than monetary worth."

"I'm sure you're right, but my friend was a scientist and a scholar. I'm fairly certain he believed this book was valuable, so I don't understand how he could be so wrong."

There was a long pause before Bram said, "I see. Well, then, if you or the new owner would care to come by the gallery sometime and bring it along, I can take a look at it. Maybe we missed something."

"As a matter of fact," Max said, "we neglected to mention that there are a number of what look like hand-drawn and hand-colored botanical plates. Also the margins have been annotated. There was a letter in the bottom of the Solander box from 1807 addressed to a doctor in Leesburg who was a cousin of Meriwether Lewis of the Lewis and Clark expedition. We assumed the book belonged to the doctor. His name is Francis Pembroke."

I heard Bram's computer keys clicking again. "You're sure those prints are originals?"

"Quite sure," Max said.

"That's rather puzzling . . . it wasn't an illustrated book."

"This copy is," Max said.

"Do me a favor and have another look at the title page. I wonder if whoever owned this book wrote his name somewhere. Look near the author's name. It might be rather faded."

William Coles's personal copy? I caught my breath.

"Give us a moment." Max got a magnifying glass from his desk and slowly passed it down the page. Near the bottom next to the quote from Genesis he pointed to something written in ink that was so pale I hadn't noticed it before.

It wasn't William Coles's name. Disappointed, I said to Max, "Can you make out what that says?"

After a moment he said, "It's very faint. I think it's 'Js. Newbon.'"

"Js. Newbon. Perhaps it could be Isaac Newton?" Bram asked.

Max sucked his breath between his teeth like a small hiss. "You mean, Sir Isaac Newton? Good Lord, wouldn't that be a find. Do you have a facsimile of his signature so we can compare?"

"There's an app for that, believe it or not," Bram said. "Hang on, I'm sending you a link. Check your e-mail."

Max pulled his phone out of his pocket and thumbed it on. He found the message and showed me the display.

"It matches," I said.

"You're right, Bram," Max said. "The book did belong to Sir Isaac Newton."

"Well, now." Bram sounded as though his level of interest had just gone up a few notches. "That rather changes things. Tell me about this letter you found."

"Sophie, you tell him," Max said.

When I was done, Bram said, "Let me check something. I'll ring you back."

"Fine," Max said. "We'll be right here."

"The suspense is killing me," I said after Bram hung up.

"Have another macaroon," Max said. "They're good for the nerves."

I grinned and took one, passing him the plate as the phone rang again.

"That was quick," I said, as Max hit the speakerphone button.

"All right," Bram said. "I just wanted to confirm a few dates, and it turns out I was right. The founder of the Chelsea Physic Garden was a man named Hans Sloane, a wealthy physician and an avid collector. When Sloane passed away in 1753, he bequeathed his collections to his country and they became the foundation for the British Museum. But he also served as secretary of the Royal Society, an organization of the world's finest scientists who came together in the late 1600s with a common interest in experimentation and scientific discovery. It still exists, as a matter of fact. But at that time the president of the Royal Society happened to be—anyone care to guess?"

"Sir Isaac Newton," I said.

"Precisely. It would seem that Isaac Newton obtained a copy of William Coles's book, but what could make it especially valuable is that perhaps it was Coles's personal working copy, one of a kind, since you say the prints are originals."

"Is there any way you can trace provenance that far back?" I asked. "How did Francis Pembroke get hold of it and how did it end up in Leesburg?"

"We can certainly look into all that for you," Bram said. "However, I would need to have the book here at Asquith's. If you'd be interested in leaving it with me, I could send a courier to Max's place straightaway with all the necessary paperwork."

Max looked over at me and nodded, mouthing, *Let him.*

"As I said, it's not my book. I'm fairly sure it belonged to Brother Kevin Boyle, the Franciscan environmentalist who died yesterday," I said. "I sort of came across it by accident."

If Bram Asquith was surprised by my vague explanation, he didn't let on. Instead he said in a smooth voice, "That shouldn't be any problem. We could get it directly to the legal owner on your behalf, if you wish. But as I said, this book may be an original—the only such copy in existence—so perhaps that person would be interested in having an appraisal of its worth, either for insurance purposes or in the event that he or she would consider the possibility of selling it."

"Someone else may be looking for this book," I said.

"It wouldn't surprise me in the least. However, if it's at Asquith's, not only do you have my promise of complete discretion, but since it will be in our vault, I assure you it will be as safe as houses."

Which is exactly what Kevin would have wanted: the book to be stored in a safe place.

"Then by all means, please send your courier to pick it up," I said. "And, even though it's not mine, I'd still be interested in knowing what you find out about the provenance."

"I'm sure that won't be a problem. And I'm glad you mentioned those colored plates. They change everything."

"So this book is quite valuable after all," I said.

"Indeed," Bram said. "To a collector, it would be priceless."

"How soon can you send a courier?" Max asked, giving me a warning glance. "I believe Sophie's book ought to be secured in your vault as soon as possible."

"I'll take care of it myself. Our armored truck will be there within the hour."

After he hung up the phone, Max turned to me. "Well, there's your answer."

"Yes," I said. "It is a book worth killing for."

9

Before Bram Asquith sent his courier to pick up Kevin's book, I took photographs of each of the hand-colored botanical prints and asked Max to make me a copy of John Fairbairn's letter to Francis Pembroke. He gave me the photocopy in a plum-colored folder with M. Katzer Fine Antiques embossed in gold and, after I signed the paperwork turning the book over to Asquith's, he added those documents as well.

It was four o'clock by the time he walked me to the front door of the gallery.

"I'm supposed to call Thea Stavros, or she's going to call me and ask what I found in the locker at the Natural History Museum," I said. "What am I going to say?"

"Thea and Bram know each other, you know, since they're both antiquarian book experts. I think you can trust her to be discreet. Frankly, I wouldn't be surprised if the Library of Congress might be interested in acquiring the book, given what we just found out."

"Acquiring it from whom? I don't know who owns it."

"Presumably Kevin's heirs."

"I think all of his possessions now belong to the Franciscans. But there's another possibility. Maybe Kevin didn't buy the book, so it's not his."

Max gave me a sideways look. "Then who did buy it?"

"Edward Jaine was underwriting all of Kevin's research expenses," I said. "He was Kevin's benefactor."

"Oh, Lord," Max said. "I hope Kevin kept good records. If the book wasn't worth much, it wouldn't be a big deal. But now—"

I nodded and chewed my lip. "Kevin and Edward Jaine were arguing the night before he died. I overheard them at a party at the Austrian ambassador's residence. Kevin didn't want to talk about it, but I wonder if it had to do with the book."

"Money's a powerful motivator, sugar." Max gave me a significant look. "Believe me, in my business I've seen my share of squabbles over estates and who owns what. People become very proprietary and petty over the smallest things. I've seen siblings argue over who gets Mom's special pickle fork."

He kissed me goodbye, and I walked back to the Vespa, hoping Max was right about Kevin's record keeping. Even a billionaire like Edward Jaine would be interested in acquiring the only existing copy of a book with the unique provenance this one had. When I worked for IPS in London, I'd occasionally photographed a rare treasure that had come to light—a work of art, a book, or a piece of jewelry, and most recently two lost Fabergé imperial eggs—before one of the big houses like Asquith's or Sotheby's auctioned it off on behalf of the owner. Those events always attracted the Edward Jaines of the world, the rarified class of billionaire whose hobby was collecting one-of-a-kind items for the sheer pleasure of knowing they had something no one else possessed.

Had Kevin realized what he owned, and if so, had Edward Jaine been aware of the book's value as well? And if Jaine did know, what would he do to acquire it, especially if Kevin didn't want to give up the book?

Would he commit murder?

My phone rang when I was halfway back to the Vespa, which I'd chained to a streetlamp on Reservoir Road. Caller ID flashed TOMMY, along with a photo I loved of my half brother standing outside a clinic in a remote mountain village in Honduras where he'd worked on a medical mission during a gap year between college and medical school. His arm was draped around a sweet-faced young girl whose arms ended as two tapered stubs below her elbows. Both of them were grinning like a couple of fools without a care in the world.

Tommy and I were fifteen years apart—I was fourteen when my mother married Harry—but we were close and I adored him, just like I adored Harry. I knew the feeling was mutual, but there was also a special bond between us because Tommy realized, just as I knew Harry did, that deep down inside our mother wished I could be airbrushed out of the family photos and that I'd never been born.

Of course she would never admit it, but there were times when I'd caught her looking at me when she thought I didn't see, and I knew she blamed me for screwing up her life. Her dark-haired, olive-skinned daughter standing next to Tommy and my half sister, Lexie, both of them blue eyed and golden haired, as wholesome and all-American perfect as apple pie. I was the unhappy reminder of her affair with a Spanish soc-cer player during a study-abroad year in college, a misbegotten marriage, and a dozen hardscrabble years as a single mother after we left Antonio Medina, my father, and moved home from Madrid.

For years I wanted to believe that this broke my father's heart, that he loved me, even if my mother did not. When I was old enough, I tracked down every poster and photo of him playing for Real Madrid without telling my mother, poring over every detail of his life I could find. The first time I saw his picture, dark and noble looking and dangerously handsome, was like looking into a mirror, and I thought, *I am Antonio Medina's daughter.* For a while I kept a small backpack under my bed, ready to leave the instant he showed up to sweep me into his arms and take me with him back to Spain, a land of heat and light and fiery passion in my young mind. Then one day right before we left New York to move to Virginia so my mother could marry Harrison Wyatt, she told me in a tight-lipped voice that a friend who kept in touch with Antonio said he'd been killed in a motorcycle accident near Seville. I unpacked the backpack and, just in time, Harry came into my life, and his unstinting love filled the empty space in my heart.

Tommy and I talked regularly on the phone and tried to meet for dinner once every few weeks. But since Christmas he had been working part-time at the free clinic in Adams Morgan in addition to taking classes as a first-year med student at Georgetown, and the dinners became sporadic.

"Hey you," I said. "What's going on? I've missed you."

"I've missed you, too. Same old same old. Work, school, sleep. Unfortunately not much sleep. Any chance you're free for dinner?"

My brother's schedule is more tightly programmed than most military campaigns. If he was free all of a sudden either something fell through . . . or something important had come up.

"You mean tonight?"

I heard a stifled yawn. "Yeah, tonight."

"Sure. Is everything all right? You sound beat. Want me to make a reservation somewhere?"

"I thought we could eat at my place," he said. "It's five thirty now, so how about seven o'clock?"

I knew what was in Tommy's pantry: ramen noodles, boxes of

mac 'n' cheese, a jar of peanut butter, and probably a big bag of Doritos. His refrigerator wasn't much better.

"Shall I cook?"

"I've got chili."

"That you made?"

"Is that a dig about my cooking?" He managed to sound indignant, but before I could reply, he said, "Relax. It's home-made. Not by me. And before you ask, she's just a friend."

"You know I never pry. A friend who makes good chili?"

"Actually, she makes amazing chili. You don't pry, but you do what you're doing now, ask an innocent question and then another and another until eventually you find out who I'm see-ing. Then Nick probably runs her through the Agency database to make sure she's not on some terrorist watch list or wanted in three states." Another yawn. "Hey, Soph, I'm still at the clinic, trying to get out of here. See you at seven, okay?"

Tommy hung up before I could say, "Sure, fine."

I know my brother. Something had happened and he didn't want to talk about it over the phone. Whatever it was, he was saving it to tell me over a bowl of amazing chili.

And that worried me.

I stopped by Safeway on my way home to pick up a six-pack to bring to dinner. Halfway home my phone rang, and it was Thea. I told her about finding the book and what Bram had said about it. The silence on her end went on so long I checked my phone for a dropped call.

"I would absolutely love to see those prints," she said finally. "Something that unique comes along once in a lifetime. If Wil-liam Coles was considering publishing a second edition of *Adam in Eden* that included those drawings, either he never got around to it before he died or perhaps everything was destroyed in the Great Fire of London in 1666. Thousands of books were lost when London burned, so it wouldn't surprise me if either the original plates for those prints never survived or all copies of the second edition—if there was one—were destroyed."

I could have told Thea I had photographed each of the prints and could send her an e-mail link to a photo gallery once I downloaded them, or mentioned the Fairbairn letter, but something stopped me. They say three can keep a secret if two are dead. Max assured me Thea could be trusted, but the matter of who owned the book still bothered me. The subject of Edward Jaine being Kevin's patron had never come up between Thea and me, so she probably wasn't aware that it could be a contentious issue.

"Bram's keeping the book in the vault at Asquith's until the new owner claims it," I said. "So at least we know it's safe."

"Well, obviously the Franciscans own it now, don't they? Anyway, Kevin's parents are dead, though I believe he has a brother and a sister living in Jersey. Once the formalities of his estate are sorted out, perhaps we can discuss the possibility of them loaning it to the library to put on display."

"That sounds like a good idea."

After she hung up, I thought about Jack's remark last night about the dangers of the slippery slope. Once you start down, you really can't turn back.

Tommy lived in the Ontario, an elegant Beaux Arts apartment complex situated on a couple of acres on a hilltop in Lanier Heights in Adams Morgan. When the Ontario was built for wealthy Washingtonians in the early 1900s, its selling point was the height of its location, guaranteeing pure air that was free from malaria. How times have changed. Now you hope the neighborhood's safe enough for you to walk from your car to your front door after dark without getting mugged.

Tommy's apartment was one of the larger ones on the fourth floor. When I knocked on the door, he yelled, "It's open."

He was in the galley kitchen, barefoot and in jeans and a gray Georgetown T-shirt, his straight blond hair still damp from a shower, standing at the stove stirring chili in a flame-colored pot with a book propped next to him.

"Is that a cookbook?" I asked, and pulled the six-pack out of a canvas bag.

"*Principles of Biochemistry.*" The kiss that was probably meant for my cheek landed on my ear. "Is that beer cold?"

"Of course." I gave him a quick hug around the waist. "The chili smells terrific. What can I do?"

"Open us some beers, if you don't mind." He pointed to the window and what looked like a small brass head of a wolf with its mouth open wide in a scream screwed to the frame. "Use the gargoyle. It's a bottle opener."

"It even has its own dedicated trash can, I see." He grinned as I opened two beers and handed one to him. "What else?"

"There's corn bread in the microwave," he said. "Can you put it on a plate?"

Before Tommy moved in, my mother had furnished the apartment—which Harry owned—in her idea of the perfect bachelor pad. To me it had looked like there ought to be DO NOT TOUCH or DON'T SIT ON THIS CHAIR signs on every surface until Tommy's weights and his unfolded laundry and his piles of books and papers slowly littered the rooms and the place finally seemed more like a home than a decorator showroom. Somehow I figured Mom hadn't seen the gargoyle beer bottle opener.

We ate in the dining room after I cleared the table of his papers and books.

"The chili's great," I said. "And when are you going to tell me what's going on?"

He passed me the plate of corn bread and said, "It's Chappy."

At least he didn't beat around the bush. My chest tightened, and I set the plate down hard on the table. Chappy was the name I'd given Charles Lord, our grandfather, the first time I met him when I was two years old and he told me that Charles was happy to meet Sophie. I'd melded the words together and he became Chappy. One of the early post–World War II photographers who worked for Magnum, the iconic photo agency, he had been hired by no less than the legendary Henri Cartier-Bresson.

Before my mother married Harry, she had sent me to Connecticut to spend summers with my grandfather since she couldn't afford day care when school was out. Those summers gave me some of my happiest and most carefree memories. Chappy had treated me as an assistant, not a child, letting me help him in his darkroom and experiment with developing my own film. When I was twelve, he gave me my first camera and taught me how to shoot. My grandfather was the reason I was a photographer today.

"Is he all right?" I asked my brother. "How come nobody told me anything before now?"

"Relax, Soph. Chap's okay." Tommy put down his spoon. He knew I was mad. By "nobody," he knew I meant our mother, who had put him up to passing on this news. "I mean, he's not in the hospital so it's nothing serious."

"Then what is it?"

"A neighbor found him wandering around Topstone Park in the middle of the day dressed in his pajamas and carrying his old Leica."

"Topstone Park used to be Edward Steichen's home. When Steichen was alive, he and Chappy were good friends. He knows that place like he knows his own backyard."

"Well, Chap, uh, seemed to think he and Steichen were going shooting together, that they had some kind of date."

I closed my eyes. Edward Steichen, another photography legend who organized the world-famous *Family of Man* exhibition in the 1950s, among many other accomplishments, passed away in 1973. Before I was born.

"Oh, my God. Is this the first time he's done something like this?"

Tommy's eyes met mine, and I knew there was more. "That we know of. Mom drove up to Connecticut this morning. Dad didn't want her to go on her own—especially making that drive to West Redding all by herself—but hunting season just wrapped up and now he's got the spring steeplechase race coming up, plus it's a busy time in the real estate market. She's thinking of staying up there for a while, and he can't afford to be gone that long."

If something were seriously wrong with my grandfather, Harry would drop everything—turn his real estate business over to his partner and get someone else to take over organizing the point-to-point that the Goose Creek Hunt, his foxhunting club, sponsored—and he and my mother would fly to Connecticut. Since he was staying behind, maybe the situation with Chappy wasn't so bad.

"Mom should have told me," I said. "I would have gone with her."

"She knows. That's why she didn't tell you. She said you'd take Chappy's side and the two of you would gang up on her."

"Take Chappy's side about what?"

He broke off a piece of corn bread. "She wants him to move to an assisted-living facility because she doesn't think he should be rattling around that big house all by himself. Chap won't have any part of it. She's not going to have the easiest time persuading him."

"An assisted-living facility? Are you kidding me?"

"Hey, calm down—"

"That's been his home for more than forty years. It would be criminal to put him in some room or suite where he doesn't have access to his studio, all those decades of photographs and negatives and slides. Come on, Tommy. His mind's still as sharp as a tack. I talked to him a few days ago, and he was telling me stories about the old days at Magnum, Capa's parties when he'd come back to New York from the Paris office and everyone would go to 21 or the Algonquin. He remembers every detail."

"Soph, Robert Capa died in Vietnam. I think it was in the 1950s." Tommy stood up. "I'm going to get another beer. You want one?"

"I'll stick with this, thanks."

When he came back into the room he said, "Look, sometimes with memory loss you remember things that happened years ago with absolute clarity but you have no idea what someone said to you ten minutes ago or how to find your way back home from church or the grocery store." He paused and added in a gentle voice, "Or how you got to Topstone Park."

"He doesn't have Alzheimer's. Or dementia. He couldn't."

The chandelier flickered as if a small electrical surge had pulsed somewhere in the building, and the light seemed to grow dimmer. Across the room, the radiator gurgled and the heat came on with a hiss.

For a long moment neither of us spoke. Finally Tommy said in a calmer voice, "I don't know anything and neither do you. Mom wants him to see a doctor, get him evaluated."

"So she can move him to some warehouse with a bunch of strangers. It'll kill him."

"Come on, Soph, Chap does need medical attention. Why don't we sit tight until we find out how that goes? Before I forget, we still have dessert. Mint chocolate chip ice cream. I bought it for you."

He was finished talking about our grandfather until there was something new to say. Nick was like that and so was Harry. Men can be so economical with their emotions. Women need the catharsis of talking it out, exploring all the possibilities and angles. Men want to move on to dessert. Done is done.

We stood in the kitchen and ate ice cream out of the carton after Tommy stuck it in the microwave to soften it.

"I'm still going to see you Saturday, right?" I said. "We could use your help translating at the shoe store when the kids come with their parents. Your Spanish is perfect."

"I wouldn't miss it. And your Spanish isn't bad, either."

"Mom wouldn't speak it after we left Spain. Mine is work-manlike, only what I remember from high school."

"It's better than that. It's a terrific thing you and Gracie are doing, Soph. I see a lot of those kids in the clinic. It's hard to imagine the kind of poverty I saw in Honduras right here at home."

"I wish we could do more. It just seems like a drop in the bucket. One pair of shoes." I pushed up my sleeves.

"What are you doing?" he said.

"The dishes. It's the least I can do since you fed me, plus I owe you for Saturday."

"No, you don't."

"Go get whatever's left in the dining room."

Tommy flashed a grateful smile and when he came back with dishes and our empty beer bottles, a copy of the *Washington Tribune* was tucked under his arm. He set the paper on the counter folded to Grace's story on Kevin.

"This fell off the dining room chair when I was cleaning up. I'm sorry I forgot to say something about Kevin when you got here. He was a good man. God, what a shame."

I set the clean flame-colored pot he'd used for the chili in the dish drainer, and he picked up a towel and began to dry it.

"I'm really going to miss him. The last time I saw him was the day he died. He promised to help me with a book on the forgotten gardens of Washington," I said. "Grace and I planned to use the profits from the book's sales for fixing up the Adams Morgan Children's Center. I'm going to be lost without Kevin's help."

"I'm sorry," he said again. He gave my shoulder a quick squeeze. "But if you're looking for overlooked gardens, the Ontario's got a great one. Plus we have an incredible communal herb garden. Kevin used to come by every so often to help one of our older residents who was a good friend of his until she passed away last year."

"He did?"

He nodded. "I'm serious about you photographing it. I'm sure the board would give you permission. It's not just your run-of-the-mill parsley, sage, rosemary, and thyme. There's a lot of exotic stuff. My next-door neighbor grows herbs for teas and uses some for medicinal purposes. I've warned her to be careful, but she says she knows what she's doing."

"Do you grow hyssop?"

"No idea. I can ask my neighbor. It's pretty common. I think it's been around since the Bible. Why?"

"I heard something today about a plant someone thought might be hyssop. It was supposed to help with memory loss."

Tommy gave me a skeptical look. "Are you thinking of Chappy?"

"Of course."

He pulled out his phone and started tapping. After a moment he said, "Looks like there's two kinds of hyssop. What you're probably talking about is called water hyssop. Listen to this. *Water hyssop is commonly used as a brain tonic to improve mental alertness and enhance learning and academic performance. The herb has antioxidant, cardiotonic and anticancer properties. It improves intellect, memory, consciousness, mental acuity, mental clarity and longevity. Water hyssop calms the mind and promotes relaxation.*" He looked up. "It's common in Ayurvedic medicine. That was from a website about India."

"When I was in India on an assignment years ago, I developed a horrible rash on my arm that wouldn't go away. I tried everything—pills, creams, even a shot of cortisone. Finally our translator took me to a woman who practiced Ayurvedic medicine. She made a salve—I don't remember what was in it—that cured it within two days," I said. "It was like magic."

Tommy slipped his phone into his jeans pocket. "Or maybe what you were taking conventionally finally started to work. Ayurvedic medicine is part of that whole constellation of alternative or complementary medicines that includes acupuncture, homeopathy, naturopathy, stuff like that. You can find practitioners here, too, but all of it's unregulated," he said. "You've gotta be careful. Maybe you were lucky."

"Or maybe that Indian woman knew what she was doing. If it's true that Chappy has the beginning of Alzheimer's, I'm going to find someone who knows Ayurvedic medicine and get him or her to make him a tea or tonic from water hyssop. So what if the FDA hasn't approved it? That doesn't mean it couldn't help. Do you think you could check and see if there's any in your garden?"

"First of all, it grows near water, so we probably have the other kind of hyssop if we have it at all." My brother laid his hands on my shoulders. "Let's not jump to conclusions, okay? Or practice medicine without a license."

"It's plants, not drugs. And I'm not going to brew some concoction myself. I'll find someone who knows what they're doing."

He gave me a swift warning look. "Sophie—"

My voice wavered. "I couldn't bear it if Chappy starts to forget everything . . . if he forgets *us*."

Tommy pulled me to him. "I know." He ran his thumb back and forth through my hair, and his voice broke, too. "Neither could I."

Harry called as I walked through the door of my apartment half an hour later.

"I just talked to your brother," he said. "I heard you two had dinner and he told you about Mom and Chap."

Harry is usually straight with me and he doesn't beat around the bush. He already knew about the dinner, and I figured he called Tommy to get the lowdown on how I'd taken the news.

"Harry," I said, "why didn't you call me and tell me about Chappy? I know Mom put Tommy up to it after she left for Connecticut."

He made a sound like air leaving a tire. "I learned when I first married your mother not to get in the middle of things between the two of you. I think it's the reason I've lived as long as I have."

"Still—"

"I'd like you to come to London with me, kitten."

"Pardon?"

"That's why I'm calling. Your mother and I had a quick trip planned, just for the week. There's an art show at Olympia, plus an old friend has a Thoroughbred running in the Winter Derby at Lingfield. Caroline planned to bolster the British economy by buying out all the shops in Knightsbridge. Now that she's with your grandfather, I wondered if you'd keep your old man company instead."

"Oh, gosh, Harry, it sounds great, you know I'd love to. But the day after tomorrow is Saturday and that's when the kids are getting their shoes at Sole Brothers. I can't miss that."

"If that's the only impediment, don't worry. It's the night flight. Please come, honey. You've been working awfully hard lately. You can visit friends, do whatever you want. You'll have fun, I promise. And I'd love the company."

I did some mental calculating. My one looming deadline was Olivia's manuscript; she wanted to meet in a week to talk about photos for "No Little Plans." I could take the manuscript with me and work on it on the plane and in the hotel.

"I'll come," I said. "I'd love to."

After Harry hung up, I got my camera bag from the foyer and brought it into the living room. Though Nick and I had transformed one of the upstairs bedrooms into an office, I often worked at an antique gateleg table that I'd moved into the alcove of a bay window overlooking S Street. When I pulled out my diary, the brochure for Kevin's symposium at the Botanic Garden fell out. "Losing Paradise: Our Endangered Biosphere and the Challenges of Safeguarding It for Our Children."

I looked again at the list of speakers and panelists, including the director of horticulture at the Center for Historic Plants at

Monticello, Dr. Ryan Velis. Kevin had been to Monticello in January, and after that he'd been in London to speak at a conference at Kew Gardens.

The other morning at the Tidal Basin he'd talked about something he'd found in London and said that he'd done additional research on whatever it was when he'd returned to the States. Had he bought the copy of *Adam in Eden* in England? Francis Pembroke, the Leesburg doctor who'd written to the head of the Chelsea Physic Garden, was a cousin of Meriwether Lewis. In my dim, distant memory of high school U.S. history, Thomas Jefferson had been president during Lewis and Clark's expedition.

I pulled out my laptop, and a moment later I found what I was looking for. President Thomas Jefferson, keen to learn anything he could about the land he had just acquired through the Louisiana Purchase, obtained funding from Congress for a western trip known as the Corps of Discovery Expedition headed by his personal secretary, Meriwether Lewis, and Lewis's close friend William Clark. Maybe Kevin had gone back to Monticello for his additional research.

Ryan Velis's e-mail address was listed on the Monticello staff page, and there was a general information e-mail address for the Chelsea Physic Garden. I wrote two e-mails, one to Ryan Velis and another to "To whom it may concern" at the Chelsea Physic Garden, explaining my connection with Kevin and asking if it would be possible to meet with someone to discuss a letter John Fairbairn had written to Dr. Francis Pembroke concerning plants from the Lewis and Clark expedition.

I hit Send and found the file for the engagement photos from the other night, spending the next hour editing them. When I got to the ones of Kevin saying the blessing, I had to stop and pour myself a whiskey before I could finish. After I was done, I uploaded everything to a photo gallery and sent e-mails to Ursula, Yasmin, and Victor with the link.

Then because I'd forgotten about it the other day, I down-loaded the Tidal Basin cherry blossom photos I'd taken the last time I'd been with Kevin. There were several of him gesturing enthusiastically, his arms windmilling as he talked, eyes lighting up, glasses slipping down the bridge of his nose, his familiar smile. I stared at them before I moved on to a series of panning shots, a complete view of the Tidal Basin. A few were blurred and I started to delete them when something caught my eye. A man stood next to the steps by the Roosevelt Memorial, star-ing right at Kevin and me. I enlarged the photo until it became too pixilated to even make out that it was a person, so I printed the picture and used a magnifying glass. But the photo was so blurred that the figure looked almost transparent, a vaporous ghost image.

Was this man Kevin's stalker? Had he been waiting for him as Kevin left the Tidal Basin that day? Kevin had said someone could have been watching the two of us, and I'd told him flat out that no one was there and we were all alone.

Now it looked like I'd been wrong.

My e-mail dinged and I jumped. It was exactly midnight. Ryan Velis had written back.

I would be very interested in discussing your letter from John Fairbairn to Francis Pembroke as well as possibly shedding some light on the background of Dr. Pembroke. If, by chance, you are willing or able to travel to Monticello, we can discuss this in person. I would also be happy to give you a private tour of Thomas Jefferson's gardens and look forward to hear-ing from you.

I hit Reply and wrote:

I can be there by 11 am tomorrow (today) if that would be convenient. I'll be driving from Washington, D.C.

He wrote right back.

Excellent. I have some questions for you as well. Bypass the visitors' entrance and drive up the mountain to the parking lot below the mansion. Someone will let you through the gate. I'll be expecting you.

I wondered if his questions had anything to do with Kevin's book.

Tomorrow morning I'd find out.

10

Ursula Gilberti's secretary called just before nine a.m. as I was navigating onto Highway 29 about forty miles outside Washington near Gainesville, Virginia. A little farther out, 29 turns into a pleasant country road that winds through Civil War battlefields, past farms, orchards, vineyards, and pastures where horses and cattle graze against the hazy backdrop of the Blue Ridge Mountains. Right now, though, I was still dealing with the headache of commuter traffic on a Friday morning.

"Ms. Medina," she said, "I hope I'm not calling too early, but the senator has asked me to tell you that Archduke Victor and Miss Gilberti were called away unexpectedly on a family matter. Any further meetings will have to wait until they return."

I merged into clogged traffic and said, "Thank you for letting me know."

What further meetings? The last time I had seen Ursula was the day before yesterday when she arrived at the Franciscan Monastery just before Officer Carroll walked me into the church for questioning. Perhaps she had assumed my presence there meant

I agreed to her terms that any further photography work I did for Victor and Yasmin's wedding would be without pay. I had already decided to stay on, not because of Ursula's vague and probably inflated promise to recommend me to all her friends, but because I'd made a commitment to Victor, whom I liked very much and didn't want to let down.

"Senator Gilberti will contact you herself next week to discuss further arrangements," the secretary said. "And she also requests that you send her the engagement party photos as soon as possible."

One of the meager benefits of not being paid was that I no longer needed to jump through every single hoop Ursula Gilberti held up.

"Please tell Senator Gilberti that I sent her, her daughter, and Archduke Victor an e-mail with a link to the photos last night, so she should check her in-box. Also, I'll be in London next week, so if there's anything else, she can contact me when I return. And you'll have to excuse me, but I'm driving and I need to pay attention right now."

"I'll look for those photos and I'll let her know you'll be away. You have a nice day, Ms. Medina."

Jack phoned next. "I was going to call last night to ask if you ever figured out what that key unlocked, but I got stuck on campus until late. Then one of the seminarians needed to talk, and that went until midnight. Any chance you're free for lunch today?"

"I wish I were, but I'm halfway to Charlottesville. I'm meeting someone at Monticello at eleven o'clock."

"Monticello?" He sounded surprised. "Work related or just taking a day off?"

"Neither."

I told him everything, including the discovery that Kevin owned an original copy of a book that had once belonged to Sir Isaac Newton.

"Are you serious?" He sounded floored. "I wonder if Kevin knew it was that valuable."

"I don't know, but the bigger question is who actually owns the book. I wonder what kind of deal Edward Jaine had with Kevin. Did he give Kevin money with no strings attached so Kevin bought the book himself, or did Jaine buy the book and Kevin was only borrowing it?"

Jack let out a long unhappy whistle. "That would be a mess. If Jaine bought it, then they'd have to sort out whether it was a gift or just a loan. And if it was a gift, Kevin should have reported it to the Franciscans."

"What do you mean?"

"Technically everything Kevin owned when he was alive belonged to the Franciscans. He took a vow of poverty, just like I did, just like all religious orders do. Only diocesan priests don't take that vow, so they can have personal wealth." He added in a dark voice, "There is a third messy possibility. Maybe Kevin didn't get around to reporting the book so the Franciscans were unaware he had it in his possession."

"And if he didn't do that?"

"Cue the lawyers."

"Seriously? Would the religious order of St. Francis of Assisi, founded on poverty and humility, actually go to court over something like that?"

"I wouldn't bet against it," Jack said. "There are only three things God doesn't know: how much money the Franciscans really have, how many communities of nuns there are, and what any Jesuit is thinking at any given time."

I burst out laughing. "You're joking . . . aren't you?"

"Only about two of the three. We Jesuits are real enigmas."

"No fooling." I smiled. "But I wish I knew what Kevin and Jaine were arguing about at the Austrian ambassador's the other night."

"Even if it had something to do with the book, I seriously

doubt Edward Jaine trashed Kevin's study room at the Library of Congress looking for it," Jack said. "He doesn't really fit the profile for breaking-and-entering, you know?"

"Maybe someone did it for him?"

"That still seems like a stretch."

"At some point Father Xavier needs to know about all this," I said. "The book, Asquith's, the room at the library . . . all of it."

"I called the monastery yesterday. They're totally swamped. Every news organization in the world wants an interview. Plus they're still trying to process Kevin's death, right in their own garden. I think you can wait a few days, Soph, to contact Xavier and add one more thing to his plate. Nothing's going to change, especially since the book is safe and sound at Asquith's."

"All right. It's probably just as well, because I'm going to London for a week with Harry." I told him about Chappy, my mother's trip to Connecticut, and her plans to move my grandfather into assisted living.

"Chap would hate that," Jack said. "He's always been so independent. I'll keep you all in my prayers. Maybe there's some other explanation for what happened. There are a lot of reasons people get confused, especially the elderly."

"I hope you're right."

"I have connections in high places. I'll do what I can. And if I don't talk to you before you leave, have a great trip."

"Thanks. Hey, I just remembered something. Kevin was supposed to drop by the Library of Congress on Wednesday after he met me and then he said he had a meeting with someone. He wasn't happy about it and said it was something he had to say now because it would be worse later if he didn't speak up. He didn't tell me who he was meeting, of course, but what if it was a follow-up conversation with Edward Jaine at the monastery?"

"You really have that guy on the brain, don't you? And then Jaine killed Kevin?"

"It could have been an accident, or an argument that got out of hand." I knew I sounded defensive, but for some reason that I couldn't explain, I didn't care for Edward Jaine. "It's not so impossible."

"Except I happen to know who Kevin was really meeting with," Jack said. "Yasmin."

"Yasmin? Why?"

He didn't answer right away and, knowing Jack, he was doing mental jujitsu about the ethics of telling me what was going on. "I suppose I'm not betraying any confidences now that Kevin's dead," he said at last, "but we had a quick chat at the party. One of the things I noticed—and you probably did, too, since you were photographing everyone—was that Yasmin and Victor were never together, almost like they weren't a couple. Then there was an incident Kevin and I happened to witness that made us wonder if Yasmin's ready for this marriage."

"You mean when Yasmin almost spilled her drink on her dress because of the guy who was ogling her?"

"You saw that?"

"His name is David Arista. Thea Stavros told me about him, and then coincidentally I met him the next day when I was at the Smithsonian. Olivia, my editor at Museum Press, says he's got a reputation among the female employees. Now he's working with Yasmin on the Smithsonian Creativity Council. Olivia says they're very close."

Jack groaned. "Kevin noticed little things here and there on other occasions when he'd been with Yasmin and Victor. He told me he finally decided to talk to her, caution her not to rush into anything, especially marriage, if she wasn't one hundred percent sure it was the right thing to do. Afterward he was going to call me and, if his talk didn't go well, we were considering taking a page out of St. Matthew's gospel."

"Pardon?"

"Then the two of us would join forces and have the 'come to Jesus' talk with her," he said. "Yasmin shouldn't be marrying Victor if she's got feelings she hasn't sorted out for David Arista, or anybody else, for that matter. Everyone's going to get hurt if she goes through with it. And in our business, you're morally obliged to say something if you see that kind of train wreck coming."

"So what happens now?"

"Well, right now I think the most immediate concern is Kevin's funeral at the monastery once the medical examiner releases his body. After that, maybe I can try to talk to Yasmin."

By the time Jack hung up, I'd reached the outskirts of Charlottesville and 29 had widened again into a multilane highway lined with ugly strip shopping plazas and modern commercial sprawl spreading like a stain toward a sweet little university town that had been founded in 1762. The weather had changed again overnight, back to a raw, gray chill that was more late winter than nearly the beginning of spring. As I made the long corkscrew drive through a fog-shrouded forest up Thomas Jefferson's mountain, I finally realized what had been nagging at me for the last few miles since my conversation with Jack.

If Kevin's talk with Yasmin hadn't gone well and she suddenly realized he had doubts about her marriage to Victor, then she could have been in quite a panic, worrying whether he might also share his thoughts with her fiancé. When I saw her at the monastery on Wednesday, she'd been early for our five o'clock meeting. Though the parking lot had been empty, that didn't mean she hadn't already arrived and left her car elsewhere before I'd seen her, maybe to seek out Kevin and urge him not to do anything that could interfere with her wedding or ruin her plans. Though she had seemed stunned at the news he was dead, maybe she was a good actress.

I'd just told Jack I thought Edward Jaine had a motive for murder. Now I wondered if maybe Yasmin did as well.

Someone buzzed me in at the security gate after I drove past the visitors' parking lot at Monticello and told me it wasn't much farther up the mountain to the small private lot near the mansion where Ryan Velis had told me to park. The gardens and grounds staff had their offices in a long rustic shed that included storage barns and a nursery. The low structure was so well tucked into the side of a steep hill I nearly walked past it until two men standing next to a tractor directed me where to go.

"End of the building, last door," one of them said. "He's in."

Dr. Ryan Velis was tall and lanky, probably around my age, with sandy hair just beginning to gray, an open freckled face that was tanned and weathered from years outdoors, and an engaging smile. He was dressed for gardening work in old jeans, a heavy dark green sweater, and a quilted vest. He rubbed his palms together before reaching across the desk and sticking out his right hand.

"How do you do? Sorry, I know it's like shaking hands with a block of ice. I'm out and about in the gardens so much I hate to heat this barn up and waste the electricity. Unless of course it's the dead of winter." He spoke with a folksy drawl as if I were an old friend who'd come a-calling, but he'd given me a sharp-eyed going over.

"I'd tell you to take off your coat and make yourself comfortable, but better not because it is a mite chilly. Do have a seat, though. And I can offer you coffee. Brewed fresh and it's hot. Warm your hands right up."

"Thanks. Milk and sugar, if you don't mind. And thank you for taking the time to see me."

His office looked like he was losing the war on paperwork, with files, magazines, documents, and books piled on every surface and overflowing a bookshelf. At least half a dozen moving boxes were stacked behind his desk in a long, low wall. He poured two coffees from a coffeemaker on a table near the window and handed me a mug with a scuffed silk-screened picture of Monticello. The milk came powdered and in a can along with the sugar.

"So," he said, wrapping his hands around his mug and leaning back in his chair, "you knew Kevin, God rest his soul. What a loss. I'll miss him."

"Me, too. It's still such an awful shock."

"How did you meet, if you don't mind my asking? You're a professional photographer and you've spent most of your career overseas with a news agency." His eyes crinkled with amusement. "Don't look so surprised. You didn't think I wasn't going to look you up, did you? Your photographs, by the way, are stunning."

"Thank you." I'd looked him up, too. I just hadn't expected him to be this direct. "A mutual friend, a Jesuit priest, introduced us years ago and we became friends. How about you?"

"I saw him when our paths crossed at various conferences over the past few years, but I only started working at Monticello the week before Thanksgiving so I didn't really get to know him until he came here for a month in January." He sipped his coffee and added as if it were an afterthought, "What brought you to me? I mean, besides the letter?"

"I saw your name listed along with Kevin's as one of the speakers at a conference at the Botanic Garden . . . 'Losing Paradise.' Plus I knew Kevin was here in January doing research."

He set down his mug and folded his hands on his desk. "Tell me about this letter."

I realized then that he hadn't known about it before I contacted him and that Kevin hadn't confided in him. But if I expected any help, I had no choice but to do as he asked.

"It's a letter from John Fairbairn, the head of the Chelsea Physic Garden, to a Leesburg doctor named Francis Pembroke," I said. "It was written in April 1807 and it's rather long."

He arched one eyebrow. "Did you bring it?"

"A copy, not the original."

I got it out of my camera bag and passed it to him. He picked up a pair of glasses and read while I drank my coffee and watched him. Though he kept his face neutral, I could see his eyes flicking back and forth over the page as though he was either surprised or startled by what he read, and my own heart started beating faster.

When he had finished, he looked up. "May I ask where the original is?"

"I don't have it."

He smiled like a patient teacher waiting for a student to figure out the right answer to the question. I smiled back.

"Look," he said, "let me tell you something about Kevin. Here at Monticello we're trying to restore Thomas Jefferson's garden to what it was in his day, no mean feat because Jefferson grew three hundred and thirty types of vegetables. You might think a man who kept a detailed *Garden Book* for nearly forty years and wrote twenty thousand letters in his lifetime would have meticulously recorded the proper names for the plants he grew, but you'd be wrong. Jefferson had a habit of describing plants by their appearance or some identifying characteristic—like 'the flowering pea of the plains of Arkansas'—that has made trying to figure out what he meant something of a botanic treasure hunt. We wouldn't be nearly so far along as we are if it weren't for Kevin, who was tireless in helping my predecessor and, for the last few months, helping me track down some of those lost plants." He leaned forward, palms squarely on his desk, and looked me in the eye. "So if I can do something to repay a debt Monticello owes Kevin, I'd like to do it."

"I see."

He sat back and folded his arms across his chest. "So that's my story. What's yours? And, while I'm at it, how'd you get hold of the letter? Kevin was in touch a few weeks ago asking questions I now realize had to do with it. He didn't say a word about this"—he tapped the letter—"so I figure he had a reason for keeping it quiet. Now he's dead and you show up. Are you working on a newspaper or magazine story maybe?"

The folksiness in his drawl was gone. He thought I was trying to cash in on Kevin somehow.

I straightened up in my chair and looked him in the eye. "No. It's nothing like that."

"Then what is it?"

I told him about finding Kevin the other day in the monastery garden, his fears of being stalked, and my belief that his death was somehow tied to the letter.

When I was finished, Ryan said in a stunned voice, "Good Lord, Kevin thought someone was after him? Who would do something like that?"

"I don't know. But the letter was inside a Solander box with a book. *Adam in Eden.*"

"Are you implying the book also had something to do with his death?"

"I think it's possible. That's why I'm here. I was hoping you could tell me about Francis Pembroke. And about *Adam in Eden.*"

Ryan looked perplexed. "I know the book, of course. The author was William Coles. Jefferson didn't own a copy, but I'm sure he knew about it. He used Philip Miller's *Gardeners Dictionary*, which was published a century later, as his primary gardening reference. Miller's book was a classic, far more than Coles's was. Anyone who was a serious gardener in those days had a copy of Miller's dictionary. Jefferson owned three editions, including the last one in which Miller finally began using the new Linnaean system of binomial nomenclature."

From high school biology I dredged up binomial nomenclature. "The Latin system for naming plants?"

"Actually for naming and classifying all living things. Unfortunately, Jefferson didn't use it or we'd know what we were looking for in his garden."

"And who was Philip Miller?"

"Curator at the Chelsea Physic Garden in London during the 1700s. One of the most influential botanists of his time. He was succeeded by William Forsyth—for whom forsythia was named—and John Fairbairn succeeded him."

"Why would the head of the Chelsea Physic Garden be writing to a doctor in Leesburg, Virginia? It was obviously an ongoing correspondence. Who was Francis Pembroke?"

Ryan stood and got the coffeepot, holding it up by way of asking if I wanted a refill.

I shook my head, so he filled his own mug. "Francis Pembroke was a wealthy physician who, as you already know, was a cousin of Meriwether Lewis. Before Lewis and Clark left on their western expedition, Thomas Jefferson, who got Congress to fund this journey, insisted Lewis have some medical training to equip him for whatever might come up in the wilderness. So Jefferson asked Francis Pembroke to train Lewis. In return, and as thanks, Jefferson gave Pembroke many of the new and unknown herbs Lewis and Clark brought or sent back, which would be of obvious interest to a colonial doctor who treated his patients with herbal remedies. Jefferson also asked Pembroke to see whether he could cultivate anything, or what use he could make of these new plants."

"There was a pressed plant in Kevin's copy of *Adam in Eden*," I said. "It was on the page that described hyssop, the plant John Fairbairn said Francis Pembroke misidentified."

Ryan gave me a thoughtful look, rubbing his fingers across his lips as though he were considering something. He picked up the letter. "I'd like to make a copy of this."

"Go right ahead."

When he was done, he returned my copy and said, "You still haven't told me where the original is. Though, presumably, it's with the book."

"I don't own the book or the letter, so an antiques dealer friend made arrangements for them to be stored in the vault of another dealer whose specialty is rare books. They're quite safe."

"How did you get hold of them in the first place?"

"I had the key to a locker where Kevin kept them."

"And—?"

"And I found the book and brought it to my friend." We were still dancing around, but he'd pushed hard enough. I hadn't told him about the hand-colored prints or that the book belonged to Isaac Newton. But until the thorny matter of who now owned it was sorted out, the fewer people who knew, the better.

"Look," I said, "Kevin didn't get to finish something he started. I want to help out if I can, do something in memory of a dear friend. That's all."

He gave me a long assessing look. "Let's go see the garden. Afterward I want to show you something in the mansion."

"I'd like that. But does the 'something in the mansion' pertain to the letter? Because you haven't explained to me why it was significant to Kevin."

He gave me an enigmatic smile. "No, I haven't." He pointed to my camera bag. "Take that with you. We won't be coming back here."

I obeyed and followed him outside. Though Charlottesville is a hundred miles south of Washington, give or take, the trees were as bare as they were at home and the grass was the washed-out yellow-green it always is at the end of winter. Thomas Jefferson's beloved mansion came into view, long and low with its octagonal dome and neoclassical lines reflecting his love of ancient Rome and the elegant symmetry of Palladian architecture.

"First we're going over to the west lawn," Ryan said, "the side of the house you see on the back of a nickel, and then to the vegetable garden before we go inside the mansion. By the time we're through, you'll know as much as I do about why Kevin thought the letter was important."

I had seen a few tourists at the gift shop on this damp, gray day as we walked over to the west lawn, but just now Monticello seemed deserted and we had the wide gravel path that Ryan called "the winding flower walk" to ourselves. Today there were only some early heirloom tulips, daffodils, and rosemary in bloom, and the brilliant yellow of the forsythia.

Halfway around the flower walk when the mansion was directly across the lawn from us, Ryan stopped and pointed down. "Look."

A brass plaque, maybe twelve inches in diameter, was set into the ground. CORPS OF DISCOVERY II—200 YEARS TO THE FUTURE formed a ring around two hands extended in friendship, a peace pipe crossed over a tomahawk, and the words PEACE AND FRIENDSHIP.

"It's based on the original silver peace medal Jefferson had the mint make for Lewis and Clark to trade," Ryan said as I knelt to photograph it. "The marker commemorates the two hundredth anniversary of the day he wrote Congress asking for funds for their trip."

He waited until I got up, and then went on. "That trip was a really big deal in its day, the modern-day equivalent of traveling to the moon. No one knew what Lewis and Clark would find, but Jefferson was passionate about exploring the new territory he'd just acquired and establishing an American presence there. So Jefferson, who thought botany was the most useful of the sciences, told Lewis and Clark to collect as many plants as they could, learn about them from the Indians, and send or bring as much as possible back to Washington."

"Including the pressed plant in *Adam in Eden*," I said.

"You're getting ahead of the story. You've got to let me tell this my way. Come on. Now I'm going to show you the garden."

We walked down the sloping lawn to the lower garden, which was cut like a terrace into the side of the hill. Directly in front of us was Jefferson's spectacular thousand-foot-long garden, stripes of pale green grass dividing large patches of tilled earth, many of which sprouted new plants pushing out of the clay soil or the straw-colored remnants of something that would be renewed in spring. Perched as if it were sitting on the edge of a cliff, where the terrace dropped away to a lower level, was a small brick pavilion with arched windows and a view of the Piedmont countryside stretching to the horizon, as wide and blue as an ocean.

"What you're looking at was a lot more than a place to grow vegetables for Thomas Jefferson's dinner table. It was a laboratory where he experimented with new crops, including vegetables Lewis and Clark brought back with them. See those markers?" Ryan pointed to a row where a small sign with the initials *TJ* also indicated it was planted with French artichokes. "Those are Jefferson's seeds. Anything with an *LC* marker, many different kinds of corn, beans, squash—vegetables the Indians cultivated—came from Lewis and Clark."

I looked at where he was pointing, row after row of neatly labeled plants.

"What made the Lewis and Clark seeds so important and exciting to Jefferson was that these were plants and vegetables the rest of the world had never seen. For the Founding Fathers, the potential economic and commercial opportunities of so many new native American species, especially trading with Europe, was huge." We had started walking along the perimeter of the garden, and Ryan went on. "Don't forget, all those men were farmers who believed the economic future of their new country would be as an agricultural nation. One of the things they did to encourage that—and Jefferson probably more than the others—was swap seeds among themselves, enclosing seed packets of new plants they'd come across in their letters to each other. Later they'd compare notes about what grew and what didn't on their various plantations."

He knelt next to a small garden bed that butted up against the hill where half a dozen planks lay in a row on top of the soil. He lifted the first one and grunted in satisfaction.

"What are you doing?" I asked.

"Checking the peas." He lifted the other planks. "It didn't freeze last night, but it came awfully close." He said with a grin, "Don't worry, the peas aren't expected to grow through the wood. We take it off when the weather warms up. Come on, let's go up to the house."

He stood and brushed the dirt off his hands. "The letter you brought me is important," he said as we retraced our steps, "not only because of the misidentified plant—and I'll get to that after I show you something in the mansion—but also because it talks about Washington and Jefferson actually doing something to establish a national botanic garden."

"What do you mean?"

"A few years before George Washington died in 1799, he wrote to the commissioners for the brand-new capital of Washington and suggested that a botanical garden be incorporated into the design plans for the city. He even proposed a few locations for it, along with the idea the garden could also be part of a national university. The next time anything happened was 1820, when Congress approved funding for the project, and James Monroe, who was the president, agreed the garden could be established on a tract of land near the Capitol."

"Where the Botanic Garden is located today."

"Nope, not exactly. They moved it later to where it is today, and let me tell you, there was blood on the carpet when that happened because of all the trees that had to be destroyed."

By now we had reached Jefferson's mansion. Ryan climbed the steps to the columned portico two at a time as though there were some urgency in what we were doing, and I followed.

"Francis Pembroke's letter, which was written in 1807, talks about Washington and Jefferson having already selected plants, or seeds, for a national botanic garden," I said as he held the door for me.

"That's right, and that's what I'm going to show you."

We stepped inside Jefferson's spacious light-filled two-story entrance hall, part museum, part art gallery with classic busts and sculptures from Europe alongside a wall with a display of Native American artifacts from Lewis and Clark's expedition. For the first time, we weren't alone, and Ryan touched a finger to his lips and motioned for me to follow him down a corridor to a steep, narrow staircase that wound to the second floor like a tight coil. To my left was a doorway that led to the balcony overlooking the entrance hall. We turned right and entered a small octagonal room.

It was a bedroom, simply furnished with a bed tucked into an alcove, a chest of drawers, and a chair. There was also a fireplace and the rectangular windows were all at floor level.

"This is what I wanted you to see." Ryan pointed to what looked like a large pine armoire. "Thomas Jefferson's seed press, made here in the Monticello joinery. He kept all his seeds in it, in vials that were hung on hooks attached to the wall or in tin canisters. Originally it was downstairs in his private suite, the rooms he called his Cabinet."

"It's very interesting," I said, "but why are you showing it to me?"

"Because it dates from 1809, after Jefferson returned to Monticello at the end of his second term as president, two years after the Pembroke letter. But here's what's interesting: We have a written account of a woman, a friend of Jefferson's who knew him in Washington and visited Monticello, who said Jefferson also had a portable seed press, which he used for carrying around seeds when he worked in his garden. It's gone, completely vanished, and we have no idea what it looked like except for her description: a wooden stand with some truss hooks and more corked vials of seeds. According to the woman, the portable press was able to hold at least one hundred different kinds of seeds, so it wasn't some little contraption."

I didn't understand where he was going with this. "Are we still talking about Francis Pembroke's letter?"

"I'm getting to that." He sounded testy. "Hold your horses. Pembroke's letter stated that Washington and Jefferson had selected seeds, or plants, for the botanic garden as you said. From what Fairbairn wrote to Pembroke, it appeared that Jefferson added many of the plants discovered by Lewis and Clark to that list, plus he was also going to incorporate an herb garden into the national garden. Pembroke, who was something of an amateur artist, intended to document those plants, which would have been why he wanted the copy of William Curtis's *Flora Londinensis* that John Fairbairn sent him, so he could see how Curtis did the same thing for the plants and flowers found in and around London."

"So there should be a book of Pembroke's drawings somewhere," I said.

"I've never come across it, but after reading that letter I plan to make some inquiries in case it's still out there. So I appreciate your making us aware of it."

"Kevin's the one who discovered it," I said. "But I don't understand how this seed press fits in with your story."

Was that what Kevin was looking for? Francis Pembroke's drawings of the plants that were meant to go in the national botanic garden?

Ryan ran his hand along the edge of the old worn cabinet as though he were channeling Jefferson. "The other thing we've always wondered," he said, "was whether Thomas Jefferson had a second seed press like this one, or perhaps another portable press, in the White House. It seems logical since he would have kept the many varieties of seeds that Lewis and Clark brought him. But, you see, we've always assumed that any seeds he might have had at the White House were eventually intended for Monticello, or else to share among friends." He turned to me. "Maybe we got this wrong. Maybe Jefferson was storing seeds for the national botanic garden, seeds that he and George Washington collected together. The Pembroke letter is another puzzle piece that would seem to validate that theory."

"What happened to the seeds?"

"The British burned Washington during the War of 1812. Almost nothing in the White House survived, including the furniture, most of which had belonged to Jefferson."

"You think the seeds were destroyed in that fire?"

He had started pacing back and forth in the little room, as though he were trying to work this out. "That's the thing," he said, almost to himself, "maybe they weren't."

"So where are they?"

"I have no idea. But I wonder if Kevin did. Dolley Madison made sure a lot of irreplaceable items like the Constitution and the Declaration of Independence were moved to Virginia for safekeeping, barely getting them out of Washington before the British showed up for their bonfire. It's possible the seeds were already stored in labeled packets, which was common in those days, meaning it wouldn't have been hard to gather them up, even if you were in a hurry, and put them in some sort of pouch. Dolley would have known how much those seeds represented to Washington and Jefferson."

"Kevin told me he'd discovered something that was more or less hiding in plain sight. Or, at least, he thought he did. That's why he was keeping this quiet until he could find out if he was right," I said. "Do you think he knew what happened to the seeds?"

Ryan's eyes were bright with interest and his cheeks were flushed. When he spoke, I could hear the growing excitement in his voice. "If he did, that would be quite a historical coup. There's a letter from Dolley Madison to Jefferson after the White House burned in which she mentioned something about 'the presidents' seeds' being safe. I always thought it was a grammatical error because she referred to presidents in the plural."

"Even if there was a seed pouch somewhere, that was over two hundred years ago. After so much time, wouldn't they be dust?"

He shook his head. "Stored under the right circumstances, they could still be viable. In other words, you could plant them and you might be able to grow something."

"That would be amazing."

He nodded. "Seeds from plants that George Washington and

Thomas Jefferson themselves collected, probably from Mount Vernon and Monticello, plus the original seeds of plants discovered by Lewis and Clark? There would be a huge amount of interest among historians, as well as in the scientific community, especially if some of the species were extinct."

Ryan still didn't know how valuable Kevin's copy of the book was, and it seemed as if Kevin might not have realized, either. So if he had been murdered, had it been because of these seeds?

"Just how valuable would the seeds be?" I asked.

Ryan's eyes met mine. "To the right people—not just historians but also pharmaceutical companies or agribusinesses—they could be extraordinarily valuable because of the potential for new drugs or new crop species. Especially if you're the one who finds them. They'd be priceless."

I nodded, wondering if the plant in *Adam in Eden* that apparently had great potency in restoring memory was one of the species that had become extinct. If so, it would be, as Kevin had said, potentially worth millions. Maybe more.

I stared at Thomas Jefferson's seed cupboard and tried to take in what Ryan had just told me. Because if he was right, there were two things Kevin had discovered that might have cost him his life.

First the book.

And now these seeds.

11

Ryan walked me to my car after a detour through Jefferson's rooms, the beautiful suite he called his Cabinet and his sanctum sanctorum. I told him I was leaving tomorrow night for a week in London and had written to the general information address at the Chelsea Physic Garden, asking to meet with someone to discuss the Fairbairn letter.

"The person you want to see is Zara Remington, the curator. She's good people. I can write her on your behalf, if you'd like. In return, I'd like to be kept in the loop of anything you find out."

"Fair enough," I said. "So, what about you? Do you have any ideas where these seeds might be?"

"No, but I certainly intend to start looking."

"And in return, you'll keep me in *your* loop." I gave him a bright smile. "If you find anything, I'd like to be the photographer who gets the first pictures. I owe it to Kevin. It's his story, you know."

He nodded. "Now I understand why he was keeping this so quiet."

I got in the Mini and rolled down the window. "If someone killed him, he wasn't keeping it quiet enough."

He looked startled. "I suppose you're right."

"Be careful."

He reached through the window and patted my shoulder. "You be careful, too."

Sole Brothers Shoes was located on Columbia Road, the main commercial drag in the colorful, noisy heart of Adams Morgan. Years ago the store had been an elegant French patisserie called Avignon Frères, in the middle of a largely immigrant Hispanic community. The Sole Brothers, whose surname was Weinstein, had managed to keep the Old World emporium charm when they renovated the place, and now the shoe store had become as popular a destination spot as the bakery had once been. That they were closing for a morning for "a private event" was a big deal, and as one of the brothers told me, "The good publicity don't hurt us, neither. Everybody in the neighborhood has been in, buyin' shoes and showin' their support. Plus, we've had a bunch of donations. We got at least another two hundred bucks for you just in the past three days."

The children arrived in shifts beginning at nine o'clock, by grade, the littlest ones first, or else we figured the store would turn into a mob scene. Grace, Tommy, and I had arrived earlier, along with every teacher in the school and the entire staff of Sole Brothers. Though I would have loved to take pictures as souvenirs for the kids, I left my camera at home. Not everyone was in the country legally and we didn't want to scare any of the parents away. The goal was for every child to leave the store with a new pair of shoes.

My phone rang halfway through the third wave of kids, the fifth and sixth graders. I had been reaching for a shoe box on a high shelf for a ten-year-old girl with a sweet smile and big dark eyes who looked enough like me that we could have been related. I answered the phone and looked down to see who was calling. A D.C. number I didn't recognize.

"Hey," a male voice said, "it sounds like you're in the middle of Union Station. I hope I'm not catching you at a bad time."

"Who's this?"

"Sorry," he said. "It's David Arista."

I handed the box to the little girl and walked to the end of the aisle where the shoe sizes were too big for any of the kids so it was quieter.

"Actually, I'm in a shoe store," I said, "and I'm kind of busy. What can I do for you?"

"I never get in the way of a woman on a shopping mission," he said with a grin in his voice. "Especially when it involves shoes. I'll be brief. My friend at the Arts and Industries Building is willing to meet us next week and you can photograph the inside of the building to your heart's content. I was just wondering what day would work for you."

I leaned against the end of a tall shelf and closed my eyes. "Thank you, but unfortunately I'm not available next week."

"Sophie?"

I looked up. Grace stood at the end of the aisle and beckoned me. I held up a finger to indicate I'd be a moment.

"You're not free any day next week? Can't you rearrange something?" he was saying. "He's making an exception to let you in. I'm not sure I can pull this off again."

"It's very kind of you, but I won't even be in the country. I'm going to London for the week. What about the following week?"

He made a noisy, unhappy sound. "I got the mountain to come to Mohammed, but I'll see what I can do. You'll have e-mail while you're away, right?"

"Yes. I'm really sorry, but I've got to go."

"All right. Cheerio. I'll let you get back to your Jimmy Choos and Manolo Blahniks. Sounds like they're giving them away if that din is anything to go by. Where are you, anyway?"

"It's a private event and actually they are giving them away," I said. "Goodbye, David."

I joined Grace, who said, "We're almost done. The older kids knew exactly what they wanted, so once that big line at the cash register is finished, that's it. I thought we could stick around and tidy up so the place doesn't look like a war zone and then I'll buy you lunch."

"Yes to everything, but I need to pass on lunch. I haven't packed for London, plus I'm going to try to make five thirty Mass at the cathedral before Tommy comes by to take me to Dulles."

"You have a sweet brother."

"I know. He was going out to Middleburg anyway since he's on spring break and the house will be empty. He figured he'd get a lot of uninterrupted studying done."

Tommy left, telling me he'd see me later, and Grace and I stuck around with several of the teachers to restock boxes that had been left in piles like snowdrifts and pick up tissue paper and cardboard shoe inserts flung about like haphazard decorations. It was just after twelve thirty when we left, both on foot, since I lived about twenty minutes from the store and Grace's house was around the corner. We exchanged hugs at the intersection of 18th Street and Columbia Road, where we went in different directions.

"What can I bring you from London?" I asked.

"I'd love some tea from Fortnum and Mason, if you have time. Any kind of tea, as long as it's English."

"I'll have plenty of time. It's a pleasure trip."

"By the way," she said, "I meant to tell you. Two things. I'm still covering the story on Kevin and I checked in with my contact in the medical examiner's office this morning. They haven't done the autopsy yet."

"Will you let me know if you hear anything?"

"Of course."

"You said two things."

"You'll have company from home while you're in London. I saw a story on the International Press Service wire this morning. Archduke Orlando, Victor's father, is in the hospital recovering from pneumonia. There was a picture of Victor with Yasmin Gilberti entering St. Mary's Hospital with a scrum of photogs around them. Yasmin's turned into quite a little media sensation."

So that's what Ursula's secretary had meant when she said Yasmin and Victor were called away on family business.

"How's his father doing?" I asked. "I knew he was too frail to come to the party the other night, but I didn't realize he had pneumonia."

"I think it came on suddenly. Apparently he's not doing well at all."

"I'll write Victor and tell him I'm thinking about him."

She gave me another hug and crossed Columbia Road. When I was halfway down 18th Street, I thought of Ursula's neighbor's remark the other night, that Ursula wished the older prince would die before the wedding so Victor would inherit his father's titles and his share of the family fortune. It had been a snide, snarky comment, but maybe there had been some truth in it.

Yasmin would marry a wealthier, more titled man and her wedding would be even more important in European royal society. And now neither Ursula nor Yasmin had to worry about Kevin doing or saying anything that might interfere with that wedding.

If it's an ill wind that blows nobody any good, maybe the Gilberti women considered Kevin's death and the archduke's illness to be a fortunate turn of events.

But I hoped they didn't.

Though I have amassed enough air miles for an upgrade on the first commercial trip to the moon thanks to work-related travel, I am still fascinated by the off-kilter view from an airplane window as cars, buildings, cities, lakes, and even mountain ranges shrink to the size of toys like the quick reverse zoom of a telephoto lens. Harry gave me the window seat on our flight from Dulles to Heathrow on Saturday night; he travels first class, a sublime luxury. We took off just after ten p.m., and before long, dusky shapes melted into deeper shadows until there were only constellations of bronze and silver lights, ghost images of cities and towns and dark-edged coastlines below. After a while even those faint winking lights vanished into the depthless void of a moonless night as we turned away from Nova Scotia and headed over the North Atlantic.

Harry ordered champagne for both of us without asking me because that's the way he is. If my handsome white-haired stepfather, a traditional Southern gentleman with a moonlight-and-magnolia sense of chivalry, could wrap his arms around the women in his life—my mother, my half sister, Lexie, and me—and keep the wicked world at bay, he would do it.

He touched his champagne glass against mine. "You're welcome to come to Lingfield on Monday to watch the Winter Derby with me, kitten. The horses run on artificial turf. It ought to be a good race. You'd meet some nice people. What do you say?"

I smiled. "Thanks, Harry, but if you don't mind, I'd prefer to stay in London. See some friends, revisit old haunts."

Though Harry knew about Kevin's death, he didn't know I'd been at the monastery that day, nor did he know anything about the book, Asquith's, or my visit to Monticello yesterday. I also hadn't told him that while we were waiting at the gate at Dulles I'd received a disturbing e-mail from Zara Remington, the curator at the Chelsea Physic Garden. According to the time stamp, she'd written me at two a.m. London time.

I would very much like to meet you when you're in London. Though the garden is closed at this time of year, by exception we're open tomorrow, Sunday, for a sale of lilies in anticipa-

tion of Easter. The sale will be finished by half three, so I can be available to see you at 4 pm. I hope this suits your schedule, but in light of the information you shared with me in your e-mail as well as further correspondence with Ryan Velis, I believe time is of the essence. I shan't let anyone know you are coming and would advise you to be similarly circumspect. Please let me know if these arrangements suit you.

I'd written her right back and said I'd see her Sunday at four and didn't plan to share that information with anyone. That included Harry. If he found out any of this, he'd insist on going with me.

"Whatever you want to do, sweetheart," he said to me now. "I just want you to have a good time."

"It's London. I'll have a wonderful time."

We got a few restless hours of sleep before they turned on the cabin lights and the flight attendant began serving breakfast. Harry had booked us at the Connaught—more luxury—and someone from the hotel met our flight at Heathrow, shepherding us to a waiting black Bentley that zipped along the motorway, eventually winding its way onto the quiet streets of Mayfair on a chilly, gray Sunday morning.

"I forgot to pack gloves. It's a lot colder than it was at home," I said to Harry as the chauffeur pulled into Carlos Place and stopped at the glass-fronted hotel entrance. A doorman in a black top hat and a smart camel overcoat opened the car door.

"Welcome to the Connaught, Mr. Wyatt, Ms. Medina."

Another doorman held the front door as Harry and I walked into the paneled lobby, where a fire burned in a small gas fireplace and the air smelled faintly of the fragrant pink and magenta roses that spilled out of a crystal vase next to the spiral staircase. A grandfather clock chimed eleven as a woman in a navy suit came toward us, holding a clipboard.

She, too, welcomed us to the Connaught in a faint Eastern

European accent that I couldn't identify. "Your rooms are ready and your registration has been taken care of. You're on the fourth floor, and James, your butler, is waiting for you. He can bring you coffee or tea, if you wish, and he would be happy to unpack your bags, which are already in your room." She led us over to an elevator across from the registration desk.

When Nick and I lived in London, we occasionally stopped into the Connaught for drinks, and once I came to afternoon tea with a couple of girlfriends. But I'd never stayed in this small jewel of a hotel, and I already felt as though we were guests at a friend's posh country home. Our rooms, furnished in understated British opulence, overlooked Carlos Place and a shallow infinity pool in which two bare-branched London plane trees grew.

"That fountain is called *Silence*," James said as we stood at the window in Harry's room after he'd brought coffee for Harry, English breakfast tea for me, and a basket of warm scones, jam, and clotted cream on a heavy silver tray. "Every fifteen minutes a mist comes up from the base of the trees and then vanishes after fifteen seconds. At night when it's lighted, it's quite magical. But those plane trees . . ." He chuckled and shook his head. "A right mess when they're in bloom. Just ask the doormen."

James left after assuring us he was available to indulge our every whim and we assured him we could unpack our own bags.

"What are your plans, kitten?" Harry set his empty coffee cup on the tray and pulled a credit card from his wallet, holding it out to me. "Why don't you go shopping? Early birthday present from your mother and me."

I closed his hand around the card. "The trip is an early birthday present and Christmas and every other holiday. Thanks, Harry. I'm just going to walk, see the sights."

He grinned. "You certainly didn't inherit your mother's shopping gene. You going to get together with anyone?"

"I called Perry DiNardo, my old boss from IPS, before I left home. He's in Istanbul but he's flying back to London tonight. We're going to meet up for lunch tomorrow. What about you? What are you going to do?"

"I might rest my eyes," he said. "Just a quick nap. Then I'm having lunch with an old friend in Covent Garden. He used to come out to Middleburg to hunt when he was with the British embassy in the sixties . . . you're welcome to join us, you know."

I kissed him. "Thanks, but if I'm not there you can talk about horses and hounds and hunting to your hearts' content. I can entertain myself . . . I'll probably just take a nostalgia tour of all the old special places."

"If that's what you want, then. Have fun." Harry knows when I'm lying, but he gave me the look that said he'd stay out of my business and respect my privacy. "What about tonight? Will you be free for dinner? I could ask James to make a reservation at the seafood place down the block. Drinks downstairs first in the Coburg Bar. What do you say?"

"That would be perfect, but if you mean Scott's, it might already be booked for this evening. That restaurant is always crowded."

Harry flashed a roguish smile. "Sweetheart, you're staying at the Connaught. If I asked James to arrange it, he'd find a way for us to have tea at Buckingham Palace."

I laughed. "Of course he would. What was I thinking?"

After living in London for more than a dozen years, I believe I'm entitled to call it home, or at least, I still feel I belong here. The doorman held the door for me and tipped his hat as I stepped outside, asking if I needed a cab or a map or directions to a particular museum or shop. I thanked him and told him I knew my way around, setting off down Mount Street and through Mayfair with its elegant banded buildings of red brick and white stone, luxury shops, quiet mews, and discreet clubs and businesses like a kid who has been turned loose in the toy store.

Let me just get it out of the way that I believe, as Samuel Johnson did, if you are tired of London, you are tired of life. As an adopted daughter of the South—Harry's grandfather and great-uncles fought with Lee and Stonewall—I grew to love Southern culture and its tradition-steeped ways, which is why I probably slipped into life in London so easily. They had a lot in common. I love this city's vibrancy and rich history, the green parks and flower-filled gardens, royal palaces and picturesque squares, the Globe Theatre, the erudition of the *Times*, the culture of Radio 4, dry British wit and understated humor, the pageantry of Trooping the Colour, strawberries and cream at Wimbledon, Christmas lights that turn the city into a fairyland, and bonfires on Guy Fawkes Day. I find comfort in putting the kettle on for a cup of tea, cab drivers and shopkeepers who call me "love," Big Ben chiming the hour, and I tear up when I hear a choir singing "I Vow to Thee, My Country" in Royal Albert Hall on Remembrance Day.

David Hockney—the modern British painter who decamped to California—says there's nothing wrong with photographers as long as you realize we see the world through one eye, or as he says, we're a bunch of momentarily paralyzed Cyclops. To me that implies that we miss a lot, or worse, we see the world flattened out in two dimensions, not fully formed in three. London, and Britain, for that matter, have their share of warts, which I'm not blind to—an ingrained class structure that can be stultifying, free socialized medicine that is worth what you pay for it, overly boiled vegetables, and more descriptive ways to describe rain and gray weather than any other country on the planet. I will never understand why the British celebrate so many days with the limp, uninspired title of bank holiday, and am still baffled by the illogical grammar of collective nouns and matching verbs so that it's correct to say, "England are winning the match."

I know they return the favor with their aversion to our loud go-big-or-go-home swagger when we travel, our gun-toting culture and accompanying violence, which scares them, the staggering cost of our health-care system, our mindless fascination with people who are famous for no logical reason, and our belief that we are at the epicenter of world politics yet most of us probably couldn't correctly fill in a map identifying the countries of the United Kingdom if our life depended on it.

But as I walked down the Sunday-quiet streets, London felt as familiar and welcoming as catching up with an old and well-loved friend. I took the side streets until I reached New Bond Street, where I lingered in front of Asquith's window and wondered if Bram had come to any conclusions about the value of Kevin's copy of *Adam in Eden.* At Fortnum & Mason on Piccadilly I bought tea for Grace and my landlady from a gentleman in a morning coat who called me "madam" and afterward spent half an hour roaming the floors of Hatchards bookstore, running my hand over the dust jackets of books I hadn't seen in any bookstore at home, like a lover who has been told it's the end of the affair. A pub lunch at the crowded, noisy King's Head—a pot of tea to warm my hands and then fish and chips with a pint of Fuller's—while a television blared the Chelsea versus Spurs match. When I left, Chelsea were winning.

Eventually I gave in to the sharp, cold sting of English weather and bought a pair of forest-green knit gloves and a matching cloche at a shop on Regent Street after I walked down to the outdoor market at St. James's Church, where I would have found something offbeat and cheaper, until I realized it was Sunday so it was closed. By then it was time to take the Underground to Sloane Square and make my way to my meeting with Zara Remington, about a twenty-minute walk through the quiet residential streets of Chelsea. The wind had picked up again, buffeting me and whipping the last dry autumn leaves around my feet like small cyclones. I turned up the collar of my coat, glad for the hat and gloves.

Zara Remington hadn't given me any instructions other than to show up at the garden at four o'clock, so I first tried the visitors' entrance, a locked wrought-iron gate in the middle of an ancient brick wall on Swan Walk. No one was at the kiosk inside the garden, so I walked around the corner to Royal Hospital Road and rang the bell at the staff entrance.

A slender dark-eyed man opened the door. Early thirties, maybe, with curly brown hair that ringed his face, giving him an innocent, angelic look. Though he was staring directly at me, one eye was focused at something off to my right. "I'm sorry, miss, the garden's closed. I'm afraid the Easter lily sale has finished."

"I know," I said. "I have a four o'clock appointment with Ms. Remington."

"Today?" He looked at me with interest. "And you are—?"

"Sophie Medina."

"How do you do? Will Tennant. Why don't you come in and I'll let her know you're here?" Will Tennant opened the door wider and called over his shoulder, "Zara, Sophie Medina is here to see you."

I stepped into a long, narrow anteroom dominated by a wall map of the Chelsea Physic Garden in the 1800s. Below it a wooden table held brochures and information sheets in neat piles. In a corner, the shade was pulled down at an information window across from a door with a STAFF ONLY sign.

A woman whose light brown hair was silvered with gray and done up in a windblown bun walked through a door at the far end of the hall. She wore Wellingtons and a quilted jacket over a tweed blazer and jeans as though she'd just come in from walking her spaniel across the moor. Her clothes smelled of the fresh chill of outdoors and Easter lilies, but more to the point, she didn't look happy to see me.

"Thank you, Will," she said, her tone an unmistakable dismissal. He nodded, giving me another curious cockeyed look before he left through the door she had just used. Zara Remington turned to me and added in a brisk voice, "We're just finishing up with the lily sale in the gift shop. I need a moment with Will, but if you'd care to have a look around the garden, I'll join you shortly."

"Thank you."

Something was wrong, because it was clear she was upset by my presence. Before I could say anything, she reached for one of the information sheets on the table and passed it to me. A map of the garden. "This ought to get you oriented." She pointed to a patch of dark green squares surrounded by what looked like dirt paths next to a pond rockery. "I suggest you start here."

I looked at the legend on the map. Garden of World Medicine. Next to it: Pharmaceutical Beds. "I'll do that."

I followed her into the other room and entered a gift shop filled with books, potpourri, seeds, calendars, and plant-related souvenirs. Half a dozen Easter lilies, the flowers just beginning to open, sat in pots wrapped in lavender or pale yellow foil on a table in the middle of the room. Will stood behind a counter at the cash register, sorting through receipts.

"The door to the garden is in the next room," Zara said to me. "Do go through."

The Chelsea Physic Garden was larger than I expected, an expansive private park with well-swept tree-lined gravel paths converging at a moss-covered statue of Sir Hans Sloane, the wealthy benefactor who bought the garden in the 1700s to ensure it could be maintained in perpetuity as an herbal garden and a place to teach. According to the map, I was looking at a large rectangle that was slightly squashed at the far end where the boundary followed the contours of the Thames and the Chelsea Embankment on the other side of a high redbrick wall. Here, as everywhere else in London, the trees were bare, but spring seemed more imminent in this rich garden with its peaty aroma of fresh mulch, vivid green carpet of grass, and the new growth of plants that had pushed through the soil.

The Garden of World Medicine was laid out in a way that reminded me of Monticello, with the same grassy pathways separating neat, tilled beds. Zara Remington found me on one knee, reading about a plant called *Hyssopus officinalis* among the Western European medicinal plants. The description on the little black-and-white marker read *For all cold griefes of diseases of the chest and lungs, helping to expectorate tough phlemn.* It sounded a lot like the hyssop plant William Coles described in *Adam in Eden.*

I stood up and said, "I'm sorry if I've come at an inconvenient time."

She pressed her lips together. I couldn't tell if she was worried or upset, or both. "I was rather hoping you would have looked at your e-mail before you arrived and found one from me asking you to delay coming until half four. Unfortunately, I didn't have your number or I would have rung you. I assumed we'd be through with the lily sale ages ago. Will stayed around to help me finish totaling the receipts . . . I suppose it'll be all right. He doesn't know why you're here and he's also one of my most trusted and loyal volunteers. He's been with me for years."

She was the first person so far who brought up the need for secrecy in discussing Kevin's letter. Maybe that meant she knew something, that Kevin had confided in her.

"I'm sorry," I said again. "I should have checked. London used to be my home and it's my first visit back in a while . . . I'm afraid I got sidetracked." I pointed to the hyssop. "About this plant—"

"Yes, we'll come back to that later." She folded her arms across her chest and studied me. "And before we go any further, I need to know about your relationship with Brother Kevin Boyle and how you managed to acquire the Fairbairn letter." She gave me a pointed look and added, "If you have the letter, you also have the book, do you not?"

Ryan had made the same request two days ago at Monticello.

Explain yourself. The difference this time was that Zara Remington knew about Kevin's copy of *Adam in Eden.*

"I do have it," I said. Then I answered her questions, except I left out telling her about Bram Asquith and that the book was now safely in his vault in Washington. But I did tell her I was fairly certain Kevin had left the Solander box with the book and the letter in a locker at the Natural History Museum because he needed to hide them.

"Kevin hid them for a good reason." Her voice was grim. "And now he's dead. He rang me the day before he passed away and told me he was convinced someone else was looking for the book. Was that person you?"

A seagull screeched and wheeled overhead, disappearing over the wall in the direction of the Thames. "No. It wasn't," I said, taken aback.

Zara gave me a searching look. "I'll have to take your word for it, won't I? And Ryan vouched for you."

I said a silent prayer of thanks to Ryan. "I'm afraid there isn't anyone else to ask. Ryan didn't know any of this before I visited him Friday at Monticello. And Kevin told me roughly the same thing he told you, that he believed someone was stalking him. You're the first person I've spoken to who knew he was worried about being followed."

That seemed to surprise her. "Do you have any idea who it was?"

"None."

"There was a rather gorgeous coffee-table book published a number of years ago called *The Beauty of Marlborough Gardens,*" she said. "Would it be too great a coincidence to assume you're the same Sophie Medina who took the photographs for that book?"

"When my husband and I lived in London, we rented what used to be the gardener's cottage on the old Marlborough estate," I said, "before the garden was turned into a private communal park for the homes in that neighborhood. I put together that book as a fund-raiser for the garden club."

"Your photographs were stunning. I bought a copy at the Chelsea Flower Show and then I went to see the garden for myself." She paused. "Now I'm really curious what brings you here. You obviously have no professional connection to Kevin."

"I'm not a botanist or even a very good gardener, if that's what you're asking." Her lips curved in a small smile for the first time since we'd met. "But I have a personal connection. He was a dear friend. And to answer your question, I thought you might be able to tell me about the letter, and since you know about it, the book as well."

"I see. Do go on."

"Ryan Velis was interested in the Fairbairn letter because it seemed to substantiate a theory at Monticello that Thomas Jefferson kept a seed press, either a portable one or an actual cabinet, in the White House during his presidency. Perhaps the seeds he and George Washington collected for an American botanic garden, plus new specimens Jefferson added from the Lewis and Clark expedition."

Zara shoved her hands in her jacket pockets. "Let's walk, shall we?"

Walking suited me, too. Zara's initial suspicion that I was Kevin's stalker, her request that our meeting be kept a secret, and her concern that one of her colleagues had seen me arrive was making me jumpy. I nearly looked over my shoulder to see if Will Tennant was watching us with his peculiar stare through the gift shop window.

"So are you here because you believe I can help you find these seeds, or that I might know where they are?" She gave me a smile like we were a pair of conspirators.

I didn't take the bait. "It still hasn't been established that they even existed."

"Kevin believed they did."

I stopped walking. "He told you?"

"He did." She gave me a significant look. "And that, my dear, is the extent of my knowledge of the whereabouts of those seeds. A week after he left here, he was dead."

"A week after——? I thought Kevin came to London in February to give a talk at Kew Gardens."

"That's right, he did," she said. "And whilst he was here, he spent a morning on Portobello Road pottering around the book dealer stalls. That's when he found the copy of *Adam in Eden* at the bottom of a box with a jumble of books on English gardens. He crowed about what a lucky find it was, even though, at the time, he thought none of it was worth much."

We were standing in front of the statue of Hans Sloane, who appeared to be smiling down on us with sightless benevolence. The pockmarked statue was covered with moss that looked like dark green trim on his long flowing robe, and Sloane's carved face was so weathered that his eyes had worn away and it looked as if he were wearing large goggles.

"At the time?" I said. "Something changed his mind?"

"It did," she said. "But before I go on, where is the book right now? I do hope it's someplace safe."

Zara Remington was the only person who knew the entire history of the book, and Kevin had trusted her. "It's at Asquith's in Washington. Bram Asquith is a good friend of a friend of mine. He's appraising it as a favor."

"Well, Bram will certainly know in a tick about the provenance of that book. I hope he doesn't talk."

"He's not going to. However, there might be some question about who owns it now that Kevin is dead."

Zara put a hand to her forehead as though she were massaging a migraine. "Good Lord. Who are our options?"

I almost smiled at her use of "our."

"The Franciscans and an American billionaire named Edward Jaine. He was Kevin's benefactor."

"I didn't know Kevin was involved with him," she said with a faint note of distaste in her voice. "There have been rumors in the British press recently that Mr. Jaine has some rather unsavory business dealings."

"What do you mean?"

"I don't recall exactly, but I believe it had to do with computers that were being shipped to Third World countries. Perhaps they were substandard, I'm not sure. You can probably find the story on the Internet."

"I'll look. But you were going to explain about Kevin's trip here the week before he died."

Zara tucked a wisp of hair that had come down from her bun back into place. "It had to do with the book. He brought it back to England because someone wanted to take a look at it. A collector. That's when he found out how extraordinarily valuable it was." She lowered her voice. "Did Bram say anything to you?"

We continued walking down a broad gravel path toward a gate set into the brick wall at the back of the garden. Except for the occasional chuntering of traffic along the Chelsea Embankment on the other side of the gate and the twittering of invisible birds in the trees above us, Zara and I were alone in what seemed like our own secret garden in this quiet tucked-away corner of London. Almost four centuries ago, apprentices of the Worshipful Society of Apothecaries had tilled this same soil, growing medicinal plants and studying their uses. Like Monticello, here the present seemed to recede to a gentler past that moved at the slow, unhurried rhythm of nature.

Only our conversation, in hushed tones, felt out of place.

"Yes," I said, "but this was before Bram had actually seen the book. He said he believed it was the personal copy of Sir Isaac Newton and, because of the original botanic prints, possibly William Coles's own copy that was meant to be a second edition."

She smiled. "Spot-on. Bram knows what he's talking about."

"So who did Kevin consult with in London?"

"I have no idea. Apparently the individual was interested in purchasing the book and wished to remain anonymous. Obviously the fewer people who knew Kevin had found pure gold in a box of dross, the better."

"I suppose you're right."

"Shall we finish our stroll and go back to the gift shop? I believe I've answered all your questions."

"You have, thank you. You've been very generous with your time."

Zara Remington had answered my questions, but she'd just added a new one. Who was the individual who wanted to buy Kevin's book? It wouldn't have been Edward Jaine.

And here was another question: Did that give someone else a motive for murder?

12

"**O**ne final thing before we go inside," Zara said. "I nearly forgot that I promised to tell you about *Hyssopus officinalis*. Let's walk back over to the Garden of World Medicine."

"Was that the pressed plant inside Kevin's book?" I asked.

She smiled. "I see you found it."

"Yes, but found what, exactly?"

We walked across the spongy grass, back to the Western European medicinal plants. "As you know, John Fairbairn told Francis Pembroke that the plant he believed was *Hyssopus*, or hyssop, as we call it today, was wrongly labeled. In actual fact, it was another kind of hyssop."

"Water hyssop," I said.

"That's right." Zara looked surprised. "You've done some research. But water hyssop goes by the Latin genus name of *Bacopa* and it's best known for its memory-enhancing properties. It grows in wet places—on pond edges, muddy shores, lakes, that sort of environment. And it favors warm or tropical climates. It's not the same thing at all as *Hyssopus officinalis*.

The plant that was pressed between the pages of Kevin's copy of *Adam in Eden* came from the genus *Bacopa.*"

"So Pembroke was right?"

"It would seem he was, but Kevin did some checking and learned that particular species is extinct. In fact he half jokingly named it *Bacopa lewisia extinctus.*"

"I get *extinctus,*" I said. "And *lewisia* for Meriwether Lewis?"

Zara nodded. "If you discover a plant, then you are allowed to name it. Karl Linnaeus, who visited this garden when Philip Miller was the curator, supposedly named plants for his friends and weeds for his enemies."

I smiled. "How did Kevin learn that the plant was extinct? Did he bring it here to you?"

"Not to me," she said. "I'm sure Alastair helped him. I know Kevin made a trip to Wakehurst."

"Who is Alastair and what is Wakehurst?"

"Wakehurst Place is a rather splendid, rather old estate in Sussex, about forty miles south of London. The Millennium Seed Bank, which is part of the Royal Botanic Gardens at Kew, is located on the property. It's an immense seed storage facility staffed by an international group of scientists. Their goal is to collect seeds from as many plants as possible throughout the world, to preserve them for future generations before the plants become extinct." Her mouth twisted in a smile. "To avoid more *lewisias.*"

"And Alastair?"

"Dr. Alastair Innes. Brilliant man. He's in charge of the department of seed conservation. He would have been able to look at the DNA of the plant specimen Kevin brought him."

"I'd like to talk to him," I said. "I don't suppose you'd be willing to share his phone number or an e-mail address?"

"I'll give you his details when we go inside."

The wind had picked up and another seagull screeched overhead. By now it was probably well past five o'clock. At home it would be dusk. Here it was still bright, although the sunless milky light had thickened as though a gauze curtain had fallen over the garden.

Zara pointed to a tidy row of beds designated for pharmaceutical plants. "The plants you see here are used in modern medicines. The beds are arranged according to what discipline of medicine the drug derived from that plant is used for."

I read the signs out loud as we kept walking. "Oncology, neurology, psychiatry, ophthalmology." I turned to her. "Are all these plants really used for such serious conditions and illnesses . . . arthritis, eczema, Parkinson's disease?"

"They are. Be glad you weren't alive in William Coles's day, when the common belief was something known as the doctrine of signatures. If a plant physically resembled a particular organ of the body, it was used to treat ailments related to that part of the body."

"A heart-shaped plant treated heart problems?"

She nodded. "In medieval times, it did. Even today, a lot of people still believe plants are mostly used in homeopathic and alternative medicine, but you'd be surprised how many drugs used in modern-day medicine are plant based." She paused and said in a thoughtful voice, "Though I did think Kevin was rather too hopeful about the potential of *Bacopa lewisia*."

"What do you mean?"

"The Fairbairn letter mentioned that the misidentified plant was going to be included in the national botanic garden," she said. "Kevin believed, or at least hoped, it was amongst the seeds in Thomas Jefferson's White House collection."

We had stopped in front of a bed with plants dedicated to cardiology. Half a dozen small pink-and-white signs with a skull and crossbones and the words POISONOUS PLANTS were stuck in the ground in a little cluster. The markers looked like they had probably once been bright red, screaming *danger, warning!* before they were bleached by the sun, but now they almost looked decorative.

I knelt and read the names on the markers. "*Digitalis lanata. Atropa belladonna* . . . My God, these *are* highly poisonous."

"More commonly known as foxglove and deadly night-shade," Zara said. "You're quite right, so do be careful. We're deadly serious—excuse the pun—with the signs and the warning on the maps. Put your hand or a finger in your mouth after touching one of these plants and it really could be the last thing you ever do."

I shuddered. "I wonder if they grow poisonous plants in the garden of the Franciscan Monastery."

Zara looked startled, but then she said, "If you're asking whether someone could have poisoned Kevin with a plant from that garden, the answer is yes. It wouldn't be hard to do. More plants than you might think are highly toxic—the leaves, the berries, the flowers."

I stood up and we walked back to the gift shop. "I don't understand what could have happened to those seeds," I said. "If Dolley Madison knew they were so important to Thomas Jefferson, why didn't she get them directly to him? Montpelier, their plantation, was just down the road from Monticello. They were great friends."

"Believe it or not, perhaps I can answer that question for you," Zara said. "I wrote my thesis at uni on the subject of the eighteenth- and nineteenth-century seed exchange between Britain and America."

She held the door and I walked inside. The room was warm after the raw, damp chill of the garden, fragrant with a pleasant potpourri of floral scents.

"Your botanic garden was originally conceived to be a showcase for American plants, all these exotic new varieties that we didn't have here in Europe," she said. "Unfortunately, the money and, it seemed, the political will were never there, and by the late 1820s, the current president, John Quincy Adams, turned the idea on its head. His treasury secretary wrote every foreign dignitary in

America asking for plants from their countries, plus sent a letter to all naval officers, instructing them to bring home seeds from their foreign travels. And then, of course, there was your famous expedition to the South Seas a decade later that sent home more than fifty thousand plant specimens." She paused and shrugged. "I suspect the idea of a garden that was strictly American became too provincial, too quaint, for the world power the United States was becoming. George Washington was dead and Thomas Jefferson, as you may recall, never returned to Washington after he left the presidency. He considered being president of the United States one of his lesser accomplishments, so insignificant it wasn't even part of the inscription on his tomb."

"So no one cared anymore," I said.

"Possibly."

"But the seeds went somewhere for safekeeping," I said. "Or Kevin believed they did."

"And that is the riddle, isn't it? Or perhaps the treasure hunt." Zara pulled out her phone and did some scrolling as she walked over to the cash register counter.

The treasure hunt. Kevin had used those same words to describe his search for the seeds that last day at the Tidal Basin. Was that what I'd gotten involved in, along with someone else? A race to find hidden treasure?

Zara scribbled something on a piece of paper and held it out to me. "Please don't tell Alastair you got this from me. Better he thinks Kevin gave it to you. I suggest e-mailing him first rather than ringing him. Don't worry, he'll be in touch."

"Thank you." I tucked the paper in my camera bag.

She walked me to the door. "I presume, since you knew Kevin so well, you heard about his sister?"

She saw my blank expression. "Ah, apparently not. Well, I believe it's relevant to what brought Kevin here, his sense of urgency."

"Please go on."

"Both his parents died of Alzheimer's disease," she said. "His sister, who was two years younger than Kevin, was recently diagnosed with early-onset Alzheimer's." My shock must have shown, because she added, "I think that made him even more desperate to find those seeds, because of the apparent potent memory-enhancing property the *lewisia* plant supposedly possessed. Obviously it's an utter long shot as to whether any seeds could be germinated, but when one is desperate and a beloved sister is going to slowly lose her memory, one will do anything in one's power to prevent it, you know?"

I thought about Chappy. "Yes, I know."

"Kevin was making some discreet inquiries amongst contacts in the pharmaceutical industry to find out about Alzheimer's drugs that were being developed, whether there was any possibility of his sister taking part in tests for the most hopeful possibilities." She held the front door for me. "He even asked about water hyssop. Good luck, Sophie. I hope you find what you're looking for. And do be careful. Someone was here recently talking to Will, another American, who seemed especially interested in *Hyssopus officinalis*, as you were. I didn't think anything of it until just now."

I froze. "An American? Was it a man or woman?"

"A man."

"Could you describe him?"

"I'm afraid not. I was in my office and happened to see the two of them together out the window, but their backs were to me. And the gentleman left through the gate on Swan Walk. I asked Will why he let him in when we were closed, and he said the chap was particularly keen to see the garden as he was only in town for a day or two. He managed to talk Will into giving him a tour since he'd come all the way from America."

"Good Lord," I said. "I wonder if his visit had anything to do with Kevin's book. Though who else could have known about the plant?"

"I thought no one knew about it except Kevin, Alastair, and me," she said. "It is possible his visit was just a coincidence."

I said goodbye and walked down Royal Hospital Road toward Sloane Square. But I didn't think the visit of another American to the Chelsea Physic Garden asking about the same plant I did was a coincidence.

Sloane Square was nearly deserted at six o'clock on a chilly Sunday evening. I walked the last half block from Lower Sloane Street to the Underground station entrance thinking about everything Zara Remington had said.

"Hello? Sophie?"

Will Tennant waved an arm over his head, signaling me from the fountain in the square across the street. A double-decker bus pulled away from a stop and cut off my view of him. When it passed, he ran across the street and joined me.

"I thought I recognized you," he said in a cheerful voice. "Have you just come from the garden?"

"I have. Were you waiting for me?"

He gave an odd laugh. "No, I've just been round to tea with a friend down the King's Road and happened to spot you. How was your visit with Zara?"

"Fine," I said. "Apparently I'm not the only American to drop by the garden before it opens in the spring. Zara mentioned you were talking to one of my countrymen the other day."

He blinked. "Did she, now?"

"Could you describe him?"

"May I ask why?"

I patted my camera bag. "I'm a photographer on assignment for a magazine. It's freelance. But I've got this competitor, you see. I think we're working on the same story. I was just wondering if it was the guy."

"What does he look like?" He gave me his off-kilter look. "Maybe I can tell you if it seems like the same chap."

"Uh . . . pretty average. In his forties, dark hair, blue eyes. A little overweight." If I made up a description, maybe he would contradict me and tell me what I wanted to know.

He shook his head. "You're in luck. This fellow was old, white hair, glasses. A bit stooped. Visiting from . . . what's that state? Missouri, I think he said. From Lincoln."

"Lincoln is in Nebraska."

Will looked surprised, but he grinned. "I guess I got it wrong. Are you walking to the Underground?"

"Yes."

"Me, too."

My pass had expired, so he waited while I bought a new one. "If you're going to be here for a while, you ought to get an Oyster Card," he said. "You can keep topping it off and it usually works out to be a cheaper deal if you pay by the week. You can use it on the buses, too."

"I know. I used to live here."

"Did you now?" At the bottom of the stairs he asked which way I was going.

"Victoria," I said.

"I'm off to Notting Hill Gate. The opposite direction. Are you staying around Victoria?"

"No," I said. "Mayfair. Here's my train. I'd better go. Goodbye, Will."

The train wasn't crowded, and when I boarded, I looked out the window at the platform. Will Tennant was gone. A moment later the bells chimed and we were advised to stand clear of the closing doors. The train left the station and I knew he'd seen right through my con and had lied to me.

What I wondered was, why?

13

Harry was asleep in the adjoining room when I got back to the Connaught shortly after six, so James brought me a glass of sherry on a silver tray while I checked my e-mail. Nothing from Nick, which surprised me. We almost never went this long without being in touch. I wrote him a quick note and told him about my day in London, though I left out the details of my meeting with Zara Remington, and said I missed him like crazy, especially here. Then I drafted a vague e-mail to Alastair Innes explaining that I was a friend of Kevin's and was interested in visiting the Seed Bank while I was in London.

Afterward I went to the website of the Royal Botanic Gardens at Kew and clicked on the link to the Millennium Seed Bank. The more I read, the more I wondered why I had never heard of this place before, an enormous underground storage vault staffed by scientists and conservationists like Kevin who were racing against the clock to save thousands of plant species worldwide—by their account, sixty to one hundred thousand— that faced extinction. So far they'd collected eleven percent of the world's plants. Now they were aiming for one-quarter of all plants found on earth, specifically the ones threatened by extinction, as well as plants that might be useful in the future.

What struck me most was the urgency of their mission. It seemed as if this particular group of scientists had more inside knowledge than the rest of us about a giant doomsday clock that really was ticking down somewhere, an awareness that there wasn't much time to finish their work, or maybe even that there wasn't *enough* time. Harry knocked on my door just then, and I closed my laptop before he could see my computer screen.

"How about a drink?" he said, smiling. "The Coburg Bar serves some first-rate Scotch, plus they've got a drinks list that goes back before 1800. What do you say?"

"I say it sounds terrific."

As we finished our cocktails by the fireplace—Harry had his Scotch, a sixteen-year-old Lagavulin, and I had a Pimm's Cup purely because it was considered the first English cocktail—my phone buzzed in the pocket of my jacket. I pulled it out as we left the bar to walk down the street to Scott's. Alastair Innes had answered me as swiftly as Ryan Velis and Zara Remington had done.

Dear Ms. Medina, If you are available, I can meet you tomorrow, Monday, at 10 o'clock here at the Seed Bank. It is an easy trip from London; trains run regularly to Haywards Heath from Victoria Station and then I suggest you take a taxi to Wakehurst as the bus only runs once every two hours. I look forward to hearing from you. Brother Kevin's death was a huge shock to us all; I trust you and I will have much to discuss about a mutual friend who was beloved here by all who knew him. Yours sincerely, Alastair Innes

"Everything all right, honey?" Harry asked. "You've been kind of quiet all evening. Something bothering you?"

I looked up from my phone. "Just a little jet-lagged is all.

Everything's great. I'm sorry, do you mind if I answer this e-mail? I'm trying to get together with someone tomorrow. It'll only take a second."

"Go right ahead. I'm glad you'll be busy when I'll be in Lingfield. Who are you seeing, if you don't mind my asking? One of your old friends?"

"Actually, an old friend of Kevin Boyle's."

Harry looked surprised. "A Franciscan?"

"No, someone involved in conservation. A scientist." I slipped my arm through his. "Tell me about your lunch in Covent Garden. Did you have a good time?"

Harry let me change the subject and evade his questions for the second time in the past twenty-four hours, but sooner or later he was going to ask what was going on. I had no idea how much I would tell him, just as I had no idea how I was going to bring up the *lewisia* plant with Alastair Innes tomorrow.

But with jet lag stealing over me—that much was true—and Harry plying me with wine and good food in the cocooned coziness of Scott's, I was feeling drowsy and light-headed, in no condition to think about any of that right now. I'd figure it out tomorrow when I had to.

I always did.

Harry and I ate breakfast in the Connaught's pretty glass-enclosed conservatory overlooking Mount Street the next morning before his friend's driver picked him up in a dark blue Jaguar to take him to Lingfield.

He kissed me goodbye in front of the crackling fire in the lobby fireplace. "There's a champagne reception and a dinner after the race, so I'll probably be back quite late. Don't feel like you need to wait up."

I laughed. "You party hard, Harry. I can't keep up with you."

He grinned. "Don't tell your mother. She'd tie me to a chair if she knew. Ever since my surgery she treats me like I'm made of glass. She's always telling me not to overdo it."

Truth to tell, his mild heart attack a year ago and a double-bypass operation before Christmas had scared me, too. But I'm like Harry. When I die, I hope my regrets—if I have any—are for things I've done, not what I wish I'd done.

"Have fun," I said.

"I love you, kitten."

"I love you, too. See you when you get back."

After the Jaguar pulled out of Carlos Place, I walked to the Bond Street Underground station and took two trains to Victoria, catching a Southern Railways train to Haywards Heath that pulled out of the station thirty seconds after I stepped on board. Perry sent me a text message as the train left London and crossed over the Thames.

Are we still on for lunch at 1? How about the Old Red Cow?
Meet at the bureau first?

The Old Red Cow was a pub near Smithfield Market and it wasn't far from the International Press Service bureau. It was one of our favorite places for lunch or a pint at the end of the day.

I wrote him back:

Absolutely on for lunch. I've got an appointment this morning
but I'll be back by 1. Probably better to meet at the pub.

As soon as I hit Send, I regretted my choice of words. Perry doesn't miss a thing. He wrote back instantly.

Back from where? You out of town?

Long story. I'll explain when I see you.

Then I put my phone away so I could duck further questions.

The rest of the journey was uneventful and I had the carriage to myself for the forty-five-minute trip, except for a young man who came through with the tea trolley and the conductor who collected my ticket.

Haywards Heath was approximately forty miles due south of London, as Zara had said, and if you continued south for another twenty miles beyond that, you'd hit the English Channel and the seaside town of Brighton. By the time we passed Gatwick Airport, the scenery had become mostly rural, black skeletal trees against a cold white sky, a somber-looking landscape of fields, and the occasional house in subdued tones of dull brown and washed-out green.

As Alastair Innes had promised, there was a taxi rank just outside the little station, which was built into a hillside and surrounded by woods. My cabdriver was from Afghanistan, and once he learned I'd visited his country, he spent the entire twenty-minute journey quizzing me about my work with International Press Service. As he turned into the private road for Wakehurst Place, he said over his shoulder, "You going to the mansion, miss?"

"No," I said. "The Seed Bank."

It was situated in a low-lying field, two industrial-looking metal structures like bunkers joined by a glass-vaulted roof. The building blended in with the greenish-yellow late-winter landscape, which was probably the point of its unobtrusive design. I went inside through the main entrance and gave my name to a young woman sitting behind a desk in a small waiting room.

"I'll ring Dr. Innes," she said after I'd signed in. "Please have a seat."

The room was as plain and unadorned as the exterior of the building except for a set of arty photographs behind the reception desk that I knew had to be seeds. Besides the front entrance, there were two other doors, both bright yellow and both closed, with pads to swipe ID badges next to them. I leafed through brochures about the Seed Bank and a colorful newsletter filled with pictures and articles about its latest projects until a petite, attractive woman in what looked like a hand-knitted Fair Isle cardigan, white blouse, and gray wool trousers opened the door nearest to where I was sitting.

"Ms. Medina?" she said. "I'm Fiona Eccleston. Dr. Innes has asked me to take you downstairs to the library whilst he finishes up with a meeting. He thought you might enjoy reading some information I've prepared for you about the Seed Bank."

I stood up. "That's very kind. Thank you."

She swiped her ID on the gray pad and, as we stepped into a corridor, the door closed behind us with a firm click. I hadn't considered there would be this much security in a place that stored seeds.

"We'll take the lift to the lower level," she said. "Follow me."

We walked through a quiet corridor and took the elevator down one level. The industrial-looking library was busier than I'd expected, and many of the tables were filled with people working on computers. A few of them glanced up when Fiona and I entered the room. She led me to a long table at the back of the room where a coffee-table book lay open next to a file folder. Inside the folder were several photocopied articles.

"These will give you an overview of our work here," she said. "Any questions, feel free to ask. And I'm sure Dr. Innes will be happy to answer anything I can't help you with."

A couple of heads snapped up at the mention of Alastair Innes and then it was eyes down. I thanked Fiona again and started flipping through the material she had put out for me. Besides the quiet clicking of computer keyboards and muted voices from nearby rooms, I heard a pervasive low hum, like an engine or perhaps a generator. When the phone rang a few minutes later, I heard Fiona say, "Of course, Alastair. I'll bring her right up."

I stood and she turned around. "Ms. Medina, Dr. Innes is free now. I'll walk you to his office."

I picked up my camera bag and followed her back to the elevator. It seemed we were retracing our steps to the reception area, but then Fiona turned down a hallway of closed doors that was as silent as a graveyard. The humming sound was less distinct here. She knocked on a door midway down the corridor.

A tall, ascetic-looking man with white hair and a neatly trimmed beard opened it. He was dressed Saturday casual in jeans, an open-neck collared shirt, and a burgundy sweater.

"Ms. Medina?" His voice sounded hoarse and he cleared his throat. "Alastair Innes. You'll have to forgive me, I'm just getting over a rather nasty cold. Do come in. And thanks, Fee, for looking after her."

Fiona left and Alastair indicated the only chair in his tiny windowless office next to the door. "Please have a seat."

The space was cramped and made Olivia Upshaw's Smithsonian office seem palatial. The room was barely big enough for his desk, a computer, two low bookcases, and my chair.

He closed the door and sat behind his desk.

"You're a friend of Brother Kevin's," he said. "You must be visiting from the States?"

"Actually, I lived in London for many years until last summer, so it feels like I've come home rather than being here on holiday."

He sat back in his chair and tilted it as though he needed to study me from a greater distance. "I see. Nevertheless, Wakehurst is rather off the beaten path," he said in a mild voice. "One must really make an effort to get to us. You're not a conservationist or a scientist, you're a photographer. So what really brings you to see me, Ms. Medina?"

I was getting used to the third degree from Kevin's colleagues and it was only fair. Who was I and why should they talk to me?

I told him what I could as honestly as possible without mentioning Zara Remington or my visit to the Chelsea Physic Garden. Then I needed to bluff.

"You helped Kevin identify the plant that was pressed in the pages of *Adam in Eden*," I said. "The one he named *Bacopa lewisia extinctus*."

He gave me a cool stare. "Did Kevin tell you that?"

"No, but it seems logical, given what you do and that Kevin was just here visiting you."

"I see. Well, as the name implies, the plant is extinct."

"How did you identify it, then?"

"I didn't identify it per se, merely confirmed the genus. I checked our database, which is linked to the herbarium at Kew Gardens, to see if there was any information about the species, but I found nothing. So what Kevin brought me was a unique specimen, though that's not uncommon. Every year scientists still discover approximately two thousand new species of plants."

I stared at him. "Two thousand?"

"Two thousand a year. Astonishing, isn't it?"

I nodded. "So you also know about the packets of seeds that Kevin believed supposedly went missing from the White House when the British burned it?"

He nodded. "Kevin told me his theory that they were among the items Dolley Madison rescued before the British soldiers showed up."

"If someone found them, I was told it might be possible to get the seeds to germinate, even after more than two centuries."

"You'd have to know what you're doing," he said. "But it's possible. You can't just stick them in the soil and wait for something to sprout. We've already done something similar at the Seed Bank. As a matter of fact, it's one of the objectives we're focusing on now, how to awaken plants and get dormant seeds to germinate when we know nothing about them."

"How do you do that?"

"By attempting to re-create the conditions of a plant's habitat, the temperature, humidity, type of soil, that sort of thing . . . whatever it would take for the seed to germinate naturally. For example, if we know a plant comes from a tropical part of the world, we try smoke or heat to simulate the climate."

"And it works?"

"Not all the time. But, as I said, we've had great success germinating a plant grown from seeds that are more than two hundred years old. In other words, roughly the same age as the *lewisia* plant."

"Where did you get two-hundred-year-old seeds?" I asked. "And how do you know that's how old they are?"

He smiled. "This particular case was extremely well documented, so we were lucky. In 1803, a Dutchman named Jan Teerlink sailed on a ship called the *Henriette*, which docked in Cape Town, South Africa. While he was in port, Teerlink went ashore and visited the famous Company's Gardens, which had been planted one hundred fifty years earlier by the Dutch East India Company. Somehow Teerlink acquired seeds from that garden, which he brought back to the ship."

"He got seeds from a garden that dated back to the 1600s?"

"That's right," Alastair said. "Teerlink stored his seeds in forty paper packets, which he placed in a red leather wallet with his name embossed on it. Unfortunately for him, the British captured the *Henriette*. Later he was set free, but the leather wallet with the seeds ended up in the Tower of London. At some point everything was moved to the National Archives at Kew, where the wallet was discovered quite by accident during a research project in 2005."

"You grew a plant from those seeds?"

"We did. Eventually we managed to unlock what are known as the germination codes and, of the thirty-two species of seeds in the forty packets, we got three to sprout. Two of them—an *Acacia* and a *Leucospermum*—are growing in the glasshouse right now, healthy as you please."

"Can anyone see them?" I asked.

"I'm afraid not. The glasshouse isn't open to the public."

"Dr. Innes, I'd be very interested in seeing those plants. And I was serious about a tour of this place when I wrote you last night. I would love to take a look inside the seed vault, too."

"I see." He steepled his fingers. "What are you planning to do after you leave here, Ms. Medina?"

"I wish you would call me Sophie," I said. "You mean, am I looking for the seeds?"

"Are you looking for the seeds, Sophie?"

"I suppose I am. Kevin wanted to find them, but he died before he could finish what he started. He told me it would be an important historic discovery and he was excited about it. He should get credit for it."

He gave me a dry look. "I presume Kevin also mentioned the massive potential financial windfall, that there would be industries and individuals who would be interested in something like this?"

"He did. But you knew Kevin. It wasn't about the money. Anything that came his way would all go to charity anyway. I know about his sister and that he was talking to pharmaceutical companies in America to find out about drug tests for her once she was diagnosed with early-onset Alzheimer's. I think finding the *lewisia* plant became personal for him."

"I agree. But what about you? Is your only motive making sure Kevin gets credit where credit is due?"

I flushed but I said in an even voice, "My mother is in Connecticut at the moment with my grandfather after he was found wandering around the backyard of a former neighbor who died forty years ago. He thought they were going to go shooting together. Photos, not hunting. I adore my grandfather, and I would do anything in this world if I thought he might have Alzheimer's. However much of a long shot it was."

His eyes flickered. "I lost my wife to Alzheimer's last year. It's a living hell to watch."

"I'm so sorry."

He studied me as though he were assessing my character, my honesty, and whether he believed me. Finally he said, "Why don't you call me Alastair?"

"Thank you."

He opened a desk drawer and pulled out a thick folder. "If those seeds are found and if they are viable, I've done a bit of preliminary research and extrapolation about what it might take to get them to germinate using the map of Lewis and Clark's journey and doing some calculations about temperature back then, and climate."

"So you really think you could get something to grow if the seeds were in good enough condition?"

"I don't know. But I promised Kevin I would do my damnedest." He stood up. "Come. I'll give you a very quick tour of the seed vault and then we can visit the Teerlink plant in the glasshouse. First, though, I need to return this folder to my safe in the lab."

"Does anyone here know about Kevin and the *lewisia* plant?" I asked.

"One or two colleagues are aware that Kevin and I were working on a project together. But no one knew any details because it was—how shall I say it—off the grid." He opened his office door. "You can leave your coat since we'll come back here. And I think we'll skip suiting up since we won't spend much time in the vault."

"Pardon?"

"The temperature in the seed vault is minus twenty degrees Celsius. With the windchill, it's closer to minus twenty-seven. We wear arctic gear when we go in there to do work. There are all kinds of alarms and safety backups in case anything goes wrong. After ten minutes, if whoever has entered the vault doesn't come out, all hell breaks loose."

The lab was in the other building, so Alastair gave me a quick tour of the glass-vaulted visitor area between the two wings, where we could watch researchers and scientists at work through a series of observation windows.

"I think the seeds they're handling today came from Chile," he said. "When they first arrive they're kept in isolation until we get a chance to examine them, test them to make sure they're disease-free and healthy enough to survive storage. After that, they're cleaned, processed, and dried."

He pointed out displays of maps and photographs hinting at the global connections and reach of the Seed Bank. In one corner of the atrium was a treelike sculpture that held business cards belonging to scientists and conservationists from botanic gardens, universities, and institutions all over the world.

"Do a lot of people work here?" I asked.

"It's a good-sized operation. On the lower level where the library and seminar room are located we have fourteen bedrooms for visiting scientists. Plus we've got a number of volunteers who are restricted to nontechnical tasks, although all of them have some kind of background in science or gardening. Don't forget, we're publicly funded, so we rely on donations and volunteer help."

He opened a door that led to the other building, and I followed him into a large laboratory where white-coated men and women sat at long tables peering into microscopes or at computer screens. The faint scent of something chemical permeated the lab, and from below us came that incessant sound of an engine humming.

"What's that noise? It sounds like a motor. I've heard it almost the entire time I've been here."

"The generators. They keep the vault at the appropriate temperature at all times. This is an energy-efficient building, but it's still an expensive operation to run. When all is said and done, we're sort of a climate-controlled Noah's Ark storing seeds for posterity. This building will be rubble someday, but the vault itself was meant to last half a millennium. It's built to withstand anything, even a nuclear bomb."

"You sound like you might be expecting the apocalypse."

He gave me a wry smile as we stepped into a room just off the laboratory. "Or at least, planning for it."

"That's kind of scary."

"We live in a scary world. There are all sorts of reasons plant species could vanish. Climate change, alien invasion—I mean predators, animals and other plants, not little green men from Mars," he said, still smiling. "Then, as you mentioned, a scenario so catastrophic it would really be the end of the world as we know it."

I shuddered as he crossed the room to a row of cabinets. He bent down and opened a cabinet door, revealing a small safe. Alastair spun the combination, pulled open the door, and set his folder inside.

"How long has the Seed Bank been here?" I asked.

"The building we're in now opened in 2000, which explains our name—*Millennium* Seed Bank. Before that, the staff used Wakehurst Place, the mansion. It's a beautiful estate, four hundred years old. Originally the lab was Lady Price's bedroom, the seed cleaning was done in her daughter's bedroom, and the X-ray machine was in Sir Henry's bathroom. As you can see, we've come a long way from using bathrooms to do our work."

I smiled as he shut the safe and closed the cabinet door.

"Come," he said. "It's time to see the vault. Afterward, we'll drop by the glasshouse."

He led me back through the lab and eventually we came to another corridor, where we stood at a railing overlooking a wall of enormous metal doors lining the back wall of the floor below. One door—the exterior entrance to the vault—stood open. A metal spiral staircase resembling something that belonged on a ship coiled downstairs.

"We shouldn't be leaving the outer door to the vault open like that," Alastair said in a low voice as we made our way down the corkscrew staircase. "It really ought to be more secure."

I glanced up at a flash of movement above our heads; some-one who had been standing at the railing now was gone. We were alone again as Alastair used his badge on another keypad that let us into a large room where brightly colored plastic crates sat on a long table and in stacks on the floor.

"This is the drying room," he said. "The vault is just through here, on the other side of this room."

Yet another door where he had to use his security badge, and this time we were in an airlock. "I should have asked this earlier," he said, "but are you asthmatic?"

The question startled me. "No. Why do you ask?"

"Three hundred thousand seeds are stored inside this vault. It's very clean but inevitably there's dust."

"I'm fine. No allergies, no asthma."

"Good. Just so you know, you're about to enter the most bio-diverse place on the planet. Nowhere else in the world do this many varieties of seeds exist in one space." He glanced at me. "Ready?"

"I . . . yes. Ready."

He swiped his card and pulled the door open as frigid air blasted out at us. Alastair bent and picked up a small piece of wood. A doorstop.

"We'll leave the door propped open since we're only going to be here a moment." He flipped a switch and lit up the entrance to the vault. As far as I could see into the yawning darkness, on my right were long rows of metal cabinets with doors spaced at regular intervals every few feet. On my left was a wall of nar-row floor-to-ceiling shelves containing hundreds and hundreds of what looked like glass canning jars. Each jar was filled with seeds.

"This is as far as we go," Alastair was saying. "The place is huge, and frankly, it goes on ad infinitum. But at least you get the idea, though it is hard to fathom just how massive it is in all that inky blackness. If we used all the space—and we haven't yet—the entire vault is large enough to hold thirty double-decker buses."

I shivered, as much from the cold as from the creepiness of thinking about what Alastair had just said—this vast vault, a huge underground cave buried in the bucolic English countryside, was here as insurance in case the unthinkable really did happen. The complete destruction of earth, either by our own means or perhaps an alien invasion, the little green men from Mars that Alastair had joked about, with only a few intrepid souls surviving. I tried to imagine them making their way to Wakehurst, opening the vault, and beginning life again.

Alastair must have noticed that shudder because he said, "Are you all right?"

"I'm fine." My nose had already started to tingle and I could see my breath and his.

"Like I said, they've got sensors in the control room so they know someone's in here. Let's go, shall we?"

He removed the doorstop and stuck it back in the corner where he'd found it. Then he turned off the lights and we stepped outside into the airlock.

"One more place I want to show you," he said. "It's not quite as cold, and I think you'd find it interesting. Are you game?"

"Absolutely."

We walked through more silent corridors of concrete floors and whitewashed walls without running into anyone. I had the feeling we were still underground. I also had the feeling that we were moving away from the hub of activity of the rest of the Seed Bank. More doors badged open and closed behind us with a definitive clink. Here it was as quiet as a tomb.

Eventually we came to a short flight of stairs. "It's just up here," Alastair said.

I followed him. "What is this place?"

He badged open another door and propped it open with another doorstop. "The rest of the vault. We can move walls back, expand to make the refrigerated vault we were just in larger as we need more space and the collection grows in size. Have a look."

The triangle of light from the open door shone partway into the enormous room. Gradually, as my eyes became accustomed to the darkness, I realized we were standing in a cavernous space that seemed to go on and on forever. About fifty feet in front of us were rows of shelves stacked with boxes that seemed to reach the ceiling.

"What are those boxes for?" I asked.

"For now this is a good place to store anything we don't need in the main facility. Come over here and have a look at this wall."

We walked over to the shelving and he pointed out the wall behind it. "You can see how it's a type of modular construction. We just bump it out as we need the space."

Neither of us heard the noise, a scraping sound, until it was too late and the triangle of light began to disappear as the door started to swing shut. We both ran for the door.

"Hey, there's someone in here," Alastair shouted.

The heavy door slammed shut, plunging the room into complete darkness. A few seconds later I heard Alastair curse somewhere near me.

"Something's jamming it from the other side. My badge works on the keypad, so the door's unlocking, except I can't open it." He paused and added with classic British understatement, "I'm rather afraid we can't get out of here."

14

The darkness in the vault was so dense and solid there were no shadows, just black and more black. A light like a tiny spotlight flicked on about two feet in front of me. Alastair's phone. The beam swiveled and found me.

Had someone moved the doorstop and deliberately barricaded us in here, or had Alastair placed it poorly and the weight of the door caused it to swing shut, so this was an accident?

"Alastair, do you—?" I started to say.

"Come here." His voice was harsh with urgency. "Hold this torch so I can try the door again. We haven't got a lot of time."

I wanted to ask "before what?" but I already knew the answer. I also knew the door wasn't going to budge.

"It's not minus twenty degrees Celsius in here, is it?" I asked.

"No. Probably closer to plus five or six." He sounded grim. "Believe me, though, it's cold enough without protective clothing."

I did some mental math and took his phone. "A few degrees above forty Fahrenheit." All I had on was a sweater, a turtleneck, and lightweight wool pants. "I suppose it's a stupid idea to suggest using this phone to make a call rather than as a flashlight."

"Nothing, and I do mean sweet bloody nothing, will penetrate this vault. Remember, I told you it was built to withstand a nuclear bomb."

"In other words, no one will hear us if we start yelling, either?"

"Not even if someone were standing on the other side of the door," he said. "Which is highly unlikely since, as you saw, this place isn't used for anything but storage."

"What about the alarm system?"

"There've been plans to install one here, but it keeps getting deferred since there's really nothing to secure. All the funds go for our work."

"Oh."

"Shine that torch on the sensor one more time, will you?" I did as I was told, and Alastair swiped his badge again and again. Each time a mechanism clicked like the door was unlocking, but when he pulled on the handle, nothing moved. "Damn and bugger. It's jammed shut from the outside."

"How long have we got?" I asked. "And is there another way out of here?"

"Between thirty minutes and an hour before hypothermia sets in. Give or take. And, yes, there is another exit, though I've never used it. It's at the far end of this room."

"Lead the way," I said. "Let me get out my phone. At least we'll have two flashlights."

"Save yours. We may need it later. But take mine and shine the light so we can see where we're walking. It wouldn't do for one of us to take a header over some piece of wood or something we didn't know was underfoot. I'll keep one hand on the wall and we'll eventually reach the other door. Take my other hand. It'll be like finding our way out of a maze."

Only blindfolded and racing against hypothermia.

I could already feel the cold seeping into my bones as we

made our way along the wall of a space big enough to contain thirty double-decker buses. The darkness never grew any less substantial, though I could make out Alastair as a darker shape in the complete gloom. He sneezed a couple of times, and somewhere above our heads I heard the rustling of something that had been disturbed.

"Bats, I should think," he said.

"I hate bats."

"They won't bother you."

"So once we open this door," I said, "where will we be?"

"Presuming they haven't changed the code on the security sensor because it's not a door anyone uses, we ought to be in a meadow on the far side of the glasshouse."

"Let's not even discuss changed security codes, shall we?"

He sneezed again and stumbled, pulling me with him. I caught his arm.

"Are you okay?"

"Yes, sorry. I'm having a bit of trouble feeling my feet."

I sucked in my breath. "We've got to be almost to that other door."

"I . . . wait, here's a corner. The door ought to be somewhere along this wall."

To keep him talking and his mind focused, I said, "Do you think someone moved the doorstop?"

"And deliberately locked us in here?"

"Yes."

"Once we get out of here," he said with conviction, "I fully intend to do a data dump on the door sensors that lead to this space. I'll find out who came through there after we did and . . . crikey, here we are. The other door. Shine the torch over here."

I obeyed and Alastair wiped the sleeve of his sweater over the pad to clean it before passing his badge across it. There was an audible click and, as he turned the door handle, he sounded relieved and triumphant. "Success. Just in the nick of time."

Then silence.

"What—?" I asked.

"Bloody hell."

"What's going on?"

"I can't open it."

"My God, it *has* to open. What's wrong this time?"

"Come over here and help me push," he said. "I can turn the handle, but there's something on the other side of the door that's physically blocking it . . . something heavy."

We both threw our weight against the door, and it moved a fraction of an inch. Or at least I thought it did.

"Try again," I said.

"On three."

But after half a dozen attempts that probably would leave us each with sore, bruised shoulders, he said, "We're running out of time and we're losing strength in this cold. I can barely feel my hands and feet anymore."

He'd begun slurring his words. Not a good sign. He already had a bad cold, plus he was older and more frail than I was. Next he'd start becoming disoriented . . . we both would.

I said, "What do you think is blocking the door?"

"I know what's blocking it. Some of the volunteers have been mulching the garden beds for spring. I saw a truck bringing in bags the other day and a couple of the workers were stacking them near places where they'd be needed."

"If bags of mulch are piled against this door, they'll weigh a ton," I said. "And if we're going to open it we need to find something to use as a lever. That way we'll have more strength."

"A bloody brilliant idea. There were some iron rods on the shelves by the other door. If we can insert one of them between this door and the jamb, we might be able to pry it open. If I'm not mistaken the ends were flattened, so I think it'll be possible to do."

His voice was weaker, but he sounded hopeful and that

cheered me up. The light from his phone suddenly dimmed like a guttering candle.

"I'll get a couple of those rods," I said. "You stay here and save your strength. I'm worried about you."

"No, it's better to stick together. I don't think we should split up."

He had a point. If he got confused and wandered off in the darkness, I'd never find him.

"All right," I said. "I don't suppose you know how long we've been in here."

There was a poignant pause before he said, "I'm not sure, but I believe it's been about twenty minutes. Maybe twenty-five."

Close to the beginning of the end, the outside edge of the danger zone.

"Why don't I lead the way this time?" I said. "Your phone battery is almost gone. Let's use mine now."

He started coughing as though he were hacking up something from deep in his chest. He wheezed and said, "All right."

I reached out and found his shoulder. "Alastair, are you okay?"

"I will be when we get out of here."

At least he still said "when."

But by the time we reached the shelving back at the other entrance, we were both shivering uncontrollably. Alastair had almost completely lost the feeling in his hands, so he kept dropping the iron rod until I tucked it under one arm and locked his hands across his chest, making him grip his elbows in a kind of mummy pose. It seemed like it took an eternity to get back to the far door, and I refused to think about how we were going to muster the strength to pry it open.

Or what would happen if we didn't.

They say in extraordinary life-or-death situations that adrenaline kicks in and wires some message to the brain so that a person possesses an almost superhuman burst of strength enabling him or her to lift a car off the ground so a victim pinned underneath can be rescued or fight off an animal to allow a child to escape to safety. Somehow, between us, Alastair and I found that adrenaline strength, and after much tugging and grunting, we managed to shove the door open so a sliver of daylight appeared. I shouted as loud as I could through the opening, and after what seemed like hours—though it was probably only a couple of minutes—we heard voices on the other side of the door. That was followed by heavy thuds as bags of mulch were flung away and the door, mercifully, swung open and we stumbled outside.

Alastair was in far worse shape than I was. Two men in overalls and mud boots practically carried us to a wooden bench near a series of raised garden beds, and a woman who was working with them called 999, emergency services.

"I need an ambulance and medical assistance," she said. "The Seed Bank. We've got two possible cases of hypothermia. Come as fast as you can."

"I don't need to go to the hospital," I said. "I'm fine."

"Let's get you inside, love, and we'll see about that," one of the men said. He reached down to pick me up in his arms. "We have to start getting you both warmed up."

"I can walk," I said. "If you'll just support me, I'd rather walk on my own."

I made it inside with someone on each side holding my arms for assistance, but Alastair, whose lips were a worrying shade of bluish-purple and his skin nearly translucent, was so weak that the two men who'd found us made a seat with their arms and carried him to the infirmary. By the time the ambulance arrived, we were both swaddled in blankets and someone had made us cups of tea. Already I felt better. But there was no doubt Alastair was going to be taken to the local hospital for observation.

"We'd like you to come as well, Ms. Medina," one of the EMTs said to me. "Though we can't insist. It's up to you."

"No, thank you. I'll be all right once I warm up. But I'm worried about Dr. Innes."

"Oh, don't you worry, we'll put him as right as rain. We'll be keeping him at least for the night."

"Sophie." Across the room, Alastair was being helped onto a gurney. Besides the EMTs, a woman in a white lab coat had joined the growing number of people squeezing into the infirmary now that word was apparently spreading about our dramatic rescue. Fiona Eccleston stood next to Alastair, her pleasant face lined with concern.

I overheard the woman in the lab coat say in a clear voice, "I'm sorry, Alastair. I'm positive."

I stood and went over to them, dragging my blankets. "What's going on?"

"Apparently there was nothing blocking the door to the storage area," Alastair said. "They want to reprogram my badge."

"There *was* something."

The woman shook her head. "I'm afraid not. Perhaps it was some sort of glitch with the card swipe reader. Obviously there will be a thorough investigation because the consequences could have been tragic," she said. "The only good thing to come out of this is that now installing a security system in that area will become a priority, rather than being deferred all the time."

"Are you ready, Dr. Innes?" One of the EMTs gave me a cursory smile and said, "We need to take him, miss. If you'd like to say goodbye . . . ?"

Alastair reached for my hand with surprising strength and pulled me close. "Watch out," he whispered. "You know what I'm talking about."

I squeezed his hand and whispered back, "Someone blocked that door. Take care of yourself, Alastair. I'll be in touch tomorrow to see how you're doing."

He gave me a meaningful look. "You take care, too."

After he left and the infirmary nurse had shooed everyone out of the room, she turned to me. "I think you should stay here and rest for a while before we let you go, my love. You've been through a hell of an ordeal."

She was smiling and there was nothing in her demeanor to suggest anything but genuine concern for my well-being. It seemed to me that as far as she knew, an unfortunate accident had been averted before it became a tragedy and all was well that ended well.

But Alastair had just warned me to be careful because he believed someone who worked at the Seed Bank had deliberately locked us in the storage room. Maybe he or she had even stopped by the infirmary to check in on us just now and neither of us had known it.

There was no shortage of people from the library who knew my name and knew I was visiting Alastair. Plus the receptionist knew as well. Tomorrow when I spoke to Alastair, I would remind him to check with Fiona and see if she remembered who had been in the library when she had brought me in.

"Thank you, but I can't stay," I said to the nurse. "I really should be leaving."

"It's going on half one," she said. "I think you should stay at least until two. I'd feel better knowing you'd had more time to recover. You didn't suffer the cold as badly as Dr. Innes did, but still it's quite a shock to the system."

"What time did you say? Oh, no . . . Perry." I pulled out my phone and discovered I'd forgotten to turn off the flashlight. The battery was down to almost nothing. "I was supposed to meet someone for lunch at one o'clock. In London."

There was a flurry of missed calls and text messages from Perry on my phone, most of them written from the Old Red Cow. The last text—in all caps—asked one final time where the hell was I and said that he was leaving for a two o'clock interview at the House of Lords. He expected to be finished no later than three if I still wanted to meet him somewhere for a coffee or a drink. I wrote a quick reply.

Unavoidably detained, please forgive me. Promise a full explanation. How about the café in the Crypt at St. Martin-in-the-Fields at 3:30 since you'll be at the other end of Whitehall?

He replied right away:

I'll be there. WILL YOU?

My screen went black and the phone died, turning itself off. I looked up and said to the nurse, "I've really got to get back to London. Do you think someone could call a cab to run me to the station? And my coat is still in Dr. Innes's office."

My coat was waiting in the reception room and the Afghan driver who brought me to the Seed Bank what seemed like an eternity ago showed up to take me back to town. He resumed our conversation where we left off on the trip here and didn't seem to notice my distracted answers, or that I kept glancing in his mirrors and over my shoulder to make sure no one was following us. I tipped him well and discovered I was just in time for the 2:12 to London, which I could hear coming into the station as I ran up the stairs.

No one else got on at Haywards Heath—I checked—nor had I noticed any vehicle following my cab on the journey from Wakehurst to the train station. I bought a cup of steaming tea from the tea trolley guy and sat in the silence of my empty carriage, trying to work out how someone had known to follow Alastair and me down to the underground storage area and lock us in.

It had to be someone who worked at the Seed Bank and had the necessary clearances to walk unchallenged throughout the facility. Alastair told me a few of his colleagues were aware he and Kevin had been working on a project together, but he seemed certain no one knew what that project was.

Somehow I didn't think that was true anymore. Someone did know. And today that person had made a bold play that could have silenced the two of us for good.

I decided to take the Underground from Victoria Station to Embankment and walk the rest of the way to Trafalgar Square, where the Church of St. Martin-in-the-Fields sat on a quiet corner across from the National Gallery of Art. Perry was already waiting at a table in the Crypt restaurant when I got there. His face creased into a broad smile, and he got up to pull me close in a big bear hug.

If you walked by Perry on the street, you probably wouldn't turn your head to notice him. He is not particularly good-looking—medium build with a slight paunch, reddish hair showing some white and going thin on top, pale blue eyes, hawk nose, large mouth, but there's something innately sensual about him that attracts women as if he were north and they were magnetized. I'd lost count of how many girlfriends he'd had. He turned fifty in January and, in typical Perry fashion, threw a huge bash for two hundred complete with music, dancing, and jeroboams of Dom Perignon at a friend's posh mansion in Holland Park. I would have gone if it hadn't been Nick's last weekend before he left for the Middle East, and I figured I'd get grief about it today. Perry lived hard, worked hard, and played hard. His workaholism cost him three marriages and a small fortune in alimony, or as he said, he had to work until they lowered his casket into the ground. But his staff adored him—me, included—and the London bureau won more press awards than any other IPS bureau, so the suits in New York thought he walked on water.

"Medina," he said, looking me over, "what the hell have you been doing to yourself? I thought you were taking it easy since you moved back to D.C."

"I'm still recovering from a decade of working for you. It'll take awhile."

He threw back his head and laughed. "Seriously, are you all right? You look a little green around the gills."

"I'm okay, but I haven't eaten since breakfast. I'm starved."

"That's what you get for standing me up for lunch. What happened, anyway?"

"I'll tell you once we get something to eat."

We got in line at the cafeteria-style serving area, where I ordered a large bowl of spiced carrot soup, a cheddar, chutney, and cress sandwich, and a pot of tea. Perry got scones, with clotted cream and jam, and a pot of coffee. While he paid for our food, I found a table in the corner and took the seat so my back was to the wall where I could see anyone who walked into or out of the café.

When Perry joined me, he threw me a look that I knew had to do with the change in seating. "What are we doing in this dark corner?"

"It was too noisy over there."

"There was no one else sitting near that table."

"It's more private here."

He glanced at the couples sitting at tables on either side of us, sat down, and said in a quiet, matter-of-fact voice, "You're watching the entrance. Is someone after you?"

"Maybe."

He busied himself with pouring coffee into his cup, heaping sugar into it, and adding so much cream the coffee looked like liquid butterscotch. Then he said, "You want to tell me about it?"

I trust Perry, I always have. He's had my back more times than I can count when I've been in the field and I needed something like a last-minute visa on a weekend to some far-flung place, a roll of cash to pay bribes—even a chartered plane. Whatever it was, he always took the heat from New York when they kicked up a fuss, deflecting it away from me and claiming it was all his idea.

I told him as much as I could without betraying anyone who had talked to me or helped me. When I had finished, he said, "That's a hell of a story. How do you connect Kevin Boyle's death at a monastery in Washington with someone locking you and a scientist in a storage vault in the Millennium Seed Bank in Sussex?"

"I don't know. At first I thought Kevin's death had to do with the book, *Adam in Eden*, but after today I believe it might have something to do with the seeds. Alastair helped Kevin identify the *lewisia*, the pressed plant in the book. According to the letter, the *lewisia* was supposed to be among the plants in the national botanic garden, and Kevin believed that meant it was also among the White House seeds. That's the connection between Kevin and Alastair."

Perry bit into his scone, which he had buried under a mountain of jam and drowned in clotted cream. He picked up a napkin and wiped his mouth. "Who knew about both the book and the seeds?"

"Before Kevin died?" I gave him a worried look. "Only one person I talked to. She asked to remain anonymous and she was the source of most of my information. Believe me, it's not her."

Perry gave me a you-don't-trust-me look.

"Never burn a source," I said.

"Fair enough," he said, "but that doesn't narrow it down much."

"I don't understand why someone would go after Alastair and me. Neither of us has any idea where the seeds are, and we haven't got the book."

"But you do know about those seeds." He gave me a pointed look. "That might be enough. By the way, you haven't finished your sandwich. You still eat like a bird."

"Thank you for trying to scare me, and my sandwich is all

yours unless you want to pour clotted cream on it, which would be really disgusting." I pushed my plate over to him.

He picked up my sandwich and bit into it. "Someone just tried to put you on ice, Medina. Literally. You ought to be looking over your shoulder. You're making people nervous. Did it occur to you whoever pulled that little stunt was only going after one of you? And I don't just mean Alastair." He pointed a finger at me.

I shivered. "It can't have been me. Whoever did that has to work at the Seed Bank. There's no way a visitor could just wander off from touring the public area and slip into the part of the facility where the underground vault is located. Besides, as Alastair told me, Wakehurst is fairly out of the way. You don't just pop in for a quick visit. I think it's more likely a colleague who targeted him."

Perry stared at a spot over my shoulder. I knew that concentrated expression. He was working something out. "Have you ever considered that Kevin left a clue to what happened to those seeds right there in plain sight and you've been looking at it all this time?"

"No. But I guess maybe I should, shouldn't I?"

"If I were you and someone just tried to put me in the deep freeze, I'd be looking at every angle."

"It's so comforting talking to you," I said. "I feel so much better."

He flashed a quick grin before turning serious. "I'm not joking around. What does Nick say about all this?"

"He doesn't know. He's still in the Middle East."

Perry regarded me with a one-eyed squint. "What's he doing there?"

"Reconnaissance for Quill Russell, the former secretary of state. He's putting together a consulting firm and wants Nick to be his energy guy."

"Nick will be set for life if he hooks up with Quillen Russell and his gold-plated address book. And, not to give marital advice since I'm so lousy at it, but you ought to tell him what's going on, you know. Nick, not Quill Russell."

I smiled. "I will. When I see him." I balled up my paper napkin and set it on the tray next to the teapot. "Can I ask a favor? Two?"

"Ask me anything, sweetheart."

"Can you let me know any new information concerning Archduke Orlando Haupt-von Véssey? He's in St. Mary's, recovering from pneumonia."

"Have we turned into a paparazza?"

I glared at him. "No, of course not. I'm the photographer at his son's wedding in Washington. I'm asking as a friend of the family. And before you say a word, I'm not turning into a wedding photographer, either. It's a one-time favor for Victor."

Perry looked at me with more respect. "I'm impressed. What's your other favor?"

"Do you remember a story in the British press concerning Edward Jaine? Something not very flattering, possibly involving computer exports to the Third World?"

He shook his head. "Vaguely. I'll check it out and either call you or send you a link."

"Thanks. I owe you." I stood up. "I probably ought to be getting back to the Connaught."

Perry got up, too. "How much longer are you staying in London?"

"We go home Friday."

"Any more news about your grandfather?"

"Nope. Mom's still in Connecticut."

He draped his arm around me as we walked outside. "One more thing," he said as though he'd just thought about it. "There's an opening for a shooter in the D.C. bureau. Monica wants to talk to you."

Monica Yablonski, the International Press Service Washington bureau chief, was tough as old boots, the kind of boss who made Perry—as demanding as he was—look like a pussycat.

"What happened? Which photographer quit or got fired? I lost track of the body count in that bureau," I said. "Thanks, but I don't need my butt kicked by Monica every day, Perry. It's nice to be my own boss for a change."

He did his best impression of looking as if I'd stabbed him through the heart. "Are you kidding me? You're not interested? Come on, Medina. You can handle Monica. Don't sit on the sidelines. You ought to still be in the game."

"Washington is nothing like working in the field. It's press release city, full of talking heads and navel gazers."

"It's a major bureau. People would kill to have that beat. Aren't you the least bit interested?" He gave me a sly look. "The opening is at the White House. You wouldn't be based in the bureau. Job's yours if you want it."

The White House. A plum job, press photographer for a major news bureau. He'd held that piece of information back until the end.

"Monica actually said that? Come on, Perry, what did she really say?"

"She'd like to talk to you."

"Thought so. She needs to find someone who hasn't heard about her reputation for eating reporters and photogs for breakfast and spitting out the bones. Some benighted soul who's been living in a cave for the last couple of years."

"Aren't you being a little harsh? Sweetheart, this is the brass ring. Talk it over with Nick if you want, but Monica's beating people away with a stick. At least promise me you'll call her and throw your hat in the ring."

"I'll think about it. I'm happy freelancing and I'm plenty busy."

"You haven't got long. She wants it filled by Friday. Tick, tick, tick."

"Typical Monica," I said. "It's another road job if the president travels a lot. And this one goes to North Carolina for breakfast, Michigan for lunch, and Prague for dinner and a summit."

A boxy black cab turned onto Duncannon Street. Perry put his hand up and the driver pulled over to the curb. He opened the door and turned to me.

"I miss you," he said, giving me a hug and a quick kiss on the lips. "Since you left no one turns in expenses for mileage on a camel or insists they didn't get my e-mails saying they couldn't upgrade their flight to first class."

"I miss you, too, and I was sore for weeks after that camel ride, and the upgrade was from Ulan Bator. The flight was full and the next one wasn't for another week."

He grinned and helped me into the cab. "She's going to the Connaught," he said through the window to the driver. "Take good care of her."

"Don't you worry, she'll be safe as houses with me, guv'nor."

Perry shut the door and the driver made one of those impossible tight circle turns London cabs are famous for. I looked over my shoulder and waved until we turned the corner onto the Strand.

"Everything all right, love?" The driver met my eyes in his rearview mirror as I settled back into the seat.

"Would you mind taking me down Whitehall? I'd like to see Horseguards Parade and Parliament and the Abbey."

"Of course. I'll take you by the Palace as well."

The training to become one of the world-famous London black-cab drivers is notoriously grueling and takes years to accomplish because it involves an intensive amount of studying, driving, and memorizing the city's maze of streets, both big and small. There are multiple exams and hundreds of routes that must be known by heart. The process even has a name: "Doing the Knowledge."

My driver, an elderly gentleman with flowing gray hair and

a neatly trimmed beard, realized at once that I was checking his mirrors. "No one's following us, miss. I promise you," he said. "And if they were, I'd let you know and I'd lose 'em."

"Thank you."

But in spite of his comforting promise, I couldn't help casting an occasional glance out the windows and in his mirrors. Because maybe Perry was right: Whoever locked us in the vault this afternoon might not have been targeting Alastair.

He might have been after me.

15

Archduke Victor Haupt-von Véssey turned away from the front desk at the Connaught as I walked into the hotel lobby shortly before five. His face lit up with his warm smile when he saw me, but otherwise he looked haggard and as if he hadn't slept much lately.

He kissed me on both cheeks. "It's good to see you here."

At home he was always well dressed, no baggy shorts, T-shirts, flip-flops, or baseball caps. But here in London there was something different about him, the elegant cut of his expensive suit, his erect posture, a confidence that made me more aware of his stature as a member of one of Europe's most distinguished royal families.

"And you," I said, smiling. "What are you doing at the Connaught?"

"Looking for you," he said, surprising me. "I had a meeting in Grosvenor Square this afternoon and then I walked around the corner to the Jesuit church across the street from here to light a candle for my father. Maybe you know it? The Farm Street Church?"

I nodded, and he said, "You mentioned in your e-mail that you would be staying here, so I dropped by on the chance you might be in and perhaps free for a drink. And before I forget, thank you for what you said about my father and for your concern. I was very touched."

"How is he? The news stories say he's quite ill."

The look in his eyes told me it was even worse than that. "My mother arrived this morning. She was on a cruise with friends off the coast of Turkey and this was the soonest she could get off the ship and catch a flight to London. He's doing poorly, but he's fighting."

"I'm so sorry. I hope he'll pull through."

"So do I." He sounded upbeat, but his smile was strained. "Are you all right? You look a bit pale yourself."

"Me? Oh, it's nothing. I was out today and didn't dress warmly enough. It's chillier here than at home."

"Come on," he said. "I think we could both use a drink. There must be something on the Coburg Bar's massive drinks menu that can warm you up and give me a bit of liquid courage."

We sat at the same table next to the fireplace where Harry and I had sat the night before. Like Harry, Victor had Scotch, but didn't make his choice until he'd had an intense discussion with our waiter about the finer points of Highland and Lowland malts. I had a glass of sherry.

"Why do you need liquid courage?" I asked as the waiter set down our drinks and we touched glasses. "Is it something to do with your father?"

He shook his head. "I think Yasmin and I should postpone the wedding."

I set my glass down. "What does she think?" One look at his face, and I said, "She doesn't know."

"Not yet."

"When are you going to tell her?"

He looked like a man who just heard bad news from a jury.

"We moved out of my parents' house on Eaton Square this morning over to the Goring and were planning to have a quiet dinner in the hotel tonight. I thought I'd tell her then."

Eaton Square was one of London's posh addresses in Belgravia, an elegant residential garden square faced mostly by terraced white stucco Regency buildings. I hadn't realized Archduke Orlando and his wife owned a house there, but they were in good company since it was a neighborhood known for its famous residents, real and fictional.

"How do you think she's going to take it?"

Victor drank some Scotch. "I think she'll be okay. My father's illness, Kevin's death, her mother's political campaign, all the problems with that . . ." He made a face like the Scotch tasted off when he mentioned Ursula.

"You mean Ursula's primary? She told me she has a tough fight against a wealthy opponent."

"Brutal would be a better word. Elections in America, my God, they cost so much. Ursula just hired a new media consultant, and all the campaign language makes it sound like this is some kind of war. I'm absolutely stunned."

"You mean David Arista's media company?"

He nodded. "He's supposed to be the best. He works with Yasmin on the Creativity Council."

If he thought there was something between his fiancée and his future mother-in-law's media consultant, he was too much of a gentleman to let it show.

I made a small circle on the table with my glass. "I didn't know your parents had a house in Eaton Square. That must be quite a large place. Did you think your mother wanted privacy and that's why you moved to the hotel?"

He gave me a piercing look. "I should have realized you'd pick up on that remark. My mother is not . . . overly fond . . . of Yasmin. Sometimes even the largest houses can seem small when there is no harmony among the people who live there."

"Is the feeling mutual, if I'm not being too nosy?"

He propped an elbow on the table and rested his chin on his hand. "Actually, I'm glad to have someone to confide in. And, yes, it's mutual, unfortunately."

"What about your father?"

"He is concerned about the age difference, but he likes Yasmin."

"Maybe postponing is a good idea with all the stress everyone is dealing with." I touched my glass against his again. "Look, you have the rest of your life to be married. A few months isn't going to change anything. Perhaps Yasmin will take the news better than you expect."

I hoped she would, for his sake.

His smile didn't make it all the way to his eyes. "Of course."

"Where is she now?"

"Working, believe it or not. You'll never guess who is in town. Edward Jaine."

"Good Lord, what's he doing here?"

"He has meetings, I believe, with some financial people in the City. Yasmin has been courting him to get him to become part of the Smithsonian Creativity Council. They're having tea together this afternoon."

I thought about the intimate exchange I'd witnessed between them at the engagement party and wondered if they were just talking business. "He'd be an interesting addition," I said.

Victor smiled. "I take it you're not a fan?"

"I'm not being fair because I don't actually know him."

"I do know him and I resented the way he treated Kevin."

"You knew he was Kevin's benefactor?"

He nodded. "I spoke to my father and asked if he'd be interested in the two of us underwriting Kevin's expenses so he wouldn't have to deal with Edward Jaine anymore. Kevin and I flew over here to discuss it with my father the week before Kevin died."

The conversation between Ursula's neighbors at the engagement party came back to me: The husband had remarked that

Victor would inherit the old archduke's art collection . . . and his library.

Was Archduke Orlando the other interested party in Kevin's copy of *Adam in Eden*?

"Did Kevin bring a book with him for your father to look at?"

He sat back in surprise. "How do you know about it?"

"It's a long story. I found it."

His eyes widened. "My God, I've been wondering what might have happened to it. Where is it now?"

"In a vault. Don't worry, it's safe." Though I already could guess the answer after what Zara Remington had said at the Chelsea Physic Garden the other day, I asked anyway. "What happened when your father examined it?"

"He made a few discreet inquiries and told Kevin it was quite valuable, one of a kind."

"Did he offer to buy it?"

Victor nodded. "As I'm sure you know, the book didn't actually belong to Kevin because of his vow of poverty. However, my father was interested in talking to the Franciscans to see if they would consider selling it once Kevin officially told his superior that he had acquired it from Edward."

"He hadn't reported it to the Franciscans yet?"

My dismay must have shown, because Victor said, "No, and if he didn't take care of that before he died, then technically Edward Jaine might be able to legally claim it's still his. It was purchased with his money."

I groaned. "Kevin hid the book before he died. I found it in a locker at the Natural History Museum."

"Then we must surmise that he hadn't reported it, mustn't we?" He gave me an ironic smile. "And now the lawyers will decide who owns it."

Jack O'Hara had said the same thing.

"The book is in a vault at Asquith's Auction House in Washington," I said. "An antiques dealer who is a good friend helped me get it to Bram Asquith, their rare-book expert."

"My father knows Bram. Good man." Victor drained his Scotch. "Would you care for another sherry?"

"No, thank you."

He shook his head at the waiter who had anticipated another round of drinks and turned back to me. "Well, if Asquith's has it, that's probably a good thing. At least it will be properly stored and cared for until the matter of who owns it is sorted out."

"Did Edward Jaine know how valuable the book was?"

Victor fiddled with a gold-and-carnelian heraldic crest ring on his right hand. "Kevin told me at the engagement party that he was going to talk to Edward the following day and tell him." He gave me an unhappy look. "I have no idea if he did or not, because that afternoon he was dead."

And before he died he met with your fiancée to urge her not to marry you if she was not sure of her feelings. For a moment I almost thought I'd said it out loud.

"I don't know if he did, either," I said. "I was with him that morning at the Tidal Basin because he'd promised to help me with a photography project. The next time I saw him was in the monastery garden. Yasmin probably told you I'm the one who found him when I showed up for my meeting with her and her mother that afternoon."

He looked puzzled. "Yasmin told me that appointment was canceled."

"It was, after everything that happened."

"Are you saying Yasmin was at the monastery that day?"

I nodded. "So was Ursula. Her car pulled up as one of the police officers walked me into the church to ask me some questions."

"How odd that she didn't tell me."

It was odd. "Maybe she didn't want to upset you since she knew how close you and Kevin were."

"You are probably right."

The waiter set a leather bill folder on the table. Victor pulled out his wallet and slipped a credit card inside the case without looking at the bill.

After the waiter left, I said, "Did Yasmin know about Kevin's book?"

"Why do you want to know that?"

I turned red. "She's having tea with Edward Jaine."

"No." It came out sharp, a stinging rebuke. "She would never betray my confidence. Not only did she not come with us to London, but books, actual physical books, are most definitely not Yasmin's 'thing,' as you say in America. Don't forget the people she deals with at the museum are technology wizards or Internet billionaires like Edward. Everything she reads these days is electronic; her files and paperwork are all digital." He smiled with regret. "Unfortunately, we don't share a love of old books, as I discovered when she suggested rearranging my library according to the color of the dust jackets." He added in a dry voice, "It was not one of our better conversations."

My mouth twitched, but I kept a straight face. "I can see why not."

The waiter returned with the bill and Victor's credit card. After Victor took care of it, he said, "I probably should be going. Yasmin will wonder where I've gotten to."

He kissed my hand in the lobby.

"Good luck tonight," I said.

"I've been considering suggesting the idea of moving the wedding to Vienna," he said. "After what happened, I think it would be too difficult, too sad to be married at the monastery. Would you stay on as our photographer? I'll fly you over, take care of all your expenses."

"I'd be honored," I said. "By the way, I forgot to ask if your father happened to say how much Kevin's book is worth?"

He gave me a knowing smile. "To answer you indirectly, my

father owns one of the one hundred and nineteen complete copies of *Birds in America* by John James Audubon, an illustrated book like Kevin's. He paid nine million dollars for it. Before he became ill he made an offer of five million pounds for one of Shakespeare's First Folios to a British university that was selling it because they needed the money for research. Kevin's book was quite rare as well."

Five million pounds. Nine million dollars. Kevin's book was worth a hell of a lot. Victor was convinced Yasmin had no interest in his copy of *Adam in Eden* and she never told him she was at the monastery the day Kevin died.

That girl was hiding something.

As soon as I got upstairs to my room, James appeared as if I'd rubbed a lamp and wanted to know if I needed anything.

"Also, Mr. Wyatt rang earlier. He said he's spending the night in Lingfield and won't be returning to town until tomorrow morning. Apparently he tried to phone you, but all he got was your voice mail."

I pulled my phone out of my pocket. "That's because my phone is dead; I'd better charge it up. Thank you, James. I'll listen to his message. And I think I'll have dinner in the room tonight."

"Of course, Miss Medina," he said. "You look a bit pale, if you don't mind my saying. You're not unwell, are you? We have a doctor on call . . ."

"Thank you, I'm fine. I probably overdid it today. Dinner and a night's sleep will put me right, I'm sure."

"Are you sure I can't bring you a sherry? Or a pot of tea?"

"Maybe some hot tea. Thanks."

By the time my phone battery had enough of a charge that I could turn it on again, I'd finished my tea and dozed off. Harry had called, as James said, but there were two other missed calls with messages, a London number and Max Katzer's cell phone, as well as an e-mail from David Arista. David's e-mail was short, asking how I was enjoying London and letting me know his friend could still get me into the Arts and Industries Building next week, but the sooner the better since they were going to begin fixing the ceiling and then the place would be off-limits for several months. I wrote a quick reply, thanking him and asking if we could meet sometime next Monday.

The London caller was Edward Jaine, asking me to phone him as soon as I got his message. I took a deep breath and hit Redial.

He skipped right past the pleasantries. "Ms. Medina, we haven't formally met, but I understand you were a good friend of Brother Kevin Boyle's. I also attended the party at the Austrian ambassador's residence the other night in Washington. Since we're both in London, I thought we might meet to discuss a certain book I understand you have. It happens to belong to me."

There was no point beating around the bush or claiming I didn't know what he was talking about, but I did wonder how he knew I had the book and who told him I was in London.

"I don't have it," I said. "I'm not sure what there is to discuss."

"Meet me tomorrow at ten o'clock at the Paramount restaurant," he said. "It's in Centre Point on Tottenham Court Road. Do you know where it is?"

"I do."

"Excellent. I'll see you there. And, Ms. Medina, don't stand me up. I assure you I will make this meeting very worth your while. Please be on time."

"I—"

But he had already hung up. In a furious mood, I listened to Max's message: He had news from Bram. I poured lukewarm tea into my cup, calmed down, and called Max, wondering if Bram's news confirmed what Victor had told me downstairs about the value of Kevin's book.

Or, if you were Edward Jaine, his book.

"Bram says that copy is worth several million, sugar," Max said after we exchanged small talk. "If he were selling it at auction, he'd ask around five."

"Edward Jaine just called me," I said. "He wants to know where his book is. Kevin may not have notified the Franciscans that he had it in his possession, so it might legally belong to Jaine. He asked—ordered—me to meet him tomorrow for coffee to discuss it. He's in London."

Max made an unhappy noise. "He might own it or does own it?"

"I don't know."

"Apparently he's not the only one interested in it. Your friend Victor Haupt-von Véssey's father was making some quiet inquiries. Bram heard about it through the grapevine," he said.

"That's because Kevin flew to London with Victor and showed it to Archduke Orlando the week before he died."

"So Kevin knew how valuable it was?"

"Yes."

"You can't get in the middle of this, Sophie," Max said in a warning voice. "What are you going to tell Jaine?"

"I don't know. I guess I'll have to tell him Bram has it. It can't be the first time Bram has had to deal with parties warring over who owns something."

Max sighed. "I know you're trying to do the right thing, but sometimes you just gotta leave things lay where Jesus flang them. The book's not your problem anymore. Tell Jaine the truth, and then you'll be done with it."

But I wasn't sure I would be done with it, especially after what had happened today at the Seed Bank.

I suspected there would be more to come.

16

Someone knocked on the door after I hung up with Max. James stood in the doorway behind a small table draped with a white linen tablecloth, place settings for two, covered silver dishes, and a bud vase with two red roses.

"I didn't order dinner yet," I said. "Did Harry change his plans and come back to London tonight after all?"

"Allow me to leave this with you, and you can knock on Mr. Wyatt's door." James gave me an enigmatic smile. "I'm sure it will all make sense."

I knocked on Harry's door. My husband stood in the doorway.

"Someone told me you might be free for dinner," he said. "I believe the butler did it."

In the thirteen years Nick and I have been married, I have learned not to be surprised when he turns up on the doorstep even though I'm dead sure he's in some other part of the world. This time was different.

He pulled me to him, kissing me until I couldn't catch my

breath, and whispered into my hair, "You have no idea how much I've missed you."

And then he took me over to the bed and proceeded to show me.

Nick and I had met in Paris fourteen years ago on New Year's Eve at the party of a mutual friend who had rented a glass-enclosed riverboat that cruised the Seine until sunrise. I remember that evening as magical, the boat gliding under lighted bridges, the fizz of champagne, the romantic cigarette-and-whiskey songs of Aznavour, Brel, and Piaf, Notre-Dame basked in floodlights, the Eiffel Tower glittering like an enormous studded jewel, and finally the pale blush of colors in the dawn sky, but mostly I remember falling head over heels in love with Nick. We spent the next day together walking the quiet streets of Paris, found a little brasserie that was open on New Year's Day in a mostly shuttered city, and eventually, as we knew we would, ended up spending the next night together in my hotel in the Latin Quarter. After that, Nick liked to joke that we had the world's longest first date, spanning two years. He proposed six months later, on a sultry summer night on the viewing platform of the Eiffel Tower, and we were married the following Valentine's Day at the Chelsea Town Hall in London.

We knew from the beginning that the secrecy that cloaked Nick's job and the clandestine nature of his work, along with my itinerant travel schedule with IPS, were going to be hard on our marriage. So whenever we got together after one of those separations, the first thing we did—before talking about work or the mundane concerns of home life, bills, our families—was go to bed together. After fourteen years, it was still as good and intense and erotic as that first night in Paris, maybe even better because we knew each other so intimately.

I had not thought to close the curtains before we tumbled into bed tonight. The soft golden light from the streetlamps on Carlos Place caught the outline of Nick's naked body as he hovered over me, silhouetting him so he looked like a perfect Greek god. I pulled him down and guided him inside one more time. He groaned and murmured my name, and before long we were touching and kissing again, starting all over.

Later, when we were lying in each other's arms, I remembered James arriving with our dinner . . . hours ago.

"What are we going to do about the meal James brought us? It's been sitting there for at least two hours."

Nick ran the back of his finger across my shoulder and down one arm. "It's okay, sweetheart. Everything's on ice and it's a cold supper: caviar, foie gras, scallop and endive salad, fruit and cheese." He sat up. "First, we ought to have some champagne."

He pulled me out of bed and led me over to the connecting door between my room and Harry's.

"Wait a minute." I tugged on his hand. "How do you know what's under those covered dishes? And this is Harry's room . . . we can't just . . . and this is his bathroom. I don't think—oh, my gosh, how beautiful."

Someone had placed lighted votive candles throughout the white-and-gray marble bathroom, and the large soaking tub was already partially filled with a bubble bath. Nick turned on the hot water and the heat released a fragrant scent, lavender combined with the heady aroma of ylang-ylang. A small bowl filled with red rose petals sat on the tub ledge and a bottle of Mumm was chilling in a silver bucket next to a tray with two crystal champagne flutes on it.

"Don't worry about Harry," Nick said. "Why do you think he's staying in Lingfield tonight?"

"You mean he knows? You two planned this?"

Nick grinned. "It's the next best thing I could do since I missed our thirteenth wedding anniversary. Harry and I couldn't have done it without James. Who do you think prepared the bath and lit all these candles?" He held out his hand. "Come on, why don't you add those rose petals to the water and I'll open our champagne?"

I picked up the bowl and scattered the bloodred petals. Then I let Nick help me into the tub.

We sat facing each other, my legs wrapped around his waist, and finally talked as we drank our champagne. He told me all about what he'd been doing in the Gulf, animated and excited in a way that I hadn't seen him for a long time.

"You seem happy," I said.

He moved his hand across the top of the water and scooped up a handful of foamy soap bubbles. "I am. By the way, Quill said I don't have to work out of the Washington office if I don't want to. We could move back here."

"To London? Are you kidding me?" I sat up and knocked the bubbles out of his hand. "When were you going to tell me that?"

He grinned and brushed the tip of my nose with more bubbles. "I just did. So what do you think?"

"You know I'd love it. But we just moved back home, we've barely settled in. I think we ought to give it a try."

"You really want to stay in D.C.?"

"I think so, at least for now." I finished my champagne and he reached for the bottle, refilling our glasses. "Perry told me today that IPS is looking for a White House photographer. Monica Yablonski wants to hear from me by the end of the week."

"Are you interested?"

"I like being my own boss."

"Is that a no?"

"Come on, you know what the White House press room is like. It's like working in a submarine, low ceilings, no windows. When it rains, the carpet gets soaked and you're jammed in there like sardines. Access to the president is strictly managed, choreographed, and parsed out by his people whose default answer is 'no' or, if you're lucky, 'I don't know.' If the president thinks he's living in a fishbowl, the press lives in a gilded cage."

He said in a mild voice, "And those are just the good points?"

I laughed. "It sounds glamorous, but you and I know it's not . . . Would you be happy in Washington?"

"I'll be happy anywhere as long as I'm with you."

James had left oversized terry robes on the back of the bathroom door. We climbed out of the tub and had dinner back in my room, where an opened bottle of Domaine de la Romanée-Conti was waiting at our table.

I gave Nick another surprised look and he grinned. "James and I had this all set up."

"I can see that."

Nick held my chair and poured the wine. "What have you been doing since you got here? Not shopping, obviously."

"How do you know that?"

He indicated the rest of the room. "No shopping bags. No Harrods, no Harvey Nicks. Not even a bookstore carrier bag. Just some tea from Fortnum and Mason."

"I bought that for Grace and India. I should have gotten some for us. Maybe I'll go back tomorrow."

Nick unfolded his napkin as though he were unwrapping something that required great concentration and placed it in his lap. "You have a hell of a set of bruises starting to come up on your right shoulder and along the back of your arm. You also winced a couple of times in bed. I tried to be careful. Why don't you tell me what's going on, what you've really been doing?"

As soon as he said that, I reached for my shoulder. It had taken a battering when Alastair and I tried to shove open the security door to the storage vault, but I hadn't realized the bruises showed much yet since I couldn't see them. Besides, I'd been too lost in Nick, in what he had been doing with me, to think about anything else.

"I'm okay," I said. "Don't worry."

"Did somebody hurt you?"

"A door. And it hurt like hell."

He set his fork down and waited.

"Eat your dinner and I'll tell you. It's a long story."

I didn't leave anything out. When I was done, he said, "I've got a couple of friends who moonlight doing security work. I'm going to call them. I don't like you walking around London unprotected. These guys are discreet. You won't even know they're there." He paused. "Unless you need them."

"Nick, I don't need a bodyguard or a babysitter. I can handle this."

"Humor me."

"All right, I'll make you a deal. Let me talk to Edward Jaine tomorrow morning. I'm meeting him in a posh restaurant, for Pete's sake. After that, if your friends want to follow me around London and carry my shopping bags—because that's what I'm going to do next—that's fine."

He smiled. "I'll set it up."

"Not now, okay? Let's have this evening just for us."

By the time James came in to take away our table and the dinner dishes and ask if we wanted a nightcap, the two of us were so tired we could barely keep our eyes open.

"I think we're all set, James," Nick said, stifling a yawn. "The meal was excellent. And thank you for everything. My beautiful wife had no clue about our plans."

"Quite true," I said. "You're very sneaky, James. I never would have suspected."

"It's one of the required courses at butler school, Miss Medina," he said. "I was top of my class."

I laughed. "I bet you were."

James grinned. "Will you both be taking breakfast here tomorrow morning, or will you dine downstairs?"

Nick gave me a reluctant look. "I've got a ten a.m. flight tomorrow out of Heathrow. I'm sorry, sweetheart."

"You're leaving tomorrow? Already?"

"I've got to, I'm afraid. I'm sorry." He turned to James. "Any chance of coffee and something to eat at six o'clock in the room?"

"Of course, sir. What about you, Miss Medina? Will you be dining with Mr. Canning, or do you wish to wait until Mr. Wyatt returns?"

"I'll have breakfast with my husband at six, please."

James left after sorting out our order and assuring Nick that one of the hotel cars would be downstairs at seven to take him to the airport. After he was gone, I wanted Nick to pull me into bed again, now that I knew all we had left was the rest of tonight.

He did.

Later, after we finished making love, I fell into a deep sleep where my dreams and the events of the last few days since Kevin's death collided in a giant, confusing pileup. At one point I must have cried out, because all of a sudden Nick was stroking my hair and hushing me, murmuring that it was only a dream, probably fueled by wine and champagne drunk late at night. But when I slept again, the dreams returned and I was alone in a long, dark arctic-cold tunnel where Perry's voice repeated what he'd told me earlier in the day at the Crypt restaurant.

Kevin left you the answer to the puzzle, Sophie. It's right there in front of you. You just can't see it.

When I woke the next morning, I was alone, the imprint of Nick's head still on his pillow and his half of the rumpled blankets turned back where he'd slipped out of bed. It was dark outside, but a crack of lamplight shone under the threshold to Harry's room. Nick's deep voice carried through the door, though I couldn't hear what he was saying. The clock on my bedside table read five forty-five.

I found my robe on the floor where I had dropped it last night. When I opened the adjoining door, Nick was sitting on the edge of a damask sofa across from Harry's bed, engrossed in a phone conversation. Somehow, he'd managed to shave, shower, and get completely dressed without waking me. He looked up and smiled as I walked in, stretching out his arm for me to join him, still listening to whoever was talking on the other end of the line.

I sat down next to him and leaned my head on his shoulder. "I owe you for that one, buddy," he was saying. "Thanks for letting me know . . . you, too . . . sure, let's get together for that beer. I'll call you."

He disconnected and kissed me. "Morning, sleepyhead. I didn't mean to wake you."

I kissed him back. "What time did you get up? I didn't hear you get out of bed."

"About an hour ago. You were dead to the world. I don't think you would have heard a bomb go off."

"Who were you talking to just now? My future bodyguard?"

"I already left a message with two guys I know. Hopefully I'll hear from at least one of them real soon." He brushed a lock of hair off my face and tucked it behind my ear. "That call was to an old friend in the D.C. office of the FBI."

"I thought you guys in the CIA and the FBI didn't talk to each other."

"The smart guys talk to each other, we just don't tell the others about it. He made a few calls for me. I'm sorry, baby. You're not going to like this, but the medical examiner is going to rule that Kevin Boyle's death was an accident."

"That's not possible."

"My buddy says Kevin sustained a basal skull fracture and that's what killed him. In other words, he cracked his skull. There were no injuries consistent with a struggle."

"Someone pushed him, and that's how it happened. I'm sure of it."

"Then call the officer who questioned you," he said. "Tell her you found a five-million-dollar motive for why it might not be an accident."

"I left her card at home," I said. "I'll wait until this afternoon when it's proper business hours in Washington and then track her down."

But once we were back in my room eating breakfast, I said, "You know what's going to happen, don't you? If I tell Officer Carroll about the book, the police are going to confiscate it as evidence."

He said through a mouthful of eggs, "Not your problem."

I shook my head. "What a mess."

Just before seven, James gave a discreet tap on the door and Nick let him in.

"Your car's waiting outside, Mr. Canning, and your luggage is already in the boot. It's been a pleasure having you stay with us, sir."

He left so we could say goodbye in private. "I'll text you or call as soon as I hear back from my security buddies," Nick said.

"I almost forgot to ask where you're going now."

"Doha."

The capital of Qatar. "Is that the last stop? When will you be home?"

"Almost the last stop. And I'll be home soon." He kissed me. "I love you."

"I love you more."

Then he was gone.

I ran to the window and waited until he emerged from the hotel to climb into the Bentley. He must have made some joke to the doorman, who broke into a hearty laugh as he closed the passenger car door. A moment later, as the big car circled Carlos Place, gliding toward Grosvenor Square, the mist from the fountain vents at the base of the two plane trees drifted into the air, perfectly timed so it seemed to swallow the Bentley. When it cleared fifteen seconds later, Carlos Place was empty.

I poured the last of the breakfast coffee into my cup and finally got "No Little Plans" from the writing desk where it had been sitting since I arrived. Olivia Upshaw had e-mailed late yesterday, asking how I was getting on. I replied just now that I was in London—with the manuscript—and promised to get in touch when I got home next week.

The author, whom I hadn't met, had done a terrific job of telling the story of the creation of the National Mall with the high-stakes tension and drama of a blockbuster novel. For the next two hours I was caught up in the egos of a parade of larger-than-life personalities and the many clashes, feuds, and missed opportunities that began with Pierre L'Enfant and George Washington and ended with the Senate's McMillan Commission, which resurrected L'Enfant's grand plan for Washington and established the Mall as it was today. My phone alarm went off at nine, a reminder it was time to get ready for my meeting with Edward Jaine. I skimmed the last pages of the book, along with Olivia's notes about the final photos she wanted, panoramic views of Washington from Pierre L'Enfant's grave, which was in front of Arlington House, Robert E. Lee's home in Arlington Cemetery, overlooking the city he'd designed.

By nine thirty I had showered and dressed, and was downstairs in the hotel lobby. While I waited for a cab, I phoned Alastair Innes. The call went to voice mail, and I left a message asking him to call me back as a black cab swept into Carlos Place. The doorman helped me into the cab and told the driver I was going to Centre Point.

I smiled and thanked him. But I really wasn't looking forward to my meeting with Edward Jaine.

The Paramount restaurant occupies the top two floors in the tower of what was once London's tallest skyscraper back in the mid-1960s. Now it is dwarfed by other buildings that have sprung up over the years, like NatWest's Tower 42, One Canada Square in Canary Wharf, and most recently, the unusual Gherkin and the exquisite Shard, which, along with the Eye are instantly recognizable on London's skyline. I gave my name and showed my American driver's license to a woman in the lobby, who phoned the restaurant to confirm I was expected upstairs and then directed me to a bank of elevators.

The restaurant and bar were on the thirty-second floor; the floor above was a glass-enclosed observation deck. When I stepped off the elevator, the first thing I saw was an enormous copper bar behind which mirrored glass shelves displayed rows and rows of bottles of alcohol. The Art Deco décor was dark and rich, sleek midnight-blue sofas and nubby gray chairs around galvanized metal coffee tables where guests could sit for morning coffee or afternoon tea or drinks at night. Beyond the bar, the tables in the empty restaurant were already set for lunch. The Paramount's big drawing card was the bank of windows that showed off a 360-degree bird's-eye view of London.

Edward Jaine was the only male in the bar among a couple of tables of women who were getting an early start on cocktail hour. He was dressed much the same as he'd been at the Austrian ambassador's home the last time I saw him, in jeans and two-tone leather cowboy boots, brown and a textured mottled skin that looked like rattlesnake. His brown leather jacket matched the boots, and a white dress shirt and a red silk scarf hung loose around his neck.

He was seated on a sofa by one of the windows checking his phone as I entered the restaurant. A manila folder and an empty espresso cup sat on the coffee table in front of him. When he saw me, he stood. "Sophie. Good of you to come. Please have a seat."

Already on a first-name basis and yesterday it had been an ultimatum, not an invitation. I took one of the chairs across from his sofa. Edward Jaine sat back against a pile of burnt orange velvet throw cushions and surveyed me like a sultan receiving a guest in his palace.

A waitress appeared, and he said, "Would you care for something to drink?"

I wanted to get this over with. "No, thank you."

He gave me a cool look. "As you wish." To the waitress he said, "I'll have another espresso."

He asked me, "So what really brings you to London?"

I folded my hands in my lap. "Personal reasons."

"You don't need to be hostile."

"You didn't invite me here, you threatened me if I didn't come. So here I am."

"All right. You have something that belongs to me."

The waitress set down his espresso and her eyes darted between the two of us. "Is everything all right, sir, miss? Can I bring you something else?"

He waved her off. "Everything's fine, thank you."

After she left, he said, "Oh, for God's sake. I know you have the book, or you know where it is."

"I don't have it."

"I'm not going to play games. How did you get your hands on it in the first place?"

"I found it. And it was Kevin's book, Mr. Jaine."

He wagged a no-no-no playful finger at me. "Ah, but I paid for it."

I had no idea what kind of deal he'd made with Kevin. "Kevin bought it. He found the book in a bookstall on Portobello Road and he paid next to nothing for it since it was at the bottom of a box of old gardening books."

Jaine seemed taken aback that I knew that much. "I gave him the money."

"If you gave him the money, then it was a gift. He's allowed some personal money, even with his vow of poverty." I hoped he didn't know how much money, because I didn't know the limit, either.

He sipped his espresso and said in an even voice, "I have the records to prove it wasn't a gift."

"I'm not going to get in the middle of that," I said. "It's between you and the Franciscans. Leave me out of it."

"I want the book."

"Talk to Father Xavier."

He set down his cup and reached for the folder on the table, spinning it around and shoving it across to me. "Have a look at this."

I opened the folder. A check with a lot of zeros after a number, a substantial amount of money, made out to cash.

"Keep it. For your trouble."

"I don't want your money."

"It's not for you. It's for the Adams Morgan Children's Center. I know you're trying to get that place fixed up. That ought to take care of it."

I felt like he'd knocked the wind out of me. The money would easily pay for fixing up the children's center, with some left over for clothes and other necessities.

"No," I said in a faint voice. "You can't do that—"

He leaned forward, elbows resting on his knees and an earnest look on his face. "I'm not the bad guy here, Sophie. Kevin was at my mother's bedside when she died two years ago. A brain tumor. Her last days were hell and Kevin was a living saint. Why do you think I offered him financial assistance for his research? I wanted to repay his kindness, that's all."

I stared out the window at the enormous green roof and central dome of the British Museum and, in the distance, the bare brown branches of the trees in Russell Square. Last night in the Coburg Bar, Victor had said he resented the way Jaine treated Kevin. But now Edward Jaine insisted his charity came from gratitude, a touching story about a debt to his dying mother.

One of them wasn't telling the truth.

"Why were you and Kevin arguing at the Austrian ambassador's residence the night before he died?"

He straightened and picked up his espresso, finishing it off and setting the cup down again with a sharp little click. "I don't know what you're talking about."

I closed the folder and pushed it over to him. "I can't accept this. And I can't help you. As I said, this is between you and the Franciscans. I'm sorry, Mr. Jaine. I think we're done here."

I reached for my camera bag and started to get up.

"Leave here without telling me where the book is and I will ask my lawyers to explore the possibility of bringing criminal charges against you."

I caught my breath. "On what grounds?"

"You've stolen a valuable item that belongs to me. It's worth millions."

"I didn't steal anything."

"Good luck proving that. I can make your life a misery." He tapped the folder again. "One last chance. Take the money, use it for those kids, and tell me what I want to know, or I'll see to it that you regret it."

I swung my camera bag over my shoulder and hoped he didn't see how badly my hands were shaking.

"I already do," I said, and left.

17

I could feel Edward Jaine's eyes on me as I walked across the restaurant and punched the elevator call button. The door slid open and I stepped in.

I leaned against the wall and closed my eyes. *Now what?*

The exit to the restaurant brought me outside to a small landing at the top of a flight of stairs overlooking a busy intersection. Just across the street was the Tottenham Court Road tube station. The morning fog had burned off and the raw chill of the past two days was gone. For the first time since I arrived in England, the sun was shining. I pulled out my phone and discovered I'd missed a call and a text message.

The text was from Nick:

Still trying to raise my buddies. Be careful.

I texted back:

Don't worry, I'm fine. Call me after you get in.

The call was from the Connaught. A woman at the front desk gave me the message. "A man who said he was the secretary to Archduke Victor Haupt-von Véssey rang here. The archduke asked if you could meet him today at noon at the Anchor pub in Bankside."

How odd that he didn't call me himself. Maybe Victor wanted to talk about how it had gone last night when he told Yasmin he wanted to postpone the wedding. Except the Anchor pub, as famous as it was, was on the other side of the Thames. It seemed like an odd place to meet.

The woman added, "The secretary asked me to pass the message along and ring him back if you couldn't make it. Otherwise, he'll expect you."

"I can just call the archduke myself. Or the secretary."

"Unfortunately that's not possible," she said. "The archduke is in a meeting. The secretary is with him."

I glanced at my watch. It was only ten thirty. Maybe Victor's meeting was in Bankside. "I can be there at noon."

"Well, then, I guess that's settled. The secretary said it was only necessary to call if you couldn't make it, otherwise the archduke will expect to see you at twelve."

I leaned against the railing, watching the people on the street below. No one looked up or even noticed me. I ran down the stairs into the Underground station, took two trains, and half an hour later got out at London Bridge on the south side of the Thames. There was still almost an hour to kill before meeting Victor.

I've always liked the hustle and bustle of this grittier part of the city, the industrial docks, wharves, and warehouses that tie it to the river, its ancient history dating to the pagan Romans, its rowdy reputation for entertainment as the site of brothels, animal-baiting pits, and playhouses like Shakespeare's Globe during the Tudor era. The notorious Clink Prison was there, and for centuries, the only entrance across the Thames to the City of London was at Southwark Cathedral, which was recorded in William the Conqueror's *Domesday Book*.

I left the Underground at the Borough Market exit and wandered past the quiet shuttered stalls. Then I walked up the street to the cathedral, where I left a twenty-pound note in the poor box and made my way along the Queen's Walk, the busy pedestrian promenade that followed the river from Westminster Bridge to Tower Bridge.

If I turned left, I'd be heading toward the Globe Theatre and the Anchor pub, where I was supposed to meet Victor. Instead I turned right toward Tower Bridge and, across the river, the massive fortifications of the Tower of London itself.

Yesterday Alastair told me that for more than a century the leather seed pouch belonging to the Dutch sailor Jan Teerlink had been locked away in the Tower. More than likely it had been put in some dark cool room deep within the complex, a sprawling fortress of multiple rings that enclosed thick-walled buildings and dozens of smaller towers. Wherever it had been, at least a few of the seeds had been preserved well enough to be regenerated two centuries later, producing plants that were now healthy and thriving at the Millennium Seed Bank.

What place back home had conditions comparable to the Tower of London, somewhere Kevin's seeds could languish undisturbed for two centuries? A building? A cave? If Dolley Madison had gotten them out of the White House before the British burned the city in 1814, the odds were good they had also been transported to somewhere nearby in Virginia along with everything else that left Washington. So why hadn't anyone discovered them during the last two hundred years? Either they were so well hidden they couldn't or wouldn't be found, or whoever had them in his possession didn't know what he had.

By now I'd walked as far upriver as the futuristic egg-shaped glass-and-steel City Hall not far from Tower Bridge. At night it was lit up with concentric rings of lights that reminded me of a spaceship about to depart for its home planet. I stayed near the bridge taking photographs of the skyline and the river until it was time to walk to the Anchor. The Queen's Walk had become busier and more bustling in the last half hour. A jostling lunchtime crowd spilled out of City Hall and other nearby office buildings to join tourists and anyone else who wanted to enjoy the warm early spring sunshine.

The Anchor pub sat in a cobblestone plaza overlooking the river, a sprawling redbrick building with fire-engine-red windows and doors, a big gold anchor hanging above the entrance, and a macabre history as the site of a pit where the bodies of those who died of the plague had been dumped. William Shakespeare had drunk and dined at the Anchor, as had Charles Dickens, Samuel Johnson, and Samuel Pepys.

Victor hadn't specified where we'd meet, indoors or outside, so I decided to sit on the embankment wall next to the beer garden where we'd be likely to see each other as he entered the plaza. While I waited, I checked my phone. Another text from Nick sent just before he boarded his flight, letting me know he'd reached one friend who was in Helsinki, so he was waiting to hear back from the other guy.

The phone rang in my hand. Perry.

"Hey," I said. "What's up?"

"Where are you? Someplace noisy."

"Bankside. The Anchor."

"I wasn't sure if you'd heard the news about Alastair Innes," he said, "but I thought you'd want to know."

I said with slow dread, "What news?"

"He was killed in an accident early this morning. His car was found at the bottom of a ravine not far from the Seed Bank. Apparently he died at the scene." There was a pause before he said, "I'm sorry, Medina."

After a moment he said, "Are you there?"

"Yes. Sorry. Are you sure it was Alastair? I mean, they positively identified him?"

"Of course they're sure. Otherwise they wouldn't release his name to the press. You know that."

I did. But I still couldn't believe it.

"Was anyone else involved?" I asked. "Another car?"

"Too soon to tell. Maybe he lost control, maybe he swerved to avoid something, an animal, an oncoming car."

"Yesterday someone went after him at the Seed Bank and today he's dead. I wonder if someone tampered with his car."

"There'll be an investigation, you can be sure of that," Perry said. "What are you doing at the Anchor?"

"Waiting for Victor Haupt-von Véssey. His secretary said he wanted to talk to me."

"Huh. Hey, before I forget, I looked up your buddy Edward Jaine."

"He's not my buddy."

"I'll say. Interpol has been keeping an eye on him."

"You're kidding me. Why?"

"He owns a company that's been shipping old electronics—phones, laptops, digital cameras, stuff like that—to Third World countries, mostly in Asia and Africa. It's called 'e-waste' because of all the toxic stuff the older items have in them. Apparently the European Union is launching criminal investigations into a number of companies and Jaine is at the top of their list. The 'used goods' he's sending are electronics that don't work. Companies do it to avoid legitimate recycling costs. He sends this crap to poor countries where people dismantle them without knowing what they're doing and get sick from lead, mercury, arsenic, and a bunch of other nasty stuff."

"My God, that's awful. I wonder if that's what he and Kevin were arguing about at the engagement party. Maybe Kevin found out from one of his environmental contacts."

"That would make sense," he said. "Jaine is in a pack of trouble. Apparently his balance sheet doesn't look so hot, either. He's trying to save his ass and what's left of his fortune."

I thought about the substantial check Edward Jaine had pushed across the table to me. If I had taken it and cashed it, would it have been good?

No wonder he wanted Kevin's book. Five million dollars wasn't much to a billionaire, but if you were broke, it probably looked like a lifeline.

"Medina?" Perry was saying. "You still there?"

"I was just thinking about all this. It seems to me it gives Edward Jaine even more of a motive for murder."

"You could be right. In the meantime, I don't think your meeting with your archduke friend is going to happen. I'm watching live television and he's walking into St. Mary's Hospital with his mother."

"Right now?"

"That's what live means."

I said, puzzled, "Then why would he ask me to meet him here?"

"Did he call you himself?"

"No. The hotel passed along a message from a secretary."

"Jesus H. Christ, Medina. You've been set up. Get the hell out of there. *Now.*"

18

slid off the embankment wall. It was still early, ten minutes to twelve, so perhaps whoever called the hotel pretending to be Victor's secretary hadn't arrived yet, or maybe he was waiting inside the pub. Either way, now I knew Victor wasn't coming, which gave me a tiny advantage if I could get out of here before anyone realized I was gone.

I didn't want to go back through the narrow streets of Bankside to the Underground station, or try to hail a cab. It would be too easy for someone to corner me. The obvious choice was to stay in the open, take my chances getting lost in the crowd. Up ahead, maybe half a mile or so, was the Millennium Footbridge, a pedestrian suspension bridge over the Thames that took you from the Tate Modern and the Globe on this side of the river and deposited you in front of St. Paul's Cathedral on the other side.

What I most wanted to do right now was make a dash for that bridge. Instead, I slung my camera bag over my shoulder and strolled out of the plaza down the Queen's Walk like I was just another tourist. When I had nearly reached the Globe, I rotated the camera on my phone so the lens faced me and held it up high as though I were taking a souvenir picture of myself in front of the theater. I snapped a couple of photos, scanning the scenery and the people walking behind me. In a split second I knew the slight man in the baggy black tracksuit, head down, nondescript baseball cap with the visor pulled low was the one. About forty or fifty feet back, moving fast, something long like a pipe tucked under one arm.

To gain access to the footbridge, you follow a zigzag ramp that gradually rises until you reach the aluminum deck over the river. I sprinted to the ramp and knew without looking back that my pursuer had sped up as well. A bunched-up crowd stood around the entrance, funneling from the wider promenade onto the narrow ramp, and that meant I was in trouble. Forming an orderly queue to wait one's turn is a British national character trait. If I pushed through those people to get ahead, there'd be a commotion and I might as well have a big neon arrow pointing straight at me. If I waited, Baseball Cap would reach me in no time.

But chivalry and decency are also quintessentially English, so I sidled up to two large men who were standing next to the ramp entrance. "I'm terribly sorry," I said to one of them in a low voice, "but there's a man back there who's been bothering me and I'm trying to get away from him. Do you think you could possibly let me pass?"

"What's 'e look like, love?" he asked, moving aside.

"Black tracksuit, baseball cap."

"I see 'im," his companion said. "Head down, coming toward us. We'll slow 'im down, my love, don't you worry. We'll turn into the Great Wall of China, we will."

"Thank you so much."

By the time I reached the deck of the bridge, I had slipped out of my jacket, shoving it in my camera bag, which I now cradled in my arms instead of letting it swing from my shoulder.

I'd also put on the dark green hat I'd bought the other day and twisted my hair in a knot, tucking it under the hat. Changing my attire and my profile wouldn't buy me much time, but if my two friends on the ramp slowed my pursuer down even a little, it would help.

The Millennium Footbridge is approximately a dozen feet wide and probably slightly more than a thousand feet long, give or take, with two-way traffic. Here it was easier to thread through the crowd because so many people stopped to take pictures or admire the spectacular views. Fortunately for me, the bridge slopes up until you are in the middle of the river, where it levels off, before gently sloping down as you approach the other bank. The result is that it is impossible to see very far ahead for much of the time you are crossing the river.

That was the good news. The bad news was that Baseball Cap and his pipe knew I had to be on the bridge because there was no place else to go.

At the halfway point, when I could see Tower Bridge on the horizon to my right, I ran. From here St. Paul's looked as though it was sitting on the riverbank, but in fact it was not. You have to cross two streets going uphill from the embankment to reach the churchyard. What's more, the main entrance, the west entrance, is around the corner. The view from the river is of the south side of the cathedral. Once I left the bridge, I wouldn't have much time to shake off Baseball Cap, but I had been to St. Paul's often enough that I knew my way around.

When Nick and I lived in London, one of our favorite traditions had been attending the annual Thanksgiving Day Service, a moving ceremony that always reduced me to tears as the Marine color guard marched down the aisle with our flag, and everyone—Americans and British—sang "America the Beautiful." And at the end of many workdays, I often walked the few blocks from IPS on Fleet Street to listen to the ethereal beauty of the cathedral choir at evensong.

I ran down the zigzag ramp off the bridge and sprinted up the street. Two tour buses pulled up and stopped at St. Paul's Churchyard as I crossed Queen Victoria Street, opening their doors to let their passengers disembark. I slipped between the buses and joined the crowd, catching a quick glimpse of the street behind me just before everyone around me surged toward the cathedral. Baseball Cap was walking my way, head swiveling from side to side. He'd lost me, at least for now. But in another minute or two he'd be right here, and I had a feeling he wasn't going to give up searching until he found me.

The tour group seemed to consist mostly of senior citizens, the majority of whom were making their way to the handicapped entrance at the south door. I maneuvered into the middle of the group and offered to push a woman in a wheelchair so that her elderly husband could walk by her side.

If you wanted to worship at St. Paul's you didn't need to pay an entry fee, but to visit any part of the cathedral you needed an admission ticket. As soon as we were inside and I could leave the lady in the wheelchair with her husband, I stood in a mercifully short queue and bought a ticket. Then I headed for the staircase to the Whispering Gallery and Christopher Wren's magnificent cast-iron dome.

The dome had three visitor galleries, until you reached the topmost Golden Gallery, from which there were breathtaking views of London. I didn't intend to climb above the Whispering Gallery, the first gallery, because what I wanted was a panoramic view of the church below. St. Paul's was built in the shape of a cross with the dome in the middle, and I knew from past visits that I'd be able to see almost all of it except the high altar and the side chapels. If Baseball Cap was here, sooner or later I'd spot him when he came out into the open.

Though the climb got steeper the higher you went, the steps to the Whispering Gallery were wide and shallow so it didn't take me long. But although I walked around the entire inside perimeter of the dome along the whispering wall that gave the gallery its name, I didn't see Baseball Cap. Either he hadn't entered the church, or he'd removed the hat so I could no longer pick him out.

I pulled out my camera to use the zoom on my telephoto, but a vigilant security guard told me in a polite but firm voice to put it away.

"I'm not taking pictures," I said. "I'm just trying to find someone down below in the church."

"I'm afraid you'll have to use these." He pointed to his eyes with his two index fingers. "Positively no photography allowed in St. Paul's, miss."

After twenty minutes, I gave up watching and waiting, hoping Baseball Cap had done the same, and went back downstairs in time to join a group from the tour bus making their way to the handicapped exit. Outside, a taxi with a lighted toplight pulled up to the curb next to the statue of Queen Anne and I ran toward it.

"Where to, love?" he asked.

"The Connaught."

Though it was only a couple of miles across town and the driver kept detouring down side streets to speed up the trip, traffic was so congested it took the better part of half an hour to get to the hotel. I had plenty of time to stare out the window, searching for anyone wearing baseball caps or black tracksuits as we slowly drove down the Strand and past the elegant gentlemen's clubs on Pall Mall.

By the time the driver cut around Berkeley Square just before pulling up in front of the hotel, I knew what I was going to do next. When I worked for IPS, I'd made a few friends at Scotland Yard and they'd helped me over the years. I didn't believe Alastair's car had gone into some ravine by accident any more than I believed Kevin slipped on the stairs in the monastery garden.

Today someone had gone after me. Even if Nick's bodyguard showed up, it was time to get help. First I'd call Washington and get hold of Officer Carroll. My next call would be to Scotland Yard.

But when I walked into my room, the connecting door to Harry's room had been flung open and Harry was on the phone, wearing out a path in the carpet as he paced back and forth in front of the window. He saw me and shook his head, a weary look on his face as he pinched the bridge of his nose with a thumb and forefinger like he was trying to stave off a headache.

"Who is it?" I asked in a whisper. "What's wrong?"

He put his hand over the speaker and mouthed, "Your mother."

I gave him a commiserating look, and he went back to his conversation.

"It's okay, Caroline, don't worry," he said. "Just do whatever you need to do until I get there . . . he's not in any pain, is he . . . Darling, calm down, I'll be there tonight . . . yes, sure, if Tommy can meet my flight . . . okay, okay . . . right. See you then."

He disconnected and said, "Your mother drove Chappy back to Middleburg today."

"She did? Why?"

He blew out a long breath. "God only knows. Now she's in a real state, worried sick about him. Afraid he's going to do something crazy like wander off or harm himself." He shook his head again. "She asked me to come home. I'm sorry, kitten. You can stay on if you want, but I've switched my ticket for the evening flight."

"I want to see him," I said. "I'll go with you."

"Are you sure?"

"I can talk to him, Harry. Mom . . . she gets so worked up around Chap sometimes. They're probably driving each other nuts. He needs someone in his corner."

Harry's eyes held mine, but I thought I saw a flicker of relief in his. "All right, I'll have the concierge change your ticket, too. You'd better get packing. We need to leave in half an hour. I've already asked James to call a car and take care of the bill." He paused and stared at me. "Are you all right, sweetheart? You look kind of . . . I don't know . . . not yourself."

"I'm fine. You just caught me off guard, is all."

I don't remember packing my bag, or much of anything, really, from that last rushed half hour at the Connaught. James brought tea for me, which I barely touched, and a Scotch for Harry, which he knocked back like it was water. When James came to take our tray, he gave me a sober look and said he was sorry to see us go and that we'd been a pleasure to have as guests. I told him the feeling was mutual.

Harry and I took the elevator down to the lobby for the last time, the little fire crackling in the fireplace, a faint fragrance from the masses of peonies in the vase next to the grand staircase scenting the air. We said our goodbyes and thank-yous to the staff as guests strolled past us into the Coburg Bar for evening cocktails.

Outside, the Bentley was waiting. I thought I recognized the driver who had taken Nick to Heathrow only this morning, though just now it seemed like days had passed since he'd left.

As the big car pulled out of Carlos Place, I looked out the window one final time for someone watching me, waiting for me. But the plaza was quiet and empty, except for the Connaught's two doormen in their camel coats and top hats. Even the fountain was still, no dreamy mist rising into the air like a genie escaping from a bottle and curling around us. As we drove through Mayfair, I leaned my head back against the seat and closed my eyes. Next to me, I heard the *rat-a-tat* of Harry drumming his fingers on his knees, a restless habit when he's thinking something through.

I reached over and squeezed one of his hands and he squeezed mine back.

"You okay?" I asked.

"I'm fine. Did you have a good time, kitten?"

I wasn't ready to tell him about Alastair and what had happened today. He had enough on his plate worrying about my mother and Chappy. Besides, I knew he was asking about my night with Nick.

"I did. You didn't have to stay in Lingfield so Nick and I could have the suite, Harry. And thanks for everything you did. I'm sure James told you I was completely bowled over."

Harry smiled. "I'm glad. How's Nick doing, by the way?"

"Fine. Coming home soon."

He kissed my hair. "That's good, honey," he said, and then he was silent for the rest of the trip.

It seemed like no time at all before our driver put on his turn signal for the airport exit off the motorway as a jet glided above us, preparing to touch down on the runway up ahead. "We'll be arriving shortly, Mr. Wyatt," he said over his shoulder. "And I've just confirmed that your flight is on time."

It all went so smoothly after that, the porter taking our bags, Harry and me breezing through security, and then cocooned in the first-class lounge with another Scotch for him and a glass of wine for me until our flight was called. Seats in first class again and then we took off over the English countryside, the scattered lights of towns and villages winking like faraway stars in the darkness, before the plane turned north to the Atlantic Ocean.

I had two glasses of champagne and more wine with dinner. Harry didn't say anything, but he watched as the stewardess refilled my glass, and I felt his little prickle of curiosity since it was more than he usually saw me drink. The alcohol did its job, and dulled my sharp-edged nerves, so when I finally slept it was heavy and dreamless. Leaving London like this—vanishing into the night as though we were stealing away—had given me a hell of a head start on the guy who came after me today, but it wasn't a get-out-of-jail-free card.

Kevin had made a recent trip to London with Victor, and a week later, he was dead. Had his killer followed him home from London? Or did whoever murdered him in Washington have an accomplice in England? Either way, that person had now found me, and I didn't think it would take long before someone started looking for me at home.

And that worried me.

There is no direct evening flight from London to Washington these days, so we landed at Kennedy, cleared customs in New York, and caught a connecting flight to Washington that departed at midnight. By the time we arrived at Dulles, it was after one in the morning, though we were still on British time so it was just after six a.m. for Harry and me. Tommy was waiting as we came through the security door, the hollows of his eyes dark smudges in the washed-out shadows of the quiet terminal. He stifled a yawn and came toward us, smiling and throwing an arm around Harry's shoulder, planting a kiss on my cheek.

"How's your mother?" Harry said as Tommy pulled our bags off the luggage carousel and set them on a cart.

"Like you'd expect. If she could lock Chap in his room, she'd do it. After she removed all the sharp objects first."

"Is he that bad?" I asked. "Would he really harm himself?"

"I don't know. He seemed pretty lucid to me, like his old self. If he's going to harm anyone, it's Mom. He's ready to kill her." He caught our alarmed expressions and said, "Sorry, bad choice of words. But she is driving him nuts."

"I'll handle her," Harry said.

"You can wait until morning," Tommy said. "When I left they were both dead to the world. I think the drive home from Connecticut wore Mom out and Chappy looked exhausted, though he still wanted me to go for a walk with him after dinner so he could take some photos of the Blue Ridge at sunset."

I dozed off in the backseat on the drive to Middleburg, catching murmured drifts of Harry and Tommy's animated conversation about the Sweet 16, the Final Four, and someone's basketball brackets being all shot to hell.

I woke when Tommy slowed down for the turn to the private road that led to Mayfield, the house that had been in the Wyatt family since colonial times. The tires crunched on the gravel drive as Tommy pulled up to the brick walkway in front of the house.

"You two go on in," he said to Harry and me. "I'll put the car in the garage and bring your bags to your rooms. Anybody want a nightcap?"

"I think I'd better see your mother," Harry said. "If you kids want drinks, go ahead."

"What about it, Soph?" Tommy asked. "Join me for a quick one?"

He was tired, but it seemed as if he was pushing for a reason. Something he wanted to tell me that couldn't wait.

"Sure. I guess I'm wide awake again."

He drove off and I followed Harry up the terraced steps of the front walk. The lighted windows of my parents' bedroom on the second floor glowed pale gold against the moonless blue-black sky, and someone had left a light on in the front hall so the leaded sidelights and fanlight surrounding the front door looked like Gothic tracery. When Harry pushed open the door, Ella, our old black Lab, was waiting, her tail thumping as we scratched her head and Harry crooned in a soft voice that he had missed his good girl.

The house smelled of the lavender potpourri my mother used everywhere and the warm, sweet smell of baking, cinnamon and apples, no doubt Harry's favorite apple pie made with apples from our orchard. A vase of yellow daffodils, probably already cut from the garden, sat on the antique oak sideboard in the hall.

"See you in the morning, kitten," Harry said, kissing my hair. "You two get some sleep. I love you."

"I love you, too. I'll wait for Tommy in the kitchen."

He came in through the back door a moment later, maneuvering our suitcases inside. "I'll get these upstairs first," he said. "Pop probably needs his bag. What do you want to drink?"

"I'll have wine. What about you?"

"There's a bottle of Courvoisier on the bar in the library."

"I'll get the drinks. Meet me in the library."

There was an open bottle of red on the dining room sideboard, so I poured a glass and walked across the hall to the library as the silvery chime of the living room mantel clock rang. Two thirty. I switched on the table lamps on either side of the navy leather sofa to their dimmest setting so they gave off only small pools of light. A bowl of pink tulips on the coffee table, that I figured were more flowers from the garden, glowed in the otherwise shadow-filled room. The lingering scent of winter woodsmoke from the stone fireplace mixed with the musty old-leather tang of Harry's vast collection of books lining the bookshelves he'd built himself were comforting remembered smells of childhood and home.

Tommy found me curled up on the sofa, my shoes kicked off and my feet tucked under me. He sat down and leaned over to clink his cognac snifter against my wineglass.

"What's going on?" I said. "Now that it's just us."

My brother swirled his drink, watching the dark amber liquid coat the sides of the glass like it was something that fascinated him. He was stalling.

"Mom told Chap tonight that she wants him to make her his guardian. That's why she came back here, to start the process." He looked up at me. "She doesn't want to deal with the courts in Connecticut because she says it'll take forever. She's planning to legally move him here so he'd be a resident of Virginia and sell his house up there so she can use that money to pay for him to be in assisted living."

I wanted to stamp my foot, hurl my glass against the stone fireplace. "That is heartless."

"I didn't say she was happy about it."

"I don't care. Jeez, Tommy. It'll kill him to leave his home, his studio. He's been there for more than forty years. What about Chappy? What does he want?"

Tommy shifted so he sat facing me. "What do you think? They had a huge blowup, both of them shouting at each other. It was pretty bad, Soph. That's why Mom wanted Pop to come home. She wants him to back her on this."

"I hope he doesn't," I said. "What about you? Whose side are you on?"

"Whoa . . . whoa, hold on there." He held up a hand. "I'm not on anyone's side, okay? I want what's best for Chap."

"Which is?"

"I don't know."

"It can't be stripping him of his life, his home, and his dignity," I said in a flat voice.

My brother's face flushed in the lamplight, but his mouth hardened into a thin, determined line. "Look, we have to find out if anything's wrong with him, first of all. Known fact: He was wandering around Topstone Park confused and in his pajamas. There isn't a doctor on the planet who would overlook something like that without trying to figure out what's going on. If Chap's sick . . ."

"Are we still talking about Alzheimer's? Has it even been determined that's what he has?"

"Mom wants him to see a different doctor," he said, still in that stubborn voice. "Someone from around here. Come on, Soph. She's just getting a second opinion. I think it's a good idea."

"Oh, for God's sake." My voice rose. "You mean a doctor who'll back her up?"

"Not so loud. You're not being fair and you're going to wake everyone."

I threw down the last of my wine and banged my glass on the coffee table. "I don't think—"

"Look," he cut me off. "You know better than anyone else in the family that Chap has a collection of photographs, a body of work, in that Connecticut house that museums and libraries would kill for. Mom says he hasn't done any planning or thinking about what he wants to do about it, and she's worried he's already been giving away some of his photos to anyone who asks him. She thinks—with his memory lapses—that he's being taken advantage of, and she wants his legacy preserved."

"I thought you said he seemed fine when you saw him today. Now you're talking like he's one step away from being bundled off to the loony bin."

"No, I didn't—"

"Let Chap worry about his legacy. It is *his* legacy, after all, isn't it?"

"Of course it is, but I can see Mom's point. She's already found some of his stuff for sale on the Internet, other people profiting off his work. He could make a small fortune if he decided to sell his entire collection."

"So this is about money," I said. "I should have guessed."

"Come on, that's not fair. It's about him."

"Then why doesn't he get a vote?"

There was a complicated, unhappy silence as my brother finished his cognac. Finally he said, "I didn't mean to get you torqued up, but I figured you should know what's going on before it all hits the fan tomorrow . . . or today, since it is tomorrow." He reached for my wrist and squeezed it. "Calm down, okay? It's late. Try to get some sleep. We're not going to solve anything tonight."

I nodded. "I know. And I didn't mean to snap at you. You know I love you."

"Yeah, I love you, too." He stood and picked up my glass. "I'll take care of these. Chappy's sleeping in Lexie's room, by the way. Not the guest room. Mom said it was closer to her room. See you in the morning."

The guest room was on the third floor, across the hall from my old bedroom. I kissed Tommy good night and climbed the stairs, avoiding the two creaky treads the way I'd done when I used to sneak in after my curfew. I paused at the door to Lexie's room and listened. From the other side I heard the faint regular sound of my grandfather's light snoring.

I almost didn't recognize my bedroom. My mother had redecorated since the last time I'd been home, this time in sophisticated shades of moss green and royal purple. My suitcase sat on a tufted mauve-and-lilac ottoman next to the fireplace where Tommy had put it. I found my nightclothes and toothbrush—it seemed like a century had passed since I'd packed them in such haste at the Connaught—and washed my face and brushed my teeth in the bathroom across the hall.

When I finally lay down in my old four-poster bed, sleep wouldn't come. The time zone change, the booze, that last conversation with Tommy. I tossed and turned for hours until finally I threw back the covers and went to the bathroom for a glass of water because my mouth tasted like I'd been chewing nails.

The floorboards creaked on the floor below as I stepped back into the hall. Someone else was awake, probably Tommy or Chappy using the bathroom. Or maybe Harry let Ella out of their bedroom because she was restless. I paused midstep and waited for a door to click shut. Instead I heard footsteps on the stairs. Not Ella, who'd step on the squeaky treads. Everyone else knew how to avoid them.

I returned to my room and checked the clock on my bedside table. Already six a.m. My bedroom was at the back of the house above the kitchen. The windows faced south and west, the south windows overlooking my mother's rose garden and the west windows looking out on the patio and swimming pool and, in the distance, a long expanse of woods and fields that ended at the Blue Ridge Mountains.

My throat tightened and I ran to the windows. I didn't see

anything at first because he kept to the shadows, but I finally caught a flash of snow-white hair as he walked onto the open lawn by the pool. For someone in his mideighties, my grandfather moved with spry agility. He opened the back gate, slipped through, and closed it again.

Then I lost him.

My clothes were in a heap on the chair next to the ottoman. I pulled them on as fast as I could and took the back staircase down to the kitchen, grabbing Tommy's old football letter jacket off a hook in the back hall as I let myself out the kitchen door.

Chappy had a good head start on me, and there were any number of places he could have gone.

If he had a destination in mind.

If he didn't, or maybe he was disoriented and thought he was still home in Connecticut, he could be anywhere. I took off running.

19

Mayfield is just over four hundred acres—four hundred and fifteen, to be precise—on a parcel of land given to one of Harry's ancestors by Lord Fairfax, which in turn was part of the original five million acres he received from his mother in 1719 when Virginia was still a colony. Over the centuries, generations of Wyatts have added on to the original farmhouse and built numerous outbuildings—barns, stables, a springhouse, a guest-house, even slave quarters—most of which are now in pictur-esque stages of ruin.

If I had to guess, I'd figure Chappy had headed for the old stone barn. The structure itself was long gone, but the founda-tion still sat on a rise of land overlooking the Blue Ridge Moun-tains, just off the gravel road between the house and the new stables. Years ago my mother had turned the floor into a patio, using the stones from the barn itself for the surrounding wall and persuaded Harry to buy the statuary of a falling-down villa she'd seen in Tuscany to grace the flower gardens she planted around the patio.

He was there, just as I suspected, sitting on the wall with his back to me where he could stare out at the mountains. In the east, the sky looked like someone had lifted the edge of a curtain, letting in a sliver of pale yellow light that had begun to dissolve the monochrome shadows into hard-edged objects. If Chappy heard me come up behind him, he didn't let on. I climbed onto the wall, swung my feet over, and sat down next to him.

The cold stone penetrated my jeans, and my sneakers were soaked from running through the wet morning grass. I snapped Tommy's jacket closed and pulled the cuffs of his sleeves down over my hands.

My grandfather was bundled up in a heavy jacket, wearing work boots and a pair of fingerless gloves. He turned to me and said as though we were continuing an unfinished conversation, "Where's your camera?"

I gave him a sheepish look and covered my mouth with Tommy's sleeve to hide a yawn. His camera was cradled in his lap. "Back at the house."

"A lot of good it's going to do you there."

"Chappy, what were you doing sneaking out of the house just now?"

With a perfect deadpan expression, he said, "I never sneak. And I didn't want to wake anybody."

"You could have left a note. I just happened to hear you when I got up for a glass of water. What are you doing here?"

"What does it look like? Waiting for the sunrise. The last time I was here I got some incredible shots of the mist shrouding those woods and the mountains. There's enough moisture in the air so the conditions ought to be right this morning . . . you can already see the fog in the trees across the meadow. If the clouds clear out or even open up a little, the light could be just about perfect."

A lot of people think professional photographers—especially the legendary ones like my grandfather—have some kind of sixth sense, knowing exactly where and when to be to make the amazing shots they get. That's crazy. What we have is passion, commitment, and the dogged determination to just keep showing up and taking pictures. There is no magic fairy dust, no special insight, just a lot of planning, perseverance, and trial and error.

That's why Chappy was here right now.

"You've got time to go back and get your camera, you know," he said. "According to the almanac, the official time for sunrise today is six fifty-seven."

For a moment I was tempted to run back to the house and do just that—I didn't even have my phone with me—and it would be like so many times over the years when I'd gone shooting with Chap, and he'd explain why he was doing something a certain way, teach me, educate me.

But his white hair was sticking up in wild tufts, and something in his pale blue eyes, the way they darted back and forth as though he were a little anxious, made me decide it was better to stay with him.

I leaned my head on his shoulder. Even through the fabric of his jacket, I could feel the sharp contours of his bones. "It's okay. I'll just watch the master at work. I was worried about you. That's why I left the house without it."

It was the wrong thing to say. He jerked away and turned to me.

"Are you checking up on me? Is that why you're here? You've been talking to your mother, haven't you? Damn it, Sophie, don't tell me she's brainwashed you, too."

Chappy had a temper, which he usually kept in check. But when someone said or did something stupid or mean-spirited, it flashed quick as a whip and then it was gone. He was angry now, but the level of anger seemed unwarranted and uncharacteristic.

I said in a mild voice, "I haven't been talking to Mom. At least, not yet. Tommy filled me in on what's been going on. I know you two had an argument last night. I'm on your side, Chappy. How could you ever think I wouldn't be?"

"Caroline's convinced I'm losing my mind," he said in that same harsh voice. "We all get forgetful as we get older. It's called aging. It'll happen to you, too, someday. Wait and see."

In the soft, gray predawn light, his jaw was set and his profile could have been carved out of the same cool stone as one of the garden statues. Though he looked more fragile than the last time I'd seen him, my grandfather's mind seemed as sharp and focused as ever. At eighty-five, he woke before anyone else in the house, studying the weather and checking the time of the sunrise to do what he'd done all his life. Show up for a photo he wanted to get. But there was something else, something that was different about him.

"I know, Chap, I know," I said, rubbing his jacket sleeve. "Tommy told me Mom's worried because you've been giving away some of your old photographs recently. She thinks you should keep your work intact and sell it to a library or a museum."

He looked perplexed. "What are you talking about? What photographs?"

"I'm not sure which ones. Photos you've taken over the years, I guess. She says she's seen them for sale on the Internet."

He shook his head. "I'm sorry. I have no idea what you're talking about."

For a moment I wondered whether he'd blanked out about our conversation or whether he meant he didn't know which pictures I was referring to.

"It's okay," I said. "We can discuss it another time."

"Discuss what?"

"Nothing. Look, it's starting to get lighter in the east. Do you want to take your sunrise pictures?"

"I don't think so," he said in the stiff, formal voice of a stranger. "It's rather chilly and we ought to be getting back to the house, don't you think? Gina will be waiting. I wouldn't like to worry her."

Gina Lord was my grandmother. She died in a car accident

when I was ten, nearly thirty years ago. I fingered my wedding ring. It had been hers.

"You mean Caroline, don't you? Your daughter?"

He turned to look at me with eyes that were now flat and dull. "No, I mean Gina."

"Chappy," I said in a gentle voice, "I'm not sure she'll be there. I think she had to leave."

"Where did she go?"

"I . . . I don't know. Let's get you back to the house, okay?"

Tommy found us when we were halfway up the road to the house, my arm around Chappy's shoulders, guiding him and listening to him talk about my grandmother as though he'd gotten out of a warm bed next to her only an hour ago.

My brother ran toward us, panting and out of breath. "Where the hell have you two—"

I shook my head. "Not now. He wants to get back to the house to see Nonna."

"Who—?" He gave me a puzzled look. "Are you kidding me? Nonna Gina? Oh, jeez. What'd you tell him?"

"That she probably wouldn't be there."

He said in my ear, "Mom's on the warpath. She wanted to call the police when she realized he was gone. Pop thought he might have gone to the stables, so he went there."

"Call or text them so they know he's okay."

"Is he?"

I met Tommy's eyes. "I don't think so."

By the time we got home, the entire house was lit up like Christmas. Through the kitchen window I could see my mother, distraught, as she paced back and forth, a phone clamped to her ear. When she caught sight of us, she whirled around and flew outside across the lawn. I looked down and saw she was barefoot.

"*Dad*. Thank God you're all right." She took my place, slipping her arm around my grandfather's shoulders. Under her breath she said to Tommy and me, "We need to get him inside before he catches his death out here."

"He's fine, Mom," I said. "Nothing happened. It's okay."

My mother shot me a reproachful look and I could almost hear her saying, *I'll deal with you later, young lady. This is all your fault.* She turned back to Chappy.

"What were you thinking? You scared the life out of us running off like that. Everyone's been worried sick about you." I could hear the dizzy relief in her voice even though she scolded him like a truant child. She looked over at Tommy and me and added, "What did I tell you? I can't trust him anymore."

She was dressed in ripped, faded jeans and one of Harry's old flannel shirts over a white T-shirt, her long blond hair loose around her shoulders, no makeup. I couldn't remember the last time I'd seen her disheveled like this—my mother always looks like she's ready for a fashion shoot even if she's weeding the garden—and in the flat early-morning light, she looked weary and worn out.

"He went to the old stables to take pictures of the Blue Ridge at sunrise," I said. "Like he did the last time he was here . . . then he got a little confused."

"The last time he was here . . . oh, my *God*!"

We were back inside the house now, Harry bursting into the kitchen after coming through the front door with Ella on his heels, meeting my mother's eyes before sweeping his gaze over Tommy and me. I'd just poured Chap a glass of orange juice and Tommy was sitting next to him at the old kitchen table, urging him to drink it. Ella padded over and planted herself in front of Chappy, who stroked her head.

"Caroline—?" Harry said.

"I'm taking him to the doctor this morning over at Landsdowne," she said, her voice hard and defensive. "Hopefully they'll admit him to the hospital and run some tests so we'll know for sure. He has a nine o'clock appointment so I need to get him dressed and ready to leave as soon as he has breakfast."

She was talking about Chappy as if he were invisible, or a child who either couldn't hear her or didn't understand what she was saying.

"I'll take you," Harry said. "I don't want you doing this by yourself."

"I'll come, too," I said.

My mother walked over to the kitchen counter and picked up an old copy of *National Geographic*. She passed it to me, her manicured index finger tapping the date and sliding down to the cover story.

"Look at that," she said.

The magazine was from May 1983. More than thirty years ago. *Thomas Jefferson's Beloved Virginia: The Beautiful Blue Ridge Mountains.* The photograph was a breathtaking view of the morning fog in whipped-cream stripes between the forest and the hazy blue mountains, the same view I'd seen at Monticello when Ryan Velis and I had been standing in Jefferson's garden the other day. I opened the magazine to the story and found what I knew I'd find. *Photographs by Charles Lord.*

"That's what he remembered," she said. "Like it's yesterday or a few months ago. He was looking at that magazine last night."

I looked up. "I'm sorry, Mom."

"He doesn't *know* anymore," she said, her voice breaking, and it seemed she was trying not to cry. "I need to take him myself, Sophie. He doesn't need any additional . . . distractions, anything or anyone to confuse him more than he already is."

Meaning me.

"Right," I said. "Sure."

"I've got class at one," Tommy said. "Soph, I can drive you back to D.C. if you want a ride. I'm going home before I head over to campus, so I can drop you off at your place."

Harry shot me a fleeting, pleading look to do this without making a scene, and I said, "Thanks, Tommy. That'd be great."

"I was thinking about leaving after the traffic dies down," he said. "Around ten."

"Dad," my mother said, "how about if I take you upstairs and get you ready?"

Chappy stood up. "Gina, where's Gina?"

There was a poignant silence before my mother said, "I'm afraid she's not here."

"Where did she go?"

My mother met Harry's eyes. Hers were anguished.

"She's . . . visiting some people," Harry said, adding to my mother, "I'll take him, Caroline . . . come on, Chap."

After they left the room, my mother turned to me. "You should have *called*, Sophie. Or at least woken someone up. Instead you let me worry myself to death."

"I forgot my phone, Mom. I'm sorry, I didn't do it on purpose."

"You always have a reason—"

"He got up early to take pictures of the sunrise," I said. "To be there for the golden hour, the first hour of light at sunrise and the last hour before sunset. He's been doing it all his life."

"I know what the golden hour is. You don't need to lecture me. He shouldn't have been out there by himself after what happened the other day in Connecticut—and God knows how many other times. I can't watch him every minute of the night and day."

"As far as we know, it's only two times. Today and last week. You can't chain him to his bed. It'll kill him."

"Don't you dare start—"

"Mom," Tommy said, "calm down. *Soph.*"

I took a deep breath and said to my mother, "I know you're under a lot of stress. But nothing happened this morning and he's okay."

"*This time*. What about the next time, or the time after that? And where will you be?" She glared at my brother and me. "If you two want breakfast, help yourselves. I need to get changed. We have to leave in twenty minutes if we're going to get to Landsdowne in time."

After she was gone, Tommy walked over to the coffeepot and filled two mugs, adding milk and sugar. He passed one to me.

"Well," he said in a laconic voice, "just another day in paradise. You want breakfast?"

"Not really. I think I've lost my appetite."

Harry found me alone in the kitchen fifteen minutes later sitting at the table with a cup of cold coffee. "We're on our way," he said. "Just wanted to let you know and say goodbye . . . make sure you're all right."

"You mean, after Mom and I went a couple of rounds over Chappy, did anyone draw blood?"

He grinned. "I wasn't going to put it quite like that."

"I'm fine. And thanks again for London."

"Sorry we had to cut it short."

"This is more important."

He gave me a rueful look. "Look, you know your mother doesn't mean half the things she says just now. She hasn't slept in days so she's snapping at everyone. Let her be, she'll calm down once we get Chap checked out and figure out what to do next."

"Sure."

"She loves you, kitten. You know she does." He walked over and pulled me to him, kissing my hair.

I slid my arms around his waist. "Will you call me after you get back from the doctor?"

"Of course. Wish us luck."

Nick phoned after everyone left. I had e-mailed him from Heathrow, telling him about Chappy and that I no longer needed the services of his bodyguard friends in London.

"My other friend already had a job, but he was making some

calls. Then I got your e-mail so I told him to forget it," he said. "I guess it worked out for the best. I'm glad you're okay and safe at home."

Telling him about someone pretending to be Victor's secretary and then chasing me across the Millennium Bridge fell into the category of things too disturbing to talk about over the phone and better saved for a face-to-face conversation.

"Me, too."

"Looks like I might be able to come home at the end of next week," he said. "I'm wrapping things up here in a couple of days, and then I've got one more stop."

"Next week? That would be fantastic. Where's your last stop?"

"Atyrau, Kazakhstan."

One of the oil-rich cities of the world, a former Russian republic on the Caspian Sea. "Just don't make any side trips across the border into Russia."

"Don't worry. I have no desire to be thrown out of the country again."

"You probably wouldn't be," I said. "I'd have to come get you out of jail."

He laughed and hung up.

Tommy and I left for Washington shortly after that. I played fetch with Ella one last time while he packed up his books and laptop, and then I fell asleep on the drive home.

I woke up when he shook my arm. "Okay, sleepyhead, home, sweet home. I'll carry your suitcase upstairs, but I'm not carrying you, too."

I sat up and rubbed my eyes. "I'm sorry. You should have poked me or something."

"I could have pushed the eject button and you wouldn't have woken up. You were out cold." He pulled into the alley next to my house and we both got out of the car.

In the few days since I'd been away, the bare-branched dogwood in the front yard was now covered with blossoms on the verge of opening and the air felt soft and fresh scented. I shrugged out of my coat. It had warmed up since this morning when Chappy and I had been out at sunrise.

"You don't need to carry my suitcase," I said to Tommy. "I can manage."

But he was already halfway up the front walk. "What have you got in here? Bricks? It wasn't this heavy last night."

I had taken Olivia Upshaw's thick manuscript out of my carry-on and put it in the suitcase. "A dead body."

The mail was still in the mailbox, since I'd forgotten to stop it. I scooped it up, unlocked the door, and headed up the stairs with Tommy following me. Even before I stepped into the foyer I knew someone had been here.

Whoever had searched my apartment knew they had time, and had been methodical. Every drawer had been opened, every cushion overturned, the books on the bookshelf in the living room were strewn all over the floor. I stared at the mess and remembered Kevin's books splayed out just like this on the floor of his study room at the Library of Congress.

Tommy was two steps behind me. "What the hell—?" He set down my suitcase and said in a tense voice, "You'd better check your camera equipment and Nick's guns. That's probably what they went after."

I blinked. He thought it was a random burglary, plain and simple. I thought it was related to Kevin and the book.

"Everything's locked in the closet in the second bedroom, the one we use as a study," I said, but I ran for the stairs.

"Wait." My brother grabbed my arm. "Maybe we'd better call the police before you go up there. And it looks like they jimmied the worthless lock on your balcony door. Which, by the way, is something I could have done if I stuck my credit card or my license between the door and the jamb and worked at it for a few minutes. I thought you were going to get that replaced."

"I meant to talk to India about it, and whoever did this is

long gone," I said. "India's visiting her daughter in Chicago, I was in England, and Max isn't here that much anymore. Someone had all the time in the world to go through the place."

The lock on the bedroom closet door had been cut and so had the locks on the cases where I kept my camera equipment. They hadn't managed to figure out the combination to the gun safe, thank God. I knelt down and opened my equipment cases.

Everything was there.

I sat back on my heels. The only other item of value in this apartment was the receipt Asquith's had given me when I turned over Kevin's book to Bram. I had left Max's plum-colored file in the top drawer of the desk. I spun around and opened the drawer.

Gone.

Also gone was the photocopy of the Fairbairn letter and the photos of the hand-colored botanical prints we'd found in *Adam in Eden* that I had downloaded off my camera and printed out. I had another copy of the letter, the one I'd brought to London, and the photos were on an Internet server, so I still had copies of everything.

But now so did someone else.

"You look like you've seen a ghost, Soph," Tommy said.

"The paperwork for a rare and quite valuable book that belonged to Kevin Boyle is gone. The book itself is at Asquith's Auction House in Georgetown."

"At least they didn't get the book," he said. "And you ought to call the police."

"First I need to call Bram Asquith." But he wasn't in, so I left a message that it was urgent he return my call as soon as possible.

Tommy left when the MPD officer arrived since there was nothing more he could do and he had class. He told me he'd call later to find out how I was doing, and I made him swear he wouldn't tell Mom or Harry what happened.

The officer, a middle-aged Hispanic man, took my statement, including everything I'd learned in London about the value of the copy of *Adam in Eden*, the death of Alastair Innes, which I felt certain was related to Kevin's death, and being chased yesterday afternoon across the Millennium Bridge. He wrote it all down and said he'd be in touch with Officer Carroll, whom I'd never managed to call from London. He also said someone would be stopping by Asquith's.

Finally, he said, "Do you have any idea who might have done this?"

I hesitated. "I don't know, but I can tell you this. Edward Jaine told me yesterday when I met him in London that I'd regret it if I didn't give him those papers, the ones that were stolen. I left town on Saturday evening, so whoever did this was here between Saturday night and this morning. I don't think Mr. Jaine has figured out how to be in two places at once, but he does have a lot of people who work for him in a big office building downtown on Farragut Square."

"Edward Jaine the rich guy? Computers, Internet stuff? That guy?"

I nodded, and he scratched the back of his head with his pen. "Well, this ought to be interesting. I think we're done for now, but I might have more questions for you."

After he left and while I was waiting for a usurious locksmith from Adams Morgan who agreed to make an emergency house call, I called Jack. He, too, was out, and I left a message.

I was reshelving books and cleaning up the mess the intruder had made when Jack phoned.

"Am I calling England?" he asked. "Are you still in London?"

"Not since last night." I told him about Chappy and returning to my apartment to discover the burglary.

"Thank God you weren't home when it happened," he said. "Especially since you're there all by yourself."

"If I had been here, they wouldn't have gotten those papers, I'll tell you that," I said with feeling. "I know the combination to Nick's gun safe."

"Whoa, there, Calamity Jane. Let's not even go down that road."

"I think whoever broke in was looking for Kevin's book. They didn't find it so they took the paperwork from Asquith's instead. I'll bet Edward Jaine had something to do with it."

"Your favorite person."

"I had coffee, or watched him drink coffee, yesterday in London. He threatened me if I didn't turn the book over to him," I said, and told Jack what I'd learned about its value. When I was done, I said, "I think it's time I talk to Father Xavier about this. He needs to know what's going on."

"I'll call Xavier," he said. "I'd like to go with you when you tell him. And, by the way, both guest rooms at the house are free. Might be a good idea for you to spend the night somewhere else since you seem to be attracting unsavory company lately. I'll even cook you dinner."

"The house" was Gloria House, the Jesuit house of formation on Capitol Hill where Jack lived with several priests who taught at Georgetown Law School and about a dozen seminarians. I'd stayed there briefly after I moved back from London last summer.

"Thank you," I said, "I accept."

"Great. I'll phone Xavier and call you right back."

But when my phone rang five minutes later, it wasn't Jack. It was Bram Asquith and he sounded distraught.

"I don't know how to tell you this," he said, "but a woman came in here this morning with the original paperwork we prepared for you when we picked up the book from Max's gallery. Somehow she managed to convince one of our employees that you wanted your book returned and, of course, I hadn't said a word to a living soul here about how I came into possession of it. I'm so sorry, Sophie. The police are on their way and we have security cameras. We'll find who did this, and I promise you, we'll prosecute to the maximum extent possible."

It took me a moment to realize what he meant. "The book is gone? Someone just walked out with it?"

"I'm afraid so. My God, this sort of thing just doesn't happen to us. It was a complete, utter cock-up. I can't begin to tell you how sorry I am. We'll get it back."

I felt numb. Part of this was my fault. I should have put the papers in a secure location instead of leaving them in my desk. Maybe given them to Max to keep in his vault before I left for London.

"I . . . sure. You'll let me know if there's any news, won't you?"

"Of course. Sorry, I'd better go . . . there's a detective waiting outside to talk to me." He still sounded stricken. "If word of this gets out . . . good Lord. I'll be in touch as soon as I know anything."

Jack called after that. "Your line was busy. Xavier's invited us for drinks at the monastery at five o'clock."

"Did you tell him what this was about?" I asked.

"I gave him a hint," he said, adding in a grim voice, "He can't wait to see us. Hey, are you okay? You sound, I don't know . . . sort of strangled."

"Bram Asquith called. I'm afraid we have a little problem."

20

The public tributes to Kevin were still piled at the outside gate to the monastery when Jack and I pulled into the parking lot across the street shortly before five. Someone had culled the dead and badly wilted flowers—I remembered heaps of bouquets from the news stories—and what remained were mostly candles, plants, and letters to Kevin or photos of him sealed in plastic sleeves. Jack went down on one knee and blessed himself while I read some of the notes, many from the children of Brookland Elementary School who worked with him in the community garden.

When Jack stood up, he said, "I still can't believe it."

"I know." I blinked hard and righted a candle that had fallen over. "I'm dreading this, telling Xavier what happened."

Jack put his arm around my shoulder, and we walked through the Rosary Portico along the colonnade to the rear of the monastery and the friars' residence. Just before the entrance to the monastery was a small herb garden, two plots on either side of the walk with white marble markers for culinary, household, medicinal, and biblical herbs. In the medicinal garden I saw what I was looking for: a small plant marker for *Hyssopus officinalis*.

"It'll be okay," Jack was saying. "Don't worry."

I took a deep breath, and we went inside the friary. Jack gave our names to a security guard who made a phone call. "Father will be with you in a moment. Please have a seat."

Xavier entered the lobby five minutes later, dressed in baggy corduroys, a pale blue dress shirt with the sleeves rolled up, and sandals. Though his smile was pleasant as we followed him down a corridor to an elevator, something in his demeanor made me think we had interrupted something that still preoccupied him.

We took the elevator upstairs to the private living quarters and walked down another quiet corridor, this one with doors on either side, until we reached a staircase.

"I thought we'd have drinks downstairs in the loggia off the chapel. We'll have it to ourselves," he said.

The loggia was long and narrow and smelled of incense and history. Its plaster walls were painted a soft, translucent gold that glowed in the late-afternoon sunshine, and faded Oriental carpets covered a terra-cotta floor. A primitive fresco of St. Francis of Assisi smiling down on a group of birds and animals in the middle of a forest filled an alcove at the far end of the room. The other long wall was a series of sliding glass doors that looked out on a high-walled Zen-like garden of flowering trees, azaleas, and rhododendron surrounding a man-made pond with a rock waterfall.

Father Xavier led us to a group of comfortable chairs pulled around a stone coffee table. "What can I get you to drink? We've got everything."

The bar was a closet in an adjacent room with well-stocked shelves, a small sink, and a mini-refrigerator. The two priests had Scotches; I had a glass of Chardonnay. As we sat down, the music of a Gregorian chant, a woman's haunting voice accompanied by a piano and violins mingled with a men's choir, filtered into the room from somewhere in another part of the friary. Kyrie eleison.

Lord, have mercy.

Jack stretched out his legs in front of him and crossed his ankles. "I think I'd spend my holy hour in this room every day if I lived here."

Xavier smiled. "It's a good place to meditate and pray."

We drank for a moment in silence, listening to the ancient music as the sunlight faded outside. Finally Xavier stirred and said, "So, my dear, Jack said you have something you wish to discuss concerning a book that might have belonged to Kevin."

He listened without interrupting. Jack sat with his drink clasped in both hands in his lap and also kept silent. I finished by telling Xavier about Bram's phone call to report that someone had impersonated a courier sent by me and the book was now gone.

"Bram Asquith seems quite sure they'll get it back," I said. "The police are involved."

"I see."

"I don't believe Kevin's death was an accident, Father. I think it had something to do with that book. Otherwise, why would someone ransack his study room at the Library of Congress and break into my apartment to steal the documents from Asquith's? I also believe that Alastair Innes's death wasn't an accident, either, and that it's related to what happened to Kevin."

"Also because of this book?"

"Yes. And possibly some missing seeds." I explained what Ryan Velis had told me at Monticello and the book's connection to the seeds that had vanished from the White House.

"Francis tells us that when we leave this earth, we can take nothing with us that we have received, only what we have given. That book, as valuable as it is in monetary terms, is not worth the lives of two good people," he said. "Nothing is as precious as human life. I will wait to hear from Mr. Asquith and Mr. Jaine, and then we will see what happens."

The sunlight had shifted so it backlit Xavier, his white hair shimmering like a heavenly apparition in this beautiful room. With perfect timing the music changed and a man's voice chanted the beginning of the Gradual and Alleluia.

Sit at my right hand until I make your enemies your footstool.

Who was Kevin's enemy? Edward Jaine? A colleague? Someone he'd believed was a friend?

As if he read my mind, Xavier said, "The police have concluded Kevin's death was an accident based on the medical examiner's report. Perhaps I need to make a phone call in light of what you've just told me."

I nodded. "May I ask a favor, Father?"

"You may."

"I would like to take a look at Kevin's papers from his study room in the Adams Building at the Library of Congress."

"They're here," Xavier said. "One of our seminarians collected them a couple of days ago. They're in a box in one of the unoccupied bedrooms upstairs. What is it you're looking for?"

"I believe Kevin had either figured out what happened to the seeds that went missing from the White House, or he was on the verge of figuring it out. Maybe there's something in his notes that might make more sense to me after everything that's happened."

He reached into his pocket and pulled out a key on a Miraculous Medal key ring, which he held out to me. "The third room on the left. This key will unlock the door. I only ask that you not remove anything, but you may look through what's there. Would fifteen minutes be enough time?"

I didn't want to push my luck. "It would be fine."

"There's something I'd like to discuss privately with Jack, so I'll leave you to it." He glanced at his watch. "We'll stop by for you at quarter to six, all right?"

I stood up. "Thank you. See you in fifteen minutes."

The empty bedroom was small and spartan. Other than a few pieces of furniture, only a wooden cross over the bed and a framed print of St. Francis, a flat two-dimensional portrait that reminded me of a Russian icon, made the room seem less sterile. Kevin's box of books and papers sat on the desk.

I removed the contents and set everything on a small dresser. Whatever I was looking for probably was among the papers rather than in a book. When I was done separating the books from the documents, I had a stack of papers about six inches high. Kevin was methodical, a scientist and a researcher, so in theory everything should have been organized by subject. But the documents had been scattered by whoever broke into his study room, and the person who packed them up—I figured it was the seminarian who'd been sent to the library—threw everything in the box like he'd been told the place was on fire.

Kevin's notes were slotted between photocopied documents, so I pulled them out first. At least they were dated. It looked like he'd been spending the final days before he died researching Francis Pembroke, the Leesburg doctor who was Meriwether Lewis's cousin and the recipient of the letter from John Fairbairn. One of the last dated pages I found was Kevin's hand-drawn reconstruction of the Pembroke family tree, which took up an entire sheet of legal paper and included relatives who apparently were still alive. I pulled out my phone and snapped a photo. There was a red circle around one of the names, Francis P. Quincy, presumably Francis Pembroke Quincy, who was the original Pembroke's grandson and had passed away in 1925. In the margin of the page Kevin had used the same red marker to write the initials *FPQ* and connect them with an arrow to another name: Charles Moore-McMillan. Three exclamation marks.

I had three minutes left. Charles Moore-McMillan. The name rang a bell. I flipped through more documents, and then I found something. A photocopy of a twenty-year-old newspaper clipping from the *Loudoun Times-Mirror*. The great-granddaughter of Francis Pembroke had donated his effects, including his medical bag and equipment, his books, his papers, and his diaries, to the Loudoun Museum in Leesburg.

Had the seeds ended up in Leesburg along with the Declaration of Independence and the Constitution? Maybe they had come into Francis Pembroke's possession. As Zara Remington had said, by that time Thomas Jefferson was wrapped up in plans for Monticello and designing the University of Virginia, but Pembroke, an herbalist who also was an amateur botanic artist, would have cared about them.

Through the door I could hear Jack and Xavier talking on their way up the stairs. I finished taking pictures and placed everything back in the box, though the top document caught my eye as I was about to close it up again. *The Report of the Senate Park Commission. The Improvement of the Park System of the District of Columbia.* The formal name of the McMillan Commission, which had been instrumental in reviving Pierre L'Enfant's plan for Washington and turning the National Mall into what it was today. I had just read about it in "No Little Plans" in London the day before yesterday. And what I remembered was that Senator McMillan's first name wasn't Charles; it was James. Kevin wasn't referring to a person with a hyphenated surname; Charles Moore had been Senator James McMillan's aide, as well as the secretary to the commission. For some reason Kevin had linked Charles Moore, Senator McMillan, and Francis Pembroke's grandson together and thought it was important enough to warrant three exclamation marks.

The door opened and the two men walked in. I slammed the cover on the box, spun around, and said to Xavier, "All done. Thank you for letting me look through those papers."

"Did you find anything?" he asked, his eyes flicking from me to the box.

"I'm not really sure. I'm still trying to connect the dots."

"Well, if you do connect them, I'd appreciate it if you would pass along what you learn." He gave me a polite smile, but his eyes were bright with interest.

Jack and I said our goodbyes, and on the drive back to Gloria House he grilled me about what I'd found in Kevin's box of documents.

"You want to explain that little tap dance back at the monastery? 'I'm still trying to connect the dots.' What was that all about?"

"What do you mean?"

"I know when you're lying. Your nose starts to grow."

"Very funny."

"So what did you find that you didn't want to share with Xavier?"

"It wasn't that I didn't want to share it with Xavier."

"Lying to a priest could earn you a time-out in that big waiting room in the sky someday. Double points when it's two priests."

I burst out laughing. "Okay. I might have an idea where the seeds are. Or at least I might have figured out where Kevin thought they could be."

Jack gave me a sideways glance. "You're kidding me. Where?"

"The Loudoun Museum."

"The little museum in Leesburg?"

I told him about the newspaper article and Francis Pembroke's great-granddaughter's donation. "Don't you think it makes sense? Maybe the seeds were in packets in his medical bag," I said. "I'll call the museum tomorrow. They're only open for a few hours on Friday, Saturday, and Sunday, but perhaps I can make an appointment to come by. I also found out there are a couple of Pembroke descendants living in the area, or at least there were twenty years ago."

"Are you going to try to track them down?" Jack asked. "Assuming they're still alive, that is."

"Yup."

"Wouldn't that be something? All this time the seeds are right under our noses in a museum forty miles away."

"Probably in their archives or in storage somewhere," I said. "I doubt they're in the museum or Kevin would have known about it."

Jack nodded and fell silent.

"What is it?" I asked.

"Xavier told me Kevin's funeral will be next week at the monastery."

"Was that why he seemed so upset?"

"Not really. He's dealing with a vocational problem, trying to decide what to do, whether this kid just doesn't belong with the Franciscans or whether he doesn't belong in the priesthood at all."

"That must be a tough decision."

"You know as well as I do we need new blood. But not everyone who believes he has a calling really does." He pulled up at a stoplight at the end of North Capitol Street and gave me one of his looks. "I trust Xavier. He'll make the right decision. He's a good man, a good guardian for the Franciscans."

"Yes," I said. "He seems to be."

"So back to my original question. Why did you lie to him just now?"

"I didn't lie. I just didn't tell the whole truth."

"Don't even go there, cupcake."

"Okay. All this time I've been thinking that whoever killed Kevin knew about his research, a colleague or another scientist. What if it was someone at the monastery?"

He hooted. "Xavier? Are you kidding me? That is flat-out crazy, Soph." He banged his fist on the steering wheel. "No way. How could you even think that? Besides, who among any of the friars would stand to gain professionally or financially from Kevin's death? They take a vow of poverty, so it's not about the money. And no one else is doing the same kind of research Kevin was involved in, so there's no professional motive, no rivalry, either."

I held up my hands like a shield. "Okay, okay. Uncle. Sorry."

"You're looking in the wrong place," he said with that same intense conviction. "Maybe you'll find out something tomorrow when you call the Loudoun Museum."

Directly ahead of us, the Capitol dome was lit up against the cobalt-blue evening sky. I stared at it and tried to imagine what it had looked like the night the British set fire to it. The dome hadn't been built yet, but the sight of the two wings of the building in flames, visible everywhere in the night sky since this was the highest point in the city, must have devastated anyone who saw it, not only because of what the building symbolized but also the deliberate, vengeful destruction. By then Dolley Madison had left town, escaping just before British soldiers marched down Pennsylvania Avenue to the White House, looting the mansion and heaping the furniture—most of it Thomas Jefferson's—into a huge bonfire.

What happened to the seeds after that awful night?

Maybe Jack was right.

Maybe tomorrow I'd find out.

21

When I finally went to bed, I slept like the dead and didn't wake up until Jack came back from Mass downstairs in the chapel. He knocked on my door and handed me a coffee mug. "Bagels in my room when you're ready. I figured you could use this now."

"Thank you. I have no idea what time zone I'm in anymore."

Twenty minutes later I walked into his suite. He had thrown open the doors to his second-floor balcony overlooking Stanton Park, letting in cool morning sunshine, a fresh breeze, and the sound of rush-hour traffic. The pages of the *Washington Post* fluttered on the seat of his reading chair. I picked up the paper before the wind blew it around like dry leaves. It was folded to a front-page story on Ursula Gilberti's primary race.

"It looks like she might not win," Jack said.

"I guess when it rains, it pours," I said. "I wonder how she took the news of Victor and Yasmin's wedding being postponed."

"Some reporter is bound to ask her about it, so she'll have to say something."

"Especially since she's been courting the press to cover it. She probably can't get away with 'no comment.'" I put a bagel in the toaster and let him refill my coffee mug. His mug said WHEN GOD MADE ME HE WAS JUST SHOWING OFF.

"Gracie's latest tacky Catholic birthday gift," he said with a grin. "You should see the card. Jesus holding out the loaves and fishes and the crowd kvetching about whether the fish contained mercury and was the bread made with organic flour."

I laughed, and it turned into a yawn, which I tried to stifle.

He gave me a sympathetic look. "Rough night?"

"I stayed up too late studying Kevin's drawing of the Pembroke family tree. I did some searching and it looks like no Pembrokes live in Leesburg anymore. Either they passed away or they moved. I did find out that Francis P. Quincy was a senator from Virginia from 1900 until 1912, and a member of the Senate Committee on the District of Columbia, which Senator McMillan chaired. But he wasn't a member of the McMillan Commission."

"I bet the folks at the Loudoun Museum can help you out since the family was local."

"I left a voice mail a few minutes ago. Maybe someone will call me back even though they're not open today."

"So now what?" he asked.

I shrugged. "The Library of Congress is just up the street. I think I'll drop by. Thea Stavros asked one of the librarians to put together a list of the items Kevin borrowed from the Science and Business Library so they could remove them from his study room before the Franciscans came to collect his things. Maybe I can talk Thea or the other librarian into letting me look at that list. There might be something about the McMillan Commission that I missed when I was there the day we discovered that Kevin's study room had been ransacked."

Jack gave me a skeptical look. "Good luck with that. What are you hoping to find, if they say yes?"

"I'm not sure," I said. "But if I'm lucky, I'll know it when I see it."

"You're going to stay here again tonight, right?"

I took the bagel out of the toaster and buttered it. "I'm over my jitters. I probably ought to go home. Don't worry, I've got Nick's guns and I know how to use them if anybody decides to pay a visit again . . . which isn't going to happen now that whoever broke in has Kevin's book."

He said in a warning voice, "I don't think you should be playing vigilante, Soph."

I waved the butter knife at him. "I'm not. But I'm not going to be a victim, either."

"Two people are dead. You don't want to be the third."

"Jack. Come on."

"I'm not kidding. First Kevin, then that scientist from the Millennium Seed Bank."

"I called Perry before I fell asleep, since he's always up at the crack of dawn. He said he couldn't get anything out of the detective inspector looking into Alastair's accident. They won't talk about an ongoing investigation."

He shrugged. "All the more reason for you to lay low. Stay here tonight and then tomorrow is Friday. You were going to go out to your folks' place for the weekend to see your grandfather, anyway."

He didn't have to push hard to persuade me. "Are you sure you don't mind?"

"I'm sure. Please stay."

"Thanks. But it's my turn to do dinner."

He brightened. "I'm up for that. What are you making?"

"Probably reservations."

He laughed. "I've got class so I'm going to take off. Meet you back here for a run at the end of the day?"

He was training for the Marine Corps Marathon, and he could leave me in the dust if he wanted. "You're on."

He kissed me goodbye, and I went back to my room to brush my teeth and get my camera bag. Before I left Gloria House, I called Harry on his mobile. He had texted me last night that Chappy was spending the night in the hospital.

"No news yet," he said now. "Your mother slept in a chair by his bed."

"Do they have any idea what's wrong?" I asked.

"His doctor in Connecticut had changed a few of his medications. So they're looking into his meds and they want to run some more tests."

"I'll be home tomorrow. I can spell Mom at the hospital if she needs me. Call me if there's news."

He promised he would, and my phone beeped that I had an incoming call. An 804 area code. Richmond . . . or Charlottesville.

It was Ryan Velis. "I'm in town for a conference at the Smithsonian," he said. "Any chance you're free for drinks or dinner tonight? I'd like to hear about your trip to London."

"I already have dinner plans, but I could meet you for a drink."

"What time and where?"

"Five at Busboys and Poets on Fifth and K?"

"See you then."

It wasn't until I was in the parking lot behind Gloria House getting the Vespa that it hit me that I'd told Ryan when I saw him at Monticello that I'd be in London for a week. Instead I came back two days early.

Was it a lucky guess that I might be home so he'd called just now? Or had someone told him I was back in Washington?

And if so, who was it?

I chained the scooter to my favorite streetlamp on 2nd Street and walked to the Adams Building. Logan Day looked up from the book she was reading at the reception desk as I walked into the Science and Business Reading Room.

"Sophie, what brings you here?"

"A favor. Is Thea in?"

She shook her head. "She's at a conference at the Smithsonian."

Maybe it was the same conference Ryan was attending. "I was wondering if I could look at the list you put together of books and research items Kevin Boyle borrowed from the library."

She gave me a wary look. "Why?"

In the past few days I had come to the almost certain conclusion that Kevin's killer knew him, that it wasn't a hyped-up fanatic who hated his environmental politics or even a drug dealer he'd displaced from a park. Whoever it was had to be someone who wouldn't have aroused suspicion if he—or she— had been seen with Kevin that last day.

In spite of what Jack said, I didn't think that left anyone at the monastery off the hook. But I felt sure it was someone who knew Kevin was working on a book about colonial American gardens and had somehow learned about the copy of *Adam in Eden*, the Pembroke letter, and its connection to the White House seeds. Kevin had told me that day at the Tidal Basin that he had been making inquiries, which I now realized must have been related to his search for the seeds. But he didn't believe anyone he'd spoken to had put two and two together and figured out the reason behind his questions. I thought Kevin was wrong: Someone did figure it out. Kevin had told me he'd asked Thea for some information, and Thea was certainly familiar with his research materials. So she was on the hook, too.

And right now I needed to persuade Logan to let me look at a document Thea asked her to prepare that was technically none of my business.

"I'm trying to take care of something Kevin didn't get to finish before he died," I said, giving her a bland smile. "It had to do with his research."

"I see." She folded her hands. "Look, I got told off after you left the other day because it was my suggestion that you take a look in Brother Kevin's study room. I'm sorry, but I haven't got the authority to let you see that list." She leaned closer and said in a low voice, "I'd like to help you, but Thea would kill me if she found out."

"I don't want to get you in any more trouble," I said. "But what if I ask you—just generally—if something rings a bell? Would you tell me?"

She stole a furtive glance around the room. There were only three people in the reading room and all seemed to be absorbed in their work. "You mean, like yes or no?" I nodded. "Okay, but that's all I can say."

"Thank you. First, have you ever heard of someone named Francis Pembroke? A colonial doctor who lived in Leesburg?"

"No."

"How about Senator Francis P. Quincy?"

"Nope."

Two strikes. "Last question. What about the McMillan Commission or the McMillan Plan?"

Her eyes widened. "Yes."

"Can you help me out with that?" I asked. "I saw Kevin's papers at the monastery yesterday. The McMillan Commission has nothing to do with colonial gardening in America, the book he was supposedly writing. It was a 1902 Senate commission that produced a report that led to the resurrection of Pierre L'Enfant's plan for Washington and, ultimately, the creation of the National Mall. According to Kevin's notes, it was the last thing he was looking into before he died."

Logan stared at her hands while I waited. Finally she looked up. "The documents Kevin never collected are still on the bookcase in the corridor by the study rooms. At least they were last night. I'm not sure why they didn't get picked up with everything else that got returned, but that's being taken care of today. It's possible the courier might not have come by yet." She gave me a knowing look. "I'd better get back to work. Have a nice day."

I knew the way to the back corridor and I remembered where Thea had found Kevin's documents on that bookcase. The corridor was deserted, so no one saw me pull the bundle of papers off the shelf. Kevin had requested three documents: a historic buildings survey written by someone at the National Park Service: *The L'Enfant-McMillan Plan for Washington, D.C.*, a dissertation on Pierre L'Enfant's vision for Washington, and finally a report from 1909 presented to the Columbia Historical Society: *The Re-Interment of Major Pierre Charles L'Enfant.*

I stared at the last report. Pierre L'Enfant had been reburied at Arlington? I tried to remember the year he died from what I'd read in "No Little Plans"—sometime in the early 1800s—but I could look that up later. I skimmed the report. It was just over twenty pages, written in flowery, effusive language describing L'Enfant's genius and patriotism, along with a detailed account of his body being exhumed from "a lonely and unmarked grave" in Green Hill, Maryland, in 1909 after Congress granted the sum of one thousand dollars to bury him in a more fitting tribute at Arlington National Cemetery. From Maryland, his body had been moved to a vault in Mount Olivet Cemetery in Washington before it was carried to the Capitol, where he lay in state in the Rotunda. Finally, he was buried with full honors on a bluff overlooking the city of Washington.

At the end of the hall, a door to one of the study rooms opened and a man walked out. I shoved the papers back on the shelf and left. The last thing I wanted to do was get Logan sacked. And thanks to her, giant pieces of the puzzle were slamming into place in my head.

Kevin had been looking into L'Enfant's burial at Arlington as well as the McMillan Plan, plus he connected Senator Francis P. Quincy, a descendant of Francis Pembroke, with Charles Moore, the secretary of the commission that had drafted that plan. I wasn't entirely sure why, but I knew someone who would be able to answer my questions.

The guard in the lobby of the Adams Building lobby checked my bag as I left. I walked outside and called Olivia Upshaw, who answered right away.

"It's Sophie Medina," I said. "I'm at the Library of Congress. I've been doing some extra research on Pierre L'Enfant and I've got a couple of questions. I was wondering if I could drop by and talk to you."

"Sure." She sounded pleased and a bit surprised at my industriousness. "I'm at an all-day affiliates conference downstairs in the west wing of the Castle. How about tomorrow, say ten o'clock?"

"I'd really like to do this today. Do you have a coffee break or a lunch break? It won't take long, I promise."

"We just started a break. We go back in half an hour."

"I can be there in fifteen minutes."

"This must be really important."

"It is."

"Meet me at the information desk in the Great Hall."

"I'll be there," I said. "Thank you."

The sudden burst of warm weather three days before the first day of spring had brought out the tourists in droves. Unlike last week, the Great Hall of the Smithsonian Castle was jammed with people milling around the gift shop and filling the tables of a café across from the information desk. Olivia wasn't there when I arrived, nor did I see her in the crowded room.

"Are you Sophie?" A woman standing behind the information desk came over to me. "Olivia asked me to tell you that she had to take a call but she'll be here in just a moment."

"Thank you."

I looked through the rack of museum brochures and tourist

information while I waited. A pink-and-white pamphlet decorated with cherry blossoms listed spring events at the Mall museums. I picked it up because one exhibition caught my eye: the exquisite blown-glass sculptures of Dale Chihuly at the Hirshhorn.

"Sophie? Sorry I was detained."

Olivia stood there, dressed in a black pantsuit and white blouse, stiletto heels, juggling a tablet computer, a phone, and a pack of tissues. She set the electronics on the information desk and reached around with a hand to flip her long blond hair so it fell over one shoulder. Then she blew her nose.

"Are you all right?" I asked.

She gave me a miserable look. "Allergies. Tree pollen. What can I do for you?"

"I was wondering if you could answer a question. Can you tell me whether the decision to rebury Pierre L'Enfant at Arlington Cemetery had anything to do with the McMillan Plan?"

"That's what you want to know?"

I nodded.

"Strictly speaking, no, it didn't."

"Are you sure?"

"Of course I'm sure. L'Enfant was buried at Arlington because of a friendship between Teddy Roosevelt and the French ambassador, a man named Jules Jusserand. Jusserand wanted L'Enfant up there in the pantheon of French heroes who helped the Americans during the Revolutionary War just like the Marquis de Lafayette. So he became a huge L'Enfant promoter and eventually, in 1908, I believe it was, Congress approved money to move the grave, and the secretary of war approved the site in Arlington where he's buried today."

"And this had nothing to do with the McMillan Plan?"

She sneezed and blew her nose again, giving me a pointed look. "Well, since you read the manuscript of 'No Little Plans'—"

"I did."

"Then you know the McMillan Commission essentially

rehabilitated L'Enfant a century after George Washington dismissed him."

"Okay," I said. "Have you ever heard of Senator Francis P. Quincy? Probably Francis Pembroke Quincy? He knew Charles Moore and he might have been involved with the McMillan Commission, even though he wasn't a member."

She picked up her tablet computer. "No, but I'll check our database." After a moment she said, "Sorry. No connection between the two."

"Nothing?"

She continued typing and said, without looking up, "Charles Moore kept extensive scrapbooks of correspondence and news clippings, plus his diaries, but I don't find anything linking him to Senator Quincy. Later Moore became head of the Manuscript Division of the Library of Congress and was responsible for bringing L'Enfant's original 1791 design for Washington to the library so it could be preserved . . ." She kept reading. "This just goes on about Moore . . . No, there's nothing."

"Olivia. You're needed in the Commons. We're about to begin the next presentation." A dark-haired woman wearing a black suit and white blouse like Olivia had joined us.

"I'll be right there."

"Thanks for the help," I said.

"No problem. I'll be in my office tomorrow. The conference goes on for a couple of days, but I only need to be here today. I'll e-mail you and we can figure out a time to get together to go over your photos now that you've read the manuscript."

I nodded. "What's this conference about? Thea Stavros from the Library of Congress and Ryan Velis from Monticello are here, too. Are all of you together?"

She seemed surprised that I knew about Thea and Ryan, but she said, "Oh, yes, the gang's all here. The subject is social networking and new media for museums, historical sites, public gardens, cultural institutions. Places that rely on donations to keep their doors open." She picked up her tablet and phone and stuffed the tissue packet into a pocket. "They're teaching us all the latest tricks to stay relevant in the digital age . . . I'd better go. See you, Sophie."

I was halfway to the mall exit when Thea Stavros called my name. I looked up as she came down the staff-only staircase next to the room containing the crypt of James Smithson, the Smithsonian's benefactor.

"What are you doing here?" she asked.

"Just leaving," I said. "I had a quick meeting with an editor I'm working with at Museum Press."

"How was London? Did you learn anything more about Kevin's book and what he was looking for?"

"How did you know I went to London?"

She smiled. "Ryan Velis told me. He also said he contacted Zara Remington at the Chelsea Physic Garden on your behalf, so I presumed you went there because of Kevin."

"I went with my stepfather," I said, "sort of a last-minute vacation. I figured as long as I was going, I'd stop by the garden."

The last time we spoke, I'd told Thea about the book, but I hadn't mentioned the Fairbairn letter. At the time I hadn't realized its significance and I hadn't yet met Ryan, who'd told me about the seeds. So Thea didn't know about them, either.

Unless Ryan had told her.

Both Thea and Ryan had been Kevin's colleagues, people he trusted. I still thought whoever killed him had known him well, and Bram said a woman had come into the gallery with my paperwork and left with the book.

Thea was still waiting for my answer to her question about whether I had learned anything more about Kevin's book and what he was looking for when I was in London. My instincts told me she was on my side.

"The book is gone, Thea," I said. "A woman walked into Asquith's with documents she got from my apartment and persuaded someone who worked there that I wanted the book back."

The horrified expression on her face confirmed it: She hadn't known until now that it was missing. "Dear God," she said, "how in the world did that happen?"

"Asquith's is working with the police," I said. "Bram is devastated. Only a few people knew he had the book in their safe."

"I will be utterly heartbroken if that book disappears forever. It should be exhibited in a place like the Library of Congress, where it can be enjoyed and appreciated, not locked up in someone's safe-deposit box forever because the owner can't display a stolen treasure." She walked down the remaining stairs and joined me. "Ryan called me after you left Monticello, and we had quite a conversation. I've been combing through our records at the library looking for any additional reference to the seeds Thomas Jefferson might have kept in the White House."

"I see."

"And what about you? Did you turn up anything new in London?"

I told her then what I learned about Kevin's sister and that I believed it had given him an even stronger motive for finding the seeds.

"The poor man. How perfectly awful for him. Kevin may have been a scientist, but he did believe in miracles and the power of prayer."

"He apparently contacted a number of pharmaceutical companies, looking for trial studies of Alzheimer's drugs that might be suitable for her."

"I wonder if he also mentioned the seeds and that he was searching for them. Obviously they could be worth a fortune commercially, to say nothing of the historical value," she said. "Do you think Kevin figured out where they were before he died?"

"I don't know. The last thing he was looking into was the

McMillan Commission's plan to resurrect Pierre L'Enfant's original design for the Mall," I said. "Do you think the seeds could be somewhere here? I mean, on the Mall?"

She looked stunned. "My God, wouldn't that be something? But where would they be? There's no monument to L'Enfant, and if they're in the cornerstone of, say, this building or the Arts and Industries Building next door, then good luck retrieving them."

"There is a monument to Pierre L'Enfant," I said. "His grave overlooking Washington."

"Yes, but surely you know what it looks like? A massive stone table set on a pedestal. It would take an act of Congress to get that moved. An act of God would be easier. If the seeds are there, it's forever."

"In other words, maybe Kevin nearly found them, but they'll stay where they were buried?"

"You'd have to have incontrovertible proof. You're talking about the National Mall or Arlington Cemetery. You don't just stick a shovel in the dirt and start digging." She laid a hand on my arm. "Let me know if you find anything and I'll do what I can to help."

"Thank you. I should let you get back to the conference."

She waved a hand. "Oh, I'm already late. I just came from a meeting with Yasmin Gilberti. The next presentation I'm going to attend is David Arista's talk at two."

"David is here?" I asked, and she nodded. "I didn't know Yasmin was in Washington. I thought she was still in London with Victor. His father is very ill."

"She came home because of David's talk and a meeting with the Creativity Council. I'm not sure when she got back. Victor stayed in England."

Maybe Yasmin flew home to tell her mother in person about the decision to postpone the wedding. Thea didn't appear to have any clue about that news, so I said in a neutral voice, "That makes sense. I'd better be going. And thanks for the offer of help."

Thea gave me a sharp-eyed look. "Are you planning to make a tour of the Mall and Arlington Cemetery?"

I nodded. "I think I might."

"Good luck. Just don't take a shovel. The Park Service frowns on people digging up federal property."

I went directly to Arlington. It seemed like the easiest and most logical place to start. The traffic lights were in my favor, so it took only ten minutes to drive around the Lincoln Memorial across Memorial Bridge to the main cemetery gate. Up ahead of me perched on a hill at the highest point of the cemetery, Arlington House and the grave of Major Pierre Charles L'Enfant overlooked the city of Washington.

Once I explained to a woman in the Visitor Center that I was a photographer working on a project with Museum Press, she gave me a map and a pass for the Vespa so I could drive through the grounds to L'Enfant's grave, instead of making my way up the steep hill on foot. The streets had names like Eisenhower, Roosevelt, Patton, McClellan, Grant, and Pershing, and the winding drive uphill past row after row of white markers was heartbreaking and haunting in its peacefulness. A few cars were parked next to the steps leading to the Eternal Flame. Maybe when I finished what I'd come to do, I would stop on the way down.

I turned on Humphreys Drive and parked in an empty lot. At eleven o'clock on a Thursday morning, the place was deserted. Here the graves were older, and it looked like a proper cemetery, no rows of white markers. But this land had once been part of a large estate, the mansion built by George Washington's adopted son and later the home of his daughter and her husband, Robert E. Lee, before the U.S. government confiscated it when Lee became a commander in the Confederate Army.

I found a more detailed map of the cemetery on my phone

and zoomed in. Perhaps the seeds weren't in the grave but somewhere near it around Arlington House. There was an elaborate flower garden next to the mansion and a colonnaded pavilion that the map called the Old Amphitheater and Rostrum, the gathering site for the cemetery before a new, larger pavilion had been built in the 1920s.

But it seemed to me that all these places were too far away from L'Enfant's tomb. I walked around Arlington House to the steep bluff overlooking the Eternal Flame far below and the view across the bridge to the Lincoln Memorial and the two other iconic monuments, both envisioned by L'Enfant: the Washington Monument and the Capitol dome. A blue ribbon of the Potomac River snaked between a broad expanse of green-tinged trees.

As Thea had said, L'Enfant's grave looked like a large table set on a substantial marble base. His map of the city had been engraved into the top slab. If the seeds were under all that marble, they really would remain there forever. A podium-like marker with a time line of L'Enfant's life and another copy of his map set under Plexiglas stood a few feet away from the grave.

I checked it out. At the base of the marker something had been set into the ground, a small metal box like a safe. I knelt and brushed away dirt. There was a keyed lock set flush into the metal surface.

I sat down hard, staring at the little safe, and thought, *I've found the seeds.*

Hiding in plain sight, just as Kevin had said that last day at the Tidal Basin. They had to be here.

My phone rang. It was Olivia.

"I've got something for you," she said. "A letter from Senator Quincy to Charles Moore dated March 4, 1902. It's just two lines. Shall I read it?"

"Yes, please."

She sneezed and blew her nose. "Sorry. Here's what it says:

Please be assured of my most sincere thanks for your efforts to per-suade the members of the McMillan Commission to accept my donation. I trust you will do your utmost to ensure that some day it is most nobly enshrined. Yours, Francis P. Quincy." She sniffled. "That's it."

"Thank you," I said. "It's very helpful."

Francis Quincy had given Charles Moore the White House seeds, and Moore had done what Quincy asked: made sure they were most nobly enshrined.

"Is this something we could incorporate into the book?" she asked.

"Possibly. We'll have to talk about it."

"Excellent. By the way, David Arista told me he could still get you into the Arts and Industries Building this week since you came back early from London. Starting next week they're going to begin fixing the ceiling, so no one will be allowed in. I think you should take those interior photographs tomorrow."

The hair on the back of my neck prickled. "Did he tell you this today?"

"No, yesterday. I haven't seen him today. But when I do, I'm going to tell him I want my bunny back." She blew her nose.

"Your bunny?"

"My *money*. My allergy medicine costs a fortune and it's not doing a bit of good."

"Sorry. I don't understand."

"It's a joke," she said. "Arista Pharmaceutical makes the stuff I'm taking."

The penny dropped. "David Arista's family owns a pharma-ceutical company?"

"You've never heard of them?"

"I've been overseas for so many years I . . . no, I haven't."

"I'd better get back to the conference," she said. "I think you should talk to David and see if you can set up that session tomorrow."

Arista Pharmaceutical must have been one of the companies Kevin contacted to ask about drug trials for his sister. And, as Thea had said, maybe he'd said something or dropped a hint that he might be able to locate seeds to an extinct plant more potent than modern-day water hyssop, something that had already proved effective in restoring memory loss. Was it David Arista who had been stalking Kevin because he already knew about the seeds?

"Sophie?" Olivia sounded impatient. "Are you still there? I said I think you should give David a call. We don't want to lose this opportunity."

"Sure. I'll do that."

"Let me know how it goes," she said, and disconnected.

Footsteps crunched on the gravel behind me, and I looked up, shielding my eyes against the sunshine.

I didn't have to call David Arista.

He was standing right here.

22

He held out a hand, offering to help me up. The smile on his face looked more like a leer. I stood on my own, clutching my phone in both hands.

How much had he overheard of my conversation with Olivia? It probably didn't matter, because I already knew it was no accident or coincidence that he was here. His eyes strayed to the ground and the freshly swept dust that revealed the little inground safe.

I caught the look of triumph before he wiped it off his face and pasted on a smile.

"Isn't this a surprise? Aren't you supposed to be at the Smithsonian?" I asked.

"Not until two." He indicated my phone. "Who were you talking to?"

I could have told him it was none of his business, but it didn't seem like a good idea.

"Olivia Upshaw. She says you can still get me into the Arts and Industries Building to take photos tomorrow." He didn't say anything, so I went on like this was a normal conversation. "Why don't we settle on a time now? I've got to get back to town for another meeting so I can't stay . . ."

He put his hand on my wrist, circling his fingers around it with unmistakable pressure. "You're not going anywhere."

"Let go of me, David."

He pulled the phone out of my hand and shoved it in his pocket. "Why don't we go for a little walk in the woods? They're planning to expand the cemetery in the next few years, right behind Arlington House. I think we ought to take a look."

He wrenched my camera bag off my shoulder and twisted my arm so it was pinned behind my back. It hurt and I knew he meant to cause me pain. The day I met him he'd talked about his mother having a Jack-and-Jesus wall in their home and how often he'd visited the Eternal Flame with her as a kid. He probably knew this cemetery pretty well. And she was devoted to St. Francis of Assisi. He probably knew the monastery garden equally well.

"Let go of me and give me back my phone and my camera bag."

He slid his other arm around my throat and leaned close to my ear. "Start walking, Sophie." He applied a little pressure. "Do as I say."

I gagged and he released his chokehold.

I refused to give him the pleasure of telling him he hurt me. Or that he scared me. "Did you follow me from the Castle?"

He gave me a heavy-lidded look. "Your GPS settings are turned on in your phone. I was able to track you quite easily." This time his smile really was a leer. "New technology. My clients teach me things all the time. Now get moving. I've got a gun."

If he brought it, he meant to use it. I said, with more bravado than I felt, "What are you going to do? Kill me? Is this what you did to Kevin? Threaten him first, then kill him?"

"I don't know what you're talking about." But his grip tightened and he shoved my arm hard enough to make me wince.

Just keep him talking, keep distracting him.

"Sure you do," I said. "You came to London, too, didn't you? You were the one who met Will Tennant at the Chelsea Physic Garden."

His expression turned ugly. "You've certainly been busy asking questions. You're smarter than I thought you were."

"Not smart enough to put the paperwork for Kevin's book in a safe place so you wouldn't find it when you broke into my apartment," I said. "They have security cameras at Asquith's, you know. Who was the woman? Who's helping you?"

"The courier who picked up that book has no idea who she got it for," he said. "I'm not stupid. Get moving."

"You came to the Tidal Basin the day I met Kevin. Neither of us saw you, but when I downloaded the pictures I took that day, I saw a man by the Roosevelt Memorial. You were only there for a moment and then you never showed up in any more pictures, almost like a ghost. But it was you."

He didn't reply, but a muscle tightened in his jaw and I knew I was right.

"Why did you lie when you met me in the Ripley Garden?" I asked. "You said you came from the Chihuly exhibit at the Hirshhorn, except it had closed a week earlier. What were you doing at the Smithsonian? Were you meeting someone?"

"None of your business."

"It had to be Yasmin," I said. "Kevin talked to her after he left me at the Tidal Basin and advised her not to go through with the wedding when he saw the two of you together at the engagement party. I think he guessed you were having an affair. Yasmin called you because she must have been panicked that Kevin found out, so you came by to see her."

"Kevin should have minded his own business."

"One of you went to talk to him later at the monastery garden. Yasmin showed up early for a meeting with her mother and me at five o'clock, but you could have gone over there, too, after you left me at the Smithsonian. I think Yasmin was so upset by the idea that Kevin might say something to Victor about your affair that either she or you tried to stop Kevin. One of you killed him."

David frog-marched me around the side of the house. "That stupid little bitch has been more trouble than she's worth," he said with venom. "She thinks she can manipulate anyone, including that fool Jaine. Now stop talking and get moving."

I ignored him. "Did you kill Alastair Innes, too? Arrange an accident for him? Or did you have help in England?"

"Shut up."

Our pace had slowed as he seemed to be working out how much I knew.

"You'll never be able to sell that book, you know," I said. "It's one of a kind."

"Don't be naïve. There are plenty of people who would be happy to buy it and keep their mouth shut. It happens all the time. You just have to find the right kind of buyer."

"You found out about the seeds because Kevin was making inquiries to pharmaceutical companies about Alzheimer's drugs. He talked to someone at Arista Pharmaceutical, obviously. Then somehow you found out about the book . . . Yasmin must have told you. The only people who knew how valuable it was before Kevin died were Victor, his father, and Kevin. Victor must have told Yasmin, and since you two were lovers, she told you everything."

"I offered to help Kevin," he said. "We were willing to pay him a fortune for those seeds, even if they turned out to be nothing more than dust."

"He didn't want your help or your money, he wanted to make this discovery on his own. So you started following him, stalking him. Were you the one who killed him?"

"I didn't kill him. He fell. And keep walking."

"You left him on those steps and he died. And now you're going to kill me."

"I don't have any choice. You're my last loose end. But I do appreciate you leading me to the seeds . . . I should have figured that out. All this time they're buried with good old Pierre L'Enfant."

To our left was the flower garden. One of David's hands still had my arm in a vise grip behind my back, and he'd used the strap of my camera bag to secure my other arm. Anyone who saw us—and there was no one—would assume we were lovers out for a walk on a beautiful sun-dappled afternoon, unless they got close to us. Down below on Sheridan Drive, one of the main roads that wound through the cemetery, a large vehicle—maybe a tour bus, if I was lucky—was coming up the hill. I could hear the whine of the engine as it got closer.

"Don't try anything," he said in my ear as his arm slipped around my neck again, "or I'll shoot."

He was bluffing. He wouldn't shoot with witnesses around. The bus came into view by the Old Amphitheater, and it was my best chance. I bit his arm and wrenched out of his grip, shoving the camera bag into his gut. He yelped and absorbed the blow with a soft "ouf" as I took off. But apparently the bus was empty or out of service and the driver didn't see me. It lumbered past the stop for Arlington House and continued down the hill before disappearing from view. I ran into the amphitheater and ducked behind a boxwood hedge.

"I'll find you," he shouted.

I heard his footsteps, so I took off running again, using the enormous white pillars and the hedge as screens. Someone had to be inside the mansion, even if I hadn't seen anyone. Wasn't it open for visitors? I ran fast, but he ran faster. He swung the camera bag, which caught me hard in the shoulder just as I rounded the corner by the L'Enfant memorial, and the blow knocked me to the ground. I skidded across the gravel on my hands and knees, ending up on the grass. As soon as I started to get up, he dove on top of me and together we rolled to the edge of the hill.

He was bigger and stronger. He gave me one final shove, to send me down the hill, and started to get up. I grabbed his ankles and yanked hard. His feet went out from under him and I held on as he landed. He kicked again, this time his blows landing on my head and shoulders. Below us I heard voices, people shouting, probably watching from far below on the plaza next to the Eternal Flame.

My head felt like someone had taken a hammer to it and I tasted blood. He gave me another hard shove, and this time I couldn't hold on anymore. I fell away, tumbling down the long, steep hill. I dug in my heels and clawed at the ground, trying to grab at something to stop my momentum. Eventually I stopped rolling and lay there, winded, bloody, and sore.

By now the sirens were everywhere, and I knew they were coming for both of us. I got to my knees, ignoring the audience talking and pointing at me down below. Halfway up the hill, two men in camouflage uniforms carrying assault rifles ran toward me.

This wasn't going to be good.

"We've already got your friend," one of them said, as the other one snapped handcuffs over the scrapes on my wrists. "You're under arrest."

23

I didn't return to Arlington Cemetery for six months, not until the middle of September, on an afternoon when the sky was so blue it hurt your eyes and the golden sunshine was warm and slanting. It took that long for Ryan Velis and Thea Stavros to call in every favor owed them in order to persuade the National Park Service to open the little safe below the marker by Pierre L'Enfant's grave. Then there was more wrangling about whose property the contents—if there were any—would be. Eventually it was decided that if there were indeed seeds inside the safe, they would go to Monticello to be cultivated, but it would be a joint project with the National Park Service. I was glad to hear from Ryan that seeds would also be sent to the Millennium Seed Bank in honor of Kevin and Alastair.

Though Thea and Olivia Upshaw pored over records and documents at the Library of Congress and the Smithsonian, no one could figure out what happened to the key that fit into the lock, which meant it would have to be drilled open. Considering Washington's bureaucracy, it was astonishing that it took only months and not years to arrange permission for someone to break open the safe. Fortunately, it didn't require an act of Congress, or I figured I could be an old woman before we'd know how it all turned out.

The months leading up to that day had been busy and tumultuous. Nick came home from his grand tour of the Middle East and moved into Quill Russell's new Washington office, and I turned down the White House photographer's job with IPS, though I told Monica to keep me in mind if she needed an extra shooter from time to time. But the truth was I liked being my own boss. I was getting more work than I could handle, and most important, a wealthy friend of Max's offered to help with fund-raising for the Shoe Project and setting it up as a nonprofit charity, so Grace and I were busier than ever with that.

In a season of bad news, scandal, and heartache, there was some happiness and reason to celebrate when the doctors in Virginia finally figured out that Chappy's mental confusion had been caused by changes to his medication, as well as Chap himself, who had mixed up his prescriptions. He stayed with Harry and my mother in Middleburg until the beginning of May, when my mother was satisfied he was his old self. By then, Harry joked that they were driving each other nuts again and that keeping all sharp objects hidden from both of them had become a full-time job. So a few days later, Mom and Harry drove Chappy back to Connecticut so she could set up daily visits from a home helper, which was the middle ground everyone finally agreed on if he was going to stay in his house independently and not move to assisted living.

We had been lucky that it turned out well for my grandfather, but Victor's father died of complications from pneumonia a few weeks after I got back from London. Jack told me Victor decided not to return to Washington and planned to stay permanently in Europe, assuming his father's responsibilities and commuting between London and Vienna. He had broken off the engagement with Yasmin after he'd learned she and David had been lovers and that David had been blackmailing her about their affair in return for information about Kevin's book. Jack said what hurt Victor the most was her betrayal, going into his private e-mail and passing along to David correspondence relating to Kevin, his father, and the book.

As for Yasmin, Olivia told me she'd been fired from the Smithsonian, although she claimed she quit in order to campaign for her mother in West Virginia. Ironically, the day I heard the news I ran into her on the staircase on my way out of the Castle.

She was carrying a small box that looked like it contained the contents of her office. I moved aside to let her pass.

She gave me a defiant look and said, "Look what the cat dragged in. What are you doing here?"

I looked her in the eye. "Working."

"Not me. I'm leaving," she said. "I'm done with this place. I'm campaigning for my mother, then I'm going to be Edward Jaine's new personal assistant. He has a private jet, you know. And half a dozen homes. I'm going to be traveling everywhere with him."

I hadn't heard about that, but I supposed it made sense. "Congratulations, Yasmin. I hope it works out for you."

"Stay out of my life," she said with feeling. "I mean it."

"I never wanted to be part of it."

"Please." She gave me a look of disdain. "You talked to Victor in London and afterward he told me he wanted to postpone the wedding. You probably had something to do with Kevin telling me he thought I should wait as well. You meddled in something that was none of your business, Sophie."

"Victor had already made up his mind, and I didn't find out Kevin met you until after he was dead."

"I don't believe you."

I gave her a weary look. "I don't care. You got someone to pretend to be Victor's secretary in London so you could get me to come to the Anchor pub, didn't you? What were you going to do? Talk to me or shove me into the river?"

Her eyes widened, but she tilted her chin and smirked. "I don't know what you're talking about. But if it had been me, I know what I would have done."

"It was you." I brushed past her and said, "I've got to go. Goodbye, Yasmin."

I never saw her again, but in June Ursula lost her hard-fought primary, in part because of her opponent's deep pockets but also because of the scandal over Yasmin's wedding and David's upcoming trial. Nick told me Quill Russell said Ursula had immediately been courted to join a competing consulting firm in the merry-go-round world of Washington politics and lobbying, plus she had a book deal lined up when she finally left the Senate in January.

In July, David Arista was convicted of the murder of Brother Kevin Boyle in a trial that was swift and tawdry, the kind of scandal that livened up an otherwise quiet summer in Washington. The star witness had been Yasmin Gilberti.

She escaped relatively unscathed thanks to Ursula's lawyers, who brokered a deal in return for her cooperation at the trial. But Yasmin had claimed—and I believed her—that the reason she had arrived early at the monastery the day Kevin was killed was to talk him out of saying anything to Victor about postponing or even canceling the wedding after their upsetting meeting that morning. She hadn't known Kevin was dead until she ran into me and Paul Zarin, but once she heard the news, she'd been terrified that David Arista might have had something to do with it. By then she'd had enough of him, so she'd contacted Edward Jaine and told him everything about the book, knowing he'd move heaven and earth to get his hands on it and thwart David's plans.

As it turned out, I'd been right that someone at the monastery had been indirectly involved in Kevin's death. Paul Zarin, the seminarian Xavier had been planning to dismiss, was David Arista's cousin. By then Paul had decided to leave the Franciscans and David promised him a job with Arista Pharmaceutical in return for keeping tabs on Kevin.

Jack showed up at David's trial every day, following it as a case study for his ethics class. He and I talked about it, of course, but the whole thing upset me more than I'd expected.

No matter how much I wanted to believe justice was being served and everyone was getting what was coming to them, it couldn't right the wrong, heal the hurt, or bring closure for me. What made it worse was that I knew Kevin would have forgiven everybody. He would have quoted Luke to me: *Do not judge and you will not be judged. Do not condemn, and you will not be condemned. Forgive, and you will be forgiven.*

But I was a long way from forgiveness.

At the end of August, three weeks before the ceremony at L'Enfant's grave was scheduled to take place, Perry asked me to fly over and help out in the bureau since he was down to a skeleton staff with people still on holiday or out sick. It was good to be back in London. By that time my American journalist colleagues had learned about the tantalizing mystery of the two-hundred-year-old seeds missing from the White House and their storied provenance, and it had unleashed a deluge of media interest. In my profession, it's never good when a journalist becomes the story; at least in London, I was able to drop out of sight for a while.

A few days before I flew home, I visited Zara Remington at the Chelsea Physic Garden, where she told me that Will Tennant was at Wormwood Scrubs prison in London awaiting trial for the murder of Alastair Innes. As I'd suspected, David Arista had been the American who had shown up at the garden asking about hyssop, and Will had lied in his description to throw me off. David had lucked out when he met Will, who not only also volunteered at the Millennium Seed Bank but was also in deep trouble trying to repay gambling debts and more than willing to accept a bribe in return for information about the project Alastair was working on with Kevin.

According to Zara, Will's ID badge had been used on the swipe pads leading to the storage area the day Alastair and I were locked in the vault. Eventually Will had been arrested and charged with Alastair's murder after a neighbor identified him as the man she'd seen leaving Alastair's garage the night before his car went into the ravine and the police found Alastair's phone in his home.

On my last night in London, Perry got tickets to the BBC Proms at Royal Albert Hall, the world-famous series of classical music concerts that begins each year in mid-July and lasts until mid-September. As it happened, it was American music night—Gershwin, Copland, and a mixture of jazz, blues, and country music. After it was over and we were leaving, Perry nudged me.

"Isn't that Victor Haupt-von Véssey across the aisle?" he asked. "And I recognize the woman he's with. Her father is the Earl of Chelmsford."

I turned in time to get a glimpse of Victor with his arm around a pretty redhead who reminded me of Yasmin. They were laughing at something with the intimacy of an established couple, and their body language suggested that they were more than just acquaintances.

"It is," I said. "I'm glad he's moved on, though she does look like Yasmin's double."

"Want to say hello?"

I shook my head. "I think I'd better not."

"You're still not over all this, are you?"

"I don't know how I could be until they open the safe next to Pierre L'Enfant's grave. I just hope the seeds are there and that Kevin was right. Or that I'm right about what I think he found."

Perry squeezed my hand. "Come on, Medina, don't be so hard on yourself. The Franciscans have Kevin's book, and it looks like they're going to loan it to the Library of Congress, at least for a while."

"I guess Edward Jaine thought it was a good public relations move to say that he'd bought it but out of charity he'd given it to Kevin and the Franciscans," I said. "It offset some of the horrible press after he got caught covering up that he was exporting toxic electronic waste to the Third World and passing it off as good equipment."

"Maybe it's why he got off with only a big fine and avoided jail," Perry said. "And the guy's smart. He'll rebuild his financial empire."

"No doubt. Yasmin Gilberti is going to be his new personal assistant."

"You still sound down in the dumps. Let's get a drink. Look at it this way. A week from today it will be all over. They're going to open that safe and you'll know for sure. Plus you get a world exclusive. That's why I've always loved you, Medina. You don't do anything by half measures." He gave me his best cheesy smile. "Go big," he said, "or go home."

The day scheduled for opening the strongbox would have been Kevin's fifty-fifth birthday, a deliberate choice and posthumous tribute. The Park Service had set up a large white events tent around the L'Enfant grave with an enormous window at one end that looked out on the city and the Potomac. With the exception of Chappy and me as the two official photographers, and Grace, and a reporter from International Press Service, all the other media had been required to stay behind a rope line and were camped out on the steps of Arlington House.

The biggest concern was the condition of the seeds after two centuries, their fragility and preserving whatever package or container they were in. In addition to Ryan, Thea, Olivia, and Logan, along with a handful of VIPs from Monticello, the

Library of Congress, the Smithsonian, and the White House, the only guests were people I'd asked to be there: Nick, Jack, Xavier, Max, and Bram Asquith. A locksmith hired by the Park Service would drill out the lock, but it had been decided that Ryan would be the one to look inside the strongbox.

Ryan surprised me by asking Xavier to say a prayer before we began, so we all bowed our heads while he asked for God's blessing on us and on Kevin. Then he quoted Genesis, a gentle reminder of what we might find inside the box: *For dust thou art and unto dust thou shall return.*

The locksmith was good, but it took a few minutes before he drilled through the lock.

"Are you all right?" Nick said in my ear. "You look like you've stopped breathing."

"I could be wrong. What if I'm wrong?"

He leaned over and gave me a quick kiss on the cheek. "Don't second-guess yourself. Everyone here thinks you're right."

I nodded and raised my camera.

"Okay, this is it." Ryan sounded tense. He reached into the safe and for a long moment, he was silent.

The only sounds were the shutters clicking from my camera and Chappy's as now everyone seemed to be holding their breath. What if someone had been there already, or something else had been stored there and we'd got it wrong, or . . .

Then Ryan pulled something out of the safe. Everyone gasped as he held up a dark brown leather pouch with the reverence of a priest raising a communion chalice. In the slanted afternoon sunlight, the leather, embossed with the initials *Th J*, gleamed like old burnished gold.

"Thank you, Kevin. I know you're watching," he said with a broad smile. "I do believe we've found Mr. Jefferson's seeds."

ACKNOWLEDGMENTS

The characters in *Ghost Image* are all fictitious creations invented for this story, with the obvious exception of historical figures such as Thomas Jefferson, George Washington, Pierre L'Enfant, Lewis and Clark, Dolley Madison, John Fairbairn, and the members of the McMillan Commission, though I have also used those individuals fictitiously. Any resemblance to any living person is entirely coincidental and unintentional. Francis Pembroke and Senator Francis Quincy never existed and there was no seed cabinet left behind in the White House by Thomas Jefferson.

The idea for *Ghost Image* came about after I heard an NPR book review of Andrea Wulf's *The Founding Gardeners: The Revolutionary Generation, Nature, and the Shaping of the American Nation* (Vintage Books), a page-turning account of the Founding Fathers' obsession with gardening, seed collecting, and farming, and the impact their passion had on shaping our country. Shortly afterward I read an article in the June 2012 issue of *Smithsonian* called "Seeds of the Future" on the work of the Millennium Seed Bank in England, which subsequently led to a conversation with Mark Verrilli, a landscaper friend with Pleasant Valley Landscapes in Aldie, Virginia, about whether it might be possible to germinate seeds that were hundreds of years old.

I was fortunate to have considerable help with this book from many people who took time out of busy schedules to answer my questions. As usual, if something is wrong, that's on me. In America I owe thanks to the following people: Scott W. Berg, author of *Grand Avenues: The Story of Pierre Charles L'Enfant, the French Visionary Who Designed Washington, D.C.* (Vintage Books), for sitting down over breakfast and talking to me about Pierre L'Enfant until it was nearly lunchtime; Rick Tagg, winemaker at Barrel Oak Winery in Delaplane, Virginia, for his help and knowledge of herbs; George Thuronyi, Copyright Division, and Jennifer Harbster, Science, Technology and Business Division of the Library of Congress; Peggy Cornett, Curator of Plants, and Mary Scott-Fleming, Director of Enrichment Programs at Monticello; Dr. Martin Gammon, Vice President of Business Development and Museum Relations, Bonhams (and a regular appraiser of rare books and manuscripts for PBS's *Antiques Roadshow*); Detective Jim Smith, Crime Scene Section, Fairfax County (VA) Police Department; as well as Dr. Carmella Moody and Rosemarie Forsythe, who made numerous constructive comments and offered advice. Also thanks to a few anonymous people who answered questions relating to Nick's intelligence career, as well as several individuals who were my resources for religious matters: You know who you are.

In England, thanks to John and Jackie Briggs, my former neighbors, who fed me and gave me a place to stay when I was in London. I also am grateful to Kay Pennick, Librarian, and Dr. John Dickie, Head of Information Section, Seed Conservation Department, at the Millennium Seed Bank; Christopher Bailes, Curator, Chelsea Physic Garden; Anna Christodoulou, the Connaught; and finally to Andrea Wulf, for meeting me for breakfast in London in between taping a show for the BBC to discuss *The Founding Gardeners* and offer suggestions and help, including her idea to invent a White House seed cabinet that belonged to Thomas Jefferson.

Several books, in addition to *The Founding Gardeners* and *Grand Avenues*, were helpful: *The Creation of Washington, D.C.: The Idea and Location of the American Capital* by Kenneth R. Bowling (George Mason University Press); *The Apothecaries' Garden: A History of the Chelsea Physic Garden* by Sue Minter (History Press, UK); *Monument Wars: Washington, D.C., the National Mall, and the Transformation of the Memorial Landscape* by Kirk Savage (University of California Press); *"A Rich Spot of Earth": Thomas Jefferson's Revolutionary Garden at Monticello* by Peter J. Hatch (Yale University Press); and *The Last Great Plant Hunt: The Story of Kew's Millennium Seed Bank* by Carolyn Fry, Sue Seddon, and Gail Vines (Kew Publishing, Royal Botanic Gardens, Kew, UK).

Heartfelt thanks to my critique group friends and fellow authors: Donna Andrews, John Gilstrap, Alan Orloff, and Art Taylor, affectionately known as the Rumpus Group, for considerable help with many drafts of this book. As always, my dear friend Tom Snyder read the first draft (and the ones that followed) with a keen eye and a sharp blue pencil.

At Scribner, thanks to Katrina Diaz, my editor, and to Susan Moldow; also to Alexsis Johnson, my publicist, and Katie Rizzo and Cynthia Merman for copy editing. I am especially indebted to Maggie Crawford for editorial help and guidance.

Finally, thanks and love to Dominick Abel, my agent. Last, but by no means least, I am grateful to my sons and daughters-in-law, but most especially to my husband, André de Nesnera, for more in my heart than I can possibly express. None of this would be possible without you, my love.

Turn the page for an excerpt from Ellen Crosby's new
Wine Country Mystery

The Champagne
Conspiracy

coming from Minotaur Books in November 2016

Chapter 1

It all started with the dress.

I lifted it out of the old steamer trunk and it took my breath away. A gossamer concoction of sea-green chiffon, hundreds of copper, silver, and pale green glass beads in patterns like a stained-glass creation from Tiffany, with a sexy zigzag hem of silver fringe that glittered, even by the light of the yellowed bulb that barely lit this dim corner of the attic. I had never seen it—you don't forget a dazzling couture number like this—but it had been beautifully and lovingly preserved, as though one of my long-dead relatives expected to pluck it out of its hiding place and shimmy off to a madcap night of too much dancing and drinking and making out with some guy in the backseat of his roadster.

When I found it, I had been in one of my periodic bouts of overzealous cleaning, which usually happened when the stress piled up and I needed to do something to feel I could restore order and control to some part of my life. Somehow, sorting through boxes and trunks of the discarded detritus that had belonged to generations of ancestors usually did the trick.

Plus—and here is the more mundane reason—there was the coat drive in the middle of January. Francesca Merchant, who ran the day-to-day operations of my vineyard's tasting room and managed all our events, had shown up at work a few days earlier and announced that Veronica House, the local homeless shelter and food pantry, was collecting winter coats. Any jacket or coat donated in good condition would be given to the guests who came to the center, especially the ones who insisted on sleeping outside in spite of the dangerous temperatures in this record-shattering arctic-cold winter.

Donations of men's coats were the most urgently needed, since the majority of people who used Veronica House's services were homeless men. So I scoured the attic, searching for whatever had been stored there and forgotten by family members. I also wrote Frankie a big check.

When I gave it to her, I told her about the dress I'd found during my attic foraging. That afternoon the two of us were sitting on one of the big leather sofas by the fireplace in the main room in the villa, the rambling ivy-covered building where we poured and sold wine and hosted our indoor events. Frankie had just placed another log on the fire and we both had our hands cupped around steaming mugs of coffee to keep warm on a day when the highest temperature would still be only a single-digit number.

"You've got to show it to me," she'd said, her eyes lighting up like a child at Christmas. "It sounds amazing. A real flapper dress. I bet it's drop-dead gorgeous."

"It is. I've never seen anything like it. It must have cost someone an absolute fortune."

"Let's go see it," she said. "I can't wait another minute. Does it fit you?"

"I have no idea." I set my cup on the heavy wooden coffee table.

"You mean you didn't try it on?" She grabbed my hand and

pulled me up. "Come on, you have to. And you're giving me a great idea."

We took my Jeep over to the house. By then I'd brought the dress downstairs and hung it on the back of the door to my closet like a guilty secret, along with a shimmery silver satin slip that was obviously meant to be worn underneath, since the dress was completely sheer. Whoever the owner had been had also had the matching beaded headband. All that was missing was a long roped strand of pearls and a little silver flask filled with illegal hooch, since the dress had to be straight out of the Prohibition era.

"It's perfect for you," Frankie said the moment she laid eyes on it. "With your dark hair and fair coloring, you'll look stunning in it."

I was sitting on the old wedding ring quilt in the middle of my bed, watching her run a hand over the elaborate beading like a professional appraiser assessing its value, her head cocked as if trying to discern its provenance.

"I don't think so, Frankie," I said. "Look at that slip. It's satin and it's as fitted as a glove. No room to wiggle around in. It's for someone who is really slim."

Frankie spun around, hands on her hips, and gave me an admonishing I-dare-you look. "Like you."

I shook my head. "It's not a dress to wear anymore; it's something to look at, like a work of art—"

But she had already taken the dress on its hanger off the hook on the closet door and was holding the short silver slip with its spaghetti straps up against me. "Size looks just about perfect, if you ask me."

"I don't think—"

"I'll leave the room so you can try it on."

I glared at her. "My bra is going to show under those itty-bitty slip straps. I'm wearing a red racer-back bra. It'll look terrible with the green chiffon."

"Enough with the lame excuses. So take off your bra. Come

on, it was the Roaring Twenties. Women parked their corsets in someone's bedroom when they went to parties, so they could be . . . available." She gave me a roguish look. "Who needs underwear?"

"I . . . uh . . . "

"Come on," she said again. "What are you scared of?"

"Nothing." Just unnerved at how the dress seemed to have bewitched us both. "All right, give me a minute."

She left and I got undressed. A few minutes later I said, "Okay. Just don't come too near me. She must have smoked like a chimney. Now that I'm wearing it, the fabric reeks of stale cigarettes."

The door opened and Frankie walked in, her hands flying to her mouth, which was open in a big round O.

Finally she said, "You perfect little jazz baby, you. Lucie, you look fabulous. I swear, that dress was made for you. Wait until Quinn—"

I held up my hand. "Hold it right there. What did you have in mind? Wear it the next time we're bottling wine? Or maybe out in the vineyard spraying for powdery mildew?"

She wagged a finger at me. "No, no, no . . . I'll tell you when you're going to wear it. At our Valentine's Day party next month. We'll make it a Roaring Twenties dinner dance. Girls come dressed like flappers with rouged knees and beaded headbands and guys with pomaded hair and gangster suits with wide ties or knickerbockers and two-toned shoes."

"What Valentine's Day—"

She wasn't listening. "And because I know you won't turn me down, because you have a heart of gold that's as big as all outdoors, we'll make it a fund-raiser for Veronica House. We'll do the villa up like a party out of *The Great Gatsby*, call it our 'Anything Goes' evening." Her eyes had a dreamy, faraway look and I knew she had already mentally planned the entire evening, right down to the gin rickeys we'd drink and the Charleston we'd dance to. "It'll be such fun, something to break up the winter doldrums. Everyone's going to want to come."

"It's a good idea, Frankie," I said, "but I'm not wearing this dress. It's probably been in that trunk in the attic for nearly a century and, like I said, it smells like it."

She came out of her reverie and snapped her fingers, a quick syncopated beat like jazz. "Not a problem. My tailor knows someone who specializes in cleaning vintage clothing. Leave it with me."

"It's too low-cut."

"It is not. You always wear jeans and T-shirts or those long, flowing dresses that cover up everything. About time you showed off what a great figure you've got."

"It's so short."

"Lucie—"

"You can see my foot."

As well as she knew me, it was the one subject I couldn't talk about without betraying how self-conscious I still felt about my twisted, deformed left foot, the one remaining injury I still dealt with after a car accident eight years ago.

Frankie was silent for a long moment, and when she spoke, her voice was gentle. "And what of it, Lucie? It's part of who you are. Let me tell you, in that dress the last thing anyone's going to be looking at is your foot. You need to stop being so self-conscious. No one else gives it a second thought."

"I don't know—"

"Wear it," she said. "I mean it. We'll keep it a secret from everyone, and when you walk into the room, you'll wow 'em all." She pressed her hands together as if she were praying and threw me a pleading look. "You need to move on. Do it in this dress. And, for the record, you've got great legs."

Once upon a time, I'd been a runner. Cross-country in high school and college. I'd been good.

I gave her a lopsided smile. "Well, at least one great leg."

She burst out laughing, and just like that I knew I was going to wear the dress at our Valentine's Day Roaring Twenties *Great Gatsby* "Anything Goes" Veronica House dinner dance, like Cinderella going to the ball.

But I did draw the line at glass slippers.

That evening, I asked my brother, Eli, who was older by two years, if he knew whom the dress had belonged to. We had just put Hope, my sweet niece and his three-and-a-half-year-old daughter, to bed, and I had asked him to come into my bedroom because I wanted to show him something.

I took it out of the closet and held it up. "Any ideas?"

Eli gave me one of those looks men give women when they think you're asking a trick question and they need to get the answer right. Then he stared at the dress, studying the sheer sea-green fabric with its intricate beading, as if the answer might be spelled out in code in the beads. Finally he looked up and said, "Probably some woman who was related to us, if you found it in the attic."

"Why, thank you, Sherlock. Aren't you helpful? *Which* relative?"

"A skinny one." He grinned and ducked as I threw a balled pair of socks at him. "Jeez, Luce, how should I know? Me and clothes? Come on. Ever since Brandi walked out on me, I have two requirements for what Hopie and I wear. No visible stains and it doesn't look like someone slept in it."

But the dress had worked its magic on my brother as well, because a short while later I heard him in the sunroom, sliding effortlessly from one jazz number into the next on the Bösendorfer concert grand piano that had been our great-grandfather's wedding present to our great-grandmother. The music of Cole Porter, Rogers and Hammerstein, Gershwin; swingy, upbeat tunes that the wearer of that dress would have danced to, doing the Charleston, or the Black Bottom, or the Lindy hop. I held up the dress against me one more time and, in the privacy of my bedroom, I hummed along to Eli's songs and pretended to dance, imagining myself wearing that sexy, beguiling dress as I wondered what life had been like in the hedonistic, let-the-good-times-roll decade that had roared.

Chapter 2

When you run a vineyard, you never know who is going to walk through your front door and ask to try your wine, maybe stick around for a couple of drinks. We get all denominations: friends, lovers, families, the rare single guest who sits alone. They arrive in varied states of sobriety or inebriation, especially if they've been touring the local vineyards all day, to drown sorrows, celebrate victories, find a new love, get over an old one, or maybe just to kick back and relax. Thankfully, what we don't usually get are troublemakers looking to pick a fight.

Until today.

To begin with, we were closed. Then there was this guy's attitude, the way he barged into the barrel room—the place where we perform the alchemy of turning grapes into wine—like a gunslinger bursting into the saloon through a pair of swinging doors. I looked up from helping Quinn Santori—my winemaker, who was filtering wine into bottles with a glass thief—as the man's eyes connected with mine across the room. I knew then that even a KEEP OUT: EXPLOSIVES sign on the door wouldn't have been a deterrent.

But what surprised me more was that I knew him. Not personally, but I would have recognized Gino Tomassi anywhere. He was California winemaking royalty, the grandson of Johnny Tomassi, one of the pioneering winemakers who had emigrated from Italy to California in the early 1900s and planted some of the first grapevines in the Napa Valley. Later, after Prohibition ended, Johnny, along with Louis M. Martini, Cesare Mondavi, and a few other iconic names, transformed the region into a winemaking empire some called "the American Eden."

What I didn't know was what Gino Tomassi was doing in my winery at ten-thirty on an early-February morning. But before either he or I could say anything, Quinn cleared his throat and set the thief down on top of a wine barrel.

"Well, well, well," he said in a deadpan voice, "look what the cat dragged in. What are you doing here, Cousin Gino?"

Cousin Gino.

I was used to Quinn's secretiveness about his past life in California—he seemed not to have one—so the idea that he was related to the Tomassi wine dynasty was about as likely as, say, discovering he was also a long-lost member of the British royal family and potential heir to the throne. Quinn almost never spoke about his family, except for his mother, who had passed away nine months ago, and once, with bitterness, about a father who abandoned him and his mother shortly after he was born.

All I knew about his mother was that she was Spanish, and when she died last spring, Quinn returned to the Bay Area for several months to take care of her estate, pack up her things, and sell her house in San Jose. If he was related to Gino, it was on his father's side.

Gino gave Quinn a grim smile, like the two of them shared a secret they wished they didn't know. "What else would I be doing here? Come to see you, Quinn. Introduce me to the pretty lady, why don't you?" His eyes roved over me.

Gino's nickname in the wine business was "the Silver Fox,"

as much because of his luxuriant silver hair as his shrewd—some would even say predatory—business acumen building the Tomassi Family Vineyard from a prominent California winery into a nationally known brand. I'd also heard a darker story about ties to the Mafia thanks to an old childhood friend who was now the biggest mob boss on the West Coast. So far, it was all just rumor and unsubstantiated claims; Gino claimed it was a personal relationship and nothing more. But as the saying goes, when you lie down with dogs, you get up with fleas.

He was standing there watching us, like a stage director casting a critical eye over actors who have just fumbled their lines. In person, he was shorter than I'd expected and stockier, but maybe that was because his flamboyant personality projected an image of someone tall and commanding. He wore an expensive-looking cashmere camel overcoat over a double-breasted navy pinstriped suit and had a white silk scarf draped around his neck. Quinn and I had on faded jeans, old wine-stained sweatshirts, fingerless mittens, and down vests to ward off the damp chill of the room. I wondered how long it had been since Gino had gotten his hands dirty in the barrel room like we did. Just now he seemed miles out of our league.

But he had baited Quinn, using me as the pawn, and I resented it. "I'm Lucie Montgomery, Mr. Tomassi. I own this winery." I glanced at Quinn. "You didn't tell me you had family." I paused and gave him my sweetest smile. "In town."

Quinn's mouth twitched, but he turned to Gino and said with contempt, "That's because the last time we spoke was—what, Gino?—twenty years ago?" Before Gino could reply, he added, "How'd you find me?"

Though I think what he really wanted to know was *why*.

Gino looked around the room. By California standards, certainly compared to the vast empire he owned, which sprawled across Napa and Sonoma on either side of the Mayacamas Mountains, my entire operation in the charming, bucolic village of Atoka, Virginia—population sixty—must have seemed like very small potatoes to him. Thirty acres of vines planted on a five-hundred-acre farm given to one of my ancestors in appreciation for service during the French and Indian War, Highland Farm sat at the foot of the Blue Ridge Mountains in a region better known for raising Thoroughbreds, hunting foxes, and playing polo than for making wine.

"I've always known where you were," he said to Quinn. "You didn't think I wouldn't keep track of you, did you? I offered you your first job, remember? Tried to give you a hand up. Bring you back into the family business."

Quinn snorted. "You've got a hell of a nerve, Gino. It stopped being my family's business after your father screwed my grandmother out of her share of it. You couldn't have paid me enough to work for you. Not then, not ever."

Gino's face looked like thunder, but he kept his voice level. "Your grandmother came to my father for help because she was desperate after your grandfather lost his shirt on a bunch of lousy business deals. My old man was struggling, but he took out a loan to bail her out and she *gave* him her share of the vineyard in return. My father helped your grandmother, Quinn. The same way I tried to help you." He shook his head and tapped his forehead with his finger. "*Testa dura*," he said to me. "Bullheaded. Always thinks he's right. Always has to do everything the hard way. His way."

I didn't disagree with him about Quinn's stubbornness, but I wasn't about to say so—at least not to Gino Tomassi. "What does bring you here, Mr. Tomassi? Surely it's more than a family reunion, or that you just happened to be in the neighborhood. Atoka's not even on most maps."

This time his smile showed a lot of teeth. "Call me Gino."

"Gino," I said, "to what do we owe the pleasure?"

"You're clever, Lucie Montgomery. Smart. I've been keeping an eye on you, too. You run a good vineyard."

So he already knew who I was. The compliment about my

vineyard shouldn't have pleased me as much as it did, especially since Quinn was obviously upset by Gino's out-of-the-blue appearance. Even I knew by now that Gino hadn't dropped by to say "How's every little thing?" He had an agenda and he was doling out information in small bits.

"I have an excellent winemaker," I said.

"I know you do." His eyes held mine, a penetrating stare, but then he swiveled his gaze to Quinn. "Okay, Quinn, you're right. I didn't just happen to stop by. I wanted to see you about something, ask you some questions."

Quinn's expression hardened. "You must be in a lot of trouble if you came all the way from California to find me."

"A bit of trouble." Gino inclined his head like he was conceding the point. "I was wondering if you knew anything about it."

"About what?"

"About why I'm being blackmailed."

Quinn had been about to pick up the wine thief and begin filling another bottle. He set it down and said, "I have no clue. The Tomassi family has enough skeletons in the closet to fill a cemetery. Which one did someone decide to rattle?" He paused and added, "This time."

"No," Gino said, "this is something different."

"Explain 'different.'"

Gino walked over until he was standing in front of Quinn and me. He dropped his voice to a conspiratorial whisper, although there was no one but the three of us in the barrel room. "I got an e-mail a few days ago. Whoever sent it called himself—or herself—'an anonymous friend.' Said they knew something about Johnny. My grandfather . . . your great-grandfather." He watched Quinn carefully, and I realized he was waiting for some reaction, for Quinn to give away that he knew what this was about.

Quinn glanced at me, his face as expressionless as a poker cardsharp. "His real name was Gianluca Tomassi, but everyone called him Johnny."

"I know who Johnny Tomassi was," I said. "But I didn't know that he was your great-grandfather."

Gino looked dumbfounded. "Are you kidding me? You never told her who you are? Never told her about the family?"

"No. I did not tell her about the family." Quinn banged his fist on the wine barrel and the thief jumped. I grabbed it before it could hit the floor and break.

"Why not?" He still seemed stunned.

"Because I didn't. Get to the point, Gino."

For a moment I thought Gino was about to reach over and grab Quinn by his shirt and tell him to show some respect for his elders. Then he shrugged. "It's a long story. And it's . . . how shall I say? Complicated."

Quinn folded his arms across his chest. "I don't know anything about any blackmail. And I'm damn sure I don't want to get involved with family problems." He gave Gino a hostile look. "*Your* family problems. Especially complicated ones."

"Let me make something clear." Gino stabbed a finger in the air, punctuating his words. "I'm not asking if you want to get involved. I'm telling you that you are. Better you hear this from me, Quinn. I'm doing you a favor by coming here myself."

"Before this goes any further," I said, shooting a warning glance at Quinn, "maybe we should find a warmer place to finish this conversation."

The two of us had been there filling bottles for a staff meeting at the end of the day, where we would decide the blend for a new wine—a sparkling white like champagne. By definition, anyplace you make wine needs to be cool and dark because heat and light destroy it. But this was early February and the bitter cold of the outdoor temperatures, in the teens, even more frigid if you factored in the windchill, had seeped into my bones in spite of several layers of clothing, heavy boots, and the fingerless gloves.

"Fine," Gino said, "but this is between Quinn and me, Lucie. No outsiders. You understand."

Quinn shook his head. "Forget it. You're the outsider, Gino. Lucie owns this vineyard. Either she stays or we don't talk. You brought her into this the minute you walked through the door. Besides, whatever gets said, I want an impartial witness. You know how I feel about the Tomassi side of the family keeping their word."

Gino's face became a mottled shade of red. "This better not get out. I mean it."

Quinn shrugged. "Apparently, it already did get out and someone does know, or they wouldn't be blackmailing you. Whatever *it* is."

Gino turned to me. "I want your word you won't discuss anything about what I'm going to say. You understand?"

"I know how to keep my mouth shut," I said. "As long as you're not asking me to do anything illegal."

He shot me another penetrating look, and I had a feeling this was probably going to come down to splitting hairs and semantics. *Define "illegal."*

"Let's go upstairs to the office," Quinn said. "And get this over with."

I reached for my cane, which was propped behind a wine barrel, and caught the flicker of surprise in Gino's eyes. But he said nothing, just followed Quinn and me to a staircase that led to a mezzanine where our offices and the winery laboratory were located. At the bottom of the stairs, my bad foot buckled and I grabbed the railing. Instantly, I felt Gino's hand under my elbow, the chivalrous gesture of a gentleman helping a lady.

I froze. "Thank you, but I can manage. You don't need to do that."

"Sorry." He withdrew his hand. "What happened?"

Most people don't ask. An old person using a cane is someone who needs a little extra help and you don't give it a second thought. Someone young like me is a different story—maybe a debilitating disease or a birth defect, possibly an accident. Either they don't want to talk about your disability because it makes them uncomfortable or they figure you don't want to talk about it because you live with it.

Gino Tomassi wasn't most people. "Eight years ago I was a passenger in a car that took a corner too fast in the rain and hit one of the pillars at the entrance to the vineyard," I said.

"I'm sorry. Tough break."

"My doctors told me I wouldn't walk again, but I did. So it could have been a lot worse."

Gino glanced sideways at me and I could feel him studying me and taking my measure. There aren't many women in my profession, so we have more to prove. A woman with a disability in my profession has a hell of a lot more to prove. "You're tough, Lucie Montgomery. I've heard that about you."

"Thank you."

We climbed the stairs together in silence, Gino slowing his pace to match mine. Quinn reached the office first and opened the door. After the raw chill of the barrel room, the warm air blasting at us as we walked inside felt good.

Once inside the office, Quinn pulled the club chairs up to the coffee table so they faced the sofa. "Take a seat, Gino," he said. "Take the couch."

Gino shrugged out of his beautiful coat and carefully laid it across the arm of the sofa. He sat and said, "I could use something to wet my whistle."

"White or red?" Quinn asked.

"Red. One of yours, of course." Gino indicated the collection of bottles on the counter. "How about that open bottle of Cab?"

Quinn walked over and picked up the bottle of our Cabernet Sauvignon Reserve. "We brought it up from the barrel room yesterday to see how it's developing." He cleared his throat. "I wouldn't mind knowing what you think."

I knew it cost him something to say that. Pouring wine for customers in the tasting room is one thing. They don't want to know what strain of yeast you used or the type of fermentation or how long you let the fruit hang on the vines. Pouring wine for a winemaker means you're going to get a critique of everything, from obvious flaws to acidity, the characteristics of the fruit, any off aromas, tannins, overall balance—technical stuff.

Gino stretched out an arm along the back of the sofa and regarded Quinn. "I speak my mind; you know that. How long has it been in your cellar?"

"Three years."

Gino raised an eyebrow. "I know left-bank Bordeaux producers who would jail you for infanticide if you opened a Cab after only three years."

Quinn turned red. "Yeah, well this is Virginia, not the left bank of Bordeaux. Three years is nothing when you've been producing wine for centuries. Virginia resurrected what was left of its wine industry in the eighties after the Civil War and Prohibition. The 1980s. Do you want to try it, or give me a lecture?"

"You don't need to be defensive. Pour already."

Quinn filled a wineglass and gave it to him. "I don't like to drink alone," Gino said.

It was 11:00 a.m.

Show me a winemaker who drinks at all hours—I'm talking about drinking, not tasting and spitting—and I'll show you someone on the road to alcoholism. It's something we've got to guard against constantly in our profession. But this seemed different, more like liquid courage before he explained why someone was blackmailing him, so Quinn filled two more glasses and handed one to me. We sat in the chairs across from Gino.

He lifted his glass. "*Cent' anni.* May you have a hundred good years."

He drank, and then nodded as though he approved, and I felt Quinn start breathing again next to me. "It's got a good balance and I can see where it could be in a few years, once the tannins settle down," Gino said. "Good fruit, but the acid is still there, as

I'm sure you know. More Bordeaux-style than California. When did a *paesan* like you start making French wine?"

I answered him. "My mother was French. She came from a family of French winemakers."

Gino set his glass down on a file cabinet next to the sofa. "Family," he said. "It always comes down to family."

"What does?" Quinn asked. "Why is someone blackmailing you about Johnny?"

Gino leaned back against the sofa again and crossed one leg over the other. "I don't know how much you know about your great-grandfather," he said. "*Really* know about him. Other than the story of the poor young immigrant arriving in America with nothing but the shirt on his back and managing to save enough money to buy land in Napa and plant some of the first vines. He kept the place going during Prohibition by making sacramental wine for the Church, instead of ripping out his vines and planting orchards like so many others did. That's what saved his bacon. Sacramental wine. After that, he and Louis M. Martini and Cesare Mondavi and a couple of others from the old country waited it out until repeal. It took a while—Americans had developed a taste for the hard stuff, not wine, during Prohibition—but eventually things started picking up."

Quinn waved a hand, dismissing him. "I don't need a history lesson about how hard Johnny worked to make California wines respected. Practically carried the industry on his back, according to family legend. Him and Nonna Angelica." He winked at Gino. "I heard other stories, too, how Angelica could be a *testa dura* herself. Run the vineyard as good as Johnny could. In fact, some people thought she did once they got married."

Gino gave a so-what shrug. "Maybe so, but she loved Johnny more than anything in the world. Did everything she could to burnish his legacy and sideline anyone who got in his way. She was tough, your great-grandmother was."

By now it was obvious why Gino was being blackmailed.

"Someone found out something about Johnny that you don't want to get out," I said. "Or Angelica. They've been dead for what, sixty years? Seventy? It must be pretty bad for you to want to cover it up after all this time."

"Lucie's right. What could matter so much now? What happened?" Quinn asked. "Don't tell me they robbed a bank and now the money has finally turned up somewhere?"

Gino punched his fist into the palm of his other hand. "Dammit, don't joke about this. Johnny was a good man, a good father, a good businessman, a good friend." He kept emphasizing *good* with more fist smacking. "Plus, he was devout, did so much for the Church, gave thousands of dollars to Catholic charities, but never wanted anyone to know. And Angelica . . . she was always all about the family. Everything was for the family. She was a good woman, too. Went to Mass every day of her life."

He hadn't answered the question, just danced around it. It seemed to me Quinn had struck a nerve, or come close to it. And like they say, going to church every day doesn't make you a saint any more than standing in a garage turns you into a mechanic.

"Why don't you tell us what it is?" I said to Gino.

He picked up his wineglass and drained it. Without asking, Quinn found an open bottle of Valpolicella on the counter and showed it to Gino, who held out his glass for a refill.

In just about every language or culture, there is a maxim about the relationship between wine and what it does to inhibitions. In the Talmud it's written that when wine enters, secrets exit. In Russia, the proverb goes that what a sober man has on his mind, the drunken man has on his tongue. And of course there is the Latin platitude everyone knows: *In vino veritas.* In wine, there is truth.

Gino drank the Valpolicella, a moody, troubled expression on his face. Finally he looked up. "Did you know Johnny was married to someone else before he married Angelica?"

ABOUT THE AUTHOR

ELLEN CROSBY is the author of *Multiple Exposure*, featuring international photojournalist Sophie Medina, as well as the Virginia Wine Country Mystery series and *Moscow Nights*, a standalone novel. Previously she worked as a freelance reporter for the *Washington Post*, as Moscow correspondent for ABC News Radio, and as an economist at the U.S. Senate. Learn more at www.ellencrosby.com.